Bruce Beckham

C000001013

Murder Unsolved

Detective Inspector Skelgill Investigates

LUCiUS

Kindle edition first published by Lucius 2022
Paperback edition first published by Lucius 2022
Hardcover edition first published by Lucius 2022

For more details and Rights enquiries contact:
Lucius-ebooks@live.com

Cover design by Moira Kay Nicol
United States editor Janet Colter

EDITOR'S NOTE

Murder Unsolved is a stand-alone mystery, the eighteenth in the series 'Detective Inspector Skelgill Investigates'. It is set in the English Lake District, in the isolated northern parish known as Mungrisdale, and also the Cumbrian coastal town of Workington.

While it is not necessary to have knowledge of earlier episodes, the reader may wish to consult book twelve, *Murder on the Run*, for references to earlier events concerning DI Skelgill's cousin by marriage, Megan Graham, and her daughter Jess.

THE DI SKELGILL SERIES

Glossary

SOME of the Cumbrian dialect words, abbreviations, British slang and local usage appearing in *Murder Unsolved* are as follows:

A&E – accident & emergency department
ANPR – automatic number plate recognition
Allus – always
Alreet – alright (often a greeting)
Any road – anyway
Arl – old
Asda – a supermarket chain
Ba'be – baby
Bait – packed lunch, sandwiches
Bang to rights – positive proof of guilt
Beck – mountain stream
Bewer – girlfriend
Bleaberry – bilberry
Blether – to chat or gossip
Bob – shilling
Boozer – pub (also heavy drinker)
Bottle – nerve (bottle & glass, Cockney)
Bowk – vomit
Bricking it – feeling uneasy
Butcher's – look (butcher's hook, Cockney)
Butty – sandwich
Chippy – fish and chip shop
Cock – mate, pal
Crimbo – Christmas
Coo-clap – cow dung
Deek – look
Dog and bone – phone (Cockney)
Dole – unemployment benefit
Donnat – idiot, good for nothing
Fish supper – fish and chips
Flait – frightened

Flicks – cinema
Frae – from (Scots)
Fret – worry
Game (the) – prostitution
Gattered – drunk (inebriated)
Gay – very
GBH – grievous bodily harm
Goolies – testicles
Half-inch – pinch/steal (Cockney)
Hank Marvin – starving
Happen – maybe
Haud – hold (Scots)
Hersen/hissen – herself/himself
Hey up – hello, look out
How! – cry used for driving cattle
Howay – come on
In-bye – enclosed pasture near the farmstead
Int' – in the
Isnae – is not (Scots)
Itsen – itself
Jack Jones – alone (Cockney)
Laal – little
Lamp – hit
Lug – ear
Marra – mate (friend)
Manx – from the Isle of Man
Mash – tea/make tea
Met (the) – Metropolitan Police (Greater London)
Mind – remember
Mither – bother
Moot hall – meeting hall
Muckle – large
NFU – National Farmers' Union
Nickt int' head – having extravagant fancies
Nowt – nothing
Offcomer – outsider, tourist
Ont' – on the

Oppo – associate
Pagger – fight
Panto – pantomime
Parkin – gingerbread cake made with oatmeal and black treacle
Parky – cold
Pash – sudden short, sharp shower of rain
Patty – battered deep-fried mashed potato
Pre's – drinks at home prior to going out
Rake – channel in a rock face
Reet – right
Sagging – playing truant
Sommat - something
Sub – loan (unlikely to be repaid)
T' – the (often silent)
Tarn – mountain lake in a corrie
Tattie howkin' – potato picking
Tea-leaf – thief (Cockney)
Tek – take
Think on – remember
Tip the wink – warn in advance
Thon – that/those
Thee/thew/thou – you, your
Tod – alone (Tod Sloan, Cockney)
Trap – mouth
Us – often used for me/my/our
Wether – castrated sheep
While – until
Whistle – suit (whistle and flute, Cockney)
Wukiton – Workington
Yard – small paved area at rear of house
Yourn – yours

PROOFS

Six months earlier

'*M*ummy – *he says they're going to rape us!*'

It is beyond Sally's worst nightmare.

She has the gun.

But the stocky, greasy-haired one has Lily. Hungry eyes, leering mouth. And a knife.

The other one, the tall one. There were the cold eyes of a killer in the slit of the mask. The foetid breath. The iron grip on her wrist.

The heavy steps are on the landing. *A cry of rage!* He's seen the ladder.

The fear in Lily's eyes is almost overwhelming. Sally's legs are shaking at the knees. Her heart feels ready to explode in her chest.

Will Lily know what to do? Everything Sandy told them. Will she remember?

When she heard them breaking in, why hadn't they made a dash for it? Sandy would berate her. She could have got Lily to the loft. They would have pulled up the ladder. With a mobile phone and the Wi-Fi they could have summoned help. And they would have had the gun.

9

The gun.

She'd known she had to get the gun.

Leaving Lily for those few moments was like having her wrenched from her womb, ripped from her arms, stolen from her side – all of those fears accumulated, hallucinated down the years, a cascade of horror seething in one black maelstrom.

Lily's desperate scream of *'Mummy!'* when she had broken away from the tall one. Wrenching free of his grasp as he momentarily relaxed. Taking with her the rank odour of exhaled beer and stale smoke and ammonic sweat.

"I'll give you my jewels! My valuables! Please don't hurt her – she's thirteen! I'll get them – you'll never find them!'

The words echo in her brain. *You'll never find them* – the corollary – that they would kill them first and then ransack the house. Or bind and torture them. And worse. Lily has just said it.

There are no jewels. Why would anyone keep jewels in a holiday home? It was the guilty thought that consumed her as she lurched from the room, striving to appear calm, trying not to hear Lily. But Lily's cries had turned to a despairing whimper. He must have put his hand over her mouth right then. Now there is a trickle of blood where Lily has bitten him, to pass on the dreadful warning. Brave little Lily. Precious Lily.

And she had thought again about Sandy. 'Anoraky Sandy' she secretly used to call him. That he had been right. One day, something like this could happen. Improbable – but better safe than sorry. Just as when they went to stay in the villa at La Garde-Freinet and he'd insisted on buying an emergency tooth repair kit from Boots at Edinburgh airport. The very next morning she had broken a crown on a baguette; it was a public holiday and the local dentist was all shuttered up.

About the gun – as usual she had humoured him. She had only half paid attention. Like when he showed her how to turn off the stop-cock if there were a burst pipe. She left those things to him, she wasn't practical. But she remembered his little metaphor. Don't try to put your finger in the dam. Eventually the crack will widen. The dam will burst and drown you. Suffer the immediate flood. Stop it at source.

Lily – the immediate flood. How could she have left her? But she did.

And she'd had to remember how to get the gun.

Sandy's words. They won't expect you to have a twelve-bore. Not in England. Not a woman on her own. An old farmer, maybe – but not a middle-class metropolitan type that drives a sports car.

And she can see in the burly one's evil eyes that Sandy was right. He didn't expect her to appear with a double-barrelled shotgun. But he's sly, and he has Lily, and the knife.

Lily's blouse is pulled out of her jeans, a couple of buttons are missing. She can't speak but tears are running, diluting the blood from the bite.

The footsteps are on the stairs.

When she left the room, the tall one had followed her. Her heart sank. But she had begun to remember.

Sandy's words again. Just a couple of yards head start. Enough to lock the en suite bathroom door. She'd called out, her voice had seemed disembodied, a note of hysteria.

'They're hidden in a safe behind the door – there's no room – *I have to close it!'*

Turn the lock at the same time as the handle to disguise the sound. Open the window wide to make it look like she had fled. Climb on the bath. Push up the little hatch. The vanity shelf as a foothold. Pull up. Replace the hatch. Step on the joists – use the rafters for overhead grip and spacing. Straight ahead for the gun safe – the seventh joist. Click the light switch. Two keys beneath the fibreglass insulation. The gun – in pieces. Lock, stock and barrel. He'd made her practise. Forget the saying: it's stock, barrel and lock. Fumbling, shaking, she'd finally done it – it had seemed an age before the three parts clicked into place. Then two cartridges. The safety catch.

The banging had started – the bathroom door. And impatient shouting. But it told her the landing must be clear. The main hatch – the Ramsay ladder that silently unfolds.

The bathroom door had splintered.

But she had slipped past the bedroom and down the staircase.

Into the living room.

This confrontation. What had she hoped? That he would let go of Lily and back away? Run from the cottage?

But he is too sly for that. He has a human shield. It is Sandy's "worse-case scenario".

And he is too drunk or drugged – too greedy to give up what they have come to take.

The steps are in the hall. She has five seconds.

Would Lily remember?

12

Jump, Lily – JUMP!!'

*

'Mum? What are you doing?'
'Sorry, darling? Oh – I'm just – proofreading.'
'You looked –'
'No. It's nothing.'
'Here's the pizza.'
'I didn't hear the bell.'
'I was waiting.'
'But –'
'It's alright, Mum – they sent a text.'
'Well –'
'Am I at Dad's this weekend?'
'Yes.'
'Aw.'
'Darling, I must get through these proofs. Janet will go apoplectic if I miss the publisher's deadline.'
'Okay.'
'Now, you'll remember, won't you?'
'Mum! There's no need to nag.'

1. APPEAL

Carlisle, 11.30 a.m., Monday, December 21ˢᵗ

'*Danny – wait!*'
Skelgill spins on his heel, producing a piercing squeal of protest from the polished tiles of the atrium that turns several heads. One or two remain watching, curious for reasons known only to them.

'Hey up, Sheryl.'

His inflection conveys a question, far more complicated than the greeting might sound to said eavesdroppers. Indeed, as she approaches he turns and continues towards the exit, causing her to hurry to reach his side, and falter as they descend the rain-washed stone steps. However, it is not solely to escape scrutiny that he sets this pace, apparently indifferent to her plight, but also to buy a few moments in order more precisely to place her. Sheryl Graham, a second cousin – or third – once removed, perhaps; Graham generations tend to be shorter than most. And to assess her. Anxious, certainly. Why is she looking for him? More to the point, what is she doing at the courthouse?

Skelgill catches sight of DI Alec Smart, smoking in a doorway, sheltering from the downpour. Skelgill is too late to avoid eye contact. DI Smart, weasel features exaggerated as he sucks in smoke and squints to avoid the tendrils that simultaneously escape from his slit-like nostrils, raises the cigarette in a smug two-fingered salute. His furtive eyes appraise Skelgill's companion.

She is unsuitably dressed. Never mind for the weather – she shows too much flesh. Get her out of sight, is his inclination.

'Fancy a mash? There's a café just by the Crescent.'

Skelgill does not seem bothered by the rain, despite the lack of any overcoat. To her credit the girl does not complain. There is the effort of keeping up, and of managing an inadequate compact umbrella fished from her bag.

Five minutes brings them to Blackfriars Street; seated; mugs of tea ordered and delivered.

'Why were you there, Danny?'

'You've not forgotten what my job is, lass?'

'Nay – that's why I want to speak with thee.'

Skelgill regards her censoriously. He has long kept at bay petitions of a potentially nepotistic nature, dispensing oblique platitudes when accosted at family gatherings. Yet, she can only have acted on the spur of the moment. His last-minute decision to attend the hearing was predicated on its convergence with a forty-mile round trip to Carlisle for lugworms.

He is tolerant, however, of the girl's question.

'I was a witness in the original trial. Nowt significant, like. I was fishing at Bowscale Tarn. I saw the smoke. Thought it were the heather – offcomers with a barbecue. Got there too late – as if it'd have made any difference – the pathologist reckons they were dead before the fire were set.' He grimaces in a macabre way, though without satisfaction. 'It were a barbecue, alreet.'

Perhaps the girl's own local accent, and his grisly reminiscences have him lapsing into the vernacular that rumbles never far below the surface of his generally moderated manner of speaking. She does not know him well enough to recognise the irony in his tone, and smiles, as if she might be expected to do so.

He gets a glimpse of her in a different light; she is quite attractive in a naïve kind of way. But why the caked-on make-up and fake tan; no one Skelgill has ever met is naturally that colour. Regardless, naïve and attractive are not words he has come to associate with the bulk of the Grahams. A man himself with hardly a mirror in the house, there have been get-togethers when he has been glad of the dominant Old Norse genes of his paternal line. Among the Grahams there are suspicions of inbreeding, a dubious survival strategy for a clan shunned down the generations – although perhaps this charge is taking things a bit far.

But the girl – she must be about twenty-three, he would guess – has a lazy eye, and now he is not entirely sure if she is engaging him earnestly or half-sheepishly looking away. Her long brown hair is damp and lank, and her nails are bitten and she has stained smoker's fingers, and he guesses he would already be conflicted if this were a blind date.

'Where are you living these days, Sheryl?'

'Still Wukiton – at me Ma's. Not far from your Jess.'

Skelgill frowns at the possessive pronoun, but does not disabuse her of the notion; no doubt word of his munificence has seeped through the conductive phloem of the clan grapevine. He avoids the direct subject of Jess, the outlier, the talented prodigy.

'Come up on the train?'

Now Sheryl Graham looks at him as artfully as her strabismus permits. This is a gateway to what she wants to talk about. Though she begins with a shake of the head.

'I chummed Jade ont' bus. It's cheaper. It's only an hour-and-a-half.'

Skelgill raises an eyebrow. Twice the time it would take him to drive. Such are the luxuries and penuries of the dispossessed. But a little light has come on. The name she mentions rings a bell. Now he is more direct.

'What were you doing at court, Sheryl?'

Perhaps to his surprise, she does not beat about the bush.

'Jade swears Dale had nowt to do wi' it.' Now she looks both at him and away from him with renewed purpose. 'She wouldn't lie to us – why would she? We've known each other since infant school.'

She folds her arms with determination, as if anticipating an unsympathetic hearing from her stern detective cousin.

'Sheryl, they found his fingerprints – his jacket with DNA – other stuff.'

'Maybe he'd stole the car for them – that's what Dale did.'

'His alibi fell apart. Your friend Jade Nelson nearly went to jail.'

But Sheryl Graham is shaking her head.

'He does have an alibi. He just can't say it. He's got film – on a phone. Proof it wasn't him.'

Skelgill sups from his mug. Across the small café he sees a woman break off a piece of parkin and pass it to a small hand that rises from a pushchair, and he wishes he'd ordered a slice. He looks back at the girl, who now seems to be waiting for some endorsement of her assertion.

'Go on then, lass.'

But she shakes her head again, rather urgently; he thinks she might even look suddenly frightened.

'I don't know what it is. Nor does Jade. But they've said they'll kill her and the bairn.'

'They?'

It is like a meeting with an informer. Her reaction – casting shiftily about – makes Skelgill think again of Alec Smart, his methods derived from some stained manual of policing that allows for descent into the corrupt underworld of crime, a tacit admission of its intransience, its denizens snouts and spies and not-very-super grasses.

Another shake of the head, her eyes cast down.

'She don't know. Dale won't tell her who they are.'

'Why would Jade believe this?'

Sheryl Graham looks up, a conflation of wonderment and disquiet creasing the cosmetic mask.

'She gets cash put through her door.'

Skelgill must inadvertently show some sign of reproach; she reacts with what seems like self-preservation in mind.

'She's only just told us – I never knew none of it.' She bites at the corner of a thumbnail. 'Dale were banking on getting his appeal. Ont' bus – she were saying – she can't have the bairn growing up without her Daddy.'

At this, Skelgill slowly exhales; without a role model – should he say it? He refrains.

'Is this off your own bat?'

She nods, and now leans forward; her low-cut top causes Skelgill to steadfastly maintain eye contact.

'Danny – you can't go and talk to Jade. Nor Dale – if you see him, word'll get out – the jail leaks like a sieve. He won't even tell his solicitor.'

Skelgill sits back and lifts his mug and drinks.

'Have you told Jade you're speaking to me?'

Now she does look alarmed. She shakes her head with extra

vehemence.

'I just said there's me cousin – I'll tap him up for us fares home.'

Skelgill narrows his eyes. But there is a twinkle, the green flecks seeming to gain a little light of their own against the grey substrate.

He pats his chest but he is marginally more smartly turned out for court and his wallet is in his regular jacket. He leans sideways and pulls a wad of reserve notes from his back pocket and lays them down beside the girl's mug.

'And I thought you were treating us. I was ready for a nice bit of cake.'

The girl is plainly compromised. A base hunger becomes tinged with guilt and gratitude; complex emotions that please Skelgill to read, despite the unyielding artificial complexion and deceptive squint. She contrives to show some dignity, holding the money as though it is not quite hers. But she rises, nonetheless.

'The bus – I've not long.'

Skelgill makes a gesture of dismissal, and it seems he conveys sufficient in his unspoken farewell that satisfies her in the achievement of her mission. She is about to back away when she makes a sudden dart – and places on the table before him a five-pound note drawn from her new-found wealth fund.

'For your parkin, Danny.'

When she is gone Skelgill spends a few moments ostensibly deep in thought, though he is merely allowing feelings to digest, to no purpose as yet. A cry from the pushchair breaks his trance, and he sees the small hand extend like a nestling craving a worm. The mother obliges, yielding her last morsel.

Skelgill's eyes shift to the counter, where a glass display case houses various local offerings. There is a general impression of ginger, treacle, spices and Demerara sugar.

Then he looks down at the fiver. Sir Winston Churchill returns his gaze, his expression enigmatic. Skelgill is reminded of something – though he cannot quite put his finger on it. But there is a small realisation – he is in Carlisle with a fiver to his name; he can't have his cake and eat it – not if he wants his lugworms.

2. HQ

'Aright, cock?'

Skelgill does not need to look up from the page on his desk in order to know that he is displeased. In fact, he does not look up. Even were he not to recognise the grating voice, or the drawling Manchester accent, or the smell that is tobacco imperfectly concealed by cologne, it is only DI Alec Smart that persists with this peculiarly unattractive salutation. Then again, were Smart to adopt the local vernacular it would be even more infuriating, doubly so, in that Skelgill is most certainly not his *marra*.

'Emma.'

DS Jones responds with more grace, although she is careful with her neutral "Hi". It is dusk outside, and the corridor light not yet on, and in his dark suit he is a shadowy form. There is a sinister smile; a glint of sharp incisors; he might almost be Count Dracula waiting for the innocent slip of the tongue that will invite him across the threshold. His eyes in their sunken sockets have marked out his preferred victim. Under such scrutiny, DS Jones lowers her gaze and shifts position. Dressed ready for an after-hours class, she wears a tracksuit top and calf-length yoga pants with trainers; she sits forward, tucking her feet beneath her chair and resting her papers on her lap.

The movement seems to prompt Skelgill to break off from his perusal. Not that he is reading; he was about to let DS Jones do the honours. But he, too, is on his guard, knowing DI Smart's appearance is unlikely to be a coincidence. It is fortunate that they have not begun; he cannot have eavesdropped during his stealthy approach. Skelgill has to resist the urge to turn over the report on his desk; to do so will sound an alarm bell. Instead he crosses his forearms over the page, and leans forward interrogatively. But this is sufficient for DI Smart to consider a sign of engagement. Light on his feet, he takes a step forward, side on like a swordsman weighing up an opponent. His eyes dart about hungrily, seeking a target.

'Didn't get chance of a chinwag at Carlisle. You were otherwise occupied, Skel.'

Skel. An epithet Skelgill detests even more than 'cock'. He imagines Smart knows it. There is no particular logic for this – Skel, or Skelly, what is the difference – only Smart's devious logic, an assumption of camaraderie that he surely cannot really believe. Now he leers at DS Jones before returning his gaze to Skelgill.

'Didn't like to interrupt your cosy little tête-à-tête.'

DI Smart's words tell Skelgill that he was followed; there was no way his passing in the rain could be so described; the girl was several paces behind him at the time. However, he declines to be drawn.

'Took your time getting back, Skel. Something juicy, was it?'

Now DI Smart winks knowingly.

Skelgill is conscious of DS Jones's scrutiny. Grudgingly, he moves to parry the devious probing.

'There's nowt juicy about a cousin wanting a sub.'

'Why not? So long as you're not planning to start a family!'

DI Smart cackles unashamedly at his deployment of locker room innuendo; and he delights to see Skelgill's discomfort.

Skelgill inwardly curses. In deflecting from the true matter of his assignation, he has merely exposed another chink through which Smart can press home an advantage.

'She looked alright to me, Skel – a bit rough round the edges, maybe.'

Now DI Smart turns to DS Jones; his eyes linger appraisingly, as though he educes some comparison.

'What can we do for you, Smart? I've got ten minutes to get a report up to the Chief.' Finally Skelgill intervenes, in the absence of a stinging riposte resorting to blunt practicality, and a blatant white lie.

DI Alec Smart clicks the heels of his immaculately polished Chelsea boots.

'Didn't realise you had present company.' He casts a languid hand in the direction of DS Jones. 'Just thought I'd get your take on the hearing. That's it dead in the water, eh?'

Skelgill still has his arms crossed over the document. DI Smart's eyes continue to rove about; they settle upon Skelgill's desk. Skelgill feels a creeping unease; his pose is unnatural, held this long. But he steels himself, and contrives an expression of bored disinterest.

'You heard the judge – no grounds for appeal.'

Skelgill stares blankly at the interloper. It is plain that DI Smart is dissatisfied, that he detects some incongruity; his nostrils seem to twitch and his bony fists clench at his sides.

Then, all of a sudden, he snaps his fingers in front of his face.

'Dale Spooner. Bang to rights. *Smart* work.'

He grins in self-congratulation, and perhaps at his little play on words. He begins to back away. His eyes linger on DS Jones's lap, where she holds her papers over her Lycra-clad thighs. Then his gaze shifts again to Skelgill's desk.

'I'll love you and leave you. Mind how you go with that cousin, Skel.'

Skelgill waits until the sound of footsteps has faded, and a little longer, just in case. Then he rises and closes his door. Rather than sit, he crosses to examine the map of Cumbria on the wall behind his desk. He seems to pay particular attention to a single location, in the vicinity of the northern fells.

'That was interesting, Guv.'

There is a note of ambiguity in DS Jones's inflection that causes Skelgill to turn sharply; he seems anxious to make a point. He reaches for the document on his desk, and flaps it in the air.

'Sheryl Graham.'

DS Jones perhaps looks a little relieved, for she is quick to catch on.

'You mean – she has something to do with it? That's why DI Smart was here?'

Skelgill is nodding. He resumes his seat. Again he refers to the report.

'Could he have got wind of this?'

DS Jones shakes her head.

'I don't see how. Sure – if you want to go into the detail, witness statements, tapes of interviews – you'd need a security code and the accessing would be logged.' She raises her copy of the report. 'But this digest is in the open library. I stood at the printer – no one could have seen what it is.'

Skelgill listens pensively. DI Smart was sniffing about like the giant in Jack and the Beanstalk, scenting blood. Quite probably he divined their inhibitions.

'Seems my cousin Sheryl is best pals with Dale Spooner's girlfriend, Jade Nelson.' He nods at the papers. 'She's in there – Jade. She tried to give him an alibi – that he slept with her all night. Except they found CCTV footage of her bowking outside a club at three in the morning. Now Sheryl reckons that Jade has told her that Spooner's got mobile phone footage that proves he's innocent. Only he knows what it is, and where it is.'

DS Jones blinks as though there has been a sudden change in the light.

'So, why hasn't he produced it?'

Skelgill grimaces.

'They're under pain of death, you might say. Their bairn, an' all.'

'From whom, Guv?'

Skelgill's tone softens into that of resignation.

'Spooner's keeping mum. And he's being paid to stay quiet – she gets money shoved through the door.'

'What – like a maintenance allowance – in return for his silence?'

'Reckon so.'

DS Jones looks alarmed.

'That makes it sound like organised crime.'

Skelgill has to nod in agreement. Although from what he recalls of the case, organised crime and Dale Spooner are not bedfellows. Dale Spooner is a petty criminal, with a record since juvenile times of car thefts, housebreaking and minor drug dealing. Rather a pathetic specimen.

'Let's hope for Spooner's sake they don't implement Plan B

before we do.'

DS Jones finds Skelgill's words to be cryptic. She was a trainee constable assigned to another department when the events occurred. She is having to assimilate several new strands of information. The first is purely factual – she had earlier read online that Dale Spooner's petition for leave to appeal had been rejected. The other aspects, however, are more subjective. There is Skelgill's uncharacteristic degree of speculation – on the strength, it seems, of a random meeting with a relative; something he would normally dismiss as hearsay. And there is DI Smart's casual intrusion – his offhand manner belying an underlying anxiety.

'Guv – what were the grounds for requesting an appeal?'

Skelgill exhales dismissively.

'Mostly procedural – flaws in the collection of evidence, incorrect interview protocol, failure to consider other lines of inquiry – usual Smart copybook stuff.'

'But no new evidence?'

Skelgill now shrugs.

'The argument being that there would be new evidence, if the police cared to look for it.'

'That sounds more like re-opening the case, rather than re-examining the legal process.'

Skelgill merely plies his colleague with a knowing look. She responds with a further question.

'Is there any chance the Chief would buy into that?'

The outcome of the morning's hearing provides the perfect justification to consign the case to history. But now there is a gleam in Skelgill's eyes.

'I can think of a reason why she might.'

Skelgill puts his elbows on his desk and rests his chin on the back of his interlocked fingers. He broods for a moment, waiting for the sentiment to find a logical expression. He speaks more ponderously now, his gaze lowered.

'Dale Spooner got life with a minimum of eighteen years. Whoever's behind the payments, they know he's innocent. They would expect there to be a successful appeal. Now that's kyboshed. Do they want to keep paying for another fifteen years?

More to the point – do they believe Dale Spooner wants to rot in a cell when he's sitting on a get-out-of-jail-free card?'

'You mean they'll want to silence him?'

Skelgill looks up, sharply.

'Think where that would leave us. An innocent bloke killed in prison – and the Badduns murders still unsolved.' He inhales suddenly and releases the breath in a long hiss. 'Might get the Chief to sit up.'

DS Jones seems to act out his words, for she shifts into a more upright position. It is plain to Skelgill that she is thinking quickly. Yet he detects some hesitancy.

'Aye?'

She lowers her gaze and frowns pensively at the report, gripping it tightly between both hands.

'We need to know we can trust the word of Sheryl Graham – and Jade Nelson – and Dale Spooner. Say it's not true about the video evidence that would clear Spooner. What if it's just a ruse – to get us to do exactly what we're considering – to get the case re-opened – to expose flaws and find new grounds for an appeal?'

When Skelgill does not reply, DS Jones looks up to see him grinning like a Cheshire cat, almost unnervingly so.

'Jones – hold up your pinkie.'

'What?'

'Do it – go on, lass.'

She obliges, lifting one hand and displaying a little finger with its carefully manicured nail. Skelgill points.

'See – there's more brains in that than the three of them have got, put together.'

DS Jones's sculpted cheekbones gain a momentary flush of colour. Skelgill is not one to scatter compliments about like confetti, but she understands this is one, of sorts. And, despite that his counter argument is basically irrational, there is something about it that is convincing.

3. BOWSCALE TARN

The northern fells, 8.30 a.m., Tuesday, December 22nd

Munching upon his bait – his sandwiches, that is, not the lugworms that he has earmarked for a juicy codling or perhaps a whiting on Christmas morning (an annual tradition) – Skelgill reflects on the tail-end of his discussion with DS Jones, when she had reprised the report they had taken pains to conceal from their prying colleague. The killing of Jake and Boris Baddun; the investigating officer, DI Alec Smart.

It was almost three-and-a-half years previously, in July, that Skelgill had been on a fortnight's holiday – else the case might have fallen to him – quite likely, given what were ostensibly rural circumstances. Although it was soon deemed that this was an urban crime, displaced from the drug wars raging in Manchester or Liverpool (although this assumption proved to be incorrect).

The 'heather fire' that he had mentioned to his cousin Sheryl Graham had emerged to be a C-class Mercedes, stolen a week before from a country house at High Harrington, south of Workington. It was abandoned on a grassy riverbank some two miles along the dead-end mountain road that runs up into Swinesdale, a little-known and rarely visited valley chiselled into the far northeastern reaches of the Cumbrian Mountains. For his part, tucked away in the corrie that holds Bowscale Tarn, Skelgill had first smelled and then, having changed position, seen the smoke. He had no mobile phone signal, and was faced by unfavourable terrain – and had taken the decision to climb Bowscale Fell and call in the fire brigade. By the time he finally made it to the scene the fire had burnt itself out, but for a few residual wisps of smoke. The car was comprehensively scorched. Much the same could be said of its two occupants, in the driver's and front passenger seats.

To cut to the chase, they were identified by forensic means as

Jake and Boris Baddun, local career criminals of no fixed address, but who operated in the arc of socially deprived West Cumbrian coastal towns, from Maryport in the north to Whitehaven in the south, once a thriving hub of iron, steel and coal, trading ports that served the New World. Now they host some of the most socially deprived neighbourhoods in the country; a stark contrast to the prosperity of the adjoining Lake District national park (although Skelgill knows plenty of struggling hill farmers who would disagree).

The Badduns boasted a string of convictions that, printed and laid out, would stretch almost the length of Swinesdale itself. In their early thirties, both had jail time under their belts. They were basically opportunistic thieves, not averse to aggravated burglary, targeting both commercial and domestic premises. They were believed to be behind many unsolved crimes, and no doubt many more that went unreported.

The manner of their deaths proved to be puzzling, and it was not until detailed pathological tests had been conducted that a cogent hypothesis had been developed. There was no indication that the victims had tried to escape the inferno – but neither were their limbs bound or their skulls smashed. It seemed they had been incapacitated in some other way. And, indeed, it was eventually concluded that they were quite likely already dead, or at least unconscious. Both bodies contained shotgun pellets – although the effect of the concomitant injuries had been impossible to determine, such was the charred and diminished state of the human remains.

The scenario that DI Smart had developed was that this was some sort of double-cross or, failing that, effectively a punishment killing for the failure to settle a debt. Some contents of the car boot had survived the blaze, and it was through forensic examination of these that Dale Spooner had been linked to the crime. A well-known car thief, Spooner – it was argued by the Prosecution – had stolen the car to order, and was still owed payment for such from the Badduns. But he had denied any involvement in their deaths.

On arriving at the grisly locus that July morning, much as

Skelgill had found himself torn – a serious crime under his very nose (which had been twitching long before he consciously recognised the smoke on the breeze) – in a sense it had been a strange relief to be able to walk away. He had left the scenes-of-crime officers to sift through the debris, and DI Alec Smart to appear in his own good time, like some imperial general come to survey the spoils of a battle, probably already having made up his mind whom he might like to find responsible.

It had been shortly after dawn when Skelgill had raised the alarm. He had not caught any fish, but there had been sublime peace. He had been happy to contemplate the two immortal trout that by legend inhabit the silent pool; who could prove they do not? And the drama of the scene itself; Bowscale Tarn is the classic mountain feature that geography students are taught to appreciate under the heading of post-glacial landscapes. Carved by ice, it would be possible to believe its origins owed more to the supernatural – warring Norse gods that hewed out their amphitheatres across the fells; here beneath the dark cliffs of Bowscale Fell; long abandoned, flooded. With a pelmet of cloud on the skyline and mist on the water, he could narrow his eyes and imagine ancient champions, Thor and Wodin, going at it hammer and tongs.

As he reflects now, he recalls a sense of foreboding. At the time he had put that down to the atmospheric conditions. The summer air was still and heavy, resonant with the occasional bleat of a lamb that had become separated from its mother, and the plaintive cries of carrion crows. He had been watching a more auspicious cameo: a newly fledged brood of wheatears, small moorland birds that flit from rock to rock exposing their characteristic white hindquarters; they had come to the edge of the tarn to drink from stone perches in the shallows. The sight had pleased him, nature succeeding in such a harsh environment.

Then rain had started to fall, heavy drops which at first imitated a sudden collective rise of trout, but which in short order had him unfurling his capacious umbrella and pulling on his leggings. The silvered tarn had become transformed into an amorphous blanket in the limpid early morning light, the sound like the continuous rush of a beck close at hand. The wheatears had disappeared; he had pondered over where they might shelter; in a sheep scrape, perhaps, beneath the overhang. He, meanwhile, had been joined under his brolly by a swarm of flying insects, enlightening from an angling perspective, since he was able to identify possible baits – mainly unobtrusive sedges, gnats and heather flies – but disconcerting in that the majority were midges, which wasted little time cashing in on their good fortune, a captive meal. Indeed, he recalls that his ears were smarting for the rest of that day.

Curiously enough, he was still under the umbrella when he first noticed the smell of burning. The slow-moving shower had crept away to the northeast, but bored by his unscheduled wait he had succumbed to the lure of sandwiches earmarked for later. He had wondered if it was just the smell of the cold bacon – but, no – despite his sardonic remark to Sheryl Graham, there had been the hint of cooked meat on the wind. That and other particulates of a more industrial and thus perplexing nature. Now he knows that a vehicle had been burned. Plastic, paintwork, upholstery. Petrol. Engine oil. Clutch fluid. The rain shower had scrubbed the air of grass pollen and mountain dust, and had enabled him to taste the complex bouquet.

Of course, the actual nature of the fire – two criminals inside a stolen car – was not the first thing that had sprung to mind. Perhaps a farmer burning miscellaneous waste – that was not uncommon, farms these days are required by law to operate an incinerator, when in years gone by dead animals were simply buried. Or, as he had suggested to Sheryl Graham, overnight campers who had carelessly left a barbecue to smoulder and set alight the dry moorland vegetation.

When he had scrambled sniffing to the rim of the tarn – literally and metaphorically following his nose – such is the elevated position of the mountain pool that he had been able to survey Swinesdale in its entirety. In the glacial floodplain, neatly walled enclosures mainly under hay, the sheep turned out in late spring from the fertile in-bye pastures to roam about the open fells. The brindled southern flank of Carrock Fell a patchwork of grey scree, olive heather turning to purple bloom in places, pale mat grass and brighter green bracken.   The lower slopes thick with gorse, unkempt, its sulphur flowers gone to straw-coloured pods; further up in the valley superseded by a formidable stand of juniper – and it had crossed Skelgill's mind that perhaps this primitive creeping conifer was the source of the indefinable smell, such is the pungency of its crushed berries and foliage.

Once he had summoned assistance, almost reaching the summit of Bowscale Fell in order to gain a signal, Skelgill had taken the decision to strike directly cross-country to the scene of the blaze. Under a mile as the crow flies, the alternative was at least thrice that back to his car at Bowscale – and then the possibility of being unable to talk his way past a checkpoint, having no credentials on him beyond a rod licence.

But, more than once, he was reminded of an old adage, handed down from shepherding forbears. "There's a path for good reason, lad." Though his fishing rig was a collapsible fly rod together with little enough tackle to fit in his rucksack, to forge through unforgiving thigh-deep heather and bracken with unseen rocks beneath is the worst of walking conditions.   He was glad of his furled umbrella as a kind of wading staff.   Midges and biting clegs arose to mither him.   The clammy air was stifling.   Only the chittering of linnets raised his spirits, birds that reminded him of his boyhood rambles, of simpler times.   Reaching the valley bottom there was the small matter of fording the Caldew – but by then he was too sweaty to care and had simply splashed across.

He had no need to endure such martyrdom – but perhaps with hindsight his actions will prove to have been judicious. Even at the time, his intervention served a purpose.   The fire crew from Keswick had arrived a couple of minutes before him, and were readying themselves to smother the smoking hulk in foam. Skelgill – on seeing its futility as far as any semblance of life-saving was concerned – had persuaded the crew manager to hold fire, so to speak: that here was a crime, a crime scene, and that it should be preserved as such.

He had waited for the arrival of uniformed police officers, who had secured the immediate vicinity and – as he had foreseen – placed a roadblock on the lane into Swinesdale. While there are few residents, and it is off the beaten track, enterprising picnickers who can read a map will identify its potential for a pleasant riverside stop off, and walkers pass in both directions. But Skelgill had no special information that required his presence; he was on holiday, and a duty inspector would get the call. Thus DI Alec Smart was assigned to the inquiry. It was investigated, and Dale Spooner duly arrested, charged and convicted with the murders of Jake and Boris Baddun. "Bang to rights", as Smart has put it.

Skelgill stares pensively across Bowscale Tarn; it must be the original infinity pool.

He is perched on the same rock where he had sheltered from the sudden pash, the short, sharp deluge that had driven him beneath the cover of his umbrella. There are no midges today. The temperature is hovering around freezing and there is a dusting of snow on the tops; the cliffs look black by comparison, and the surrounding vegetation is more sombre without its summer greens; though there are still sheep about; he watches a line of them high above, silhouetted against the skyline of Tarn Crags, a little ragtag band of nomads, hardy Herdwicks, inured to the worst of the weather.

He has not come with any specific purpose in mind. His role as a witness was comparatively incidental. The time of morning was probably the most useful piece of information that he had been able to provide; his discovery of the smoking wreck and its charred contents indicating that the actual fire and events preceding it had probably occurred several hours before, perhaps as early as midnight. No, his coming back to Bowscale Tarn – his first visit, he realises with some regret, in the three-and-half years since – has a more nebulous motivation; yet it is potent, nonetheless.

Like a gundog will investigate a side path where once it has put up a covey of partridges, Skelgill knows always to cast again into a swim where before he has had a bite; the fish was there for a reason; the spot has some significance not necessarily apparent to the human observer. So, while he does not expect up here in the silent wintry fells to be confronted by some blatant clue, he knows intuitively that in Swinesdale there is meaning. There is a reason the burned-out car came to be here, and that reason was never satisfactorily established.

Ironically, it was a fact the Defence never got to grips with. The Prosecution had simply averred that the isolated dead-end was chosen as the ideal rendezvous, for a drugs deal, or a carving up of spoils. But, if Skelgill were a criminal, he would not view it as a perfect place. Isolated, yes. Getaway – a basic rule of the misdeed – no. One small police car – or a competing gangster's saloon – was all it would take to block the single-track lane. The Badduns would have been rats in a trap. They were not the sort to flee across country. For Skelgill, as an interested observer, this aspect had never stacked up, but the Prosecution had successfully glossed over it. Yet, there had to be something else.

He drains his tea and packs away his flask. He thinks about climbing Bowscale Fell. It is a shame to come up this far and not finish the job, especially after last time, when he got even closer. Wainwright recommends the broad grassy slope beneath the shoulder of the hill – but there is a much more severe rake, a steep rocky gully that bisects the crags, that he has always fancied having a go at, but has never quite got around to. However, though this might still be his own time, he has a sense that nevertheless he is 'at his desk', and it would be both too much of a self-indulgence to complete the climb, and moreover the 'wrong sort of thinking' – the degree of concentration that he needs will be better served by the less challenging descent via the path back to Bowscale hamlet.

"A typical Lakeland dale in miniature" is how Wainwright describes Swinesdale. On its north side the unclassified single-track lane extends along the foot of Carrock Fell, eventually to peter out into a stony track impassable by vehicular means. Thence there is a fork for intrepid walkers; north, past abandoned mine workings for the Caldbeck Fells and ultimately the village of Caldbeck itself; or west into the heart of Skiddaw Forest. The rushing River Caldew makes its escape from the massif through the dale, swinging north at Swinesdale Bridge to thread its way sedately through a vast rural tapestry to its confluence with the Eden beside Carlisle castle.

The light is poor; it is partially overcast, and at this time of year precious little sun reaches the floor of a valley so deeply cut and unfavourably oriented. Yet there are inhabitants. Arriving a little earlier than he had anticipated Skelgill had continued past his intended parking spot and taken the lane from Swinesdale hamlet. The settlement itself continues initially, first with an advertised "Moot Hall Café" dating from 1702 (not the café, he had assumed, though he had logged its presence for future reference). A modest country estate offers various forms of tourist accommodation. Then there is the first of three farmsteads that are strung at intervals along the valley. A small party of fell ponies had impeded his progress at one point, making hay from a manager intended for sheep, a band of hairy hill-dwellers come down in search of forage. Three quarters of the way along, a secluded property is shrouded by dark pines. Finally, not far from the lane's terminus, stands a cottage that perhaps owes its construction to the old lead mine, but now serves a shepherd, judging by a mud-spattered quad bike fitted with a dog box.

Now Skelgill can survey this arrangement as if he were a cartographer, the features laid out before him like an Ordnance Survey map. He watches as – in miniature, like the dale – presumably the same quad bike makes slow progress down the lane, moving in and out of view, a brace of collies aboard, their ears pricked, going by their posture. From his elevated position he can see the property that was obscured by trees; it has an open aspect onto the River Caldew; built of old slate, there is the dark glint of glass suggestive of a pricey conversion, the sort of thing that keeps the local architects busy and the planning authorities on their toes; second homes in the Lakes are a mixed blessing – few properties run to rack and ruin, but even fewer locals can afford them. Skelgill can only dream of owning such a place, with fishing on the back doorstep. Accordingly, he avoids the temptation to muse and turns his mind to the more tangible conundrum.

Why Swinesdale?

The victims, the Badduns, were here for a reason. The perpetrator – Dale Spooner says not he – was here for a reason. And the explanation – or at least a fragment of it – must surely lie in the dale spread before him. And that fragment, like a sliver of bone to the archaeologist, once understood might be extrapolated into a three-dimensional representation of its whole. For the time being, the whole – and indeed the sliver – must remain a mystery. But of one thing – two, in fact – Skelgill is sure. The first is patently obvious: that in investigating this case the last thing DI Smart will have done is to climb to Bowscale Tarn; he would not take an overview; he would not bide his time. The second is more intuitive on Skelgill's part. While DS Jones was quite right to cast into question the veracity of Sheryl Graham's unofficial and unauthorised testimony, what is not in doubt is the reaction of DI Smart. Even by his own prying standards, he had shown a most unnatural interest in Skelgill's activities immediately following Dale Spooner's unsuccessful hearing. And that, above all, tells Skelgill there is something amiss.

On which discordant note, he had better go and face the music.

4. PLAN B

Tebay, 1 p.m., Tuesday, December 22nd

Expediency rather than force of habit finds Skelgill and his colleagues at a motorway services café. They did not even leave together for fear of word of a team exodus filtering back to DI Smart. To complement his internal network of watchers, he has an uncanny knack of wheedling information out of the unsuspecting and gullible. Skelgill had briefed the stand-in for Sergeant George Appleby on the front desk that he was going to buy fishing tackle, and so in-character was he that he set off driving in the wrong direction, debating in his mind the merits of the pulley versus the paternoster rig.

Now, however, his subordinates find him in a reflective mood as he recounts the details of his meeting with the Chief. He had approached the matter with considerable trepidation. His apprehension became amplified when met with a blank stare, in raising that one of his own relatives, honest herself but admittedly of disreputable provenance, had hinted at potentially explosive evidence: that, as most diplomatically as Skelgill could phrase it, on the Chief's watch there may have been a miscarriage of justice. She had listened him out from behind the same unbending countenance.

His account was suitably succinct.

Dale Spooner claims to have evidence that would clear him of the Baddun killings. He has thus far declined to produce it. The reason, the threat to the lives of his girlfriend, Jade Nelson and their young daughter. His silence has been further secured by illicit 'maintenance' payments to Jade Nelson.

But Dale Spooner has now failed to achieve an appeal against his sentence.

Reading between the lines, whoever is relying on Dale Spooner to keep quiet might now anticipate that he will fall back on his 'get-out-of-jail-free' card. The corollary: that Spooner is at risk, as are his dependents. Moreover, if Spooner suffers some 'accident', the evidence that could clear him may be lost forever.

Skelgill had become conscious of the Chief regarding him with an expression that was only partially familiar. Partially, in the sense of the fiery redhead with laser eyes, a cobra poised to deliver a fatal bite at the slightest misstep. Skelgill has survived such scrapes before, and perhaps instinctively knows to stay out of range. But he had felt, too, an inexplicable pull, that he was being reeled in by the hypnotic gaze, that it had a subtly different quality to it. Or, was it just a ruse to lure him within striking distance?

Then she had nodded.

He looks pointedly at each of his sergeants in turn.

'We're not questioning the conviction of Dale Spooner. Alreet?'

DS Leyton, who has listened with evident disquiet, makes to speak – but he realises his mouth is functioning ahead of his mind and merely makes a sound that might have been a choked "But – ?" Skelgill stares at him for a moment, and then continues.

'Not in any way that Smart would judge it.'

DS Leyton finds his tongue.

'What's going to be our headline? He's bound to be nosing about. He needs to know every unit's business in case there's profit or loss in it for him.'

Skelgill mirrors DS Leyton's facial expression. Implicit in the Chief's unspoken guidelines was that she could not tolerate a situation where one officer is clandestinely operating to undermine another. And, yet, she had shown no inclination to call upon DI Smart, nor did she actually define any areas as off-limits. But she was at pains to make plain the implications of his theory. Show their hand, make one false move, and they could find themselves in a deep quandary.

In that respect her analysis was no different to his own. Nevertheless, a perplexed Skelgill had pondered the Chief's reaction – and her ultimate acquiescence. It was not often he presented her with conjecture; but maybe that was what made the difference.

He has not answered DS Leyton's question, but now DS Jones raises an affiliated query.

'Is there any issue that it's your cousin who has brought this forward?'

Skelgill seems suddenly distracted. He had, of course, come clean with the Chief – but again perhaps this added to the credibility of his petition. He gazes towards the serving area of the cafeteria, and speaks somewhat absently.

'If one of my distant relatives being somewhere in the picture was a problem, we wouldn't be able to touch half the cases in the county. It's them that keeps Cumbria police in business.'

And, as if to prove such ubiquity, he raises a hand and whistles, and calls out, "Harry!" – for seeking them is a waiter cousin, bearing a tray of teas and bacon rolls. There ensues a small hiatus – Skelgill's rule of not competing with the arrival of the tea lady (or teenage tea boy in this case).

But the interlude suits Skelgill, for DS Leyton has hit upon a practical difficulty for which there is no perfect solution (another tentative lob that the Chief unceremoniously belted back into Skelgill's court).

'You need to stretch your existing cases. Use your imagination.' He turns first to DS Jones. 'The agricultural thefts that you're looking at – gives us licence to roam. Start where it all kicked off. Cook up a reason why you need a trip to that neck of the woods. Just don't mention Swinesdale itself.'

DS Jones nods positively.

But DS Leyton regards Skelgill with more limited enthusiasm. He has already worked out his likely angle of attack, and that it may be problematic.

'Stolen motors?'

'Aye.' Skelgill sounds a little surprised that DS Leyton has hit the nail on the head. 'Spooner was probably the most prolific car thief in West Cumbria. Who's filled his shoes? Chances are it's someone we've got tabs on. If we can get their client list – it's the first step to finding out who Dale Spooner was with that night.'

Skelgill inspects the remnants of his bacon roll. He raises it, deciding he can despatch it in one go.

'I'll ride shotgun, as and when.' He wipes his mouth with the back of his hand and swills down the last of his tea. 'In between, I'll break the habit of a lifetime – drop in on the relatives.'

Saying this, Skelgill senses some unease brewing about him. He moves to justify his contradiction of his own warning.

'Look – Sheryl Graham's got an in to Jade Nelson. I'm probably the only person in Cumbria police who can visit Sheryl in plain sight. She's already tapped me up – she's hard up, Christmas is coming. They all know I helped out Jess.'

He speaks with a questioning inflection; his colleagues nod in tandem to confirm their understanding.

DS Jones is first to respond.

'So, do you think she could find out about Dale Spooner's secret evidence – through Jade Nelson?'

But Skelgill now rows back, he folds his arms and his features become creased.

'I couldn't put Sheryl in the firing line. Remember – like she said – approaches to Spooner will set alarm bells ringing. But, you're right – within reason, Jade Nelson can have confidential contact with him by phone. I'll just have to play it by ear – see how the land lies.'

DS Leyton interpolates a cliché of his own.

'Surely the geezer can be persuaded to spill the beans, Guv?'

But Skelgill's countenance is grim.

'Three-plus years, Leyton – and he's not flipped yet.'

DS Leyton rubs at his thick dark hair in a gesture of frustration.

'It must be one scary cove he's up against.'

Skelgill now grins in a rather macabre fashion.

'That's your department, Leyton.'

'Yeah, cheers, Guvnor.'

DS Jones's mind is clearly ticking over at its normal advanced rate.

'I guess we need to look at everything that was reported – not just that night – but before and after as well. Perhaps a month either side – arguably anything at all that relates to key locations, right up to the present day.'

She is making notes in shorthand and she glances up to see looks of concern on the faces of her colleagues. She grins wryly and taps her pad with her pen.

'Don't worry – consider it done.'

DS Leyton makes an exclamation of relief. He is about to tender his formal thanks, but DS Jones has another thought. She looks more pointedly at Skelgill.

'I could have a word with Kendall at the Gazette.'

Skelgill cannot suppress something of a glower from occupying his brow – though he knows she has a point. The press often get leads that the police do not. And, the fact is, they – the police – are shooting in the dark. But it is DS Leyton that voices his concern.

'Can we risk rattling his cage? You know what young Minto's like – terrier with a rat – loose cannon, to boot.'

DS Jones is watching carefully for Skelgill's reaction. When he looks at her, he finds the tables turned from yesterday – she is ready for him with a shrewd smile.

'I think he's adequately terrified of us to be trustworthy.' She pauses sufficiently for Skelgill to absorb her meaning. 'I'll steer him away from the actual date and location. So long as he has no inkling that it's about Dale Spooner, I don't see any risk. And the prospect of some future scoop ought to be enough motivation.'

Skelgill appears to relent. DS Jones continues.

'He'll be able to access shared files – Press Association, Reuters – you never know.'

DS Leyton now has a suggestion.

'Is there anything in the case against Dale Spooner that we could look at another way?'

He turns to Skelgill, but Skelgill holds up his hands, palms outwards.

'Leyton – I was just a witness – I turned up in court for an hour. I had a lot on my plate.' He gestures to DS Jones, who has a printout on the table before her. 'Just what it says in there.'

DS Jones understands that she already probably knows more about the investigation than her colleagues, despite her recent introduction to the facts. She turns the cover page and glances at a summary.

'The top line is that Dale Spooner was convicted on the strength of forensic evidence that associated him with having been at the scene of the fire. He didn't take the stand at his trial. A charred jacket that belonged to him was found in the boot of the Mercedes, along with a spare key from another car that was never identified – his thumbprint was on it and his fingerprints were found on the inside of the boot lid. That's what led to his arrest in the first instance.'

Now she flicks through the document, but does not make direct reference to it.

'I looked at the Prosecution's case. There were some notable anomalies. Foremost, of course, Dale Spooner when interviewed had claimed not to have been at the scene of the fire. He had no car of his own – at least, not that was known. So, there's the question of how he got from an isolated dale back to Workington – a distance of over thirty miles – probably after midnight, and without being seen. The first sighting of him was on CCTV coming from Workington bus station the following evening.'

DS Jones pauses to brush a stray strand of hair from her cheek.

'Secondly, the Badduns were almost certainly incapacitated or possibly killed with a shotgun prior to being set alight. There were no pellets in the vehicle, nor were any found in the immediate vicinity, so they were shot elsewhere. Dale Spooner was not known to use or possess a shotgun, and no trace of one was found. The pellets themselves were of a relatively uncommon type, a tungsten alloy that is more expensive and generally purchased for sporting or gamekeeping purposes.'

DS Leyton is looking doubtful.

'It don't sound all that convincing to me.'

DS Jones nods.

'I don't think it was the strongest of cases. But his credibility was fatally undermined when his alibi collapsed shortly before the trial. His girlfriend Jade Nelson had claimed she spent the night with him, but CCTV footage was found of her outside a club in Whitehaven at three in the morning. She was forced to admit she got the nights confused. By then Dale Spooner was committed to the lie – and perhaps that's what made the jury believe he was guilty.'

DS Jones looks inquiringly at Skelgill.

'One thing that struck me as potentially odd, Guv – did you know the fuel used to set the fire was analysed and found to be red diesel? The car itself was a petrol-engine model.'

Skelgill has been listening pensively; the general gist of what DS Jones has been relating, he knows. But here is a fact that has his antennae twitching.

'What was said about that?'

DS Jones turns a couple of pages, her eyes scanning the densely printed text.

'Well – it's another thing that I'm surprised the Defence didn't make more of, but they seemed to shy away from it. On the other hand, the Prosecution speculated that Dale Spooner must have stolen it, possibly from one of the nearby farms. But there is nothing in the court records that indicates any such enquires were made, or thefts reported.'

She makes an expression of frustration.

'If only we could see the statements. The investigating team must surely have interviewed everyone who lives in the vicinity?'

She fans the air with the document, making the point about its flimsy nature; that while it remains the case that they cannot be seen to be re-investigating the Badduns' murders, all they have to go on is the internal summary and public court records. Skelgill seems less concerned.

'I doubt there's above thirty properties up there – Mungrisdale, Bowscale and Swinesdale combined. In upper Swinesdale there's a country house, three farms, a holiday home and a shepherd's cottage.'

DS Jones nods reflectively. She understands he means that it is a manageable task to revisit them.

'Some people may have moved on though, Guv.'

But Skelgill remains phlegmatic.

'Less likely among the farming community. And that's our main point of interest – as far as red diesel goes.'

DS Jones acquiesces.

'Okay.' She leans forward a little. 'What do you think our

approach should be?'

Skelgill regards her questioningly.

'What have you got that's been stolen lately?'

'Well – nothing in that geographical area.'

'Even better.'

She hesitates – then sees his angle of attack.

'Oh – you mean, we ask if anything has been offered for sale?'

'Aye.' He grins. 'Then it's just a matter of using our skills of diplomacy.'

Skelgill becomes conscious that DS Leyton glances from him to DS Jones and back, as though he is making some sort of assessment about the extent to which such abilities are shared between his colleagues. But, for her part, DS Jones appears satisfied with the plan.

'There's plenty to go on – we have outstanding thefts ranging from a flock of sheep to a tractor. And I suppose for non-agricultural properties there are items like lawnmowers and garden tools. Ten mountain bikes were taken last week from the outdoor centre at Whinlatter.'

Skelgill nods in satisfaction, but he detects continued dubiety on DS Leyton's part.

'Alreet, Leyton?'

DS Leyton is surprised by Skelgill's apparent concern.

'Yeah – no – I mean, I get it, Guv. It's kind of like beating about the bush with no mention that we know the little jailbird Dale Spooner's sitting there in the middle. Bird in the hand.'

Given his subordinate's convoluted metaphor, Skelgill might be inclined to provide a longer answer, but settles for a short one.

'Aye.'

5.
RECONNAISANCE

Swinesdale, 11 a.m., Wednesday, December 23nd

'That's red diesel.'

Skelgill reaches up and with the side of his fist thumps the white polyethylene bowser. It makes a dull sound, resisting his attempt to gauge its contents, although stepping back he sees it is sufficiently opaque to reveal the waterline, the dark liquid within stained with dye to mark its tax-exempt status. 'Must be a couple of hundred gallons in there.'

DS Jones leans to read a specification plate.

'It says capacity one thousand litres.'

Skelgill growls suspiciously. His breath condenses in the cold air like the funnel of smoke produced by a cartoon dragon.

'What's that in proper money?'

His colleague grins; she knows he is perfectly capable of performing the calculation – she has witnessed him convert the weights of fish from metric to imperial. He can do the sums when push comes to shove. But obstinacy as regards the old ways is a matter of principle, and she suspects he secretly enjoys being something of a Luddite.

'I'd say you were spot on – since it's not quite full. British gallons, that is.'

Her rider wins his attention.

'Is there another kind?'

'American.'

He looks at her doubtfully.

'What's the difference?'

'We get an extra pint and a third.'

Skelgill looks startled – if vaguely pleased.

'So, an American gallon's – what – six and two-thirds pints?'

'Eight, actually.'

Now he regards her with reproach – he suspects the same species of wind up as his pet assertion about there being only one lake in the Lake District.

'Alreet, then?'

Skelgill wheels around. A man is standing in the shadow of the doorway of an outbuilding. His intonation suggests less of a greeting and more of a 'what are you doing?'

However, that they have parked in the farmyard at least demonstrates no clandestine approach was intended. Although, since no dogs have barked or appeared Skelgill has assumed there is no one at home.

'Mr Watts?'

He has his warrant card ready. The man approaches. He is short and stocky, and yet wiry in a contradictory way. He wears a bottle-green boiler suit and a black quilted gilet with a tuft of white stuffing protruding from a right-angled tear, of the sort inflicted by a brush with barbed wire. He has on a thick woollen bobble hat, striped yellow and black with some kind of embroidered crest that might feature mating bees.

He steps close to read Skelgill's ID card and then sways back with a frown, as if he has been optimistic with his focal length.

'Danny?'

Skelgill is caught unawares – the card reads "D.I. Skelgill" – he reciprocates with an expression that conveys he does not share the apparent recognition, but is willing to be enlightened.

'Aye?'

The man tugs off his hat to reveal a distinctive crop of red hair, cut short, receding at the temples. He taps his chest with the knuckles of one hand.

'It's *Forty* – I were at school wi' thee. Brian Watts.'

Sure enough. The blue eyes, the ruddy complexion. And the nickname – actually endowed by their design and technology master. A little kaleidoscope of memories, none of which are individually distinctive, flashes across Skelgill's mind's eye. But he does recall that Brian 'Forty' Watts was a useful rugby league player;

like most folk of farming stock about twice as strong as they look.

Skelgill cobbles together a suitable cluster of moderate swear words to admit his failing.

'That's reet – I remember now – you'd be off for the tattie howkin' every October. Your arl feller was a farmer.'

Brian Watts makes a resigned clicking noise with his tongue.

'Aye. He passed away, nigh on three year it's been. Just us and the Ma now. How about thee?'

He looks at DS Jones, rather admiringly – almost as though he has forgotten the formal introduction that Skelgill initiated, and is expecting him to introduce her in a personal context.

Skelgill wonders what to say. Despite this reunion they were not really friends, as witnessed by two decades of not needing to see one another. He half turns and gestures towards the farmhouse, as if to indicate he refers to his own domestic circumstances.

'Same – you might say.'

He tries to impart a degree of solemnity – but then he finds himself rather inadequately introducing DS Jones, making the implication that he is perhaps accompanying her for training purposes.

'But the lass can speak for herself.'

He suspects that she flashes him a dirty look, unseen by their prospective interviewee. But she takes up the baton smoothly, and in a manner that accepts the onus.

'Mr Watts, I'm investigating agricultural thefts – in particular the attempted resale of stolen property. We're simply asking residents of this area whether they have been approached with what they may believe are stolen goods – farm machinery, animals, even.'

Her question is delivered in the third person and without hint of accusation, although it does seem to elicit a flicker of apprehension in the keen blue eyes. She has of course discussed with Skelgill that there is a downside to their approach. Any farmer who does happen to have been tempted by a bargain at an auction or shepherds' meet or country show, or even by a passing hawker, is quite likely to retreat into their shell.

The man twists his woollen hat between short but strong-looking fingers; their flesh is a healthy pink and he does not seem to be feeling the cold.

'These long nights – cover of darkness – a lot of animals are down in-bye.' He glances at Skelgill. 'But I reckon we've got off light, touch wood.' He taps his temple with a knuckle, and grins. 'Not many folk come up here. Flait o' the hillbillies.'

It is something of an oblique and incomplete response, but in fact DS Jones is not perturbed – that he has referred to thefts rather than the fencing of stolen goods is closer to their interest. She moves to bolster the credibility of their inquiry.

"There have been over a hundred quad bikes stolen in Cumbria this year.' Her tone finds a compromise between the unspoken contentions that farmers ought to be more diligent and the police more vigilant.

'Fuel is one of the most frequent thefts – it's so easily resaleable.'

Now Brian Watts seems more content to respond directly.

'Hereabouts, we're all in Farmwatch – I've not heard of owt lately. Some fly-tipping along at Mungrisdale. We even get off light, wi' that.' He scratches his head vigorously, as though he suffers a delayed itchiness from wearing the close-fitting hat. 'Suppose they don't tek it any further than they need to before they dump it.'

DS Jones is forming the view that there persists a sense of complacency in this isolated dale. She notices that Skelgill is staring at the diesel tank, and she makes the decision to cut to the chase.

'Mr Watts – something that would have affected you – there was obviously the incident a few years ago – the car that was set alight –'

As she pauses, a little uncertain of her next move, the man is quick to interpose.

'Oh, aye – but first I knew, it were all cordoned off – and we never got a look in – even though it were technically on our land.'

'Were you asked at the time about thefts related to that incident?'

Brian Watts appears puzzled.

'But that were a gangland thing, weren't it.' He states it as a fact. 'The arl feller were still alive then. Your detectives mainly spoke to him about it. Can't say as I recall there were owt.'

He lowers his gaze, and seems to ponder for a moment. Then he looks up at Skelgill, an optimistic gleam in his eye.

'It's not them you're after now, though, is it!' He intones cheerily. 'Got their come-uppance.'

There is an exchange of looks, Skelgill's inferring that he could not possibly comment.

DS Jones has a folding clipboard, like a market researcher. She is wearing black woollen gloves and it takes her a moment to find the edge of the cover. It opens to reveal a printed table that contains a list of entries.

'Mr Watts – we're taking the opportunity to check that all licensed shotguns are still in the safe possession of their registered owners. There have been some instances where people who haven't used their weapons lately have been unaware of them being stolen.'

The man grins amenably.

'Nay danger there, Sergeant.' He looks again at Skelgill, as though he considers him the person to satisfy. 'I were shooting t' pigeons ont' bottom field, yesterday. I'm trying out some winter oats.'

He jerks his head to indicate they should follow him. Skelgill notices a limp. Across the yard under the cover of an open shed – the end section of a barn used as a car port – stands a dilapidated Land Rover Defender. He yanks open the rear door; it creaks in loud protest, and he has to back into it to hold it open against a slight slope.

The interior is muddy and strewn with miscellaneous tools, a dented red metal jerry can, and various hanks of blue baler twine. On a hessian sack lies a dated-looking side-by-side shotgun and a handful of live cartridges.

Skelgill looks at the farmer and indicates with an open palm.

'Mind if do, Brian?'

'Be my guest.'

Skelgill lifts the weapon somewhat gingerly and turns away from the other two, pointing it at the ground. He raises an eyebrow –

the safety catch is off. He breaks the barrel to see that there are two cartridges in place – with a thumbnail he prises them out and briefly examines them; they too are live. He hands them to the farmer. Then he rotates the firearm until he locates the model number. Squinting, and tilting the gun into the light, he reads it off to DS Jones.

She confirms it corresponds to their records, and, perhaps conscious of the farmer's anxious scrutiny, they both give the impression of satisfaction, perhaps even relief. Skelgill hands back the gun.

'That's like a relic from the Civil War, Brian.'

'Aye – it were the arl feller's. His arl feller's before that. Happen they had pigeons int' Civil War, just the same, Danny.'

Skelgill grins ruefully and watches as the man rather casually replaces the gun and steps away to allow the door to clang shut under the force of gravity. They collectively drift towards Skelgill's car, as though there is an unspoken consensus that the visit is reaching its conclusion. Skelgill catches DS Jones's eye – he can detect a look of frustration. He steps on a frozen puddle and the ice makes a sharp crack.

'That bowser, Brian – does it ever freeze up?'

The farmer follows Skelgill's gaze to the tank, which is supported at a height of about five feet by a rusted steel frame of more ancient pedigree.

'Aye, it can do – when it gets reet parky, like.' He casts a hand casually in its direction. 'That's the trouble with these new plastic 'uns. They just deliver 'em full now. We used to have a steel 'un – the tanker came and filled it. When that froze up you could just hold a cigarette lighter under t' pipe.'

DS Jones makes an exclamation of surprise.

Brian Watts regards her with a look of amusement.

'Diesel – it's not like petrol. It's hard to light. That's why diesel engines work on compression instead of a spark. You can stand in a pool of diesel and drop a lighted match.'

Despite initiating the conversation, Skelgill seems to have lost interest in the subject. He has moved around to the driver's side of his car and has the door open. But something seems to prompt another thought on his part.

'When we turned up, Brian – I was surprised no dog came to meet us.'

The observation seems to strike a nerve, for the man rather winces and drops an arm, so that he stands a little lopsidedly.

'I've got a gammy leg, Danny. Did my ACL playing for Wath Brow Hornets.' Now he raises the bobble hat and Skelgill makes the association, the yellow-and-black livery. 'About eight year back, it were. Can't get about like I used to.' He gestures again with the hat, indicating between the farm buildings to the mountainous skyline. 'We've got Jacob – lives up yonder – he's the shepherd for all three farms int' dale. Got off to a bit of a rocky start – but he seems to have the hang of it now. I'm knackered and t'other two are getting on a bit. But you'll have seen 'em, aye?'

Skelgill nods.

'Aye, we called in.'

He makes a sign to suggest it was the same kind of brief visit as that he now moves to conclude; he works on the hill folks' principle that no formalities are needed, and turns the hand gesture into a wave of farewell. DS Jones takes her cue and climbs in on the passenger side. But just as Skelgill is about to duck inside, the man speaks.

'Thou were big on fishing, as I recall, Danny.'

Skelgill hesitates, his interest inevitably piqued.

'Aye – I'm still flailing away when I get chance.'

Brian Watts seems to seek to be helpful.

'There's nowt much up here. Few little brownies int' beck.' He grins, knowingly. 'There's some daft folk as go up to Bowscale Tarn – must be nickt int' head.'

*

'Moot Hall Café, Guv?'

But Skelgill screws up his features, his front teeth protruding like those of a gerbil faced by a choice of celery or pepper. Then he veers left out of the farm gate, when the former moot hall is to the right. There is the momentary rattle and crash of the cattle grid,

48

and he holds back his reply rather than compete with the noise.

'I've got the Kelly. I'll show you the spot.'

'Of the car fire?'

'Aye – might as well, while we're up here.'

DS Jones rubs the back of her gloved hand against the windscreen. The condensation from their breath has quickly outstripped the car's heater.

'I think we might need a can of diesel to keep warm. Was that right – what he said about it being hard to light?'

Skelgill, having produced a rather disreputable-looking cloth, is also scrubbing at the glass.

'Aye. The flash point's something like a hundred and forty.'

'That's in proper money?'

Skelgill glances sideways to see his colleague grinning at him. He relents.

'Sixty Celsius.'

'I knew you could do it.'

Skelgill makes a scoffing sound.

'Fahrenheit's far more use – typically you've got double the graduations.' He grimaces through the inadequate porthole he has made. 'Older folk where I grew up, generations before them – farmers, stonemasons, weavers – they measured their work as they went. Your thumb's an inch across. A hand – a foot – they speak for themselves. A yard's your belt, or from your nose to your thumb. Or you can pace a yard. What's the use of a metre, unless you're a giraffe?' He glances indignantly at DS Jones. 'In fact, why are metres quoted at all, when it's illegal to put up a road sign in kilometres?'

DS Jones is nodding.

He has a point. And she has watched him measure distances on a map – in thumb miles – although she knows enough of cartography to understand that paradoxically the Ordnance Survey National Grid uses kilometre squares.

She gazes reflectively at the frosted environs.

'I think zero for freezing is handy. It's a good practical benchmark. When I hear someone say it's fifty, I don't know if that's warm or cold.'

'Summer's day in the Lakes.'

She finds Skelgill keeping a straight face. But before she can respond she sees his gaze attracted by something ahead and to their left. At the roadside stands a red mailbox printed with white lettering that reads, "Fellbeck". It marks a short stretch of unmetalled track that leads to a five-barred gate at the fringe of a cluster of conifers. Parked on the nearside of the gate is a quad bike, and seated on it a man, well wrapped up against the elements, but perhaps in his early thirties. There is the impression of a beard, curls of black hair escaping a beanie hat, and dark, bright eyes. Leaning on the gate from the other side, and less well attired, is a woman who might be in her early forties. She has her elbows on the top rung, her hands clutching her shoulders, a suggestion that she is unprepared to be out of doors. DS Jones can see the clouds of their breath as they speak, dispersing slowly on the lightest of breezes. It is tempting to be distracted by two dogs that cavort in the tussocky grass that borders the track, but DS Jones is struck by the incongruity – the man looking every bit a rural labourer, the woman dressed and coiffured more like a smart-casual metropolitan office worker. They break off from their conversation to gaze at the passing car, their expressions neither curious nor hostile, a kind of practised neutrality of keeping one's options open.

'Happen that's our Jacob.'

While they have the personal details of registered gun owners, those of the other Swinesdale residents remain to be established. But Skelgill can now put a name to the shepherd whom he has previously observed from afar.

DS Jones hesitates for a moment; plainly something has jarred with her.

'That woman seems familiar.'

'The pair of them look familiar.'

She realises he means familiar with one another – that there was something of a tête-à- tête in progress. It would make some sense, given the woman's willingness to bear the cold. Although there is no reason to think that it was anything other than innocent – the man in passing might have seen her coming for her mail and saved her the extra walk.

They drive on in silence and after a couple of minutes they approach the old miner's cottage.

'That's the shepherd's place.'

'It can't be far from where the fire occurred.'

'Quarter of a mile.'

The dale has grown increasingly wild, the level grey-walled in-bye enclosures left behind for steepening fellsides and a narrow bed, the beck and the lane meandering, unsynchronised, at times just a few yards apart. There are plenty of grassy pull-ins where summer picnics could be had, or vehicles parked up for overnight camping – and it is onto such a mini plateau that Skelgill swings his shooting brake.

'This is it.'

While Skelgill raises the tailgate and rummages for his storm kettle, DS Jones is attracted by the rush of the beck. Despite the frost on the grass this is groundwater that emerges at a constant few degrees above freezing. There is a low concrete weir, breached long ago, by the look of it, though it still forms something of a pool.

'This looks industrial, Guv.'

'Aye – it'd be related to the mining. Power for the cottage – or just to secure a reliable water supply.'

Skelgill's voice sounds strained and DS Jones turns to see him some yards from the car, foraging at the base of a creeping evergreen shrub. He rises with an involuntary groan, and pushes at the base of his spine with a clenched fist. He returns grasping a handful of dry tinder; the fist he unfurls before her to reveal a cluster of tiny purple berries, their surface hazed with a pale powdery bloom.

'Try one.'

DS Jones eyes him suspiciously.

'Go on lass, it's not Deadly Nightshade.'

She pulls off a glove and gingerly picks the least scarred fruit.

'Bite into it.'

Skelgill watches with interest as she complies with his instruction.

'Wow – what is that? It's really distinctive – zingy. It tastes of – well – *gin.*'

'Got it in one.'

'Juniper?'

'Aye.' He casts about, randomly. 'Stacks of it grows here. Relic of the Ice Age, so they say. Another?'

He proffers the hand.

'Er – no, thanks. It might overpower my tea. It's quite astringent.'

Skelgill looks a little disappointed. But he surely confirms her fears by tossing the remaining berries over his shoulder.

'Reet, let's get this mash on.'

When Skelgill pours meths from a Sigg bottle into the chimney of his kettle and follows it with a lighted match, DS Jones notes he takes care to jerk his hand away. With a pop the spirit ignites and in seconds flames from the dry tinder are licking out of the soot-blackened mouth. In microcosm it recalls the lethal inferno of three-and-a-half years ago.

'Guv, what do you think – having seen that tank of red diesel?'

Skelgill seems transfixed by the flames, and is methodically adding twigs. It takes him a moment to react. His tone when he speaks is oddly philosophical.

'There was everything we needed there to reconstruct the crime. A loaded shotgun in an unattended vehicle – and as much fuel as we could carry – no lock on the tap.'

But DS Jones is not fooled that he in is in any way suggesting a connection; she understands he merely makes the observation.

'It's no wonder there are so many farm thefts. To criminals the countryside must seem like a self-service supermarket with no checkouts.'

Skelgill, crouching over his dented contraption, looks up at his colleague. He seems half-amused by her analogy – but his own provenance obliges him to adopt a more partisan stance.

'What use is a gun to a farmer when it's locked in a safe? The fox has bolted. When you're scraping a living, working round the clock, why would you chain and unchain every gate, or find the money to pay for CCTV and immobilisers and security lighting?'

DS Jones is nodding. He makes a valid point. There is a Catch 22, a poverty trap of sorts. And a too-thin blue line of law enforcement to protect everybody, all of the time. Skelgill continues.

'Any road – at least we know it weren't the Watts' gun that was used. They've obviously had that for donkey's years. No fancy cartridges, either.'

DS Jones might reasonably wonder if her superior sometimes sees the inhabitants of the more obscure fells and dales through rose-tinted glasses, a relic population to be cherished for their stoicism in the face of the hardships associated with their time capsule. However, he is correct in what he says; indeed, all of the firearms they have checked this morning have been in continuous ownership since long before the incident, and none have quietly slipped off the radar in the past five-year licensing window.

Now the kettle, as is its habit, suddenly boils and without warning begins to gush ferociously from its spout. Skelgill yanks it off the fire base and, half-kneeling, fills two tin mugs that steam in the chill air. He passes one up and DS Jones cups it gratefully in her gloved hands. She gazes reflectively about the barren winter hillsides.

'What was your first impression, Guv – when you got here?'

Skelgill rises with a grunt, almost losing his balance, but contriving with an improvised dance not to spill any precious tea. Without needing to ponder, he relates his long-held view. He gestures with his free hand in the direction of the rising valley.

'Last place I'd pick for a rendezvous with someone I might not trust. There's no back door. First principle of the criminal. Even your common-or-garden burglar knows that.'

DS Jones regards him intently.

'So, what do you think they were doing?'

Skelgill is about to dip his nose into his mug; he hesitates for a moment.

'I reckon they were here for a reason.'

He drinks and then does not elaborate.

'Do you mean you think they were killed and then driven here for a reason? That it was symbolic?'

But Skelgill frowns.

'If it were gang-related, I reckon they'd have gone the other way and a done a professional job – there'd be no trace of the bodies.'

DS Jones nods pensively. The way the case was framed, petty criminal Dale Spooner had made a far from professional job of it. The corpses were easily identifiable by forensic means, and he left compelling evidence of his apparent presence at the scene of the fire. He had a putative motive, and no alibi. She looks about, her expression revealing something of the hopelessness that she wishes to deny. Skelgill seems to detect her sentiment.

'Listen, lass – if we'd just driven up here and found a dog, shot dead – what would we reckon?' He does not give her time to answer. 'We wouldn't think it's someone brought their pet up here to put it down – we'd think, hey up – this stray's been worrying sheep, and it's got what was coming.'

His sergeant has turned to face him, and is staring with some alarm.

'What do you mean?'

But Skelgill shrugs and turns away. He takes a few steps towards the beck and gazes at the pool, taking long sips from his mug.

'All I'm saying is, don't push it. Not yet. Finish your tea.'

They do not linger. A blanket of cloud, moderately high, well clear of the tops, has slid over like the retractable roof of a great stadium. There is a premature dusk; a preternatural atmosphere grows in the stillness of the valley. No birds are calling; there is just the ripple of the beck. The air is cold and heavy, almost clinging. Such claustrophobia presses them on their way.

However, Skelgill slows the car as they reach the shepherd's cottage.

'His quad's not there.'

'Maybe he's still at that Fellbeck place?'

'Let's see.'

They continue on, but when they reach the mailbox marking the track down to the stand of conifers there is no one about. Skelgill turns in. He brings the car to a halt at the gate. It is of recent construction; its hinges and latches look well maintained, and there is a new-looking galvanised steel cattle grid. But he suggests they get out and walk.

Beyond the gate the track curves for a short distance through the trees to reach the property that Skelgill had overlooked from Bowscale Fell. It is an old slate-built house, reasonably substantial, of two storeys with a high, pitched roof and capacious eaves, a style that endows many of the Cumbrian villages with their alpine feel. There is the impression of fresh pointing, and of timbered windows and doors replaced in keeping with tradition. To one side stands an open parking shelter, built of rustic pine with a corrugated iron roof, but no vehicle beneath it. Skelgill approaches the front door – he notes a bell with a viewing camera – but he gets no response.

They skirt the building, taking a gravel path that hugs a single-storey extension. On the river side it is entirely glass-fronted – the reflection that he saw from high above. The room is set out like a relaxed study, with both a desk and a settee facing outwards to the view. It looks neat and tidy, and tastefully furnished. The far wall is lined with bookshelves, packed with books.

'Looks like's she's flown the nest, an' all.'

Skelgill turns to survey the scene. Close at hand, down a steep bank the embryonic Caldew runs. It strikes him that a weir might create a pool deep enough to fish.

'I guess I can come back.'

DS Jones's remark breaks into his musings – her tone lacks conviction, and as such attracts his notice. He thinks about responding, but refrains.

'Howay, lass.'

Driving off, they glimpse a small red van just passing out of sight, further down the dale.

At the junction of the private track and the lane Skelgill halts and gets out. He rounds the car to the passenger side. DS Jones lowers her window, wondering what he is up to. The answer – he lifts the lid of the mailbox and pulls out an envelope. He glances at the front and then holds it for her to see.

'There you go.'

There is just a name, the property – Fellbeck – and a postcode.

'Katrina Darkeness – ?' Something causes DS Jones to falter, and she stares for a moment until Skelgill returns the letter to the box. She reaches for her clipboard and makes a note. 'Thanks – that ought to help with a phone number.'

Skelgill resumes his seat.

'You've got Brian Watts' mobile on the shotgun register – he'll give you a contact for the shepherd.' Skelgill inclines his head in the direction of the hamlet. 'Else the postie's a good bet.'

DS Jones nods. She still appears somewhat distracted.

'Reet – what was it you said about that café?'

*

'This would be so much more sensible if we had the original statements.'

DS Jones speaks in hushed tones; though alone, they cannot be sure of privacy. Their surroundings are curious. The low-ceilinged room contains just four tables, cramped by cupboards and shelves that display items which make it seem half-workshop half-apothecary. They have kept their jackets on. There is no obvious heating, although a couple of powerfully aromatic candles supply an illusion of comfort.

There are packets and bunches of dried herbs labelled for both culinary and medicinal purposes – and some perhaps just plain horticultural. The assumption is that these items are for sale, although the majority look old and faded, and there would be no prizes for merchandising.

Their welcome was correspondingly lukewarm. Summoned by a traditional sprung doorbell their host materialised clad in a brown storeman's overall, his manner reserved and his bearing stiff. Aged in his fifties, tall and gaunt, heavy browed and sunken cheeked, his eyes dark and baleful, he is something of a ringer for Frankenstein's creation.

From a restricted menu they have selected under pressure of silence Lonsdale scones with bleaberry jam, accompanied by filter coffees as a change from their only recently consumed tea. The order now delivered, the proprietor has retired behind a carved wooden screen, and for all they know could still be within earshot. Skelgill has immediately set about his snack; he makes a face of surprised approval, but DS Jones's appetite seems dulled.

Skelgill regards her reflectively. She is not one ordinarily to complain, but he understands that this unstructured pussyfooting around goes against the grain. She possesses a falcon's acuity that is at its best when the facts are flying thick and fast, when she will interpret a complex pattern and swoop to its crux. For his part, he is less inclined to try to make sense of things – experience tells him that they will eventually make sense of themselves, and, if they don't then they probably were not worth pursuing. Of the three farm visits they have made, only the Watts' place provided any semblance of information that was little more than contextual. With this latter aspect in mind, he addresses his colleague's dissatisfaction.

'Cheer up, lass. This was just a recce – give you the lie of the land.'

He waves his half-eaten scone; there is the suggestion that he includes the café as an important find in its own right.

She nods, if a little reluctantly.

'Yes, I realise. It will help. I'm getting a frame of reference. I'm just not optimistic, I have to be honest. I hadn't appreciated the extent to which our hands are tied.'

Skelgill shrugs casually, and readies himself to eat his last morsel.

'Then again, you might have cracked it already – you just don't know it yet.'

His unexpected contradiction elicits a rueful smile from DS Jones. His words might be glib, but there is a truism therein – a vital piece of information is often not recognised as such until much later, a lightbulb waiting for a battery, wires and crocodile clips.

Skelgill raises his earthenware mug. It is large, and wins his approbation. The café and its owner might be somewhat offbeat, but the fare served up hits the spot. He takes the opportunity to diverge further from their present obstacles. He indicates the mug.

'How come you're the expert on American weights and

measures?'

DS Jones is momentarily baffled.

'Oh, well – you know my Mum likes to bake? She has a favourite American cookery book, inherited. That's how I know the difference. An imperial pint's twenty fluid ounces and an American pint sixteen. But, to confuse matters more, the fluid ounces are different, as well. And then a lot of American recipes refer to measurements in cups, half-cups and so on.'

Skelgill is looking rather wide-eyed; it is a more elaborate answer than he bargained for.

'It's enough to drive you to metric.'

But when DS Jones might chastise him for such opportunistic duplicity, there is plainly something that diverts her. Skelgill inhales to speak when she interjects.

'We wondered if you'd like to come on Christmas Day – I mean, I know you've got your fishing planned – and the things you normally do. But Mum's baked a Christmas cake – we were thinking around tea-time, something like that? Early evening – ?'

But DS Jones's entreaty rather tails off, for she sees that his brows are knitted.

It would not be in Skelgill's nature to think of first thanking his associate, or of more generally letting down a person gently – instead, the preoccupying thought takes precedence.

'I've promised I'll go over to Big Mags Graham's – she's Sheryl's Ma.'

The significance of his words takes a moment to sink in, and only checks rather than hides the disappointment that has begun to gain sway on DS Jones's face.

'For Christmas dinner?'

Skelgill gives a choked exclamation – although it is plain he does not mean to disparage his colleague's naivety.

'Aye, if you take your own turkey sarnies. But you're more likely to gain admission with a couple of bottles of vodka.'

He grimaces and casts about the room, as if he is imagining his presence at the festivity, and already seeking a means of escape.

'They always have a bit of a shindig – open house – turn up any time after midday, once they're awake. They nag me every year to come.' He returns his gaze to DS Jones, and makes what might be a further attempt to soften the blow of rejection. 'Sheryl will be there, obviously. Jade Nelson, maybe.'

DS Jones seems uncertain of how to react.

'Yes – I see.'

There is a silence, and Skelgill is prompted to fill the void.

'I can't promise anything. But there might be a few loose tongues before midnight.'

Now she responds.

'Oh – do you think it will go on into the evening?'

DS Jones's voice sounds rather distant.

'Like I said before – I'll have to play it by ear.' He folds his arms, and scowls. 'I mean – I don't want to be there any longer than I need to. But it has to look natural when I clear off. They'll be shocked enough when I show up in the first place. No doubt someone'll be wondering what I'm after.'

'Does she live in Workington – this Big Mags?'

'Aye.' Skelgill nods. 'See – I'll be fishing from the breakwater above the slag banks – Coke Point. If I turn up in angling kit I'll have a good story, for starters. If I catch owt, even better. I can make a present of it.'

'Maybe you should buy something, as back up?'

That she has switched into analytical mode is to DS Jones's credit. Skelgill seems to appreciate her comment, and he responds light-heartedly.

'Have confidence – I've never blanked yet on Christmas morning.' Then he makes a rare face of self-effacement. 'Mind, it helps when you're the only one daft enough to be out feeding the fish.'

DS Jones is regarding him keenly. There is an inner arm-wrestle taking place behind the hazel eyes. Her combative nature gains the upper hand.

'Why don't you take me with you?' She twists her lips in a sign of determination. 'It would mean you could have a drink. And we could pop back to my Mum's for Christmas cake if there's time afterwards.'

But Skelgill now shifts uncomfortably in his seat.

'Look – they know I'm a copper – but they know I'm family before that.' His explanation is not exactly grammatical, but it serves to cover the bases. 'When the first person asks, what'll you say you do?'

DS Jones remains defiant.

'I'll tell them I'm your personal trainer.'

Skelgill cannot suppress a sudden laugh.

'That's so ridiculous they'd almost believe it.' But any hope he might hint at, he plays down with the raising of his palms. 'Look – Jess is back from college. Pound to a penny she'll be there. She knows who you are. We can't rope her in on this, an' all. I'm going to have my work cut out with Sheryl, as it is.'

DS Jones makes a face that acknowledges she is thwarted, of half accepting the situation – though Skelgill knows she does not give up easily.

'Look – I'll try and get away. Tell your Ma –'

But he is interrupted by the soft-soled arrival at his side of the cadaverous café owner; he bears more scones on a plate. It appears he does have an interest in the bottom line, after all.

'Another Lonsdale scone, sir?'

Skelgill needs no further encouragement.

The man glances at DS Jones's plate to see her cake untouched, and turns away. But she calls him back, a note of frustration in her voice.

'Excuse me? I'll take another one, please.'

6. DOCKS

Night comes early to northern Britain around the time of the winter solstice. Cumbria shares lines of latitude with Alaska, and folk who work indoors may spend several weeks without seeing the light of day. Stars are a more likely accompaniment to the commuter, and a particularly bright one – the Christmas star? – attracts DS Leyton's attention, striking for its radiance amidst an otherwise all enveloping velvet firmament. He wonders if he can use it to navigate – Skelgill would know how to do this – as he picks his way by the faltering beam of his torch through spiky grass that is characteristic of the coast and sand dunes. Somewhere ahead, he knows, must be the southern bank of the River Derwent – or, estuary, he supposes it would be by now, this close to the sea. From there he ought to be able to get a view of the docks.

A little voice is telling him to call it a day, that this is a wild goose chase. His shift has technically finished and he has the thick end of an hour's drive home. More to the point he has promised to take the family to see the new Christmas movie at Rheged. And it turns out there is a Santa's grotto – a source of great excitement at breakfast, albeit a risky move at the eleventh hour, with no time to react to a heartfelt request that comes out of the blue, an American Girl doll, or a Spiderman outfit. Maybe Santa will need to be tipped the wink.

He sighs and struggles on with renewed purpose. He is not quite ready to give up. His quest has been one of frustration, when he had set out in the bright hope that he would find something to please Skelgill – a gift of sorts; that he would be able to coast into the festive break with a win under his belt, knowing that starting back in January he would hit the ground running, belt loosened by a notch. But he has largely drawn a blank.

He had arrived at Workington armed with a reliable list of known car thieves, and a less-than-reliable list of their last-known addresses. The latter aspect had soon begun to assume greater prominence. Indeed, it was not long before he found himself, on the clear frosty morning, striving valiantly to stay ahead of a cloud of growing depression – the feeling that his limb of the strategy was not going to bear fruit.

In several instances he suspected the address was actually correct. It was simply that he had no authority beyond knocking on the door and, if it were opened, inquiring from without. Not surprisingly, a person of a dubious disposition is unlikely to answer; anyone they send by proxy will deny their presence. And so it was. Despite that Workington is a town of just twenty-five thousand souls, a mere fraction of which the criminal fraternity – its members inevitably familiar with one another – it seemed he had arrived during an epidemic of collective amnesia. "Who?" "Never heard of him." "Can't remember when I last saw him." These were typical responses. Meanwhile a leery eye would stare from a bent venetian blind or the crack in quivering curtains.

Having notched up a series of failures, DS Leyton had come upon a pair of undersized semi-identical terrors noisily 'joyriding' inside the wheelless shell of an old Saab Turbo, its axles propped upon piles of engineering bricks in a weed-infested front garden. The address was one on his list. Taking the two chocolate bars from his packed lunch he had approached casually, the confectionery on prominent display.

"Alright lads. Know where Mason is?"

"Aye – he's up t' arcade. *Aargh, Darren – me bleepin' lug!*"

The younger, perhaps aged six, had blurted out this answer – and exclamation, oath edited.

The older one – Darren – maybe a year the senior (and logarithmically a decade wilier) had instantly cuffed his sibling around the ear – evidently for grassing up Mason (presumably their elder brother). But seeing the cat was out of the bag, he opted to cut their losses.

"Give us the chocolate, Mister."

DS Leyton had gladly obliged, and had retreated under a hail of profanities; an impressive command of Anglo-Saxon for skinheads of such a tender age. That said, hailing himself from London's East End, he had merely observed that there is little new under the sun; he almost felt a pang of nostalgia for his old stamping ground. Indeed, in being assigned to what might be considered an urban mission, he considered that at least in some respects he was playing to his strengths. A change from clinging grimly to Skelgill's coattails, riding a rollercoaster of unfamiliar fells and the impenetrable dialect of their taciturn inhabitants. It had given him succour, and, after half a day of trying, he had now scored his first success.

However, his problems did not end with the locating of a target.

The first issue was that Mason Milburn was barely sixteen. While car theft does not have a lower age limit, there were associated impediments. Improved vehicle security tends to mean that higher-value cars are stolen by criminals with access to technology that is both expensive and hard to come by. Accordingly, the thieves tend to be older and associated with organised gangs. While a teenage joyrider would have no difficulty in obtaining a smaller budget model with little in the way of alarm or immobiliser, that is not the kind of vehicle a seasoned criminal wants. Moreover, while Mason might have started young, when the Badduns affair took place he would have been twelve. It is stretching the bounds of credibility to expect him to have knowledge of that time.

Not that DS Leyton had intended to make direct reference to such. And this, of course – the embargo upon mention of Dale Spooner or the Badduns or even the specific juncture – was an even greater hurdle. And it had grown in stature the more DS Leyton had driven dejectedly around the sprawling council estates of Workington. Just how do you unearth information when you're not allowed to dig for it? Even trickier when the unwilling interviewee is likely to slink away like a fox at the slightest whiff of the hound.

He had tried unsuccessfully to bottom this conundrum with Skelgill. But his superior had merely repeated his refrain that his sergeants were at liberty to use their imagination. *Imagination?* Where was that in the job description? Not so easy for a bear of very little brain.

However, in spite of his reservations, DS Leyton had arrived at an idea of sorts. Why not play the crooks at their own game? He was not arresting or charging anyone here, nor 'fitting them up' for some crime they had not committed. So, why not invent a fictitious scenario that suited his purposes? Provided it contained a grain of truth it would harm no one. If it sounded dubious, so what? The last thing a small-time villain will do is turn up at the local police station to complain.

Given that DS Leyton's underlying aim was to identify a crew in the market for stolen cars, this had to be the nub of his inquiry. Organised car crime is something he knows about; he is involved in an ongoing nationwide case monitoring the smuggling of vehicles between Scotland and London, using the M6 motorway through Cumbria. Taking joyriding out of the equation, cars are stolen for three main reasons. The first is to re-sell; often abroad – typically in Eastern Europe – but sometimes to order in Britain, where their identities are switched. Second is for parts; the vehicle is stripped down in a 'chop shop'. And third, of course, is for the purpose of a further misdemeanour. The car thief's shopping list typically comprises the marques of Audi, BMW, Mercedes and Range Rover.

Cars stolen for the latter purpose – to commit an offence – are usually abandoned and burnt out. This means that the type of vehicle – or, at least, its intrinsic value – is less of an issue. The main reason that DS Leyton can think of that a criminal would want a high-value car for a robbery is speed of getaway. Otherwise, something ubiquitous like a white tradesman's van would be more suitable – it blends in – it is harder for the police to find – and, frankly they are perhaps less likely to look for it than a Mercedes costing six figures.

Indeed, this aspect of the Badduns' potential crime – which they may or may not have successfully completed before meeting their fate – had struck DS Leyton as incongruous. Notorious serial villains they might have been, but they were basically small-time crooks. Their stock in trade were thefts of the order of a few thousand pounds at a time. Sometimes just hundreds. So why would they take on board a Mercedes worth a comparative fortune, with the intention of abandoning and torching it? Why not just sell the car and put up their feet for the night?

Something there did not stack up.

DS Leyton did not have an explanation for this anomaly. Adopting a leaf from his superior's book, he had 'parked' it, so to speak. Perhaps it would come to make sense in due course.

But the nature of the Badduns incident had helped him formulate his tactic. His gambit was designed to frighten the prospective car thief into coughing up the information he needed.

As he struggles through waist-high vegetation he reflects upon how his story might be going down with Mason Milburn. He had sidled up to the boy as, transfixed, he fed coins into the greedy mouth of a purring gaming machine at the local arcade.

"You see, young Mason – what it is, we've had word from Greater Manchester Police that there's a team with their eye on Cumbria. Not a crowd you want to cross. Stop at very little. They're taking out the local kingpins and forcing the minions to slave for them – under threat of disfigurement, or worse. You know what disfigurement means, yeah?"

Mason – a boy it seemed of few words – had continued implacably to play the one-armed bandit. He displayed some facial abnormalities already – albeit not easy to tell which were congenital and which were a product of nurture.

But DS Leyton had noticed him swallow.

"Then – when they've bled an area dry –"

He had embellished his tale with a little mime – his forefinger drawn across his throat.

A licking of the lips was elicited from Mason.

"Strange as it might seem, Mason – we're doing the local villains a favour. Our Chief reckons, better the devil you know."

Grimacing, eyes fixed on the screen, the boy had redoubled his efforts at playing the hard man.

"But in order to do that – we need to know who we should be keeping tabs on – for their own good. Who's in the market for decent motors in this manor?"

Now, a further narrowing of the boy's eyes.

"See – the thing is, Mason – the next caller you get might just be one of the gang, come to ask the same question as me. That would leave me to visit you in West Cumberland Hospital to return your Hampsteads in a clear plastic evidence bag."

DS Leyton had paused to let the somewhat cryptic warning sink in.

"You know what I'm talking about, yeah? Hampsteads?"

At last, perhaps a faint shake of the head; certainly a hiatus in the boy's gaming, for the insatiable stainless-steel squab had issued sounds that hinted at an imminent payout, urging the player's feeding instinct.

"Hampstead Heath. Teeth, me old son. Teeth, and the bloodstained pliers used to extract them."

At this the boy had involuntarily drawn back his lips, revealing an undistinguished set of dentures, but probably worth preserving, nevertheless.

DS Leyton considered himself a reasonable judge of this sort of personality, and had concluded that his words had probably struck home – hopefully the sentiment ahead of the logic, the latter being not entirely free of flaws when put to critical scrutiny.

"Have a think about it over Crimbo, Mason. Just let me know. It's no skin off your nose – not yet, anyway – *hah!*"

He had left the boy with simple verbal instructions for how to contact him. And a £20 note deposited on top of the slot machine. The chameleon-like eyes had shifted; DS Leyton would not have been surprised had a sticky tongue flicked out and snatched it – and there was a sense of a deal being sealed. No doubt the paper consideration is long converted into silver and consumed by the bloated monstrosity.

Escaping the strained environment of the amusement arcade, DS Leyton had replenished his stock of chocolate bars and bought a copy of the local newspaper, and had eaten his lunch in cramped discomfort at the wheel of his car parked in the deceptively bourgeois Portland Square, something of a gentrified market-town oasis in a wider desert of urban decline. However, the Times &

Star cast the town in a more pragmatic light, being a repository for all that is heart-rending and shocking, juxtaposing hope and despair; in one article both, the story of an invalided miner who climbed one-legged every single Lakeland peak for charity, only for the cash collection to have been callously stolen amidst the finishing line celebrations.

At around two p.m. DS Leyton had brushed crumbs from his lap and, muffled against the cold, set off on foot to tackle the last three names and addresses on his list, the remainder located in the cramped back streets around the town centre.

The first of these, a flat above a kebab shop, and then the second, a ground-floor property reached by a dank alley – a "ginnel" the girl he had asked for directions had called it – at the back of a butcher's and beside what appeared to be a small abattoir, had fallen in with the underlying pattern of the day: no response. The third, an apartment over a working men's club by the name of Steelworkers Welfare, was looking the same way. There was no apparent means of ingress. In desperation he had entered the establishment, squeezing between two ample-bellied smokers at the doorway, eating pies between drags of their cigarettes, and looking as little like working men as he could imagine. (Working on their blood pressure, maybe, and so much for welfare.).

The interior was commensurately monochromatic. Three solitary patrons were spread about the poorly lit room. A handful of unappetising-looking pies remained in a heated glass cabinet on the bar, like a vivarium at a poor zoo; beyond loafed a scrawny, weaselly faced man watching horse racing on television.

DS Leyton had approached, conscious that he stood out as a stranger, and prepared to do more so when his accent revealed him as an "offcomer" as Skelgill is fond of calling him. There was also the paradox that he was an actual working man. He had decided to be upfront with his credentials, and he had explained he was trying to contact a certain "James Hawkins", whom he believed to live above the establishment – but that he could not find the door – perhaps it was reached from within?

The mustelid features – pinched mouth, narrow-set eyes, straggly facial hair – were building up to a rejection when there had come from behind a creaky voice.

"He were t' barman afore thee, Ryan." DS Leyton had turned. An elderly man – the nearest of the three lone drinkers – was pointing a crooked finger upwards. "He had thon flat."

DS Leyton had instructed the barman to supply whatever the man was drinking, and a soft drink for himself, and had carried them across.

"Mind if I join you, sir?"

"Nay, sit theesen down, lad." There was a gleam in the old eyes at the sight of the treacly Demerara rum.

DS Leyton had taken it as read that the man had overheard his introduction, and knew he was a police officer. For his part, he had experienced no little relief that, for the first time in the day, he had been met with an amenable response.

It had transpired that DS Leyton's object of interest, the said James Hawkins, had for a period of a few months worked as a part-time live-in barman, the small flat upstairs coming with the job. The situation, however, had not lasted and Hawkins had been replaced by the present incumbent, Ryan, some eighteen months earlier. Unfortunately, the man's knowledge became attenuated – DS Leyton had rather begun to suspect that the elderly chap's initial forthrightness had been designed to reel in a captive listener.

He had proceeded to announce that he was ninety-two, "Wukiton born and bred" and one of the few survivors who had worked with the archaic Bessemer converters, built in 1872 at the Moss Bay site. His was a proud family tradition, a long line of steelmen. His grandfather had been crushed to death by a slag-tipping locomotive when the chocks failed and it careered over the edge of the slag bank, and his father had met his fate when engulfed by a spillage of molten iron. It had placed the word "survivor" into a different context.

"If thou go out t' slag banks – as far as the eye can see there's nowt, from Coke Point reet down to Moss Bay. There were a time when that were like a town itsen, used to light up t' sky for miles around – like Las Vegas it were. Now there's nowt fer folk round here to do."

It had been a much longer soliloquy, and DS Leyton had

swooped upon this opportunity to segue into his own burning question.

"So, how about the Hawkins fella – where's he working now?"

"Word is he got a job on t' docks. That's handy – for some."

The man had tapped the side of his ample nose and had fallen silent.

DS Leyton had realised that it was a cue for another drink, and he had signalled to the barman.

Unfortunately, the second rum (of course, it could have been the twenty-second of the day for all DS Leyton knew) had only succeeded in eliciting another industrial history monologue.

"A little fishing quay grew into one of England's biggest ports. Two centuries of coal and iron. They built Lonsdale Dock in 1865. Before long, Wukiton rails were holding t' world together, lad. *Holding t' world together* – think on that! But it all went down tubes int' 1970s. Nowadays they get the odd bulk carrier in and out. Open storage and warehousing. Undersea cables, wind turbines, timber, shredded tyres – *hah!* Most of the time, it's like a ghost town."

Each new iteration of the tale has a familiar ending. But there was nothing more as far as James Hawkins was concerned, and dusk was setting in when DS Leyton, following his satnav had spotted signs for "Port of Workington" and "Lifeboat Station". The main docks lie on the north bank of the River Derwent, at its confluence with the Solway – the huge inlet of the Irish Sea that comprises the upper stretch of Cumbria's coast. He had crossed the new Northside Bridge, taking a moment to remember the tragic loss of a brave colleague when its forerunner had been swept away by devastating floods.

Indeed, the thought of those black waters running beneath him had sent a chill down his spine. Growing up near London's Docklands and the mighty Thames had done nothing to instil in him an affinity for water; the opposite if anything, and his mental images of those tidal reaches are dominated by snatches from Dickensian TV dramas, of Gaffer Hexam whose living was to scavenge for corpses, and of the menacing escaped convict Magwitch smeared in the foetid black mud.

Folk memory also informs DS Leyton's sense of the long and infamous history of docks and men and misdemeanours. Docks and crime go hand in hand, and have done since time immemorial, whenever that was. The water is an accomplice to the criminal like no other; a surreptitious means of coming and going: a global network of corrupt harbourmasters and conniving stevedores; no limit on size or amount of goods, and all manner of disguises and deceptions; and retreat to the impunity of the high seas, an escape beyond reach of civilised jurisdiction.

His first impression on approach was that the place looked more like an abandoned military base. There seemed to be mainly waste ground behind relatively low-security fencing, chain-link held up by concrete posts angled inwards at the top and strung with three strands of barbed wire. In the rapidly waning light he could make out the shapes of hangars, rusted shipping containers, fuel storage tanks and silos – but it was a sparse arrangement. A solitary crane was silhouetted like a great marsh bird, its namesake, against the strip of pale sky low on the western horizon.

Meagre street lighting had petered out, and there was only the occasional external bulb on a building, and the single red eye of the iron crane bird.

He had reached a gatehouse of sorts. It was unmanned, and the passage open – just a sign warning of private property and no entry except on business. He had supposed, if there was nothing easily portable to guard, then the way might be left clear for the lifeboat station – for the volunteers to gain access as swiftly as possible should the alarm be raised. They would all have been hoping for a quiet night on Christmas Eve – that sailors and anglers shared their inclination to hang their stocking over their hearth and put up their feet in front of the television. It reminded DS Leyton of his impending commitments.

Cautiously, he had driven in.

The words of the old man at the Steelworkers Welfare had come back to him – not exactly to haunt him – but that the place was like a ghost town. As the beam of his headlights played around one deserted corner and then another, he fancied he could imagine the scenes described: the hissing steam engines that brought their loads of still-hot iron rails from the rolling mills across the river; the gnarled men heaving with their longshoremen's hooks and hauling at ropes; a maelstrom of shadowy oil-lit activity, against a volcanic sky illuminated by the distant foundries.

And then in the darkness a tiny conflagration, unimagined. In a nightwatchman's cabin, little more than a sentry box, someone had struck a match. He could see the orange glow of the cigarette tip as the person inhaled. The cigarette moved out and in as the person stretched their arm.

Acting without a particular plan DS Leyton had driven slowly up and lowered his window. The watchman had stepped out of the cabin and taken a few paces towards him, but then had stopped as if by a moment of caution.

"James Hawkins?"

"Ha-hah!" There had come an abrasive cackle. "Blind Pew, more like. Who wants to know?"

DS Leyton was not entirely ready for this kind of retort, but he had remained steadfast to his own agenda.

"I was told I could find him here."

He could not see a lot of the man's face. He seemed to be in his forties, short and heavily built – the age and height could be right – but DS Leyton could hardly call up and compare the photo on police records.

"As thou can see – there's no one."

This of course was not entirely factual – DS Leyton was looking directly at *someone* – but the man had elaborated.

"The docks are shut down for Christmas. Finished early today – that's why I'm here now instead of ten o'clock."

"Sounds like you've drawn the short straw – a long shift."

"While midnight."

Until midnight. That had not quite stacked up. Although for no particular reason that DS Leyton could think of – maybe it was just the way the man had said it. Or maybe it was the manner in which he had glanced aside – in the direction of the quay – and had done so more than once during their short and rather unsatisfactory interview.

And yet it was not entirely unsatisfactory. The instincts that had taken DS Leyton to the docks, and which have now brought him to a location from where he might surveil them, are telling him there is something in the offing – perhaps literally so, if only he can get to a point where there is a half-decent view of the estuary mouth.

The man had been evasive – he had not volunteered his identity, a stalemate that DS Leyton had settled with, sensing he should not reveal his own. Of course, he could check with the port authority after Christmas. But who was to say that the man was legitimately employed? And with the evasiveness came a twitchiness – as though he wanted DS Leyton out of the way. There was the cigarette – the timing of it – the man must have heard his car coming – there was the odd way it was waved about. Was that a signal? What better time than Christmas Eve when the docks are unmanned for the exchange of some kind of contraband. Could he even have been awaiting the delivery of a stolen car? It could be slipped out of sight into a rented shed.

And now his ears prick up.

Is that the throb of an engine?

His nose begins to twitch.

The acrid smell of diesel in the salt air?

But these clues are elusive, they come and go; now there is just a distant murmur of traffic from the direction of the town, and the sporadic cry of a marsh bird, perhaps passing overhead in the darkness.

DS Leyton forges on. He has parked on the unlit road that runs parallel to the south bank of the Derwent and terminates at a little headland in a walkers' car park. Beyond is a breakwater and the Irish Sea. He is perhaps a quarter of a mile short of the headland, at a point he estimated would be opposite to the docks on the northern shore. And now, wading through the soft sand and spiky waist-high grass, he gets a glimpse of the red eye of the crane. And then – *darn it* – he is partially thwarted – he realises there is open water before him, but it is a natural tidal pool. In the faint light of the stars and his ineffectual torch he can just discern small boats, yachts and dinghies, tilted and marooned in the glistening mud, though there are creaks and squelches, and the tide must be creeping in. But his view beyond is obscured by the spit that curves around to form the lagoon.

For a moment he wonders if he hears a sound behind him. He swivels, almost losing his balance in the soft substrate underfoot. But his beam, for what it is worth, reveals nothing but the undulating mass of the marram, the noise perhaps the irregular susurration of the breeze in the swaying foliage.

Then he recognises an opportunity. Close by is a boat larger than most – an old tub by the look of it – it must be ten feet from its keel to its deck – and it seems to be reachable by a rickety wooden pontoon. From that height he will surely be able to see across to the docks.

He goes gingerly. The pontoon is wet and slimy with weed and algae, and the deck of the boat likewise, and tilted to make matters worse. There is no superstructure to hang onto – it seems to be an abandoned wreck – and his smooth-soled business shoes are about as unsuitable as footwear can get in the circumstances. Skelgill would berate him.

But the view is opening out – the channel indeed – and there goes that engine again – definitely, the dull reverberation, approaching under cover of darkness. And no navigation lights – why would a boat have no lights when they are a mandatory requirement?

And was that not a flicker of light from the quay?

The deck rises ahead of him – if only he can reach the prow he will be able to watch what is about to unfold. Arms outstretched for balance he slides one foot at a time, like a novice skater in slow motion. He turns his head from side to side, understanding that his peripheral vision will be first to detect any signals.

The Christmas star is shining more brightly than ever, highlighting the contrast that night has descended like an impenetrable blanket; even at this early hour, all about there is the quality of midnight.

He edges forward, straining to see.

Then suddenly – a shooting star? *Aargh* – no – shooting *stars*. A galaxy. Vertigo. Gravity.

And blackness.

*

His next impression is also of blackness.

And feelings that tell him time has elapsed.

A dull throb at the back of his skull. Numbness in his left foot. A burning sensation in his right wrist.

Water – creeping, cold, chilling to the bone – is that what has brought him round? Water around him – up to his chest. He struggles to find his footing. Mud and slime seem to be sucking him down.

He slips backwards and goes under. He comes up; his gasps echo in the darkness around him.

What is happening?

Is he in a tank? In a barrel? A convict ship – a hulk?

He sees the grinning face of Magwitch – feels the pawing of Gaffer Hexam.

He recoils in half-shock, half-fear. Claws at the air. Cries out.

The water level is rising.

Wait!

A pale portal overhead – an inverted black hole. Suddenly – a fine shaft of light – the Christmas star?

He staggers, falls, rises, splashes, chokes, splutters and staggers again – the fine beam becomes a blazing supernova – he reaches up.

A fist comes down.

7. SLAG BANKS

Workington, 8 p.m., Thursday, December 24th

'Cor blimey, Guvnor, I thought I was a f-flippin' g-goner. Swallowed by a wh-whale – something like that.'

As Skelgill clambers back into his car he presses a tin mug of steaming tea upon his colleague. He cranks up the heater and stamps on the accelerator pedal to give the engine a boost.

'Get that down you, Leyton. You're still talking coo-clap.'

Skelgill switches on the interior light and glares his sergeant, wrapped in two army blankets and an outer shell of a foil survival cape.

'Hey up, Leyton – I reckon you've got some useful bait in your hair. I'll pick that out and have it for the morning.'

'Whoa – leave it out, Guv. It's bad enough me falling into that f-flamin' d-death trap – never mind the ruddy creatures that want to eat you.'

Skelgill inhales sharply – but he checks himself. It is not the right moment to cross-examine his befuddled colleague about what he fears happened. And, after all, it might not.

But his assessment of DS Leyton's present state of confusion is certainly accurate.

'Where the f-flippin' heck are we, anyway, Guv?'

'They call this stretch the slag banks.' Skelgill jabs a hand to indicate to their left, although there is nothing visible in the darkness. 'From this headland, down to Moss Bay.'

'Oh – Moss Bay? Yeah, of course. They used to ship the slag from the Moss Bay works by steam locomotive, Kerr Stuart 683, fifteen-inch by twenty-inch cylinders – two-foot gauge railway from the foundry. The loco would reach the rail-stops and the driver would uncouple the ladle and connect the ladle-chain. Then he'd reverse to tension the chain and tip the ladle. The molten slag poured down the bank like a volcanic eruption. Workington's own Vesuvius, it was!'

Skelgill is agape.

'Leyton – you'd better let me double-check that bang on your nut.'

DS Leyton instinctively touches the spot; he flinches, but shakes his head determinedly.

'Nah – I'm fine, Guv – straight up. Right as rain.'

Skelgill is not convinced by his colleague's protest. He reaches across and pulls a half-eaten packet of chocolate digestives from the glove box.

'Here – dunk a couple of these – the extra sugar'll give you a boost.'

DS Leyton begins to do as ordered – then a realisation strikes him.

'Wait a minute – what time is it, Guv?'

Skelgill glances at his dashboard clock.

'Back of eight.'

DS Leyton splutters and looks like he would jump out of the car, were he not so well swaddled and balancing the scalding tea and biscuits on his lap.

'It's Christmas Eve!'

Skelgill regards him suspiciously.

'Aye, it's Christmas Eve.'

Skelgill plays down the fact – but his colleague becomes more agitated.

'I'm taking the nippers to Rheged – to the flicks – and Santa's grotto. I've gotta get back, Guv. But I'm late – the film started at seven. Cor blimey – oh, no – I'll get earache from the Missus! She'll have had to go by taxi or something.'

Skelgill places a calming hand on his shoulder.

'Leyton – it's all taken care of. Jones has driven them. She's stayed with them. She's good with your bairns, mind?'

'What? But – ?'

DS Leyton is nonplussed – but then he seems to experience a moment of clarity, understanding that contingencies have been unfolding in his absence.

'Whoa – wait a minute. Eight o'clock? I went to that – that boat thing – that was before five.'

'Aye – so I've gathered.'

'But, Guv – the Missus – she'll have been worrying her socks off.'

Now Skelgill makes a face that might be slightly sheepish but which at the same time conveys stern necessity.

'Not exactly, Leyton – we told her you were doing some secret last-minute Christmas shopping with me.' Skelgill grimaces and gives a twitch of his head. 'I reckoned you'd turn up. She knows you're okay – I just texted Jones while I was waiting on the Kelly.'

DS Leyton's malleable countenance is something of a moving feast, suggestive of the disjointed thoughts that swirl beneath the surface. After a few moments' reflection he suddenly raises the packet of biscuits.

'You not having one, Guv?'

'Aye, maybe I will in a minute. When I get you a top-up. You'll be dehydrated, swimming in salt water all that time.'

DS Leyton makes a growl of consternation in his throat.

'How did you find me?'

Now Skelgill grins wryly.

'Leyton – it looked like an elephant had trampled through the marram from your car. When I got to the shore I heard what sounded like a hippo wallowing about inside that wreck.'

DS Leyton gives an ironic-sounding groan; but he seems to be perking up. The sweet warming tea, the fluid and the simple carbs are taking effect, as Skelgill has predicted.

'Yeah – but – I mean – how did you find where I was – my motor?'

Skelgill slumps back in the driver's seat and folds his arms.

'You've got Jones to thank. She wanted to wish you Merry Christmas – couldn't get you. Your wife phoned at half-five and Jones took the call. We agreed there might be an issue and Jones checked when you last logged on and compared it to your itinerary. I got on my bike – in the meantime she got back to your wife to put her mind at rest.'

DS Leyton exhales, first with relief, but there is a hint of renewed exasperation.

'She'll be hopping mad if she thinks I've done a bunk with you, Guv – left her in the lurch. She'll reckon I've let you talk me into going down the boozer.'

Skelgill shrugs off this concern – though he refrains from actually pointing out that it is probably a preferable species of anxiety. Besides, if not exactly a false alarm, it would have been in vain. He opts to distract with the facts of his trip.

'I started following your tracks. Steelmen's Welfare. Drove all round the docks. No sign of you there – thought – what would I do myself? Maybe have a deek at the lagoon. Flood tide – it's when the boats come and go.'

The suggestion that his sergeant had taken the course of action that he too saw as logical is, however, a little disingenuous. For if Skelgill were entirely honest, what he would have done himself – so near to the breakwater he intended to fish in the early hours – is go and have a look, tempted by the spring tide, possibly even cast in a speculative line – if only to catch some spare bait for the morning. But he skirts around this knowledge.

'Sure enough – there's your car, parked on the verge. A trail leading into the dunes towards the foreshore.'

DS Leyton is looking pensive.

'You say the tide was coming up, Guv – that thing must be holed.'

Skelgill nods. He had calculated himself that the abandoned craft simply sits on the bottom and alternately fills and drains with each movement of the tide. But he puts a positive spin on the matter.

'I reckon if it weren't half full of seawater I'd never have got you out.'

He reflects upon the moment when he shone his torch into the hatch and lowered a clenched hand to create a slip-proof grip for his floundering colleague to grab onto. But, he must admit, not all the credit is due to him – he doubts his dodgy back would have survived the hauling out of his none-too-slender associate without the man's own survival instincts kicking in, disoriented and half-drowned or not.

Skelgill suspects that DS Leyton does not recall much of getting back to the shooting brake and driving the short distance to the secluded parking area overlooking the headland. He was at his lowest ebb. Skelgill had scavenged materials from his camping and mountain rescue kit, and set to with his Kelly kettle. He had determined that any injuries were not life-threatening – and that a combination of hypothermia and dehydration posed the greatest threat – and these he could remedy most quickly himself. Perhaps less altruistically, there was also the issue that if DS Leyton was carted off by ambulance to Whitehaven he would not get the story until tomorrow morning.

That said, he has decided not to attempt to de-brief or question his colleague unduly – not least, the answers may be unreliable (or just off-the-wall), as illustrated by some of DS Leyton's delirious ramblings hitherto. However, his sergeant now seems to suffer another flash of semi-lucid recall.

'At the docks, Guv – did you see that nightwatchman – the Blind Pew geezer?'

Skelgill narrows his eyes. He had searched and seen no one – dressed for panto, or otherwise. He shakes his head.

'Happen he was doing his rounds. I didn't hang about when I figured you'd gone.'

Another white lie. What had in fact crossed his mind was that it would be an easy place to conceal an unwelcome vehicle and its occupant – in one of the sheds, hangars, warehouses – or off the edge of the quay.

But DS Leyton persists.

'Something was queer, Guv. You know how you get a feeling? That's why I drove round to this side of the river – so I could watch. I'd swear there was a boat coming in with no lights showing.'

Skelgill does not respond, and a silence ensues. It is a minute or more before DS Leyton speaks again.

'What's that – shining out there – a lightship?' He nods to indicate ahead, beyond the windscreen to the darkness of the Irish Sea.

'That's Venus, Leyton.'

'Nah – nah, Guv – I mean lower down – the one that keeps flashing.'

Skelgill adjusts the trajectory of his gaze.

'It's the lighthouse at the Point of Ayre.'

'What – Ireland?'

'Nay, Leyton. Isle of Man. It's only thirty-five miles as the crow flies.'

DS Leyton gives a short whistle.

'I think of it as a foreign country. It's all millionaires and cats with no tails, ain't it?'

Skelgill might well look askance – that the rambling has resumed – were it not that these are a trio of facts of a sort.

'Aye – it's a foreign country, alreet. They have their own team in the Commonwealth Games.'

'Hah – I bet they're good at the three-legged race, Guv!'

Skelgill regards his colleague with a look of encouragement.

'There you go, Leyton – that tea's working wonders – you're starting to tell bad jokes again. Give us your mug.'

Skelgill disappears behind the car. After a few minutes he raises the tailgate and there are clanks as he replaces his kit. He reappears with two full mugs to find DS Leyton patting himself down, over the blankets.

'Guv – I reckon I've lost me old dog and bone.' He scoffs in self-reproach. 'It must have gone flying when I fell through that ruddy hatch.'

Skelgill regards him intently. His sergeant's words rekindle his smouldering concern.

'Jones said it wasn't ringing out when she first tried you, about five-thirty. After that, I couldn't get anything.'

He hands over the two mugs.

'Hang on to these – we'll drive back down and I'll have a deek. Most likely you dropped it when you got out of the car.'

DS Leyton looks doubtful. But Skelgill already has them on the move. He drives judiciously the short distance and comes to a halt, nose to nose with DS Leyton's car. He grabs up DS Leyton's keys from the central console.

'I'll check inside, an' all.'

He leaves the headlights on, and the engine running for continued warmth – though it seems his colleague has largely recovered his wits, commensurate with restored fluids and the raising of his core temperature. Compared to mountain rescue casualties, Skelgill is amazed he has come out so well after several hours languishing in chilling mud and slime and subsequently rising seawater.

When Skelgill had first arrived – the empty car, unlocked and with the keys in the ignition – he had suspected it was a case of answering the call of nature – that DS Leyton would not have strayed far – and perhaps had met some mishap, a twisted ankle or suchlike, something that had incapacitated him. They had received no warning – no indication that he was about to do something dangerous that would merit calling for back up.

In the beam of his superior torch he had followed distinct tracks through the marram grass and undulating sand dunes – and soon came upon the boat and heard the cries of distress. His overriding priority had become the salvaging of his partner – and to get him back to the sanctuary of his own car. But a series of niggling clues had lodged themselves in his mind, and these he now wants to double check. His sergeant thinks he went to the boat alone, and trod on thin air, and cracked his head as he fell through the hatch. Given his fragile condition, Skelgill has not wanted to disabuse him of this notion, to shed doubt upon it – and, besides, he has no actual evidence to the contrary.

But there is an alternative scenario. If DS Leyton had inadvertently stirred unrest by poking about the criminal underbelly of Workington, perhaps someone was on his tail. Whether they thought he was a police officer or indeed some interloper might make no difference. He could have attracted such attention at any time of the day, right up to his last call at the docks. Or it could have been cumulative, with the jungle drums monitoring his progress. Finally, his car moving along the unlit road towards the headland would have been an obvious target – the beam of its headlights visible from the port, for instance. Who comes up here on Christmas Eve – except perhaps some sad fisherman with nothing better to do? He could have been followed. He could have been bumped on the head. He could even have been dumped into the hulk. Local knowledge in play – that the wreck was scuttled and would fill with water. A death trap indeed.

Despite that he chastises himself for such extreme fancies, Skelgill takes care as he picks his way through the sharp-tipped grass. Unfortunately, soft sand does not accept prints – merely an amorphous disturbance. There is plenty of that, and flattening of the grass – but between him and DS Leyton they each passed this way twice – four sets of footfalls. Any others would easily be subsumed. And at the narrow foreshore the tide has now covered the smooth silt that would be more revealing. He examines the slimy pontoon. Clearly it too must become inundated by the highest tides. In the light of the torch he can see streaks and scuff marks, but there is nothing conclusive. It is the same on the wooden deck – plenty of signs of activity – but he dragged his colleague over the boards and tumbled backwards himself. They were both floundering about; it is impossible to tell if someone else has been here.

He clicks off his torch and stands for a moment in the darkness.

The sky is clear and the stars bright, though they make little impression on the landscape. It is always lighter at night near a town if there is a layer of cloud to reflect the light pollution. Overhead a calling curlew passes, and a flock of oystercatchers piping to maintain contact. He knows that birds will move with the tide, to be first to the food on freshly exposed mud. He casts about with his torch. The water is still high, but – yes – perhaps it is dropping. His beam alights on a nearby vessel – he gives a small rueful laugh. 'Danny Boy' is still for sale.

It seems to prompt him, and he turns and makes his way back down what is little more than a rickety gangplank. Sure enough, there is a tidemark, just a foot or so of freshly wet sandy silt below a line of fine debris and foam. And then – what is that? A silver flash. Always alert for fish, Skelgill moves closer. But it is a mere disc, small – like a very large scale, at best. He bends over. No – the monarch's head. It is a coin. A ten-pence piece. Remembering the motto about good luck he reaches and picks it out of the mud and rubs it pensively between his fingers. Then a second thought strikes him, and he turns it in his palm. It is tails up – but only in a manner of speaking – for the engraving is of a tailless Manx cat. Now, there is a coincidence.

A couple of minutes pass before he re-opens the door of his car, rousing a drowsing DS Leyton. He proffers a mobile phone.

'Guv! Where was it?'

'In your motor. In the hands-free. Turned off.'

'Stone the crows – I must have done that when I went to the docks – so as not to attract attention if it suddenly rang.'

Skelgill clambers in and fastens his seatbelt.

'Time we got our skates on, Leyton. What say we drop in at A&E for a quick once-over? While I'm waiting, I'll sort a pick-up for your motor.'

DS Leyton rolls his shoulders and rotates his neck, like a prop forward who has just endured a particularly demanding scrummage.

'Nah – I'll be fine, Guv. If I've got concussion there ain't much they can do about it – and now I'm off for a few days.' He picks rather gingerly at the outer layer of blanket. '*Huh* – I'd maybe do it if I thought they'd give me a dry change of clothes – me whistle's sodden.'

Skelgill reverses his car and then crunches it into first gear without braking.

'Tell you what, Leyton – Asda's still open. They'll have suits going cheap at this time of night – red, with white trimmings.'

8. CODLING

Big Mags Graham, Skelgill is thinking, must once have been plain Mags – or Maggie, or maybe even Margaret – for surely there was a time when she could not have merited the additional descriptor. At a little over five feet, it is not height that attracts the epithet, while that other dimension (which presumably does) to the best of his recollection has been steadily inflated since adulthood was reached. Unless, that is, the 'Big' has some other meaning and origin altogether. Though he cannot think what – at somewhere between his own generation and that of his mother (although much closer to him in age), Big Mags is hardly a matriarch of the clan. There are plenty of more elderly females who could be ascribed that title, a whole committee – which is in fact probably more representative of how the soft power is distributed in this half of the family. Notwithstanding, she is a force to be reckoned with in her own domain, and has been thrusting this way and that about the throng like a small carnival float done up as a tinsel-trimmed Christmas pudding.

He is relieved of the conundrum by the interjection of an inebriated uncle.

'Alreet, Danny Boy?'

Skelgill raises his bottle of alcohol-free beer. With his long fisherman's fingers covering the label it looks enough like the genuine article.

'Alreet, Fred.'

'That's a gay fine codling int' fridge. Catch it theesen?'

'Aye. This morning.'

The man scowls disapprovingly.

'Someone ought to get it ate, lad – it's teckin' up room for ale.'

Skelgill had identified the problem upon his arrival, under one arm laden with a multipack of nondescript lager and a seasonal 2lb box of Milk Tray for Big Mags, which seemed to be well received – certainly with more enthusiasm than the fish; she had clung to the chocolates, and instructed him to deposit the rest in the refrigerator. But this was a modest contrivance and, though apparently cleared of food for the purposes of the party, it was more or less jammed solid with bottles and cans. The outside temperature being just a few degrees above freezing, he had opened the back door, thinking he could hang the fish on the handle in its carrier bag, and leave the lager to chill on the step. But two small scrawny cats had run out, as if divining his intentions, and he had been obliged to retreat with the codling and reorganise the contents of the fridge.

'Ont' real ale, then?'

Now the man has turned his sights upon Skelgill's choice of beverage, which he purchased last evening along with other merchandise. Uncle Fred's tone is suspicious, as if Skelgill is flaunting the use of some new-fangled substance. He is about to trot out his stock sermon – that there is no such thing as real ale in a bottle (a reason he hardly ever drinks at home) – that it is as much an oxymoron as alcohol-free beer itself, when he is saved from such pedantry.

Someone has put 'Sweet Caroline' on the sound system and the man, in tandem with just about everyone else, suddenly breaks into raucous song and is sucked into the seething multitude as the compelling chorus sweeps like a tsunami through the small terraced property. Skelgill is left thinking that, if just one of them has a disease which is as remotely as infectious as the tune, they will all go down with it before long. But, hey – so far so good, so good, so good – he has avoided questions about the singularity of his presence. And, so far, no one has asked him for legal advice.

He figures he ought to get out of the kitchen.

He squeezes beneath an archway – the rest of the house is knocked through into one long room with an added conservatory. He sees a green top-knot bobbing over the sea of heads and he catches the eye of Jess. A guy of about her age has an arm around her shoulder – she is looking good. She reacts with a demure smile and Skelgill raises his bottle and makes a hand gesture and facial contortion that is intended to signify that they must talk at some point, but recognising that at the moment there is little prospect of getting close or of even hearing the other person. One who did not know better might estimate that Skelgill has arrived near the crest of the first wave of party mania, and that in due course there will be a trough to allow for interaction. But Skelgill knows otherwise. He has attended these events before, and the best that can be expected for several hours is a plateau – these folk know how to tank up and stay tanked up. There may be a prevailing antipathy to work, but no lack of vim when it comes to letting the hair down.

The whole place is pretty well jammed. Older relatives sit blinking, marooned on sofas, armchairs, and dining chairs which have been pushed against the walls. In between it is standing room only. The crowd flows out into the narrow hall, where people are perched on the stairs. Circulation is nigh on impossible (other than by employing Big Mags' ice-breaker technique) and the tendency is to get stuck with the nearest person. Then, as Skelgill has already highlighted, there is the near-impossibility of trying to have any form of intelligible conversation, and not just due to the deafening noise. Healthy respiration is hampered by a progressively thickening fug of cigarette smoke and human smells, only masked by perfume in some cases.

This kind of thing is far from Skelgill's natural habitat, and not one he frequents often. And though he is the youngest of four brothers himself, the Skelgill lineage has been historically attenuated, the Y-chromosome at one time passing through generations of only-children, five successive males, defeating the laws of statistics; it is a rare genome – he has met no others in the Lakes or elsewhere; only in the Lakeland topography does the name appear, hinting at its Old Norse origins. As he considers the prolific clan around him, his mother's side, it suddenly strikes him – and prompts a wry smile – just look what happened when Skelgill fastidiousness met Graham fecundity! He has to tip his hat to his Ma; she will be at her sister Mary Ann's in Cockermouth, with a good number of that generation, enjoying a more placid Christmas dinner; although knowing Minnie Graham as he does, were she here right now she would be up with the best of them belting out *"Bam, Bam, Bam!"*

A man whom he does not recognise but who evidently knows who he is buttonholes him and seems to be complaining about speed cameras, although his accent is so broad and his voice so thick that Skelgill can only nod at what he estimates are the right moments. In the circumstances there are basically two ways of losing an individual one becomes lumbered with – to express the urgent need either for a new drink or to go to the toilet, which engender roughly equal sympathy. Skelgill invokes the latter tactic, as it is less likely to have the man volunteer to come with him. The only bathroom is upstairs, and Skelgill forces his way out into the hallway via the kitchen, rather than the congested lounge route.

The staircase may once have boasted a bannister, but it is long gone and he finds himself eye to eye with his cousin Sheryl, whose presence he has noted but not yet had chance to engage with. She is seated six steps up beside another young woman, whom he identifies as Jade Nelson, a slim peroxide blonde with immaculate make-up and a distinctive diamond-studded choker that emphasises her slender neck. The pair are clearly well oiled, and have attracted a gaggle of younger blokes who occupy the lower steps and the standing room near the front door, and it is not difficult to see why. Sheryl is dressed in the fashion of his previous encounter, and Jade likewise, both wearing tight micro dresses that almost might as well not be there. The view from his angle is alarming enough; from directly ahead, no wonder the young men are goggle-eyed, as the animated pair writhe about in laughter, their tanning-salon-coffee-coloured lower limbs flaunting the normal rules of decorum. Sheryl has not yet noticed him, as he wonders how he will navigate this particular human log jam.

He is just beginning to think that the back lane might be a more practical expedient, when someone beats him to the punch. A clearly drunken male, dishevelled and overweight and in his mid-forties pushes out into the hallway and begins to force an assault on the stairs. He scrambles over the acolytes who throng the lower steps. Reaching the girls, his gaze falls naturally upon their naked legs. Their scowls register disapproval, but they rise to create a gap for him to pass. A step below, his eyeline now at bosom height he turns to face Jade, and it seems is about to put a hand where he should not.

'Hey!'

A sharp slap rings out. It sounds painful, but he merely leers knowingly.

'Nice diamonds, Jade – are thee back ont' game?'

He reaches again.

In a sudden of flurry of movement Jade knees the man in the groin, doubling him up, and pours her sticky-looking pink cocktail over the back of his head and shoves him with the sole of one foot, sending him toppling through the bodies on the stair. There is an outburst – evenly divided, Skelgill determines, between a roar of approval for Jade and jeers of come-uppance for the man. But in the same moment the fight dislodges Sheryl from her precarious position and, there being no bannister, she topples backwards onto Skelgill.

Her glass goes flying past his head and shatters off the wall, and he reacts by reflex and catches her – she is no waif, but his muscle memory is fresh from manhandling DS Leyton, and she assists by instinctively wrapping her arms around his neck and (less instinctively, it seems to him) sucking hard on the side of his face. He staggers under the force, but his legs hold firm and he senses she seems pleased with the situation, her body settling against his and a mixture of perfume and perspiration enveloping him. In the back of his mind a little voice which he attributes to DI Alec Smart cackles contemptuously, and he becomes aware that, with one forearm under her knees and his other hand beneath her backside he can feel only bare flesh. He is conscious that in the ongoing melee there has been flash photography, and that some of the jocularity has transferred to his predicament – one warning of the damage Sheryl's weight will do to him and another remarking that it saves the bother of chat-up lines. Most evidently do not know who he is.

But now there is a further distraction for the audience. Word has got through to the powers that be. Just as the man kicked down the stairs is picking himself up, gulping deep recovery breaths and flinching under cruel jokes comparing him to a wether sheep and recommending a cold sponge – Big Mags comes out swinging from the lounge. From frying pan to fire. With a volley of blows and invective, she drives him out of the front door, landing a solid parting kick in the well-padded rear.

Skelgill has perhaps rather inexplicably hung on to Sheryl, and now with what is more of a slobbering kiss in his ear she informs him that this is Eric, her mother's latest boyfriend. Latest, and not the last, it would seem. There has been a lull in the music, but now a new track bursts forth and Sheryl starts waving her arms about, clubbing style. Skelgill does not want to appear as a middle-aged killjoy (albeit he can be little more than a decade older than Sheryl and the coterie of twenty-somethings). And perhaps he subconsciously takes pride in showing his strength. He whirls around in the cramped space and sees that Jade is staring straight at him, smiling in a reflective kind of way, and he notices full on just how strikingly good looking she is, and he can't help wonder how did Dale Spooner net a girl like her.

As they spin Sheryl reaches and high-fives her friend and then sinks back against him and presses her mouth to his ear.

'Why don't thee come round to mine later? It'll just be me and Jade – she's staying the night. Her Ma's looking after t' bairn.'

Skelgill sees that Big Mags is eyeing them curiously, and he lowers Sheryl to her feet and makes a face of trepidation to her mother. Perhaps he successfully conveys the protective role in which he has just joined with the older woman, in saving the two girls from the wandering hands of her wayward beau, for she smiles in a manner that he takes as reassuring, at least to the extent that a gap-toothed grin can be so, and she reverses whence she came. Skelgill moves swiftly. He makes brief eye contact with Sheryl but then hauls himself athletically up onto the staircase, avoiding the lower steps, and smiles at Jade and heads quickly onwards.

His outwardly calm demeanour conceals the fact that his head is spinning, and he wants to reach the temporary sanctuary of the bathroom in order to digest if not understand what he has just learned.

When he descends cautiously a few minutes later there has been a change of personnel in the crowd on the stair. He weaves through the bodies and enters the lounge in search of Jess.

She is pleased to see him and he thinks she has blossomed and she looks happy to be with a boyfriend she has brought home from Sheffield. Skelgill's heart becomes an immovable lump in his throat when he learns she has been called for trials for Team GB – but conversation is restricted amidst the incessant racket of raised voices and the cranked-up sound system that must be shaking the neighbours from their sofa as they sleep off their Christmas dinner. He gleans that the boyfriend, Tom, a tallish thin lad who has a modest way about him is studying anthropology. "You've come to the right place," is Skelgill's observation – the boy is not quite sure if he is joking, but Jess digs him in the ribs and he realises he should laugh. Skelgill suggests they join him on his planned Boxing Day hike up Haystacks – but she explains they must leave shortly to drive to Tom's parents' place in Northamptonshire – and in a way Skelgill is secretly relieved, wondering why he suggested something that for him is out of character.

The party rocks on, as Skelgill has foreseen showing no signs of decline and perhaps not even the plateau, as if the premature falling of winter night locks them in and confirms the only thing to do is get well and truly gattered.

And, despite being in many respects a fish out of water, he begins to find a strange comfort in the packed throng, in knowing – if only in a subliminal sense and not actually factually – that he is related to the majority of the people in the room. There is no need for forced conversations, or – and something he enjoys increasingly – the requirement to enunciate clearly. Instead he can let the underlying mode of speech that he always hears inside his head hold sway, forget about pronouncing aitches and the 'g' of '-ing'; use lazy local contractions, and insert dialect words that make little or no sense in the formal environments in which he spends much of his time. The swinging atmosphere takes hold of his inner rhythms like a jazz recital, a loosely structured flow of sounds that seems to engage with his brainwaves in a way he cannot explain, like rafting down a river, rushing here, slowing there, turning on an eddy, quickening, breaking free and drifting on. His thoughts pass to DS Leyton, who occasionally gets away with playing a few snatches of this sort of music – until Skelgill winds down the window, preferring fresh air and whatever external sounds might be worth hearing – and he wonders how his bruised sergeant might be faring today. Last night he had hobbled heroically down his path, the family silhouetted at the front door, an inviting glow behind and Christmas lights flickering in the bay window, laden with extra gifts and capped by the Santa hat that Skelgill had insisted upon buying for him.

And now the image brings to mind DS Jones, and Skelgill finds himself checking his watch – for the first time, he realises to his surprise (as is the passage of hours) – but someone sees him in this act and uses it as an excuse to drag him into a dance. There is no great distinction between who is and who isn't actually dancing, and no designated dance floor or otherwise – but by now he has weakened to the extent of having downed a couple of beers – safely within the driving limit – but nonetheless, on a largely empty stomach and perhaps with the smoke and possibly other substances mixed in he feels a little light-headed, and he goes with the flow.

There is another thing. The person who has grabbed him is an unlikely ally. It is Megan Graham, single mother of Jess, and not a blood relative. She, too, is looking better than when he last saw her – much, much better – such that he feels a great wave of relief, joy almost (perhaps this is something for Jess, as much as the woman herself, and perhaps the blooming of Jess has played some role in her mother's recuperation). Her hair is glossy and her skin unblemished, and she has put on weight that he now realises was depleted. Her make-up is subtle and stylish and she wears jewellery and a nice blue dress that shows off what is an attractive figure. Only the scarlet lipstick hints at her former self – and perhaps knowledge of such is what causes a moment of frisson for Skelgill – and he senses she recognises his reaction and turns it to her ends, for she draws him close; though the packed room provides cover for any such proclivities.

'Now I know why Jess is looking happy.'

Skelgill's words may be ambiguous, but his tone is not and Megan Graham narrows her eyes in a way that is both appreciative and reproachful. She stands on tiptoes to speak into his ear.

'I hear thew've taken a shine to Jade.'

Skelgill is shocked. He has to wrestle with an affected recoil, denying any such interest. But Megan Graham has remained intimately attached and now she lets him off the hook he mistakenly thought he was on. She whispers again.

'What man wouldn't, she's the double of Paris Hilton.'

Despite that Skelgill could play innocent and ask why she is referring to a French hotel, he senses the line of least resistance is simply to go along with the woman's assertion; after all, he is streetwise enough to know she is, in a roundabout way, fishing for additional reassurance. She is pressing closer to him, rather than leaning back to gauge his reaction. He feels his pulse rate rising, though he is not sure of the cause. He is reminded that, while she might be Jess's mother, by the truncated nature of Graham generations, she is near to his own age.

'Experience is what counts, Megan.'

He hopes the statement is sufficiently ambiguous that she can take from it whatever compliment she desires, while it does not commit him to some sentiment to which she might seek to hold him. But she seems to have more to say about their mutual cousin's friend.

'That Jade – they say she's not what you think.'

Skelgill has been puzzling over whether others might know of the predicament that Sheryl had brought to him outside the courthouse. He takes a chance on a question.

'Has Sheryl said something to you?'

'Aye – Sheryl – she's allus dropping in for a mash.' The woman jerks against him, although he cannot quite determine the purpose of the movement. 'I don't believe half of what she says – she'll say owt for attention – she's outshone by Jade – who wouldn't be?'

It could be more fishing for compliments; Skelgill certainly does not think that Megan Graham has commandeered him for a purpose related to his clandestine mission. Though she is largely in control of her faculties, there is no doubt she has had plenty to drink, and he senses a rather loose tongue is acting without a great deal of conscious direction. And the subconscious direction seems to be manifesting itself increasingly in the movements of her body.

'Why don't thew drop in, later? We can catch up. I'll be going back soon – got to get my beauty sleep.'

Skelgill is caught off guard by the sudden and specific proposal – and not least the experience of déjà vu – but he manages to quip that it is obviously working (the beauty sleep, he means) – and for a second time he plays the call-of-nature card, and succeeds in detaching himself in a way that he endeavours will seem temporary.

On his way back down he takes a detour into the kitchen, resolving to retrieve one of his alcohol-free beers from outside the back door. He is conscious of not overplaying his hand – he is fully assimilated into the rowdy, milling gathering, but there are many people here whom he does not know or even vaguely recognise. Family members are unlikely to ascribe covert motives to his presence, but he cannot be so sure about outsiders. Besides, there is the unnerving undercurrent in his own mind that has been stirred by some of the things he has heard, without trying too hard to interpret their meanings. One aspect of these, however, he is obliged to confront more directly when he slips out of the back door – but first he discovers his remaining bottles scattered across a patch of uneven paving slabs, one of them broken.

He is about to blame the cats when he notices that the multipack of lager has also gone, despite that the refrigerator, hauled open as he passed, is still comparatively well charged. And now a double-sound wins his attention – the crack and hiss of a tin being opened. He traces it to a shed that leans precariously in one corner of the narrow yard.

In the dim light filtering through a grimy pane, he finds seated comfortably in a plastic patio chair and surrounded by discarded empties, an old rug over his knees for warmth, Eric – the vanquished boyfriend of Big Mags. The man greets him amenably.

'Alreet, marra.'

He seems to suffer no shame, either at having crept back with his tail between his legs or being exposed by Skelgill – though presumably he would be ignorant of the fact that it is Skelgill's lager that he has singlehandedly despatched (and not that Skelgill would care). Skelgill reciprocates his greeting. The man sees he has a bottle in his hand.

'Sit theesen, down.'

Skelgill can think of worse scenarios – there is no knowing who might collar him next – and he lowers himself onto what might be a microwave oven. The man watches with interest as he uses the Swiss Army knife on his keyring to flip the crown cap off the bottle. The man offers his can.

'Cheers, marra.'

'Aye, Merry Christmas.'

Skelgill doubts that Eric knows who he is, or even recognises him from the incident on the stairs, when his eyes were on stalks that faced in one particular direction, followed by a period of tumbling and disorientation in which much of the time his hands were protecting his bowed head from the blows rained upon him. He must have sidled off down the street and rounded the terrace of properties by the back lane; it seems unlikely he would have had the temerity to seek re-admission through the front door. That said, brass neck he certainly does possess, as witnessed by his return of sorts – and, of course, his earlier pawing at Jade. And now he catches Skelgill on the hop.

'She yer bewer, aye?'

'Eh?'

'Sheryl – is she yer bewer?'

Evidently he had taken in more of what ensued in the hallway.

'I'm Sheryl's cousin.' Skelgill tries to sound mildly offended.

'You looked well in there, lad.'

'I didn't have a lot of say in it.' Skelgill opts to turn the tables. 'Besides, I were watching you getting into a pagger with your missus.'

'*Huh.* I'm history. There's nay missus about it.'

'Nay – I reckon Big Mags made her point. She only told you to get lost – she didn't say owt about not coming back.'

The man seems unconvinced, but not all that bothered, and takes a long draught from his can.

Skelgill capitalises upon the limited momentum he has gained. He contrives to sound vaguely disinterested, as though he is just making conversation.

'What was all that with Jade, then?'

Eric plies him with a drunken leer.

'Is that what thee are after? *Hah* – joint t' queue with your wallet!'

It is an oblique rejoinder, but Skelgill makes an inference, having witnessed the prelude to the man being kneed in the nether regions.

'She took umbrage – she don't look that sort of lass.'

'Huh – does she look like she's ont' dole to you?'

The man has a point. To put it more plainly, he suggests that Jade is clearly living above her means. He adds a rider.

'Thee didn't see t' fur coat she turned up in, neither – all t' lasses were tryin' it out.'

He rests his case with another noisy slurp of lager.

Skelgill is about to respond when the kitchen door opens and they hear someone come out. They exchange watchful glances, co-conspirators in the darkness. Eric looks apprehensive – Skelgill wonders if he is fearful of being caught by Big Mags. Unsteady footsteps approach the shed. A figure shuffles close to the window. They freeze, each holding their breath – evidently the person cannot see them seated low in the shadows. The figure sways from side to side. The person – it is a man – clears his throat vigorously. He leans to rest his forehead on the pane. Then Skelgill realises it is his uncle Fred. Now comes the sound of liquid against the wooden slats, and splashing copiously on the ground. Steam rises.

Skelgill grimaces. Still, it could have been more awkward – it could have been an amorous couple.

*

A church clock strikes one just as Skelgill taps gently on the front door, and beneath the pallid street lighting glances down to check his appearance. He realises a shoelace has come loose and crouches to tie it.

While he does so the door opens and into his field of vision step bare feet with neatly manicured glittering toenails; shapely bronzed lower limbs ascend to disappear into a knee-length towelling gown printed with snowflakes, which might also be a seasonal variation.

Skelgill rises. He raises one arm and holds aloft a supermarket carrier bag. He grins a little sheepishly.

'Get the chip pan on, lass. Rod-caught codling, fresh from the Solway.'

There is a moment's silence, a pause, becoming pregnant; there is no telling what might be the reaction to his eccentric suggestion.

Then a repressed chuckle escapes from lips reproachingly pursed.

'You're going to eat fish and chips – *and* my Mum's Christmas cake?

'Try me.'

She knows Skelgill well enough; it is not a bet to take.

'It's in an Asda carrier bag.'

'That's another story.'

9. HAYSTACKS

Lorton Vale, 11 a.m., Saturday, December 26th

'Maybe we should take it a bit easier, Guv?'

Skelgill seems startled by DS Jones's exhortation, to the extent that he stops in his tracks and looks at her vacantly. Then he turns and stares back down the fellside. Some fifty yards below, DS Leyton labours valiantly, slip-sliding in the snow, making progress – but also clearly limping.

'This is the last stretch. Scarth Gap.' He inclines his head. 'It plateaus out after these rocks. There's no actual summit on Haystacks.'

'That looks tricky.'

But Skelgill ignores her concern and calls out.

'Howay, Leyton – hotpot tastes better when you've made it to the top. And you'll qualify for seconds from me Ma.'

DS Leyton raises a hand in response, and trudges laboriously on.

'Guv – you don't realise how fast you go.'

Skelgill regards DS Jones quizzically – he realises that she is breathing heavily, despite that she must be one of the fittest police officers in the county.

'I get into the zone.' He frowns, perhaps wishing to show a sign of self-reproof. 'I were miles away.'

DS Jones chuckles.

'You would be miles away – and I shouldn't like to have to navigate each time the snow comes in.'

Her hazel eyes reflect the terrain ahead of them, and she might almost be cognisant of Wainwright's description of the mountain when viewed from a distance: *"Black are its bones and black is its flesh"*. The bones – certainly – indeed they could not be more jet in contrast to the snow; but the flesh today is white, and the irregular musculature softened and landmarks erased. Not least the path, to which she refers; but Skelgill plainly knows the lie of the land by heart.

He is surveying the scene with a critical eye.

'It's not the biggest. It's worth it for the view, though. You'll both be glad you came.'

DS Jones nods to signify her faith in his assertion. A little earlier, speaking with uncharacteristic reverence he had shown them 'Wainwright's Window' in the tiny church of St James, Buttermere, with its view to Haystacks, the legendary Lakeland biographer's favourite fell. Skelgill had revealed that he makes an annual pilgrimage – "just a quick stretch of the legs" – his version of the traditional Boxing Day stroll, a prelude to turkey hotpot, open house at his mother's modest abode in the village – a more sober affair than that he attended on Christmas Day, although one gaining energy by the year as a growing brood of grandchildren increasingly run riot; perhaps the Skelgills will rival the Grahams in generations to come.

But he does have a more serious motive, a rationale for summoning his colleagues. That they are all off work until January 6th causes him to fear their present mission will be overturned, derailed at least – for they are likely to be confronted on return by furious mob, hammering at their doors, demanding satisfaction. And events of the past couple of days have left him feeling incomplete, without quite knowing the explanation, or even whether he should be concerned for the viability of the investigation. Is it simply that this is a case he has personally brought to the fore, and thus the onus lies upon him to prove its validity? "Get our ducks in a row," is as much as he has confided in his associates.

DS Jones poses a tentative question.

"What were you thinking about? Was it something you heard yesterday?'

But now Skelgill grimaces. He glances back down the hill.

'You're right – we'll wait for Leyton. Discuss it at the top – on the way down, any road.'

DS Leyton, shrouded in a small cloud of condensation and

puffing like a train pulls up alongside them.

'You make it seem easy, Guv – just when I think I'm catching you, I look up and you're off in the mist again.'

'Come on, Leyton – last leg.'

'I'm on me flippin' last legs, Guv.'

Skelgill immediately moves away – more judiciously however – picking a safe route as the incline steepens. There are other walkers about, and they will not be the first to reach the top of Haystacks this morning – but nonetheless Skelgill seems to find virgin snow. It is not particularly deep, and in fact of a consistency that produces a satisfying crump underfoot, and takes a grip – though they will require to apply caution descending. And Skelgill reminds them of this rule as he leads them across the mystifying plateau just as a flurry blows through, limiting visibility to a dozen yards; the maze of summit tors is very much the "fairyland" of which Wainwright wrote.

The trailing edge of the snow shower blows through like a curtain swept aside by a great unseen hand to reveal a vertiginous vista, and they realise he has brought them to a precipitous cliff. A thousand feet beneath curves the great ice-scoured basin of Warnscale Bottom, its slopes rising parabolically to the snow-capped spine of Fleetwith Pike opposite. To their left the dale runs out, the ribbon lake system of Buttermere and Crummock Water, once contiguous, now separated by walled pastures, fertile grazing that since ancient times has put milk in the churn and the butter in Buttermere. Smoke rises from the tiny hamlet.

DS Leyton is so overtaken by the view that he is halfway through an exclamation of an industrial nature before he readjusts to something more printable.

'Stone the crows – will you look at that! I better take a selfie – prove to the Missus we climbed a mountain.' He moves with an alacrity that belies the sprained ankle that has hampered his ascent. He sounds genuinely awestruck. 'Imagine you growing up here, Guv – the only time I ever got a view was when I went round to one of me mates who lived in Tower Flats. Nearest I'd been to a mountain was Muswell Hill.'

DS Jones, knowing London, laughs. He refers to what is

thought of as a pleasant residential district rather than as a place that could be considered lofty.

'Don't step any closer, Leyton, else you might find yourself back where you started.'

DS Leyton grins amiably.

'Come on – everyone in.' He beckons to his colleagues. 'Rose between two thorns.'

Skelgill manages to defeat his sergeant's suggested composition by ending up in the centre of the trio. For a moment they stand a little apart, until DS Leyton breaks the ice – he produces his red Santa hat and insists they huddle in. But Skelgill is still self-conscious – this is alien to him – and it is only when DS Jones wraps an arm around his waist and then DS Leyton grabs him likewise, that he rather gingerly reciprocates. He sees his alarmed face, sharp on the little screen, and is taken by just how photogenic DS Jones is, her high cheekbones flushed pink, her eyes bright, her bronzed hair escaping the Christmas bobble hat with snowflakes. She looks like a model in an ad for a winter break. Rose is right.

'Come on, smile – *Swee-eet Car-o-line!*' DS Leyton sways and breaks into song; he has a clear tenor voice.

They complete the chorus, Skelgill lagging by half a beat, and off key.

He is quick to detach himself from the embrace.

'Where'd you get that from, Leyton?'

'Where did *I* get it from?' DS Leyton grins and winks at DS Jones. 'Guv – I could hear you – you've been humming it all the way up.'

Skelgill looks at DS Jones. She nods, smiling. Skelgill scowls.

'Aye – they played it yesterday.'

'I'll be whistling it for the next week, Guv – I'll blame it on you when I get grief from the Missus.'

Skelgill looks slightly irritated.

But DS Jones explores the little opening.

'How was the party?'

Skelgill's expression does not markedly alter. For a moment it looks like he will answer, but they know him well enough to see that he reads into the question a degree of difficulty that significantly exceeds its casual nature. Instead he turns away and signals for them to follow him.

'Quick tour – before the next shower.'

He plainly has an aim in mind, for he leads them over and around snow-covered undulations with dark protrusions of heather to a small irregular body of water, hardly a stone's throw across, seeming more like a large rockpool exposed by the tide.

'Innominate Tarn.'

After a second or two of silence DS Jones dutifully responds.

'That means it has no name.'

Skelgill regards her, almost gleefully.

'Aye.'

She nods slowly, and snatches a glance at DS Leyton.

'I feel a pub-quiz question coming on.'

Skelgill snaps his fingers and turns away triumphantly.

'And now you know the answer.'

He leads them safely off the summit plateau by way of a shortcut close to the rocky step he will forever think of as 'Jess's Jump' – remembering when she trusted him and took off like a bird.

His pensive expression provides another excuse for an inquiry.

'Penny for your thoughts, Guv.'

He responds to DS Jones with a reluctant grimace – he seems to appreciate that he can no longer escape the subject for which, after all, he has convened his team for what is a busman's holiday of sorts. And now they are comfortably descending, line abreast, only DS Leyton is panting mildly; there is no excuse for avoiding a conversation. But he continues in his mode of deflection.

'How far did you get with historical crimes?'

DS Jones looks a little surprised – that he has reverted to an aspect which, had she unearthed anything remotely significant, he would certainly by now be apprised of. However, she interprets the question as a means of bringing up to speed DS Leyton, who of course spent the last official working day of the year otherwise occupied.

'Well – I got nowhere – but that actually might mean somewhere.'

She pauses, as if puzzled by her own words. DS Leyton certainly is.

'This sounds like another pub-quiz question, girl.'

She raises her hands to indicate she will explain.

'Firstly, in relation to the Badduns, a minor crime wave ended when they died. The graph of middle-ranking burglaries nose-dived. A reasonable conclusion is that they were responsible for up to ten unsolved break-ins. But when you look at the nature of those robberies, they bear little relation to either the locality or the circumstances in which the Badduns were found. They didn't steal from farms – nor were they known to deal in drugs or associate with other criminals. According to the court reports, they were reclusive and had been living together in a caravan on waste ground near the Northside speedway track.'

Skelgill raises an eyebrow, but does not speak. The site to which she refers is just to the north of the Port of Workington, a sprawling area of derelict land. DS Jones continues.

'I spent the whole of Christmas Eve going through the archives. I looked for anything that might have a connection with West Cumbria, with organised crime or with the type of activities that the Badduns might have dabbled in – but, to be honest, there's nothing that stands out. I know I need to come at it from a different angle, but it feels like we have one arm tied behind our backs while we can't access the Spooner case files.'

DS Leyton makes reference to their earlier discussion.

'Did you get any joy with the Minto cove?'

DS Jones glances sideways at her colleague. She is conscious of Skelgill's scrutiny.

'Oh, no – I didn't – I haven't contacted him yet.' She grins a little awkwardly. 'I want to get a better grasp of things myself before I risk letting him off the leash.'

Indeed, she had decided not to approach the precocious reporter, a contemporary of schooldays, prior to Christmas. Knowing Kendall Minto, he would take it the wrong way and turn up with an extravagant gift that embarrassed her into agreeing to something she might regret. She addresses Skelgill directly.

'I'll concentrate on the Swinesdale area. I'll repeat the house-to-house inquiries. There must be a chance that something went unrecorded. The original team might just have been a bit too blinkered for their own good.'

This view wins Skelgill's approbation. He has no doubt that DI Smart had made up his mind from an early stage; he would have been interested only in 'facts' that fitted his case. His tone is encouraging.

'You've got more leeway there.' He gestures to encompass DS Leyton and himself. 'Dealing with Spooner's connections – professional and personal – we're dancing in a minefield. One foot wrong and Spooner gets it. But up in the fells – there's no one with owt to do with him. I reckon you can be straight about the timing – even the incident. Just don't let on that we think Smart got the wrong man.'

DS Jones regards him keenly. She nods, a light in her eyes. This is progression compared to their 'recce', when he had been cautious about revealing their underlying motive. Perhaps he has become sympathetic, having participated in the unsatisfactory interview with farmer Brian Watts.

And DS Leyton has a further suggestion.

'Use a bit of poetic licence, girl – that's what I've been doing. I told Mason Milburn there's a mobster from Manchester coming to get him, and he'd be better off playing ball with us.'

'Look where that got you, Leyton.'

There is something about the way that Skelgill interjects – his tone suggestive of unwelcome repercussions – that causes both his sergeants to start, DS Leyton in particular.

'What are you saying, Guv?'

But Skelgill returns his colleague's inquiring gaze with a blank stare.

'Leyton – you were there – you tell me what happened. Tell Jones. About the boat.'

DS Leyton ponders as they continue to descend. A tricky section of snow-encrusted boulders delays him. Some people pass and they exchange compliments of the season.

'Thing is, Guv – I don't know what I don't know, do I?'

'Well, what do you remember?'

For the benefit of DS Jones, DS Leyton recaps, broad-brush fashion. How he was mainly unsuccessful in tracking down known car thieves. His interview with the young tearaway Mason Milburn and his search for James Hawkins – possibly successful – "to be continued" as he puts it. But of course it is the final act of the day that is of most salience.

'I remember making my way out towards the shore. Thought I could hear a boat coming in. Climbed up on that there wreck to get a better view.' He hesitates, staring at the ground, plainly racking his brains. 'I dunno – I just remember how dark it was – and the stars – suddenly seemed bright – and flashing – and, then – ' He tails off and looks at Skelgill in bewilderment. 'Next thing – chocolate digestives, Guv.'

He sees that DS Jones is regarding him with equal puzzlement.

'What's that word, girl – you know – when you lose your memory?'

'Amnesia?'

DS Leyton is about to confirm, when Skelgill interjects.

'Aye, well – you'd been lamped on the head, Leyton.'

'What – ?'

Skelgill realises he has doubled down on his earlier assertion, and tries to row back, but the damage is done. Before he can revise his words to suggest a more passive explanation, DS Leyton expands upon his query.

'Is there something I don't know? About what happened?'

'I'm not saying owt, Leyton.'

'Is that why you went back, Guv?'

'Leyton, I was looking for your phone. There was nowt to indicate you were attacked.' His sergeant's eyes are widening by the second. 'But I had to consider the possibility. Poke about in a cesspit and don't be surprised when you-know-what happens.'

DS Leyton is suddenly animated.

'But – that's a good thing, Guv – surely? It's best if I were – lamped one.'

DS Jones is perplexed by the perverse logic.

'What do you mean?'

'Well – I only made contact with two geezers. If something

came out of that, maybe it narrows down the field.'

For his part, Skelgill is scowling.

'It doesn't guarantee a connection to either of them, Leyton – or Spooner. Unless you let slip his name.'

DS Leyton shakes his head decisively.

'Nah – that's one thing I was careful about, Guv.' He thinks for a moment. 'It could be a step in the right direction. I was only looking for known car thieves. And – if what you say is right – it caused a serious reaction. There's two pieces of the jigsaw.'

Skelgill is looking agitated. As far as he is concerned, his slip of the tongue has been taken too literally. But DS Leyton continues, seemingly unperturbed by the possibility that someone might have attempted to eliminate him.

'I need to find out if the Hawkins geezer has filled Spooner's shoes. And whether that was him at the docks. The more I think about, the more I reckon something dodgy was going on there.'

DS Jones has a question.

'What about the young boy – Milburn?'

Now DS Leyton looks uncertain.

'I dunno – I'm half expecting to hear from him – *aargh!*'

He loses concentration and makes a false step. Instinctively, DS Jones grabs his sleeve to steady him.

'You must be careful.'

Though wincing, he eyes her mischievously.

'You know me, girl. Cat with nine lives.'

She frowns reproachfully, but does not offer an estimate of how many remain intact.

Meanwhile Skelgill has drawn away. He is conscious that DS Jones has tried three times to get him to be forthcoming. She would have good reason to think that he is holding back some awkward detail – but his reticence has more to do with the incomplete nature of his understanding. Much as he had hoped the walk would generate some clarity, during the periods of striding alone his mind has wandered off track. It is a perennial problem – tell himself to think about something specific – and the next thing he comes to wondering whether the *Bibio* is best used as a point fly or on a dropper (on the top dropper, surely?). It is as though his subconscious takes the view, "That's homework – do it later".

Yet he has to admit he is unnerved – the party hangover made him feel like he had woken this morning from a troubled dream, in which the images were real ones. A spectral world of shifting shapes where nothing could quite be discerned. Uncle Fred, a hazy grimace at the shed window; deep in shadow Eric guzzling beer and nursing his nether regions – and females, of course, their soft bodies hot with insinuation, their faces too close to read.

But one face was crystal clear – the beautiful – yes, definitely beautiful – Jade Nelson. Perhaps it was seeing her in the flesh. There was the expensive way that she was dressed and bejewelled, her majestic bearing suggestive of privileged status. Something doesn't stack up.

His understanding that she is receiving hush-money maintenance payments has been badly shaken. He cannot ignore the hints and innuendo to which he was exposed at yesterday's gathering. And, accordingly, he has been guilty of flaunting his rule that all items of evidence are equal until proved otherwise, or proved irrelevant.

'How'd you get on yesterday, Guvnor? Manage to smoke out anything of interest?'

Skelgill turns to look over his shoulder. From the ingenuous expressions on his subordinates' faces it is plain they have conspired to work as a tag team. DS Leyton is having a go in the ring.

Skelgill waits for them to catch up.

'I was just about smoked out myself, Leyton.'

Skelgill knows he must sound like he is playing for time.

'What – like someone sussed you out?'

'Nay – not that. I kept a low profile.' He glances from one to the other to see DS Jones is regarding him with a smile forming at the corners of her mouth. 'There was no point wading in with my size twelves – but just turning up could have put me in the spotlight, right enough. I picked up a few snippets – got the lie of the land. It weren't the time or place to have a conversation – never mind you could hardly hear yourself think.' After what seems like second thoughts, he adds a rider. 'I reckon I've got a couple of openings.'

DS Jones is eager to explore this point.

'Did you get an introduction to Jade Nelson?'

But Skelgill remains guarded.

'Not directly. I passed the time of day with Sheryl Graham while I was queuing for the loo. Jade was with her.'

'Do you think you'll be able to approach her directly?'

Skelgill frowns.

'Jade? I'll need to sleep on it.'

They all, including Skelgill himself, know he does not mean this, either literally or metaphorically – a more accurate answer would be that he does not know, and is unlikely to do so as things stand. His colleagues, however, wait patiently, just in case there is a development. After a few moments, he brightens abruptly.

'Jess sends her regards.' He gestures behind them. 'She would have come today – but she's got this lad with her – they needed to get to Corby, to his folks.'

The scene of Jess's triumph looks a bit different, wintry serenity when there was a frenzied crowd, torrential rain, flailing limbs and a mud bath; while, high on the fells, a blood bath, almost.

Skelgill indicates ahead of them; they are nearing the small settlement. Someone has just switched on twinkling Christmas lights above the door of the inn. He glances at his watch.

'Happen there's time for a swift half. Hotpot'll keep.'

10. CONNECTION

Swinesdale, 1.50 p.m., Monday, December 28th

Turning into the lane to Swinesdale, DS Jones is surprised to see that the Moot Hall Café is open. A sign has been dragged onto the snowy verge – the chalkboard type used by pubs, and handwritten "Open Monday 11-2" and beneath a slash "Milk – Bread – Stores". No gritter has yet made it onto the narrow byway and perhaps a moment of trepidation causes her to slow. She has neither a 4x4 nor special tyres, and certainly not the snow-chains that Skelgill carries – and while thinking about it she pulls into what is a walled parking area designated for café visitors, a facility she had not previously noticed – Skelgill had stopped on the verge a little past the property. She realises there is a car already – white with black trim, it blends with its surroundings, although it is clean of snow, a small sporty Mazda, not really the sort of vehicle she would expect to see – a pick-up or a Land Rover would be more likely – but of course there are thousands of tourists right now spending Christmas in the snowy Lakes; she has heard that most accommodation is sold out for the entire festive period. The car looks brand new, but the personalised registration disguises its age and provenance. The plate catches her eye – MX5 KTD – and then, as she sits pondering her next move, the owner of the car emerges around the side of the low stone building and DS Jones finds herself shrinking back against her seat.

Her instinctive reaction comes as a surprise. There is no particular justification for such, despite that she does recognise the person. It is the woman they saw talking at the gate of the property called Fellbeck – and once again she feels an inexplicable sense of familiarity. She pictures the envelope that Skelgill had fished from the box. "Katrina Darkeness" the name had read. That could almost explain the registration plate.

The woman is today more suitably dressed for the elements – a colour scheme matching the car of short white quilted jacket, and black skinny jeans and Ugg boots, white woollen hat and gloves. It is the attire DS Jones would associate with a middle-class tourist or a wealthy landowner. She carries two milk cartons hugged with one arm, a red top and a blue top, and she strides purposefully, seemingly unhindered by the slippery conditions. When she reaches the roadster she delves for her keys. Something small and almost invisible flutters to the ground; maybe a note. She stoops urgently. Only now, having risen, does she extend her horizon – and makes immediate eye contact with DS Jones. It is fleeting, and strangely expressionless, as before. She slides into the driver's seat and departs without a second glance, turning up into the dale.

This latter action takes DS Jones's mind off whatever has distracted her – if the woman can get up there in the sports car, she ought to have no problem in her front-wheel-drive hatchback. After all, the gradient is mild, the trick is just to keep moving. She can always reverse downhill, if the worst comes to the worst.

However, she finds herself sitting in silence – not thinking, exactly, but neither in a usefully meditative state; she feels inexplicably anxious. Then she notices the time on her dashboard clock and determines first to enter the café. Seeing the milk has given her an idea – or, an excuse. For what, she is not entirely sure. Follow your nose; do as Skelgill does.

She is not surprised to discover the small room empty.

The scented candles are burning as before. However, it seems even colder, and it is hard to imagine anyone would come out for coffee and scones today – although perhaps it would seem a haven to a passing walker. Or Skelgill at any time.

She glances about the displays of herbs and preparations. She notices, behind where she sat last time, a section of shelves given over to useful staples. There are a few loaves of sliced white bread and some cartons of milk – it is unrefrigerated – long life. And there are other items, little essentials that she supposes locals may run out of and not want to drive to the nearest shop, which is probably Keswick, ten miles away – or that visitors who have rented a holiday let might need. Matches, candles, cigarette papers, batteries, paracetamol, envelopes – that kind of thing – and a shelf given over to used paperbacks that is marked 'Book Exchange'. Her eyes dwell for a moment, the authors and titles revealing of the demographic profile of staycationers hereabouts – older, female, educated, she would say.

'Can I help you?'

It is the soft-soled cadaver man. His tone is bereft of enthusiasm.

DS Jones wheels around – too quickly – she realises there is guilt in her movement.

'Oh – hello – I saw you have milk.'

In these couple of seconds she wonders why she has decided at this juncture neither to announce who she is, nor to conduct an interview.

There is a pause. The tall man holds her gaze. In the gloom his long face with its sunken eyes and hollow cheeks and pasty complexion gives him the demeanour of a Victorian lawyer. She feels cross-examined.

'Just help yourself.' Then he contradicts himself. 'It's a maximum of two per household. Until I can get more stock.'

'Oh – one is fine, thank you.'

DS Jones turns away and selects a carton, the green top, semi-skimmed. The prices are marked.

'I have the right money.'

As he watches unmoving, she digs for change in the zip pocket of her top.

'It ought to be called semi-whole.'

She glances up, uncertain.

'I'm sorry?'

He regards her blankly.

'Instead of semi-skimmed. It contains half the fat of whole milk. It contains four times as much fat as skimmed. Quadruple skimmed. Semi-whole.'

She turns the carton to read the small print.

'I've never thought of it like that.'

'You still want it?'

She senses his gaze has dropped from eye contact to body

contact. She feels just a trifle uncomfortable. She has to resist the temptation to turn the tables and produce her warrant card.

'Yes – it'll be fine, thanks.'

'You're not with your boyfriend today.'

She is wrong-footed by the unexpectedly personal observation.

'My boyfriend?'

'You came in on Wednesday. Are you staying in the area? You've got your Christmas weather. Have to sleep off your hangover this time of year. Is that for his breakfast cereal?'

The progressively eccentric string of phrases both invites and defeats response. The man is standing six inches too close for her liking; the space is confined.

She steps decisively past him and keeps walking towards the exit.

'Yes, that's right. Thank you. Goodbye for now.'

She feels his eyes follow her out of the door.

The fresh air is a relief, but she is feeling somewhat disturbed. Not intimidated, but certainly unnerved. As much as anything because the man was so hard to read. Was it low-grade sexual harassment or just plain awkwardness? Or was there a more sinister motive at play – the man's slant intentionally oblique to see what it would flush out from her – or simply to drive her away? If so, it succeeded.

She finds herself standing beside her car. Perhaps the experience has sharpened her senses; she notices for the first time a tall timber gate that butts up to the back wall of the stone property. She supposes it might be access to a tea garden for summer use, although there is no such invitation. The gate has no latch, but a bolt is visible, drawn across the narrow gap between its edge and the first post of a high fence that disappears into a thick hedge of Leyland conifers, a little unsightly as non-natives.

She takes a deep breath and realises she can still smell the sweet musky aroma of the candles; perhaps the particulates have clung to the artificial fibres of her outdoor gear. She cannot shrug off a peculiar foreboding – but she puts it down to her knowledge of DS Leyton's uncertain experience – the possibility that strange things can happen. The notion that someone unknown to them might be on their tails. She nods; that is how the cadaver man has made her feel.

She regards her superfluous carton of milk and climbs into her car. She should push on. It might snow any time – there is more forecast, from mid-afternoon, though the weather in the fells is a law unto itself. She smiles – probably the law that Skelgill understands best. Thought of him brings her focus back to her mission. If she is to speak to everyone in the eight hamlets that make up the parish of Mungrisdale who may be germane to the investigation she had better get going. Today – officially off duty, of course – she has resolved to tick off the two remaining households in upper Swinesdale and to make a start with the hamlet.

Later in the week she proposes to visit the next most proximate settlements: Bowscale, Mungrisdale itself, Berrier and Rowrah. These lie on the way back south to the A66 – by far the fastest access to Workington – and she estimates more likely to be productive than those others – Haltcliffe Bridge, Heggle Lane and Hutton Roof in the more obscure northerly direction towards Caldbeck, a route that logic dictates neither the Badduns nor Dale Spooner were likely to have used.

She drives carefully. There has been a gradual accumulation of snow, about four inches hereabouts, and a single set of wide compacted ruts makes steering comparatively straightforward. However, pulling aside into a passing place offers a challenge; hopefully an oncoming – down-coming – vehicle would have the sense to give way. Meanwhile, the sky is hard to read. Whereas in recent days it has been possible to see the advancing showers as opaque smudges beneath distinctive masses of cloud, the afternoon is uniformly overcast; if it were not for the demarcation where the white fells disappear into the amorphous grey, no detail would be discernible.

The first house on her list is the last in the dale, the old lead-miner's cottage. The occupant's full name is Jacob Floxham, which she has garnered, along with those of about half of the householders in the parish from a call to farmer Brian Watts. But her mind keeps returning to her non-interview with the café owner.

He, she knows to be called Hugh Larkfield. Just what was it that made her withdraw so meekly? Sure – the guy is creepy – she noticed that on her first visit with Skelgill, but in her job she comes across plenty of creepy guys. And, besides, the decision – to the extent that it *was* a decision – she made without any particular reference to the man himself. Was it seeing the woman emerge with the milk that threw her plans into abeyance? Now she considers to what extent she has made matters difficult for herself. It will be embarrassing to go back and announce herself formally. Metaphors come to mind. While she has not exactly burnt her boats – she is a police officer, after all – she has certainly queered her pitch – a circumstance that the proprietor himself contrived to amplify.

The miner's cottage is austere. It has no fence to keep sheep at bay, no pretence at a garden, it simply rises out of the uneven turf like an outcrop of the underlying rock. Clearly it was constructed as a purely utilitarian dwelling. Yet she muses that is something that must apply to most of the old cottages and farmsteads in the Lakes. Homes were raised from materials closest to hand, to provide basic shelter and often for accommodation of animals, too. They bear no relation to modern living. Nor was there an eye to the future, no thought to look quaint and bucolic in order to drive 21st century second-home seekers into a desperate feeding frenzy – yet it is intriguing how antiquity bequeaths a desirable quality. Demand is insatiable and prices sky high, way beyond the reach of locals.

The quad bike is parked at a tilt on rising ground in front of the house. Tracks show it has moved a number of times, and it is clean of snow. The key is in the ignition. There is a bale of straw in the dog box; she notices it is tied with the same blue twine that Skelgill often carries. With circumspection she climbs out of her car; she stands for a moment, holding the door.

She feels the colder air on her face, a sign of the altitude she has gained. But she is well dressed for the conditions – indeed, more than adequately for a walk on the fells. It is an all-black ensemble. Walking boots. Thermals under an outer layer of tailored softshell neoprene stretch top and pants that Skelgill recommended. She has windproof gloves and a close-fitting hat. She considers that she might appear like a walker asking for directions, were it not for the car.

She closes the door and immediately dogs commence barking. They sound close behind the front door of the cottage, which is centred between two small windows set into the squat stone fascia like unseeing eyes. She steps forward. She has her warrant card at the ready. The front door opens.

'Stay there!'

For a second she thinks he means her. But he is commanding the dogs.

It is the man they saw previously. He is a little above average height. He has an athletic frame, well proportioned. He is clad in a waterproof navy overall with the hood drawn up. But DS Jones can see enough of the face to recognise him – tanned, the dark beard and curls, very dark almost black eyes.

He emerges and closes the door. The dogs have fallen obediently silent. He looks surprised to see her, as though he were already on his way out. He carries a plastic tub by a wire handle; it has a photographic image of a sheep on its label.

He exudes an engaging confidence. Perhaps it comes with knowing he is handsome – and here is what, a damsel in distress on his doorstep? For her part, she is wondering if he can possibly recall seeing her, as a passenger in Skelgill's car.

He is not remotely alarmed when DS Jones displays her ID and introduces herself. Instead, he surveys her with a kind of quizzical impudence.

'You look more like you're from Black Ops.'

DS Jones frowns in mock reproach.

'Well, they haven't issued me with a Type 25 yet.'

He grins approvingly and is about to say something more – but it appears he thinks the better of it. DS Jones is wondering about his accent. He is well spoken – when she was expecting a local brogue, and a manner less worldly – though without good reason, she realises. In his mellow voice there is the hint of an antipodean inflexion. She moves to explain the purpose of her visit.

'I wonder if I could ask some questions? It will take just five or ten minutes.'

He makes a face that seems to want to convey both cooperation and disappointment. He raises the tub to shoulder height.

'I have to place a mineral lick up on the fell.' He swings the item in the direction of his quad bike. 'And put that bale in a manger. There's not a lot of forage to be had in these conditions.'

DS Jones nods, she understands the importance of his mission. He speaks again before she can reply.

'Then I'm meeting the vet at three at Watts' farm – he's on a tight schedule. We have a couple of sick brood ewes.' He chuckles. 'He's up to his elbows at this time of year.'

DS Jones is staring at the quad bike. She does not seem to absorb his attempt to make light of the matter.

'Why don't I come with you? You can ride and talk?'

Jacob Floxham shows his admiration that she is up for it. He makes a face of exaggerated disbelief.

'Can you ride and write?'

'I have a good memory.'

He is quick to reply.

'That's only half the answer – but I'll try to make it memorable.'

DS Jones reins in the conversation before it runs off at a tangent.

'I'm on a tight schedule, too.'

He bows his head, at first in acknowledgement of her formal task – but the movement extends to a subtle once-over of her figure.

'Nice outfit.' He grabs at the breast of his overall with his free hand. 'But you'd be better with one of these on top. There's still mud in places, where groundwater crosses the track. Keeps your kit clean – and defeats windchill.' Now he tosses back his head. 'I've got a spare inside.'

'Sure – thanks – that sounds good.'

He turns and mounts the broad stone outer threshold.

'I'll shut the dogs in the kitchen. They're alright – but they'll be all over you.'

He glances over his shoulder – and flashes a smile.

DS Jones follows as soon as she sees the way is clear. The man pulls an overall from a peg in the narrow hall and directs her into what is an all-purpose living room, a sort of workroom come lounge, though it is largely empty of effects, clean and tidy. She casts about as much as is fitting for the nature of her invitation. There is a wooden bench in front of the window, upon it some tools and an oil can spread on a sheet of newspaper. A settee crouches before an open hearth where embers glow. Angled in the corner is a TV monitor, and she notices a games console. On the mantelpiece there is a church candle that has melted out of one side, a quarter-full bottle of Glenmorangie, a signed rugby ball and a carved wooden effigy she recognises as a Maori tiki. Okay, so the accent is perhaps explained. There is a stack of paperbacks – mainly thrillers, although one title, 'Raising Sheep' would seem less so. Her gaze would dwell but he has shaken out the suit and is holding it up for size. She takes it and steps into the legs.

Curiously, it is a good fit – snug without being tight at the armpits – too small for a man of his build. It makes her want to know his backstory. There are no obvious feminine personal effects on display, and as far as she knows he lives alone. It also strikes her that there are no Christmas trimmings. He watches her, though she feels his scrutiny is practical rather than in any way voyeuristic, and he makes an approving murmur as she swiftly completes the job of dressing.

'Better get our skates on, if you don't mind.'

'Hopefully it won't come to that.'

He grins again.

'The quad's a four-wheel-drive.'

She makes a face of suitable relief.

Once outside, he straddles the machine easily and starts the engine; it is throaty, but like all sound in the dale, its rumble is damped by the blanket of snow.

DS Jones realises there has been no offer of a helmet – but she reminds herself of the times she has ridden on horseback, bareback, footloose, her hair trailing in the wind. The seat is designed for two, but she can see it is a cosy fit. The dog box is on the front, and there is no rear support. She has ridden pillion on Skelgill's motorcycle, which at least has a sissy bar for grip – but then they will hardly be speeding.

But immediately it feels fast as Jacob Floxham confidently pulls away. The quad with its massive tyres seems to handle the conditions as he foretold.

DS Jones reflects upon her situation. She is much closer than she bargained for when she made her rather rash suggestion – but it was out of a kind of desperation, of not wanting to draw successive blanks. Though she can put pressure through her feet onto the running boards, the curvature of the pillion means their bodies are touching, her thighs against his buttocks. And she dare not lean back. Without actually holding on to him, she must bring to bear her equestrian skills; it has to be done from the waist down.

He notices her silence and calls out.

'Fire away.'

He means with her questions.

They are moving down the lane at a steady pace, the route is smooth and conversation is perfectly possible with raised voices. She opts to couch her inquiry in plain terms.

'I believe you lived here at the time of the incident that was known as the Badduns Murders.'

Does she imagine a stiffening of the man's body – or is it just that the curvature of the road requires strain through the shoulders to hold the quad bike on course? He turns his head a little to one side.

'I've been here almost five years. I trained as a shepherd in New Zealand. I got a part-time job with Brian Watts – then the cottage came up and I took over all the flocks in the dale.'

He has answered about timings, when she has anticipated he would home in on the drama itself – or to question her interest, or ask what it has to do with him. Instead, he waits patiently.

It is time to unleash what DS Leyton described as poetic licence.

'We've received information that the brothers who died in the incident had earlier committed a high-value robbery. It may have included gold items that would have survived the fire in some form – but no trace was recovered. We are exploring the idea that they came to Swinesdale to hide their haul.'

She pauses and this time he interjects.

'Isn't it more likely they were robbed themselves? I understood they'd been shot before the car was set alight. The convicted killer was a known criminal.'

He does not hide that he is familiar with the detail. Albeit surely everyone who lived in the vicinity would have followed events at the time.

'We would have expected the items to have resurfaced on the black market before now.'

'What if the killer melted them down?'

'Their intrinsic value was as artifacts, not so much the precious metal.'

She is glad she has thought this through in advance – but it suddenly strikes her that, just say – *just say* – the infinitesimal outside possibility that he knows something about this – then he would also know she is spinning him a yarn. And yet the sensation that grips her is not so much anxiety as the thrill of lying and its incumbent risk – as she heads for the hills with a flamboyant stranger and little to protect her!

But she shrugs off the idea as quickly as it comes – for the bike slews off the road and she is jolted against him as they halt. His strong back absorbs the impact.

'Would you mind getting the gate?'

She recalls Skelgill's point of view, about time-consuming security barriers. Although this one has no lock, merely a straightforward latch, the snow beneath makes it difficult to heave open. As she stands by, Jacob Floxham remarks that he is glad she has come.

They have entered a large empty enclosure that first declines to a narrow, arched packhorse bridge over the Caldew and then rises deceptively steeply, tilting her backwards, more so as he accelerates to cope with the gradient. Instinctively she presses with her knees, as she would for grip on horseback – but she senses it is not enough and she has no choice but to grab hold of the man's overall at the waist – it has belt loops and she hooks her gloved thumbs into them. He reacts, he glances approvingly over his shoulder – as though he is pleased she has relented and done the sensible thing.

After a minute they crest a bank and turn right, onto what is a gently rising snow-covered trackway traversing the mountainside. On their left side is a cutting and, as he suggested, occasional springs percolate across their path. She sees that he is looking at the ground ahead – and perhaps not just to navigate ruts and potholes. There is plenty of evidence of sheep – and perhaps deer – but she realises he is watching a line of walker's prints in the fresher snow along what is the verge, a long stride, purposeful, and associated pole marks. It never ceases to amaze her, the times and places people will hike in the fells, and she recalls Skelgill bemoaning mountain rescue call-outs that are never when he is short of something to do, though that is a truism.

'What is it you want from me?'

She is a little surprised by the question, unaware that her attention to the subject has dropped off as they dealt with the more challenging aspects of the terrain. The course once more is fair, if bumpy.

'I'm speaking with everyone in the area. It's a general enquiry.' She wonders if she tries too hard to make it seem as though she has no special interest. 'Is there anything that has occurred since, or occurred to you since, that could be related to the incident?'

She sees that after a few moments he shakes his head.

'I don't know what that would be.'

DS Jones leans forward so that she may more easily be heard.

'For instance, something out of place. Masonry dislodged, an outbuilding disturbed, a drain cover shifted. Crimes – burglaries in particular – are often not discovered until long after. An item may be hidden and the location poorly remembered in the heat of the moment. Sometimes stolen goods are abandoned in haste, or less valuable parts discarded – such as a picture frame or a jewellery box.'

She would like to say, how about shotgun cartridges of an unusual make (and that they can last for years), but something tells her not to highlight this particular detail, perhaps because it is too leading a suggestion. She sees he is nodding, but he does not offer up any ideas.

'Where were you at the time of the incident?'

He rises abruptly in his seat and half swivels towards her, a broad grin revealing even white teeth.

'Surely you've read my statement?'

DS Jones's eyes widen – more because of his devil-may-care antics – they are ploughing on and he is looking the wrong way; although there is something about his amused manner that suggests he thinks she might be trying to catch him out. And, of course, there is the small nail that he has inadvertently hit on the head: she has seen neither his nor any of the official statements.

To her relief he turns back to the track ahead. She fudges as best she can.

'At this stage, we're trying to look at the investigation afresh. The original focus was on securing the murder conviction. That necessitated a particular approach.'

It does not sound convincing to her. But he seems to accept the explanation. He calls back.

'I was here. I didn't know about it until the morning. One of your officers knocked me up at about eight.'

He slows the quad bike and holds it on the clutch. He indicates to their right, down into the dale.

'It was at the end of the road – see where there's a kind of half-barrier across the river?'

DS Jones recognises the spot that Skelgill took her to. She wonders if the point Jacob Floxham is making is that it is a good distance from his cottage, if not exactly out of sight, then out of earshot, at least. Her gaze tracks the lane back towards Swinesdale hamlet. After the miner's cottage there is Fellbeck, partly surrounded by what seem almost black conifers against the snow and in the waning light; then the sequence of farms, one after another; beyond which she can just make out the buildings of the little settlement.

Jacob Floxham makes an exclamation. She realises he is looking in the opposite direction, across the rising flank of the fell.

'Nut job.'

'I'm sorry?'

He leans back, pressing against her, and stretches out his left arm so she may look along the line of sight. There is just the hint of a body of water, grey against the white of the snow, beneath sharply rising walls of rock and scree. Snow is beginning to flurry, obscuring the view – but now she homes in on the object of his scorn – in the distance, a green fishing umbrella.

'Bowscale Tarn – they say there's no fish in there.' He laughs, as though he does not care. 'And last time I looked the season closed in September.'

It makes DS Jones think of Skelgill. She smiles to herself. Neither of these reasons would be much of a deterrent. But the fine snow that is materialising becomes something of an imperative, and Jacob Floxham drives on another hundred yards or so to a small exposed cliff where a spring spills into a half-sunken galvanised trough. Beside it stands a rickety wooden crib-like manger. He hauls the bale into place with casual ease and cuts the twine with a pocket knife. Then beneath it he inverts the tub of mineral lick; its contents come out as a solid yellowish block.

Their return to the lane, downhill as far as the river, is accomplished in just a few minutes. The extra speed and the rough terrain preclude further conversation, but as they join the smoother final leg, for a second time he queries DS Jones's silence.

'No more questions?'

'You have answered. I only really had one question – whether there is anything new.'

'I'll keep it in mind – maybe something will jog my memory while I'm out and about.'

When they stop outside the cottage he waits for her to dismount on the flat before he runs the quad bike up the slope, into the lee of the building. DS Jones unzips and steps out of her borrowed overall; he approaches as if to assist, but she is too quick.

'You were right, I think this made a big difference.'

He makes no effort to take the garment from her.

'You ride well – confident.'

She lowers her gaze under the scrutiny of his penetrating dark eyes.

'I was in a riding club as a teenager – there seem to be some similarities.'

'Expect the unexpected.'

She makes eye contact and smiles obligingly. But before she can contrive a suitable rejoinder he indicates with a thumb across to Bowscale Fell.

'That fisherman – I guess three days of Christmas was enough for him. Cooped up with the wife and kids and mother-in-law.'

His manner is conversational, but the subject is out of context.

DS Jones defends her sex.

'It could have been a fisherwoman.'

'True. Is that why you're not home?'

She realises she has fallen into a little trap – unless she is imagining things – but there is no doubt that his gaze drifts to her left hand; but it is gloved.

'I have a backlog – it comes with the territory.'

She suddenly shivers – inadvertently, when it might be affected, but for sure she has become chilled in twenty minutes or so of exposure, sitting still, despite her layers.

'Come in for a hot toddy.'

His tone is insistent – only the Kiwi inflexion gives the proposal the propriety of a question.

Now DS Jones returns his gaze; her eyes narrow a little.

'Don't you have the vet?'

'Ah – cripes!' He feigns to look at his wristwatch, though it is inaccessible. 'The vet.'

DS Jones steps forward and presses her overall into his hands.

'Thanks – and for your cooperation.' She grins wryly. 'I shouldn't leave the keys in your quad – that's official police advice.'

The shepherd watches while she performs a three-point turn. He nods to her parting wave and she sees in the mirror that he enters the cottage.

She has barely a minute to ponder if there really were a vet's appointment before she reaches the mailbox that marks the turn for Fellbeck. She hesitates to make the manoeuvre. The track slopes down more sharply than she had appreciated – but she supposes if the roadster can make it back out, then surely she will be able to. She moves forward and shifts into third gear to rumble slowly downwards, crossing the cattle grid and entering the cluster of trees.

The white car is parked beneath the shelter – it might be of rudimentary construction, but it comes into its own when it snows. DS Jones pulls up cautiously in front of the cottage. She climbs out and casts about. The main building is two-storey, white fairy lights are strung around the pitched canopy above the front door. In the growing dusk it is a homely scene, with snow clumped in the pines and woodsmoke hanging about the upper branches like an evening mist. The air is still and there is almost complete silence, but for the faint splash of the beck behind the property, and the churr of a wren somewhere in the undergrowth.

The front door seems to open quickly in response to her polite knock.

There are as many ways that people occupy their threshold as there are people, and body language is spoken even if no words are uttered.

Intuitively, DS Jones knows this is always an important moment, when she must be poised to translate that subliminal message to her advantage. But – once more – her best intentions are overwhelmed by a wave of familiarity, more powerful than ever, now that the two women are face to face. For her part, the householder does not appear surprised to receive a visitor – and perhaps she recognises DS Jones from their earlier, if fleeting encounters.

'Katrina Darkeness?'

'That's right.'

'I'm DS Jones from Cumbria Police – I wondered if you were able to spare a few moments?'

'Of course – come in.'

The woman has deep blue eyes and a clear complexion, wavy shoulder-length brown hair and regular attractive features, in particular full lips that make her look like she is preparing for a kiss. She is slim and small-boned, and DS Jones thinks probably a couple of inches shorter than herself; her waist in the skinny black jeans looks tiny. Her manner is confident – and yet strangely expectant.

'You look frozen – would you like cocoa? I have some almost ready.'

DS Jones feels she ought to decline on principle – it does not seem appropriate. But there is a maternal reassurance about the older woman that defeats her resistance. Besides, she would like cocoa, and what harm can it do? Only break the ice, surely.

As she steps inside she detects the same sweet musky smell as of the café, and she wonders if the woman has bought one of the beeswax candles that seem permanently to advertise their aroma. While Katrina Darkeness fastens the door she takes in the stone-flagged hallway; beneath aged beams white-painted walls are hung with abstract watercolour landscapes that have a local feel. On a row of hooks, jackets and hoodies in feminine colours and, below, a neat arrangement of women's boots and trainers, all in new condition and none bigger than a size three, by the look of it.

'Just go ahead, please – past the foot of the stairs.'

DS Jones does as bidden. She catches a glimpse into a room to her right, softly lit, a comfortable-looking lounge with a polished oak floor partly covered by an expensive Persian rug, on which a chesterfield settee and traditional armchairs cluster around a broad hearth. Arranged on the mantelpiece three collectible china dolls wear tinsel tiaras, and alternately between them burn two lighted candles – the source of the fragrance.

The woman follows her into a small internal kitchen where she slides a pot from the simmer plate onto the hotplate of a maroon Aga. She positions two earthenware mugs and stirs the pot gently with a spurtle. DS Jones sees the milk cartons standing on the adjacent worktop. Perhaps the woman notices her attention.

'It's whole milk – is that okay?'

'Oh – yes – perfect, thank you.'

DS Jones is still hovering in some state of faintly suspended reality. She cannot quite put her finger on what it can be, although she is aware that she is accumulating a series of left-field experiences this afternoon.

'One minute – then we'll go through to my study – it's more comfortable.'

There is a small pine table that only seats two, and that at a push. The kitchen has been tastefully refurbished and equipped, like a high-class holiday home – within its exposed slate walls it seems to have all the right things that would appeal to the upmarket visitor. Alongside the Aga there is a deep Belfast sink and a trio of gadgets which, if DS Jones identifies them correctly, make bread, pasta and ice cream respectively.

'Sorry – here we go.'

The woman is ready with both mugs and indicates with a twist of her narrow shoulders that DS Jones should accompany her through an arch. They enter the room that she and Skelgill had nosed into from outside. It is as appealing as it looked – more so, in fact, in that the view through the glass wall over the rocky beck and rising snowy fellside is one great living tapestry – changing even by the minute as the light fades and perhaps some glimmer of low afternoon sun reaches the higher slopes and finds its way by diffusion into the valley. There is the writing desk – and the comfortable-looking sofa before which the woman places the mugs on a coffee table. There are some magazines and a folded Daily Telegraph with the cryptic crossword completed – and this is something that would ordinarily attract DS Jones's interest – but her gaze – stare, indeed – is focused laser-like upon the cover of a well-thumbed paperback novel.

Not for the first time today – nor even for the second – but for the third and because it is the third a penny drops with one great clang – she almost imagines the woman beside her hears it. The first time was in the café – the shelf of used books for swaps. The second time on top of the pile of thrillers in Jacob Floxham's cottage. And now here – the same black cover with orange flashes, a pattern that wraps around the spine. The same title. The same author. She looks up to find the woman is watching, her lips just fractionally parted.

'Excuse me – but, are you K.T. Darke?'

Now the woman smiles. She bows her head so that her hair falls across her face. It is the act of a modest and patient apology.

'It's hardly a pseudonym in the class of John le Carré, I'm afraid, or even Lynda La Plante. Not so easy to hide behind. I was called Katy as a child – hence K.T.' She smiles disarmingly. 'And you are a detective, after all.'

DS Jones prides herself on her level-headedness. But she is

awestruck.   K.T. Darke is among Britain's best-known contemporary crime-writers. Moreover, she has a reputation for privacy which in itself creates headlines. While most authors would not be recognised in the street, and despite that she does not participate in magazine features or give television interviews or display her face on her book covers, occasionally her guard has dropped, and she has fallen prey to paparazzi. Of course, her good looks make her a more prized target still. And DS Jones is aware of some stories about her personal life – her marriage perhaps.

She is also a little confounded. There is the woman's demure and delicate appearance, and this place – refined and pristine. Yet her stories are notorious as gritty thrillers that pull few punches when it comes to sex and violence. A spiky punk persona and a chaotic Bohemian retreat are closer to what she would have imagined.

The woman seems to detect her confusion.

'My main residence is in Edinburgh. But it is essential to have somewhere to escape to. I'm sure you can understand.'

DS Jones nods obligingly. Somewhere a faint and rather futile voice is trying to remind her that she is here for a reason; but the woman seems to be in no hurry, and surely there is an invitation in her words.

'It must be wonderful to write here – hours on end without distraction.'

'Oh, no – there is a golden hour.'

DS Jones knows she must appear wide-eyed – and yet the author willingly elaborates.

'Yes – I only actually write new material for an hour a day. Just after dawn. Often before daybreak at this time of year.'

DS Jones finds herself consumed by curiosity.

'Is that all it takes – I mean, surely to write a whole novel – ?'

'Five hundred words a day – it soon adds up.' She nods at DS Jones, as if she is imploring her to perform the mental calculation. Then she chuckles wryly. 'If only it were so easy. Sadly, in its own way it is a full-time occupation. I have other sessions. Sifting. Knitting. Pruning. Kneading. Polishing. Patching. I take printouts and sit on the hillside – away from the laptop. And I walk and think.' She gestures with her mug towards the desk. 'I can be in here at five in the morning, and back again at nine at night making adjustments. Entirely the wrong kind of nine-to-five.'

'Do you ever get writer's block?'

DS Jones has asked this question before she can reprimand herself for her impertinence. But the woman answers immediately, her expression sincere.

'You know – I can't help feeling it's just another form of laziness. When you adore something, how could you ever get stuck? Imagine – you love the outdoors. Put on your boots. Leave the house. Start walking. The journey soon takes care of itself.' Her gaze transfers to the scene beyond the window. 'The poet A. E. Housman would drink a couple of pints of beer and take a stroll through the countryside. He could return home with entire stanzas completed. He said he hated it when they were unfinished and he had to complete the poem himself.'

DS Jones wants to ask: but how does she develop the story – the complex plot pursuant to the novel that is in progress? This woman produces acclaimed crime dramas, televised and filmed. Surely she doesn't just dash them off in a dreamlike state?

She realises Katrina Darkeness is looking at her with something between an amused smile and a concerned frown.

'Are you warming up? You should take off your top. If you're chilled the insulation will trap the cold in. And drink your cocoa.'

The woman is well spoken and her soft voice is persuasive. DS Jones finds herself complying. At least, she unzips the front of her jacket and takes several long sips at the cocoa; it is very milky, and sweet to the extent that Skelgill might even approve. She wonders, Fellbeck itself was clearly visible from the mountain track – could the woman possibly have seen her, passing across the fell on the back of the quad bike? How else would she suspect she is in fact so cold, when it is apparent she arrived by car? While DS Jones still has her nose in the mug, the writer again hints at her thinking.

'I've been researching hypothermia and cold shock response for my latest book.' She gestures loosely towards the snowy scene. 'Although all one needs to do at the moment is spend a few minutes outside in the wrong clothes. Or dip one's toe into the stream.'

She says stream and not beck – but neither burn – for, to the best of DS Jones's knowledge, K.T. Darke – Katrina Darkeness – is a Scot. Perhaps she is an alumnus of one of Edinburgh's renowned independent schools.

'Do you write in the café?'

'What – at Swinesdale village?'

'Yes – I was thinking –' DS Jones tails off, realising it is the sort of naïve question with which the woman must be repeatedly regaled when she is signing books at a festival for a queue of admirers.

Katrina Darkeness smiles understandingly.

'No. Maybe I could in a very busy one – where there is just the background hubbub. But – well, you know?'

DS Jones nods – though she is not quite sure that she does know – perhaps that someone would soon take a photograph, or ask for a selfie. Before she can reply, the woman has a question of her own.

'Would you like to write?'

DS Jones is a little tongue-tied.

'Oh – well – I suppose – you know, most people probably would like to write a book. But I did study English at university.'

'Ah – a literary detective. You could rival Morse. And you would have so much salacious material.'

The author brushes her tongue along her upper lip, as though the prospect excites her.

But DS Jones plays down the suggestion.

'I think it would bore readers if they knew how much time is spent on procedure and routine. Whereas – well – you can make up anything you like.'

'What makes you think it's made up?'

The woman's response is sharp, not reprimanding, but in the sense of a reflex reaction that she is accustomed to providing, for reasons of professional pride – although DS Jones feels stalled for a moment – and the author does not seem to wish to expound.

'But don't you have to – I mean –' DS Jones waves a hand in frustration. 'Sadly, we don't solve all of our cases. At least you can always reach a resolution.'

The woman's expression becomes earnest, and she leans a little closer to DS Jones.

'My female detective isn't averse to laying off – if she thinks justice has been sufficiently served. You could say it's one of her trademarks – others might use the term quirk.'

'Oh – I see.'

DS Jones is not so much troubled by the moral aspect (it is fiction, after all), but that her ignorance reveals she has not read any of 'K.T. Darke's' novels. She scrabbles about for words that will develop the point, that there are cases when the sheer cost of resources required to produce evidence outweigh its potential value, and that such qualitative decisions exist equally in the real world of police work.

But they are both now diverted by the sound of an engine.

DS Jones is surprised that the noise penetrates the old stone building – and the double-glazed viewing wall is surely soundproof – but then she notices that a small side window is ajar, for ventilation presumably. The vehicle is passing – it is hard to tell in which direction – but she recognises its signature throb as that of the quad bike. Perhaps he is returning from meeting with the vet.

She clutches at this small straw.

'I spoke with your neighbour – Mr Floxham?'

'Aha?'

Katrina Darkeness turns back to look at her visitor – she seems to understand that they must address the hitherto unspoken purpose of her call.

'You see – I'm conducting inquiries in relation to the Badduns murder case – which you will know about?'

'Yes, naturally. I was here.' She waves a hand in self-reproach. 'But, of course, you will know that.'

DS Jones smiles resolutely.

'I'm trying to establish if there was any other criminal activity at the time.' She mirrors the older woman's penitent gesture. 'Obviously, that should have been picked up – but the extreme nature of the incident put the onus on solving the murder.'

'What sort of crime?'

'We're keeping an open mind. But, as you may know from what was reported, the Baddun brothers had a history of housebreaking and commercial theft. Burglaries are often not noticed until a later date. There is also the possibility that they came to Swinesdale to hide something of value.'

'But, no leads, no line of inquiry?'

DS Jones gets the impression that the woman has shifted into detective-writer mode, and is trying to be helpful. It occurs to her that 'K.T. Darke' has spent many more years than she, in wrestling with mysteries of this nature.

'I'm basically asking everyone to rack their brains, and also to be vigilant.'

The woman nods pensively.

'I woke to the aftermath. Jacob called me – he told me the police had sealed off the lane and we were all to remain indoors.' She looks at DS Jones interrogatively. 'You weren't involved, I take it – you look too young?'

DS Jones is not quite sure how she ought to react. The rider might be a compliment, which out of politeness she ought not to ignore. But she opts to deal with the substantive point.

'I was assigned to a different department. I'm rather playing catch-up.'

'Maybe you will have greater success with one of the farms? A farmer is more likely to notice the sort of thing you mention – or perhaps a shepherd.'

It is an interesting statement – not so much for its practicality, but in its implied finality – that the woman herself has nothing to contribute. Indeed, she continues quickly, glancing at the fading light beyond the glass wall.

'Do you have more calls this afternoon?'

If she were a salesperson, this would be her closing line. Thanks to the woman's unaffected friendliness, DS Jones has become more at ease – though she has remained conscious of outstaying her welcome in such celebrity company, and time has subtly been called. She has finished her cocoa, and she checks her watch.

'Yes, I do. And I had better get going.' She rises and finds the two ends of her zip. 'Thank you for your time – and hospitality.'

Katrina Darkeness smiles graciously. They move into the hallway and she opens the front door and steps aside.

'I really must read one of your books.' DS Jones has blurted this out before she knows it, and wishes she had not. She must surely sound obsequious and starstruck.

But, if anything, it is a flash of alarm that crosses the author's countenance in response.

'Wait.'

She hurries away, back into the study. A few moments later she returns, clutching a paperback that looks to be in mint condition. It has the orange and black cover design.

'Please, have this.'

DS Jones reacts with surprise.

'Oh – I can't take it.'

'No – you must – I have boxes of them in the loft. The leftovers from promotional signings. They can't be sold, they have no barcode. If I return them to the publisher they will be pulped.'

'Well – if you're sure – that's very kind of you.'

'It's signed. You could always pass it on as a gift if you decide it's not for you.' Now the woman smiles archly. 'Unless you're having trouble sleeping – then it might help.'

'No – I'm sure that's not right.'

'Well – more seriously – you are not my target profile. My lady detective is a fifty-five-year-old firebrand. She doesn't take any prisoners, and she bends all the rules. She would probably drive you crazy.'

DS Jones is thinking that a good two-thirds of this sounds perfectly familiar.

'How many are there – in the series, I mean?'

The woman raises her eyebrows in a cautionary fashion.

'There will be eighteen soon.'

'Oh, wow.' If DS Jones gets through a book every couple of months at the moment, she is lucky. 'Shouldn't I read them in order?'

'No, there is no particular need. I couldn't possibly expect anyone to do that. Try just that one – do.'

For her part, DS Jones knows she has not sounded convincing, and rather regrets her suggestion. However, she bows a farewell, holding the paperback reverently in two hands.

When the front door is closed she rounds to the passenger side of the car and slips the novel carefully into the glove compartment. Then she stands for a moment, absorbing the cool air and thinking about what has just taken place – not especially analytically – in fact less thinking and more feeling the vibes of the encounter. But night is closing in. The fairy lights above the door are twinkling brightly, and they draw her gaze.

And then – a little to her surprise – she catches sight of what is surely a face in an upper window, an unlit room – the hints of the pale complexion and the long dark hair. Is the woman watching to make sure she leaves? But almost immediately the figure draws away – if it were a figure – or was it just a trick of the Christmas lights? Yet is that not a patch of condensation on the cold pane?

She shrugs and rounds to the driver's door, as she opens it she notices a light go off – it is the small side window of the extension that houses the study. She hesitates – something about it strikes her as odd. But flakes of snow are beginning to fall, and she climbs inside and pulls away. She wants to get out of the driveway before it becomes too difficult. She may not have a mobile signal, and it would be awkward to have to go back to ask to use the landline to summon assistance.

But perhaps her ride on the quad bike stands her in good stead, for she takes a run at the slope and makes it successfully onto the lane. The fresh snow affords a little extra grip, although if it comes on heavier it will grow to be an impediment. Indeed, she questions the wisdom of staying in the parish any longer. The road down to the A66 is little better than this lane, and will be low priority as far as the gritters are concerned – especially during this holiday period. Maybe she should call it a day, bank her gains.

There are two remaining households along the valley, and these both at its mouth, at the edge of the hamlet. First she will pass the country house that offers guest accommodation. She knows from her research that it changed hands two summers ago – and the present owners came from outside the district – reasons to be pessimistic about their value as potential witnesses. Then there is the Moot Hall Café. She certainly does not relish the prospect of another encounter with the proprietor.

Her thoughts shift to reflect upon the interviews she has completed. Both have been decidedly unconventional, in a chalk-and-cheese kind of way. A mad dash on a Kiwi shepherd's quad bike and a cosy chat with a famous author. She wonders how Skelgill would have handled these instances. Jacob Floxham, he would probably have simply demanded he stay and talk – she wonders why she did not insist on this herself – was it some inner devilment that got the better of her? As for the interview with Katrina Darkeness – one thing is for sure, Skelgill would not have discussed writing. The only printed matter he ever looks at voluntarily is one of a map, a Wainwright guide or the Angling Times.

But did her own method serve any purpose? That she went along with the flow was an intuitive act, when her normal method is logical, rational, fact-oriented. In consequence, in neither case did she get to the nub of the matter – exactly what they heard and saw at the time of the Badduns murders. Yet she has been left with an indefinable feeling of unease – as though she has been presented with unwelcome information. Or is it simply a hangover from the unsettling conversation with the café owner in the first place? She is reminded of one of Skelgill's metaphors, about walking on solid ice but hearing distant creaks that reveal all is not quite right underfoot. She wonders what Skelgill is up to right now.

There are occasional lights at the farms, on outbuildings; but it looks like everyone is hunkered down, anticipating turkey fry-up for tea and willing it to be time for a sherry now that darkness signals the premature evening is upon them. The falling snow is certainly getting thicker, despite that she is gradually losing altitude. And some of the more intense flurries reflect her headlights and cut visibility to a matter of yards. She switches to sidelights; it is not as if she will meet anyone on the road.

And yet, as she nears the hamlet there seems to be a flickering of distant headlights, certainly there is the impression of movement. It is off slightly to her right, from just beyond the café parking area. The old moot hall building is in darkness. The effect is curious, a shimmering in the air almost like the aurora borealis.

Level with the opening for the car park she draws to a stop. Emanating from behind the fence and hedge, and she realises now that it is not the light that is moving, but the snow. As flurries shift and eddy, they are picking up fine beams that otherwise would pass unseen through the black ether. But what on earth is the source of the phenomenon?

She checks herself. Under normal circumstances, this sight would not merit investigation. There are plenty of reasons people have lights in and around their properties, especially at this time of year – indeed some homes become minor public attractions for their Christmas efforts. Besides, she ought not delay her passage from fell country to the comparative safety of the A66 corridor.

But perhaps it is because it comes on top of her succession of intangibly odd encounters that she turns off her engine and pulls on her hat and gloves.

All in black, she would ordinarily be invisible, like a svelte cat burglar slipping gracefully around the wall of the Moot Hall Café to the back gate. But the snowy environs scatter diffuse light, and as her eyes become accustomed to the conditions she finds herself occupying a preternatural twilight, a ghostly dreamlike monochromatic world, where everything is just visible but nothing entirely clear.

She recalls that the gate was fastened on the inside. She might be able to slide the bolt by inserting her fingers into the gap beside the post. But when she feels for the bolt she finds nothing – and under the slight pressure of her hand the gate moves. It is open.

Anticipating a telltale creak, she pushes it just sufficiently to edge through. But she succeeds in silence. While there is more light here, she is confronted by a scene that takes her a moment to process. About thirty feet away, across what is a kind of yard, stands a touring caravan, of medium size. It is hard to discern its condition, but she can tell that the nearest tyre is flat. However, there are footprints crossing to its door from the moot hall building, and a subdued glow behind a plain curtain. She can hear what sounds like a television. Could this be where Hugh Larkfield lives?

But the caravan is not the source of the strange lighting effect. Beyond, perhaps twenty yards further, she can make out the shape of a long, low barn – and she sees the explanation. The interior must be illuminated by fluorescent tubes, and tiny shafts and beams of light are escaping from cracks and knotholes in the planked walls. It looks like a typical broiler house.

She relaxes, quietly exhaling, a breath she is unaware she has been holding. But upon inhalation her policeman's nose is alerted – literally so – for there is the smell again. But not quite *the* smell – not the all-pervading candles but another musky sweetness entirely – *Cannabis sativa.*

The lights. The shed. Bread – milk – but no eggs. The strange character. The slightly surreal dale. Drugs. Crime. Turf wars. Murders. The unsolved case.

For a moment it is like the lightshow has invaded her thoughts – these fragments swirl kaleidoscopically — but she waits for the turbulence to pass. She must check that she is right. Then, retreat and regroup.

Only a tiny voice of dissent causes her to hesitate – the charge that she is driven by an irrational desperation to find something that will activate the case – not to mention that she is alone and officially off duty, her whereabouts unknown.

But she brushes aside such lingering doubts.

She could make a beeline for the chicken shed, but it would mean passing close to the caravan. She detected no hint of a dog on either of her visits to the café – and surely if there were one it would have barked by now. She opts to follow the line of the evergreen hedge, knowing she will blend into its shadows should eyes look her way. It seems to angle back towards the shed, perhaps enclosing it completely. It must be ten or twelve feet high, and protects the compound from prying eyes.

In thirty seconds she reaches the corner of the long outbuilding. The snow is coming down more thickly and consistently, and she feels cocooned in a protective veil. She places her palms on the boards at shoulder level and begins to edge along, seeking a gap sufficiently wide that it will afford a glimpse inside. She comes upon a large knothole from which a beam of light shines out to illuminate the falling flakes.

She leans close, on tiptoes, turning her head to see with her right eye.

She gasps – perhaps a sign of surprise, or satisfaction that she finds what she desires.

Then a strong hand wraps itself around and over her mouth.

＊

Skelgill reflects that, had he not hissed the words "Don't scream, lass" at the same moment that he did his best to make sure DS Jones did not scream – by covering her mouth, quickly but gently (it seemed to him), he would probably not be sitting comfortably by the fire in the cosy bar of the Mungrisdale Inn nursing a pint of cask ale. It would have been another kind of nursing, in A&E at Keswick cottage hospital, for a not dissimilar complaint suffered on Christmas Day by the emasculated Eric. In the instantaneous tensing of DS Jones's body, he had been reminded that she punches well above her weight. Not to mention knees, elbows – and bites, even.

He has resisted her questions thus far, having urged a swift and silent retreat from the vicinity of the Moot Hall Café – and maintained radio silence until safely ensconced in a private alcove at the welcoming local hostelry.

DS Jones squeezes past him with their drinks, and makes herself as comfortable as the wooden settle allows, her back to the wall.

'Cheers, lass.'

'You're welcome.' She tilts her own glass. 'I'm having a G&T. That was some afternoon.'

She is about to take a sip, but hesitates, seeing that Skelgill is regarding her with an eyebrow raised in inquisitorial fashion.

'How was your quad ride?'

'What!' She puts down her glass. 'How do you know that?'

He cocks his head sideways and makes a clicking sound with his tongue – for a moment it appears that he intends to keep his secret – but then he relents.

'You saw the umbrella?'

'What?' She repeats her exclamation, more mildly. 'Was that you, fishing?'

'Did you see a fishing rod?'

'Er – I don't know?'

'Fishing for non-existent trout in December? I'm not that desperate. Besides – a furled brolly makes a decent walking pole.'

Now she raises her glass and eyes him over the rim as she drinks.

'Guv, what were you doing in Swinesdale?'

Skelgill reacts as though he is just a tad offended – perhaps that she implies he was cramping her style, or at very least shadowing her. He shrugs and looks away.

'Great minds think alike, eh?'

DS Jones regards him suspiciously, her eyes narrowed. But his glib rejoinder is hard to contest – and she knows there is no point trying to get him to admit he was keeping tabs on her. And that she is nettled is tempered by the notion (if not exactly put into form) that there was a guardian angel of sorts – and could she blame him, especially after what might have befallen DS Leyton on Christmas Eve?

She nods slowly, and plies him with a resigned grin.

'Okay – so fast forward. What were you doing at the back of the Moot Hall Café?'

'I've got the same question for you.'

He might still be being evasive, but he has a point. Whereas Skelgill is renowned for drawing little distinction between 'on' and 'off' duty (his argument being that crime, especially in the fells, does not work shifts – although she knows it to be more complex and personal than that) – today she has taken a leaf out of his idiosyncratic copybook. She is even dressed like him. They look like a pair of climbers who have dropped in to quench their thirst after a challenging hike. She accedes to his enquiry.

'To cut a long story short, I'd had a succession of peculiar interviews, and to cap it all I saw these strange lights. In order to satisfy myself it wasn't my imagination, I went to investigate.'

'You were right to.'

She is a little surprised by his vehemence – that to do anything less would have been a dereliction of the unconventional code by which he operates. His indignation prompts her to admit to her motivation.

'You know how you say you don't necessarily know it when you see it – but if you don't see it, you'll never know it … ?'

'Do I say that?'

He pulls a strange face, revealing his front teeth, as if he is not sure that he wants to own this adage.

'Well – I'm kind of paraphrasing – it's your approach, at least. How about if I said something like, if you don't cast, you don't catch?'

'That's more like it.'

'Well – I think that comes into it somewhere – what I did.'

Skelgill raises his pint to take a drink.

'I reckon you're getting the hang of this detective malarkey.'

She gives a little nervous laugh.

'Okay – so what about you – Detective Malarkey?'

Now Skelgill grins.

'I don't need any more nicknames, thank you.' He pauses for a moment of introspection. Then he shrugs. 'There was no snow on the roof.'

'I beg your pardon?'

Skelgill casts a hand at the small casement window set deep into the distempered stone wall at DS Jones's back. Beyond, falling snow can be glimpsed, caught in an external light.

'I noticed that shed the other day. Didn't think too much of it – assumed it was just a store. Today, viewed from the fell, it stood out like a sore thumb. A heated shed with no windows – and he's not keeping animals. Not difficult to make a guess.'

DS Jones is nodding.

'Not to mention the smell – I think I know now why he has those candles burning.'

They are facing one another, and Skelgill seems to stare at his colleague with an unusual degree of intensity. DS Jones brushes self-consciously at her hair with the fingers of both hands; it is damp and dishevelled having spent much of the afternoon pressed beneath a close-fitting hat. But Skelgill's fixed gaze does not follow her movements.

'What is it, Guv?'

He starts.

'Happen you might have cracked it.'

DS Jones gives a sharp intake of breath.

'What do you mean?'

'The Chief. The statements. This might do the trick. If Smart missed a drug farm, what else did he skip?'

'Oh, I see – I thought for a second you meant – well, something more comprehensive than that – something I hadn't appreciated.'

'This is enough to be going on with. Let's not count our chickens.' He stifles a laugh. 'There were none in that shed.'

DS Jones frowns. She was hoping not to have to curb her enthusiasm. It is quite a breakthrough after a day of frustration and incomprehension. Yet also slightly perplexing is that he is not claiming a share of the credit. She tries a less controversial tack.

'Do you think we should bust him?'

Skelgill grins, in what can only be described as a Machiavellian fashion.

'If Smart didn't bother, why would we?' DS Jones knows he makes the statement part in jest – but a related thought clearly strikes him. 'Does he know we're police?'

She takes a considered sip of her drink.

'He asked me if I was buying milk for my boyfriend's hangover.'

'Boy – hangover?'

Skelgill switches phrase mid exclamation. He scowls.

'I think he has us down as holidaymakers, Guv.'

DS Jones decides not to elaborate. She had noted the way Skelgill had glared at the man when his eyes had lingered upon her during their initial visit.

Right now, he contemplates the remnants of his beer.

'Keep our powder dry, I reckon. He's not going anywhere, is he?'

DS Jones nods in accord.

'I checked the business rates and property registers for Swinesdale. As far as I can establish, Hugh Larkfield has been running the Moot Hall Café for almost ten years.'

Skelgill does not answer, but while it is clear he is mulling over the situation, she knows he will not hurry to any conclusions.

'Guv – can I count just one chicken?'

Skelgill glances up. He regards her with affected reproach.

'Something tells me you're going to, any road.'

She chuckles, and holds up her hands apologetically.

'I know – but, seriously – when you think about it – a turf-war-type double-murder and a drug farm in the same tiny dot of a dale. It's a giant coincidence.'

Skelgill does not look convinced.

'The Badduns were burglars, not drug dealers.'

But DS Jones has thought this through. She rests her palms on the table and leans forward, regarding Skelgill earnestly.

'Guv, Hugh Larkfield may be peddling the odd packet of weed under the counter to locals, using his herbal remedies as cover – but if he's producing cannabis on a commercial scale he must have an organised outlet. Maybe the Badduns broke into his shed. There'd be no point in stealing the plants – but the value of the crop wouldn't pass unnoticed. Say they tried to muscle in on it – get a cut of the profits? They could have been tricked into a rendezvous at the head of Swinesdale.'

The corollary does not require elaboration. The flaming fate that befell the Badduns is consistent with what could be anticipated. And far more likely at the hands of a drug gang than hapless car thief Dale Spooner.

But DS Jones understands where Skelgill is up to. She leans back and claps her hands together.

'Oh – and, by the way – I've had my Ennerdale moment.'

Skelgill frowns.

'Come again?'

'When DS Leyton met the film crew? I've just interviewed a famous author. The woman who lives at Fellbeck – Katrina Darkeness – it's her writer's retreat. She's the novelist, K.T. Darke – that's her pen name.'

Skelgill looks blank. Then, after a moment he speaks.

'She's kept that quiet, hasn't she?'

'It looks like she bought the property about six years ago – it was purchased through a company, Lakeland Holdings – it sounds like it's something to do with holiday accommodation.'

'Sounds more like a tax dodge, to me. They earn a fortune, don't they, these writers?'

A small furrow creases DS Jones's brow.

'I'm not so sure. Maybe the elite few. I've read that for most it's a labour of love.'

Now Skelgill grins – DS Jones senses a pun is coming.

'So, what's her story?'

She smiles obediently.

'If we're talking non-fiction, then she admits she was present at the time of the murders.' DS Jones understands she should quickly supply the caveat. 'But it's the same as for all of the householders – we got there first. They only know what they saw in the media.'

Skelgill looks like he has mixed feelings about this. After all, it was down to him that the scene of crime was discovered and sealed off before anyone was abroad. But he offers a crumb of comfort to his colleague.

'Happen there'll be more to go on when we see the statements. Folk forget things.'

DS Jones nods pensively. Then she iterates her thoughts.

'The shepherd, Jacob Floxham – he seemed to have good recall. When I mentioned valuables possibly being stolen from the Mercedes he reminded me that Dale Spooner was a known criminal.'

Skelgill is listening attentively.

'He's not a local?'

It sounds like he already knows this.

'I didn't go into detail about his background. But he said he trained in New Zealand, and came to Swinesdale five years ago. He appears to be on top of the job.'

Skelgill sits up in his seat, he seems a bit sniffy. DS Jones might reasonably wonder if it is that he considers an 'offcomer' cannot be a pukka shepherd – but, then, there is also her somewhat unconventional interview, which he has observed from afar. She opts to move the conversation off the subject – to another small mystery that she has not yet got to the bottom of.

She smiles and raises her glass to her lips.

'Guv – how did you get into the yard behind the Moot Hall Café? I'm sure the gate was bolted when I called there earlier.'

Skelgill takes a second or two to reply.

'I found a way through the hedge.' He glances over his shoulder towards the exit from the bar. 'Remember what I said – first principle of burglary – make sure your getaway's clear. Comes in handy for when it's your round.'

DS Jones is about to speak, but Skelgill stands up and swallows the dregs from his pint. Then he stoops a little to peer over her head, squinting through the little window. Now she anticipates his concern.

'Do you think we ought to leave?'

Skelgill folds his arms, though his expression is curiously inscrutable.

'On the bright side – it'll cover the tracks we just left.' He turns and steps away, reaching for his back pocket. 'Another drink and I reckon we'll be snowed in, lass.'

11. MEGAN

Workington, 12.30 p.m., Tuesday, December 29th

'Only four days late – did thew have bigger fish to fry?' Skelgill grins, a little sheepishly.

'I took you at your word – you said you needed your beauty sleep. Not that I agreed with that. I thought I must have met your classy twin sister.'

He sweeps a hand towards the woman who stands upon the raised threshold – she is smartly dressed and made up as if she is ready to go out.

Megan Graham frowns but Skelgill can see she is gratified by his gauche chivalry.

'I've got to be at work at one. Thew should have phoned.'

'I tried – it was unavailable.'

She makes a face that hints at a pained memory.

'I've got a new number.'

But Skelgill remains upbeat.

'A new life, it looks like, to me.'

He casts about – the exterior of the house has been tidied up and painted, there are new curtains, a new gate – beyond her in the hallway he can see new carpets where before there were bare floorboards.

'Where are you working?'

'At Turner's Paints – I'm doing their books.'

'Today? That's keen.'

'Just this afternoon – a spot of overtime. There's a vacancy – a chance of a promotion to Finance Manager.' Her eyes narrow with a hint of belligerence – as though expecting he won't believe her. 'I'm a Certified Accountant – I qualified at night school after I left secondary.'

Skelgill misses the opportunity to further commend her. He is thinking of his own practical objective.

'Turner's? I'll give you a lift – it's only five minutes. Save you walking in the snow.' He jerks back his head to indicate his car parked in the ungritted side street. 'Time for a mash, eh, lass?'

She hesitates.

'Aye – I suppose.'

She steps back to admit him. He notices she leans out to glance about – an old habit that has not yet died? A male stranger in the middle of the day – what will the neighbours think?

The interior, too, is recently decorated, fresh-smelling – no smoke, just a floral fragrance – there are bright, functioning lights and attractive shades. The kitchen is almost unrecognisable; it gleams more like an advertisement for a proprietary cleaning product; there are new appliances and a sparkling stainless-steel sink. She gestures for him to sit at a new pine table.

'You've fair turned it round, Megan.'

She is filling a kettle, her back to him.

'I've got thew to thank for that.'

'Howay, lass.' Skelgill raps his breast bone with the knuckles of his left hand. 'There's only one place will-power can come from.'

'Thew taught me what I needed to be for Jess.' Now she turns, and regards him earnestly. 'She's been coming home – when she's back from uni.'

Skelgill feels a lump forming in his throat. It takes him a moment to fashion a reply.

'Seems like a decent lad she's knocking about with. Bit of a brainbox.'

Megan Graham seems to start – Skelgill is alarmed that he appears to have triggered an adverse reaction. She inhales sharply, in the manner of a reformed smoker that still gains some solace from the physical act.

'I'm mortified that I let that Connor get his claws into her. It were just as well she moved out.' She sighs, and looks fiercely at Skelgill. 'And just as well thew killed the –'

Whoa! The expletive she uses for the deceased drug dealer rocks Skelgill back in his seat. Some things she has not put behind her. But now he finds feelings of his own, unknowingly submerged, breaching the surface. He wants to stand up – perhaps to punch the wall, perhaps to put an arm around her; he grips the sides of the table. Consumed by a rising fury he is reminded that, when it comes to family, emotion does not merely hold sway over rationality but obliterates it entirely. Megan Graham might not be his blood relation, but her daughter Jess is. And he realises that such feelings extend to the mother, too.

His reaction is as much of a shock to him as her outburst. He thought he had filed away the incident as a matter of duty, as a case of self-defence. His long-held attitude is that 'proportionate force' is a naïve legal construct when one's life may be at risk. And there is even a professional detachment when it comes to an offender – he rarely carries a grudge if justice is done. Here, then, is an exception.

'He had Jess in his sights. Happen he'd have left you for dead, an' all – once he'd bled every last penny out of you. Truth be told, Megan, it was the least he deserved. He was evil.'

The kettle clicks off and it prompts Megan Graham to turn. The tension in the small room seems to dissipate – she gives an abrupt laugh.

'Shame you're not the sheriff round here, Daniel. There's a few others that folk would say good riddance to.'

Skelgill blows out his cheeks – but he is content with the diversion.

'That would be a no-win situation – some of them would turn out to be relations.'

The woman joins him at the table with a tray of tea things. He watches while she dispenses their drinks and answers mechanically her questions about milk and sugar. The recalled incident seems to have left them both with something of a delayed numbness. Now that she is seated just across from him, Skelgill finds his thoughts reverting to the transformation in her lifestyle. Given his last remark, perhaps she is sensitive to his renewed scrutiny.

'There'll be no going back to all that.'

Skelgill takes a gulp of his tea; she waits in silence for him to pass judgement.

'Jess is on fire – and you're a big part of it, Megan – I can see it in her eyes.'

Megan Graham seems to relax; she eyes him more candidly.

'So what is it I can do for you – now that I owe you?'

'You owe us nowt.'

She smiles consolingly.

'Aye, if you say so – but there is sommat.'

He feels a small pang of guilt – that she assumes an ulterior motive underlies his visit. He has not rehearsed a clever line of attack; it comes more naturally to him to fly by the seat of his pants – he would rather remain mute than spout insincerity. But he is pretty sure that if he confides in her he can trust her not to slip up – and one hundred percent so that she would take his corner.

'It's about Jade Nelson.'

Megan Graham darts out a palm to place it upon his forearm.

'Thew want fixed up wi' her!'

She has slipped into a more colloquial mode. She is unselfish, he thinks, in her reaction – for he is sure he detects disappointment behind the 'why-didn't-you-just-say-so' smile.

'Howay, Megan – I'm your age, not hers.'

His rebuttal is swift – and he is right, it seems, instinctively to link the pair of them, for now she regards him with mock suspicion, her eyes narrowed – though it leaves him wondering, just how old is Megan? He has always assumed she is a few years his senior – but, Jess is still only eighteen, and Graham generations can defy the national average.

She taps playfully upon the back of his hand.

'Why not, then – good-looking bloke like thew?'

Skelgill makes a scoffing sound – but he does not wish to get drawn into the wrong argument. He must feel his way around this distraction.

'Look – it's to do with work – something that I can't personally investigate. Connected with a remark that was made at the party. It's nowt that Jade's done wrong.'

He hesitates. He is struggling to find a credible explanation for his particular interest. Megan Graham offers a prompt.

'What then?'

Skelgill scrapes back his hair with the fingers of both hands and rubs vigorously at his scalp. He is unsure if he is intentionally trying to give the impression that he does not fully understand himself what he is hoping to get at, but it makes him feel more comfortable, all the same.

'You said you know Sheryl pretty well – that she comes round?'

'Aye – she drops in from time to time – not so much now I'm at work.'

'Well, Sheryl's big pals with Jade, am I right?'

Megan Graham nods but does not elaborate.

'Jade's looking pretty well-heeled these days.' Skelgill pauses for a second, conscious that this comparison is not really something he would know. But he has reached the point of no return. He presses on, grimacing as if to suggest he is uneasy with the pedalling of gossip. 'There's the suggestion that she's dabbling in the – er – the escort business.'

He picks up his mug and looks into it with a frown, though he knows full well the state of its contents. When he meets Megan Graham's gaze she is smiling in a way that is at once wry and wary.

'It's not been declared illegal, has it?'

Skelgill shifts in his seat – and rather hastily he adds a caveat.

'Look – what I mean is through Sheryl – that she might be able to tell you about Jade.'

It seems to him that Megan Graham shrugs casually.

'Aye – I can ask Sheryl, easy enough. But I can think of another way.'

Her reaction comes as a surprise – free as it is of the consternation that he anticipated. He nods tentatively. She continues.

'Like I said – I've got a new phone. But I've kept my old handset – with all my old contacts. I can ring round – there's one or two as likes the younger lasses. I expect they'd tell us, soon enough. It's a small world.' She sees that Skelgill is a little lost for words. 'I can do it when I get back from work. I could let you know later.'

She gestures loosely, indicating their surroundings.

'Why don't thew come for tea?'

Skelgill regards her questioningly.

'Alreet – I'll bring fish and chips. Six o'clock, aye?'
'Make it eight.'

*

To kill several hours in a largely unfamiliar town at a time of year when few folk are abroad and most attractions and amenities closed, and in weather which albeit fine and bright is hardly conducive to sauntering, would for most be an unappealing prospect. But Workington has a coastline, and Skelgill has a fishing rod. He also has the means to make lunch.

He takes the estuary road to Coke Point, above the slag banks, where he fished on Christmas morning – and indeed earlier parked with DS Leyton while the latter recovered from his bone-chilling experience inside the hull of the abandoned wreck. Once again it seems he has the place to himself. He reverses to position the tailgate seawards. He fires up his Trangia and in short order has a coiled Cumberland sausage sizzling in the pan. He tears open a large oven-bottom cake and, when the sausage is cooked, fries the two halves of the bread before assembling his sandwich, adding a generous dash of brown sauce. In the meantime his Kelly kettle has reached a rumbling boil and he pours instant tea into a tin mug, having employed the Nepalese method of brewing up all the ingredients together.

He makes some space and settles in half repose upon the flatbed, only the soles of his boots protruding from the vehicle. He pulls a part-folded army blanket over his legs. He balances his tin plate on his thighs, and the mug upon an inverted galvanised bucket. He eats and drinks methodically, although unhurriedly, for he is in a contemplative state.

Indeed, he only really comes to his senses as he washes down the last of his sausage sandwich, and wonders if – now warm and comfortable – he can be bothered getting up to refill his mug. He curses that he did not leave the kettle within reach. But he is detained by the question that is forming in his mind – and he considers what is the corollary of his ruminations, and of the brief meeting with Megan Graham.

Of course, that answer is really yet to come. And while he does not wish to pre-empt the outcome, he does harbour some anxiety about what will be his cousin-in-law's findings. Perhaps what has most unnerved him is that – while Jade Nelson's own reaction to the slight cast upon her by the inebriated Eric had been unequivocal – Megan Graham, upon hearing the suggestion had reacted with ambivalence. It was as though she would not have been at all surprised were the allegation true. A small counterpoint might be that Megan's own background means that she is inured to such a notion, and therefore took the claim in her stride, while the average person would have been tripped up. Notwithstanding, if there does prove to be substance in the claim, it potentially casts into doubt the account he has received from Sheryl Graham, concerning the source of Jade Nelson's income. If Jade has lied to Sheryl about that (for obvious, understandable reasons), what else might she have lied about – and what does it mean for the case?

He had summarily dismissed DS Jones's speculation of a conspiracy between Sheryl and Jade – but that was largely on the strength of his limited knowledge of Sheryl. But how well does he know Jade? Answer, not at all. Sheryl might easily have been taken in by her story.

He is further troubled that his unease feels greater than this simple point – as though it opens a window on a deeper, more sinister aspect – something that he can appreciate, yet cannot begin to fathom, a dark shape that patrols the depths, but which may surface at any time with gaping jaws.

Skelgill gives a shake of his head, rather like a horse that is trying to disperse nuisance flies. There is no point in speculating when he may know more later. And there is now a bigger picture to consider. While Jade Nelson's story has been the catalyst, it is perhaps no longer pivotal. Since they began investigating, his team have turned stones that suggest there is a wider landscape, like an expanse of mud flats only just beginning to be exposed by the ebbing tide. It is to this that he can make a contribution; but he must be patient; see what Megan Graham has to say.

He rolls out of the car and stretches his spine. The half-sitting half-lying position was not what the physio would recommend.

Squinting, he stares out to sea. The sun is low above the southwest horizon, ineffectual, only a week past its seasonal nadir. The water surface is calm, and the Isle of Man looks closer than its thirty-five miles distance. It seems to rise in the fashion of a mirage, and it stretches too, to occupy more of the seascape than he remembers, and he is obliged to recall it compares in size and population to his present location, the Borough of Allerdale, and in Snaefell it boasts a fell the same height as Causey Pike in the Newlands valley. Although, as DS Leyton had alluded to, where the mini-nation tax haven differs is that the average income of its inhabitants is quadruple that of Workington.

He removes his knuckles from his lower back and slides his hands into his pockets and immediately feels something cool between the fingers of his left. He extracts it. In his palm he finds the coin that he had picked up from the shoreline – the Manx cat on its reverse. It prompts him to return his gaze to the island of its origin, across the Irish Sea. The high tide, lagging by four hours since Christmas morning is still flowing. He deems it would be a good time to fish. And perhaps there is something else he can usefully do.

He turns and stares into the back of his car. From the bewildering jumble of rods and tackle boxes, and camping gear and survival equipment, he assembles a lightweight spinning rig and equips himself with an extra layer of cold-weather clothing. He hooks a couple of spare lures onto his outer gilet and clips a brown polyester bass bag onto a carabiner on one of his belt loops.

He fishes initially from close to Coke Point. The mouth of the Derwent is asymmetrical, its lower southern mandible projecting further out to sea, a spit extended by a modest pier with an abandoned lookout station, and a breakwater of immense boulders, a giant's causeway of sorts. It offers a variety of possibilities for the angler, but the main attraction is to reach those pelagic species that will not venture into the small estuary.

Perhaps of most note to Skelgill is the absence of maritime traffic, or of vessels of any kind. But the becalmed conditions were forecast, and those who sail for pleasure will have remained by their firesides, or maybe headed east into the fells, to take some exercise or sledge with the children while there is snow on the ground. Across the watery grey plain there are scant clues to where fish might lurk. Skelgill watches a distant bird paddle about, its dark silhouette long and low, occasionally disappearing below the surface. Though it is too far easily to identify, he knows from its habit of sliding from sight (rather than performing a little leap) that it is a species of diver, a loon as it is called across the pond. He marvels that a bird can succeed in such an alien environment.

And a few more birds begin to attract his attention. Small groups of waders head north, flying low and purposefully over the surface, turnstone, dunlin, redshank and the like – they are returning to the upper reaches of the Solway, where shortly the turning tide will expose fresh mud and invertebrates that have not yet retreated to the safe depths of their silty burrows, still greedy for a last morsel. Skelgill grins ruefully; it is all about eating.

And then at last a boat heaves into sight. In fact, he realises, it must have been approaching for some time, but from the southwest, where he is facing north. It is a small freighter, painted in royal blue, and the throb of its diesel engine seems to roll over the water out of proportion to its size. The engine note changes as it turns to starboard to enter the port, although Skelgill's view is obscured by the pier and lookout building, and he does not see its final movements. His guess is that it will berth and remain; he is not sure how navigable is the channel once the tide has ebbed.

The distraction seems to prompt him to opt for a change of scene. He picks his way back along the breakwater and past where his car is parked to rejoin the shoreline. Initially the access road runs close by, and he continues on foot until it veers away, and the undulating expanse of dunes provides a more secluded backdrop for the angler. He continues walking, however, until his direct progress is thwarted by the inlet, the oval tidal lagoon that viewed on the map looks like an appendix to the river's principal intestinal windings.

The lagoon is flooded and its moored boats are afloat – all that is, except the dreaded hulk, the scene of DS Leyton's adventure. And Skelgill sees now the danger that was posed. Only a foot of the slanting deck protrudes above the waterline, and the hatch into which his colleague tumbled is entirely submerged. It really is a death trap.

He mounts the pontoon where it joins the shoreline. Its timbers are rotted and slimy, and were it not for having seen it exposed, and having successfully crossed it several times, he would not otherwise trust it with his weight. DS Leyton had assumed, rather erroneously it seems to Skelgill, that he would get a better view of the port – but his lack of local knowledge – of the sort that Skelgill has gleaned over the years, not least from fishing but also a more general instinct to roam about – cannot really be criticised. And it is true that the elevated position does help – Skelgill can see across to where the freighter has docked, its superstructure just visible above the strip of land between himself and the main quay. Indeed, he sees that a crane is beginning to rotate, and he watches with detached interest as it raises a red ochre shipping container and swings it around and lowers it out of sight, presumably onto the deck of the ship. He makes a face, a rueful grimace – DS Leyton could not have hoped to see anything like this in the pitch darkness of the winter night. It was a rather optimistic mission that he took upon himself; truth be told, more foolhardy than sensible – and Skelgill experiences a twinge of culpability, that his colleague had rather naïvely put himself at risk in the pursuit of his brief.

Skelgill's gaze shifts across to the east, over the rooftops of Workington to the snow-covered fells. Like the Isle of Man, they seem to loom disproportionately large, as if he were peeping through a telephoto lens that compresses the distance. And yet the nearest of them – the ridge that forms the western side of his home dale – begins to rise just eight miles from his present position. So close, and yet in what splendid rural isolation he was raised, oblivious of the proximity of this post-industrial hinterland that curves in a swath around the Cumbrian coast, where medieval fishing villages were swamped by a wave of industrial revolution that swelled their ports with coal and iron and then retreated to leave its unwelcome legacy, a flotsam and jetsam of abandoned mines and limestone workings, redundant dockyards, and structural unemployment that remains undismantled to this day.

He inhales deeply and then releases the breath slowly, pensively.

But his thoughts are pricked when his gaze falls upon the small blue craft, Danny Boy, and its perennial 'For Sale' sign. Dilapidated, worse for the weather since he last set eyes upon it in daylight, but evidently seaworthy, it seems to be a metaphor for the district. If only somebody would set about it, invest some cash and elbow grease and it could return to its former glories – whatever they were. At about thirty feet it is somewhere between a cabin cruiser and a lobster boat – a hybrid that would offer the perfect combination of overnight camper and one-eighty-degree rod-fishing from the open deck at the stern. Skelgill cannot help but feel his pulse rise a little. But there is that feeling, too – that sense of preparedness for disappointment that often precedes a purchase of any substance – buyer's remorse, he has heard it called – but it strikes him before he buys, and, in most cases, puts him off.

He is just fishing for his mobile from inside his outer layers – thinking he ought to save the advertised number – as if there will be some other occasion when the decision has more attractive nuances – when a man's voice interrupts his scheme.

'Thee won't catch owt there, marra.'

Skelgill suppresses the instinct to swivel about, and instead he continues to stare across the water in the direction he had been looking, towards Danny Boy. Then he gives a half shake of his head, as one might ruefully reach some conclusion, one unconnected with the advice that has been proffered. He shoulders his spinning rod and unhurriedly makes his way back down the landing stage, his eyes watching the slippery boards as he goes. Only when he reaches the more reliable shingle does he pay proper attention to the visitor.

'What's that, you say?'

The man regards him suspiciously. He is short and stocky, square jawed, with small eyes and flared nostrils, a belligerent personage, clad in what looks like two layers of grey tracksuits, certainly going by the hooded tops, the inner one of which is pulled up to cover much of his head. On his feet are what Skelgill would consider to be unsuitable training shoes. He leans a shade to the right, the heel of his hand pressed down upon a natural wood walking stick, a twisted briar with a heavy rounded end. At his left side he swings a heavy chain dog's lead, and with the same knuckles grips a small bulging black polythene bag.

He is the first person Skelgill has encountered since he reached the area an hour or more ago. He has heard no cars on the coastal lane. From the man's position it looks like he must have emerged from the marram grass; Skelgill is sure he would have caught his eye had he come along the shoreline. Neither has there been any sign of a dog, the usual harbinger of a human. He does not immediately respond to Skelgill's request for clarification, but perhaps since Skelgill shows no sign that he will weaken, but merely eyes the man in silence, he is obliged to expand upon his charge.

'Like I say – there's nowt in there. No one fishes there.'

Skelgill is half tempted to treat this as an unwarranted admonishment – some busybody telling him what he can and cannot do, when Magna Carta has enshrined an Englishman's rights to fish from the shore for the best part of a millennium. He takes a step forward, to within reach of the man.

Then he smiles – but it is plainly a forced smile – more of a grimace. He notices the man seems to tense up, and he glances to one side – although if he is looking for his dog, the mouth of the lagoon and view across to the docks would seem to be the wrong direction.

Skelgill unclips the bass bag from his belt loop. The man seems to flinch as Skelgill's arm comes up. Skelgill maintains eye contact.

'Depends what you're after – and the state of the tide. If you want codling, whiting, dogfish – aye – then Coke Point. But your best bet for bass – this time of year – high pressure –' (he prods his rod skywards) 'the immature fish stick close to the coast – they'll chase a shoal of fry into an estuary – a basin like this –' (he gives a slightly manic laugh) 'it's like shooting fish in a barrel.'

The man is looking perplexed – but no less threatening, in his own uncommunicative way. He stares at Skelgill's lightweight tackle, as if believing he is on the receiving end of some fatuous flim-flam. He glances again, with the same anxiety, in the direction of the port.

'Here.'

Skelgill thrusts out the bass bag; it falls open at the mouth.

Inside is revealed a gleaming silver fish.

The man's suspicion shifts down a notch, to mere scepticism. Grudgingly, he looks at what is under his nose.

'What's that, then?'

'It's yourn for a fiver.' Skelgill chuckles. 'Cost you double in Tesco. Fresh rod-caught sea bass. What do you say?'

The man takes a step back, as if to remain otherwise engaged would mean he has entered the negotiation.

'Nay – you're alreet.'

He makes a peculiar face, as though fish might disagree with his stomach – although perhaps it is simply in lieu of possessing the conversational skills that would enable him to disengage from the interaction in a more regular manner – for he merely half-turns and lurches to one side, and sets off trudging along the shoreline in what will become the upstream direction, should he circumnavigate the lagoon. More likely, Skelgill thinks, he will cut in towards the coastal lane, or perhaps to the parking area beside the old Town Quay.

Skelgill observes his progress – and, indeed, now some way off, he does head at a tangent and disappears into the marram-swathed dunes. Skelgill nods reflectively.

To blend in at a public park or popular walking spot all one needs is a dog's lead to swing by one's side (no dog necessary, it will appear to be off foraging); a pebble-filled poo-bag adds considerably to the aura of authenticity. To investigate the coastline, the equivalent accessory is a fishing rod, and a freshly caught sea-bass puts the icing on the cake.

A wryly grinning Skelgill turns and retraces his steps along the rickety pontoon. More of its structure, and the rotted black hulk are exposed. But he stops short of the wreck – it is sufficient to get a view of the port. The blue freighter with its rusty shipping container aboard is nosing out of the dock. It seems it is running with the ebb tide, while the going is still good.

A sudden sucking sound emanates from the hull; the water must be draining from a fissure in the planks. The noise unnerves him, and he wonders where DS Leyton is now – probably replete with turkey sandwiches and, armed with a tin of lager, watching the

East London derby on the sports channel from the comfort of the sofa, the kids engrossed in their new computer games, the wife jiggling the bairn, the mother-in-law snoring. The image is reassuring, though he is not sure what he thinks about it himself.

*

Good to his word, Skelgill returns to Hempstead Avenue bearing fish suppers at seven minutes after eight p.m. However, what might be considered polite lateness has a less altruistic explanation. He has consumed a cheese patty, a substantial side order purchased to prevent his breaking into the tantalising newspaper-wrapped main meals during the short drive from the chippy.

While he waits for the door to be answered he rubs with one hand at the stubble around his mouth and brushes at the front of his shirt. The parcels are still reassuringly hot against his flank, and he shivers a little; the sky is clear and there is the crunch of frozen snow underfoot as he shifts his balance.

Megan Graham has on the blue dress she wore on Christmas Day. Her hair is brushed and she has applied fresh lipstick. He detects her perfume over the smell of the food.

'Hey up – I'd have brought lobster and hired a tuxedo if I'd known we were going all posh.'

She reacts with an awkward coyness that suggests she is out of practice. She tugs downwards at the sides of her dress just below her hips.

Skelgill hands over their dinner – but when she steps back he hesitates. He jerks a thumb over his shoulder.

'I've got a bottle of wine in the car – just a Christmas present, like.' His tone is tentative.

Now she plies him with a slightly injured frown.

'I've climbed a mountain, Daniel – I have to keep sommat to give up in my old age.'

He suffers a small tremor of doubt – but he remembers she was drinking on Christmas Day, and seemed to have it under control; she was responsibly merry.

'You've climbed Everest, lass – and at least you'll get an old age now.'

It is a backhanded compliment, but she seems content with his frankness. She waits at the door while he returns to and from his shooting brake.

'Thew want it on a plate?'

The patty has only staved off his appetite for so long.

'I always reckon it's best out of the paper.'

He follows her into the kitchen and puts the wine in the refrigerator. It is well stocked, with alien provender; there is salad, yoghurt, hummus and tzatziki.

The small table is laid and she places a parcel at each of the settings. She gestures for him to sit.

'Help yourself to bread and butter. I'll get this mash poured.'

Skelgill does not stand on ceremony. He burrows into last week's Times & Star to begin eating with his fingers. Megan Graham, when she joins him, uses cutlery with more decorum, taking care not to smear her dress. Skelgill is preoccupied – a fish supper must be eaten piping hot and he tucks in while the batter is still crispy. It is only when he pauses to feed his last few chips into a butty that he glances up to find she is watching him.

Her expression gives him a jolt – there is a sudden glimpse of his mother, not a woman to overdo affection, but who is known to show grudging satisfaction when one of her brood drops in, angling for a plate of hotpot. In Megan Graham's eyes he discerns a yearning, too – can it mean so much just to see a man eat heartily in her kitchen? It surely has to be the right kind of man, one whom she trusts and respects. He is unnerved by his unexpected insight – he feels compelled to say something – he can hardly extol the cooking; he could say how good she is looking – but when the words come out he finds he has dodged the issue altogether.

'Happen I've gate-crashed your evening – you'll be missing Ennerdale.'

She seems amused by his apology – and further surprises him with her response.

'Thew've not long missed Sheryl.'

She points to the work surface beside the sink. There is an

empty half-bottle of prosecco and two lipstick-kissed glasses.

Skelgill stops eating.

'Aye?'

Now she must sense his unease.

'Don't fret, Daniel – I would have texted if she were still here. And I've not mentioned that you're interested in Jade. Sheryl dropped off a scarf I left at her Ma's. But I reckon she used it as an excuse to come by. She were obviously at a loose end – looking for a blether – and the funny thing is Jade were one of the things that were mitherin' her.'

She looks for reassurance; Skelgill nods for her to continue.

'She says they were supposed to be going to the Town Sports Bar – but when she was approaching Jade's place she saw her come out – all dolled up, like – and jump into a big black limo and it drove off. Sheryl says she wouldn't have been all that fussed – it'd been Jade that had wanted to go out – but what riled her was she swears Jade blanked her. Looked her in the eye as she got in the car.'

Skelgill is not sure he likes the conclusion that this story seems to be building up to.

'Was it a taxi?'

Megan Graham shakes her head decisively.

'I asked her that.'

'What kind then? What make?'

'She just called it a limo. Why would Sheryl know? I wouldn't know.'

Skelgill hesitates, wondering how to manipulate this conversation in a way that keeps his in-law both largely in the dark and yet still onside.

'What does Sheryl think she were up to?'

But now Megan Graham cuts to the chase.

'She's not ont' game, Daniel.'

Her words are decisive; Skelgill, for his part is at a temporary loss for what to say. She fills in.

'Like I said I would – I've spoke to folk who'd know.'

Skelgill nods compliantly. There are questions stacking up in his mind, but he feels unable to rake over coals that will impinge upon Megan Graham's former private life. Indeed, he is concerned he may have placed her in a vulnerable position. That aside, there is some relief in what she says – until a small bombshell lands.

'Only thing I can think of, is maybe she's got a sugar daddy. She's a looker, isn't she?'

Skelgill plays as green as he can manage.

'Run that by us, again?'

Megan Graham smiles patiently. But she seems to have the measure of his disquiet. She rises and crosses to a cupboard and takes down two glasses.

'Should we open that wine?'

Skelgill looks at his chip butty. Tea is really the thing – but he senses he ought to acquiesce.

'Aye – why not?'

She hands him the bottle, even though it has only a screw-cap. He pours conservatively as she resumes her seat.

'Thew're too young to know what a sugar daddy is, I expect.' She smiles, watching him a little impishly over the rim of her glass. 'It's all the rage online. The lass keeps herself for one or two rich clients. She gets perks in return.'

'Perks?'

'Handbags, shoes, jewellery.'

Skelgill, content to appear ill informed, makes a practical observation.

'You can't feed yourself on handbags.'

Megan Graham chuckles. She waves a hand casually.

'There's a monthly allowance, obviously.'

'What – like pocket money?'

'More like a regular wage, Daniel.'

He ponders for a moment.

'Did Sheryl say much else?'

The woman begins to shake her head, but then remembers a point.

'She said she's seen Jade in that car before – she couldn't remember exactly when – she didn't think too much of it at the time. I can ask her more, if you want. I said I owe her a drink – since she brought round the bottle she'd got for pre's for her and

Jade.'

But Skelgill is not sure what he thinks about these latest revelations; other than they reaffirm his scepticism of hearsay. As for undermining the foundations of the case, the nagging questions remain. Would Jade really have fabricated the story of the tape, just to explain away her enhanced income? Surely she would not have tried to pull the wool over the eyes of such a close confidante as Sheryl?

He takes up the reference to the drinks.

'If you don't mind me asking – how did you get rid of Sheryl?'

She plies him with an old-fashioned look.

'Don't fret – I didn't mention who was coming.'

Skelgill nods appreciatively. But it seems Megan Graham is not quite ready to drop her interest in Jade Nelson.

'Was it thew that arrested Dale Spooner for those murders?'

'Nay – one of my colleagues, DI Alec Smart. I had no involvement in the actual investigation.' Skelgill feels guarded, but he finds himself making conversation. 'That can't be easy for Jade – her bloke inside and a bairn to look after.'

Megan Graham looks at him sharply.

'I wouldn't so much call him her bloke. That were just a flash in the pan, so they say.'

Skelgill detects another little alarm bell. He strives to seem suitably detached.

'I had the impression they were a couple – a family – from what I know of the court case.'

Megan Graham does not appear suspicious; but she does seem to understand that she has been unofficially enlisted by Skelgill. She takes small sip of wine and tilts her head to one side. She closes her eyes for a moment.

'I heard he chatted her up one night – she'd had a few too many vodkas and he'd turned up in a fancy car – gave her a lift home from the pub – maybe they tried out the springs in the back seat.'

It crosses Skelgill's mind that the vehicle was unlikely to be Dale Spooner's own set of wheels – but it is not the main thing he is thinking. Meanwhile, Megan Graham has more to add.

'They might have gone out a few times. But she's way out of

his league. Did you know Dale?'

Skelgill shakes his head. This at least is something he can be entirely honest about. His cousin-in-law elaborates.

'I've known his Ma for years – she's a dinner lady up at the high school – I used to see her outside the gates. Not that that made much difference – he were always sagging off. All he were interested in was fixing up some old banger he'd got in the lane at the back of their house. Turned out he were a bit of a natural – word got around and folk used to take their cars for Dale to fix on the cheap. He dug his own inspection pit. He more or less started his own little mechanic's business. His Ma were hoping it would keep him out of mischief – but he got into trouble a couple of times for using black-market spares. Then he fell in with the wrong crowd – graduated to stealing cars. Easier money, I suppose.'

She takes another sip of wine; Skelgill civilly mirrors her action, though he has to conceal the fact that he will never understand what people see in the stuff. She continues.

'His Ma reckons it was because he's got a heart of gold – he didn't like to disappoint anyone. He were easily led. Happy-go-lucky. From a lad he were a scamp, but he wouldn't hurt a fly. She reckons someone must have tricked him over those murders – she swears blind it couldn't have been him.'

Skelgill remains pensive.

'I thought Jade were standing by him – what with the bairn, an' all.'

Megan Graham shakes her head doubtfully.

'He were arrested before the ba'be were born. From what Sheryl's told us it's mainly Jade's Ma that looks after her.' She makes a face of resignation. 'The laal lass might not even be Dale's.'

Rather abruptly she pushes back her chair and rises. She gestures at the prolific debris upon the table.

'Do you want to go through to the living room? The gas fire's on. I'll clear this – take your wine.'

Skelgill is half distracted by indistinct thoughts and feelings – and perhaps too the first flush of the alcohol – he drinks beer of a much more modest strength. He obliges and collects the bottle and both glasses.

In the cosily lit lounge there is a three-piece suite and a coffee table set before the hearth. He is faced by the question of where to place the glasses – but after a moment's debate he sets them down opposite the sofa. However, he remains standing, and rounds to the fireplace. Taking pride of place on the mantelpiece is a familiar trophy and beside it a framed press photograph of a bedraggled Jess in her mud-spattered green vest valiantly breasting the tape; Haystacks forming the mountain backdrop. He raises a hand to his heart. It was a moment he missed – but he was, of course, otherwise detained.

'You've got a call.'

Skelgill turns on his heel. Megan Graham is in the doorway from the hall. She has his mobile phone by her side – he realises he must have left it, on silent beneath the chip wrappings. She looks a little perturbed. Her voice is hushed. 'Sorry – I must have answered it by mistake.' She reaches over the back of the settee. Her expression conveys uncertainty. 'I think he said Douglas.'

Skelgill looks blank – but he takes the handset – he checks the screen but the number is displayed as unknown. He gives his name.

He listens.

Alarm spreads across his features.

When he speaks, there is disbelief in his tone.

'Douglas?'

He glances at Megan Graham – and he reads the dismay in her eyes.

12. DOUGLAS

Workington, 11.30 p.m., Wednesday, December 31ˢᵗ

'Is that a wetsuit you're wearing, Guv?'

'Don't fret, lass – you'll be keeping your feet dry. Just switch off your interior light before you open the door.'

DS Jones, still perplexed, looks up out of the lowered window of her car. Skelgill is a dark shadow against the night sky, a black patch that interrupts the Milky Way. As ordered, she has driven the last mile along the coastal lane to their rendezvous without headlights.

'What exactly are we doing?'

Skelgill raises a finger to his lips. It is a sign that suggests all will become clear.

'Did you find everything?'

'Yes – it was where you said it would be. It's all in the back.'

'Reet, let's get it shifted.'

Presently, an even more bemused DS Jones finds herself standing alone beside the lagoon – indeed, bemused may be an understatement; perhaps incredulous would be more accurate. Skelgill, to her astonishment, has waded into the water and swum into the darkness.

But, it is Skelgill – should anything surprise her?

She has a powerful torch, and has to resist using it. She is under strict orders not to break their cover. It is freezing cold – inquisitively, she stoops to test the saltwater, and it is warm to the touch of her fingertips. Around her on the shingle is an assortment of objects, some lugged from Skelgill's car, others from her own, articles that upon directions supplied in Skelgill's late evening phone call, she has collected from his garage en route. Perhaps most notable – and puzzling at the time – are two large jerrycans which she has filled with diesel, and a hessian tool bag containing among other things a pair of heavy-duty bolt-croppers, a hacksaw and a hefty crowbar – it is the sort of thing that convicts must dream of, falling from the heavens into their prison compound. During her journey she had tried to piece together these clues in an attempt to fathom their purpose. Now something begins to take shape – for out of the silent darkness comes the sudden splutter of an engine. A boat!

Choked and stuttering at first, after a couple attempts at starting, the engine note settles into a regular put-put. Anxiously, DS Jones casts about. She grasps well enough that Skelgill does not want to reveal their presence; light is far reaching, but sound reaches those who are not looking. Perhaps that is why the throttle is being held back to a minimum.

In about a minute the prow of the craft becomes visible – moving very slowly, it noses up against what she realises is a dilapidated landing stage. It stops roughly halfway along – perhaps as close to the shore as Skelgill dare approach. Then comes his hissed instruction.

'I'll hold her here – bring the gear. Don't overload yourself. Watch your footing.'

DS Jones's head is full to bursting with questions, but she understands these will be answered the sooner she plays her part. The fuel is the heaviest – the jerrycans each hold over four gallons – Skelgill would no doubt be able to tell her their weight in pounds – but despite the slippery planks she takes both, for balance, she tells herself. Skelgill shifts to and fro, stacking the items on the afterdeck and dodging into the wheelhouse to bring the boat back against the pontoon. After several trips, it is she that he finally hauls aboard, not standing on ceremony and grabbing her around the waist and swinging her bodily around his hip. She gives a surprised squeal.

'That's one way of getting on.'

But Skelgill is immediately back at the helm, reversing the boat and peering into the gloom, slowly but surely picking a course between shadowy moored yachts and cruisers. DS Jones watches fascinated as they join the Derwent, opposite the few lights of the port: on shadowy buildings, and the red eye of the crane. The surface is calm, though there is a sense of undercurrent, of a great force beneath them that was not present in the lagoon. And now they are heading for the open sea.

She joins Skelgill. He has not spoken. She sees that his eyes are set determinedly upon a distant blinking light. Clearing the coastline, he opens up the throttle. He turns to her with a grin – she sees relief in his inscrutability.

'Guv?'

'Aye?'

'Where are we going?'

'Douglas.'

'Douglas? The Isle of Man Douglas?'

'Aye, that's the one. Leyton's got himself into another pickle.'

*

It is approaching three a.m. when DS Jones consults her watch. Beneath her, Skelgill swarms up the cold iron quayside ladder from a loosely moored Danny Boy. He dumps the tool bag in the snow at her feet and scrambles alongside her. She takes in what she can of their environs – they are on the southern side of what is an extensive harbour and ferry port, well lit and too big and too busy – even at this time of year – for there not to be workers on shift and the coastguard on standby. "We're within our rights, period," has been Skelgill's pithy advice. She has acquiesced to his argument. The Isle of Man might be its own country but its price as a British Crown Dependency is the free movement of British and indeed Irish citizens. No special permissions are needed for them to turn up like this. And, if they have been seen, they have not been challenged.

That said, two individuals clad all in black disembarking surreptitiously from a private craft in the small hours might attract an interested eye. And, not least – as they move swiftly ashore – that one of them is toting a long tool bag.

'Just act normal, lass.'

'I'm desperate to break into a sprint, Guv.'

'It's two hundred yards – fair wind and we'll have him out in two minutes and be back on board in another two. If the tide's turning, we don't want to come back to find the boat dangling.'

DS Jones squints along the dimly lit road ahead of them.

'What if there's a guard?'

Skelgill seems to renew his grip on the bag.

'Leyton reckons not.'

They stride on, purposefully. To their left is a railing and a drop into another more informal section of the harbour where a few small pleasure boats bob amongst the many buoys. To their right is a terrace of domestic properties that fronts directly onto a narrow kerb – all who may reside here appear to have long retired to their beds.

Then DS Jones notices a round patch of condensation in an upstairs window – it alarms her, she is on tenterhooks, although she can see nobody. She is reminded of the same sense of being watched when she left Fellbeck – another misted pane, as if someone had peered out – and there was the impression of the face. But, it must have been her imagination, for how could Katrina Darkness have moved about the house so swiftly?

'Here's the lifeboat station.'

Skelgill's voice jolts her back to the present.

They have studied the map on his phone. The lifeboat station is set high on its own pier, jutting out from the harbour road. With its curved roof it looks like an oversized gypsy caravan. There are lights in a couple of upper windows, but no sounds or signs of life; if there is a skeleton crew it seems to have partied itself out.

'Think they'll have CCTV?'

Skelgill harrumphs. 'Can't say as we'll have to worry about that.' But DS Jones notices that he leads them past as far across as the roadway allows.

'There, Guv – on the right.'

DS Jones refers to a sign, weathered and fading. It reads "Marine Riggers."

The houses have ended and a long high stone wall topped with iron stakes strung with barbed wire now borders the right-hand side of the road. They reach a massive rusty iron-barred gate, secured with a sturdy chain and padlock that affords a view into an unlit compound stacked with nautical equipment, anchors and buoys, and a small boat on chocks made from pallets. At an angle they can see that the main building is a stone-built workshop, set parallel to the wall, apparently windowless, but with a high, pitched roof that accommodates stable doors beneath the front gable, achieving clearance that would have allowed a carriage to enter in bygone times, and now is suitable for a high-sided vehicle or more likely a boat on a trailer. DS Jones slows, but Skelgill urges her on.

'Keep going. There's less likely to be any security at the back.'

Skelgill is tall enough to see over the copings of the wall. He reaches a point twenty yards further on and stops. For a few seconds he peers into the gloom.

'I don't see any cameras. Or security lights.' He gives a sarcastic growl. 'Makes sense, when you think about it.'

He stoops to place the bag in the snow and pulls out the pair of long-handled bolt-cutters. Without further ado he reaches up and snips the two strands of barbed wire. He replaces the tool in the bag and lifts it and drops it over the wall.

'Wait here.'

Were there a CCTV camera – perhaps on the side of the lifeboat station pointing in the appropriate direction – it would now record the two black-clad figures perhaps in a short exchange of views. But then the taller of them turns away and hauls himself up on the wall and disappears from sight. Ten seconds pass before the second, the smaller of the pair but clearly lacking nothing in agility, follows suit.

Approximately one minute later the second figure reappears on top of the wall, and drops down easily, before rising to assist what is plainly a third person – clad in a business suit and long overcoat, somewhat ill-fitting if the observer were being critical, but given a stocky build that is always a challenge. With some difficulty and valiant assistance from his more slender associate, he slides down the wall, sinks into an ungainly heap, and struggles to his feet with renewed support, brushing snow from his knees and blowing on his gloveless hands. The pair now wait, plainly in anticipation; they exude a sense of urgency – they cast about as if time is of the essence. And then the tool bag comes flying over the wall, causing them to take evasive action, followed by the first figure, the taller, who leaps from a standing position on the curved coping stones, lands catlike, grabs up the bag and strides ahead, leaving the two in his wake, the one helping the other. In a few moments, they have passed out of sight.

*

'What are you doing with a flippin' boat, Guvnor?'

Skelgill, leaning over the helm, his features grim, his eyes unblinking, answers swiftly and decisively.

'Never mind that, Leyton. Get that tea down you while I set a course. Then I want your story, first.'

Skelgill has a compass on a chart beside him, and keeps checking the bearing. He makes slight adjustments to the helm, and cranes his neck to see the sky to their port side; he is looking for the Plough, and the North Star. Satisfied, he sits back in the skipper's seat, and takes a couple of deep breaths. However, he remains vigilant, constantly scanning the dark offing. Realistically, there is little danger of being run down at this hour, and the main shipping lanes between Great Britain and Ireland run well to their north and south. It is too early for the passenger ferries to be plying their routes, and the satellite tracking shipping app on his phone reveals only 'Golden Plover', a tanker and 'Henry Hoover', a fishing vessel as boats of any size remotely in their vicinity.

He checks his watch and makes a mental note of the time – it is three-fifteen a.m. as they pass the Point of Ayre lighthouse, abeam to port – he can use dead reckoning to verify their position later, if necessary. The conditions remain perfect, the waters calm under the high pressure that has settled upon the British Isles.

DS Jones brings him a tea.

'I can see St Bees lighthouse – highest in England. If we make fourteen knots – couple more hours and we'll be there. He taps the pitometer dial with a knuckle. 'If this tub holds out. I feel like I'm thrashing her.'

DS Jones puts a hand on his forearm – it seems to be a gesture of support, of congratulation. She has her mobile in her other hand and has been monitoring their progress on her running app. She raises the handset so that he can see the screen.

'This says we're doing sixteen miles per hour.'

Skelgill nods.

DS Jones retreats to the galley area. She has been boiling water one mug at a time with the lightweight trekking stove that Skelgill had included amongst their kit. Skelgill has worked out the rudimentary heating system, and the cabin of Danny Boy is becoming decidedly cosy – although DS Leyton, for the second time in under a week has found himself badly chilled. She brews another mug for her colleague, and he seems ready to answer Skelgill's request.

'That rotten little tea-leaf Mason Milburn phoned me with a tip-off. Reckoned there was a stolen Land Rover Discovery in one of the transit warehouses on Workington docks.'

Skelgill turns to his subordinate.

'Leyton – you were supposed to be on holiday.'

DS Leyton makes a face of resignation and hunches his broad shoulders.

'I know, Guv – but – no pun intended – I was getting flamin' cabin fever. You know my lot – and there was no escape from the old – the Old Dear.' He exhales in exasperation. 'I tell you. Once she gets hold of the TV remote, forget it – might as well try to prise a leg of wildebeest out of the jaws of a crocodile.'

Skelgill is scowling.

'You might have got in touch.'

DS Leyton waves a hand apologetically.

'I didn't want to disturb you during the holidays, Guv. I only intended to do a bit of admin while the office was quiet. Cost of Christmas an' all that – I reckoned a bit of overtime would come in handy. Then I got this phone call – I thought, I'll go and have a butcher's – can't do no harm. Went and parked up by those gypsy caravans north of the port. Got myself togged up – the nippers got these explorer sets in their stockings – I borrowed a pair of plastic binoculars that were in the back seat. Walked down the shoreline until I reached the docks.'

'You pretended to be a birdwatcher?'

Skelgill's voice has taken on a note of disbelief.

'That's right, Guv. When I reached the docks I cut inland – you have to, anyway, because of the harbour wall – so I would have just pretended I'd lost my way if anyone collared me. But I was on my Jack Jones. I found the holding warehouse – a side door was open and sure enough there was the motor. I nipped round the back to get the plate number – take a photograph on my mobile – and suddenly I heard voices – at least a couple of geezers.'

'Local?' Skelgill interjects.

'Yeah, I reckon so, Guv. Then the main doors started to slide open and all I could think of was to hide – you know how these Discos have got a door on the back – I opened that and ducked in. Held it to, without slamming it. There was a load of picnic gear and I hid under this tartan rug.'

He looks from one to the other of his colleagues, somewhat wild-eyed.

'Next thing – someone's jumped in, started her up – and within about thirty seconds – *clang!* I'm inside a flippin' shipping container!'

'Did you recognise the voices? Hear anyone say owt?'

'Nothing I could rely on, Guv – once I was inside it was more or less soundproof. And pitch black. Thankfully it wasn't completely airtight – *hah!* – and I had the interior lights of the car. But the mobile signal – dead as a doornail. I realised I just had to wait it out. I switched off to save the battery. Eventually – back on dry land – I figured I might be able to make a break for it. But, no sooner than the container was opened, the motor was driven out and straight into that workshop – took no more than a minute. Slick little operation they've got going, Guv.'

'What did you hear – or see?'

'I just kept my head down, Guv. I reckon it was only one geezer who shifted the car and locked up and cleared off. I suppose whatever they planned to do with the motor could wait until tomorrow – later today.'

'When did you twig where you were?'

'Soon as I switched my phone back on – the maps app. Obviously, I waited until I was sure I was alone. I was guessing it must be Liverpool – somewhere like that. Until I zoomed it out and found I was on a flamin' island! Stone the crows. I discovered I was well and truly locked in – that's when I phoned you, Guv – and you said to sit tight. I'd assumed you'd call in the local uniformed squad.'

Skelgill frowns, as though he detects a criticism – or at least a complaint. But, having thus far successfully executed his plan, he is more convinced than ever that it was worth putting his colleague through a few hours' extra hardship. Besides, when he had scanned about the workshop, he had noted there was a sink with running water, of which no doubt DS Leyton had availed himself in more ways than one. They have succeeded in springing free their colleague without either notifying the authorities (who surely would have acted precipitously) or alerting the gang.

And now DS Leyton has a question along these lines.

'What were you up to, Guv – when you hung back in that yard?'

Skelgill casts a furtive glance in his sergeant's direction.

'I broke the lock on the main doors and hacksawed halfway through the chain on the gate – just left it at that. So it looks like we tried to nick the car and got disturbed. Abandoned. They might be suspicious – but there's no way they'll guess they brought a passenger with them.'

DS Leyton seems satisfied with the prognosis.

'Their local rivals might feel the heat of that, Guv.'

Skelgill nods pensively.

'You might be closer to the mark than you think, Leyton.'

'How's that, Guv?'

Skelgill glances again at DS Leyton.

'What time was it – when you were loaded into the container?'

DS Leyton has to think for a moment.

'Round about two-thirty, I suppose.'

Skelgill is nodding. It corresponds to the departure of the freighter and his confrontation with the dogless dog-walker.

'I reckon I got a visit from one of their heavies.'

He is conscious that he attracts the heightened attention of his colleagues. DS Leyton pursues the question.

'What do you mean, Guv?'

Skelgill relates his account of fishing, of noticing the freighter, and of the coincidental appearance of the thuglike character. He does not mention that, at the very moment DS Leyton was involuntarily setting sail, he had half-enviously, half-disparagingly envisaged his colleague lounging at home, watching the football.

'Here – catch.'

He brings out from his pocket the little silver coin and flips it to DS Leyton. It falls to the floor but his sergeant bends to retrieve it, emitting an unintentional grunt.

'What is it, Guv?'

'A Manx coin. Two bob in old money. I found it on the shoreline on Christmas Eve – when I went back to look for your phone.'

DS Leyton stares at the object, tiny in his broad palm.

He curses, the more printable words, "rat" and "Milburn".

Now DS Jones interjects.

'But surely it wasn't him?'

However, she sees that Skelgill is nodding.

DS Leyton turns to her to explain.

'Pound to a penny Milburn's riding two horses. He gladly took a sweetener – then I bet he tipped off the gang that I was looking for them on Christmas Eve. Next thing he's ringing me about this latest hot motor being shipped out.' He addresses Skelgill. 'Then I reckon he warned them that we might be sniffing around – so they sent out their scouts and one of them found you, Guv.'

DS Jones is looking alarmed.

'Could they have suspected you, Guv?'

Skelgill is watching the distant lighthouse on St Bees Head. It flashes twice every twenty seconds. He narrows his eyes pensively. There is always the outside possibility that he will be recognised, just for who he is, a local man with his share of run-ins with the criminal fraternity. Although, unlike DI Alec Smart – not a local man – he has eschewed the limelight, the interviews and the cameras, the basking in the glories of successful arrests and convictions.

He revisits the encounter in his mind. He believes he gave a pretty convincing account of himself. Surely the sea bass trumped the poo-bag as cover stories went? The thug was plainly not the sharpest knife in the drawer. But he cannot be entirely sure.

'You, Leyton – they knew you were a cop – you didn't hide that from Milburn, or in most of your enquiries. You put them on notice about your Manchester gang – that might be where they'd think I'd come in.'

He sighs a little. He certainly shan't take any chances in future. He looks round at DS Leyton.

'If we're right about this and you were belted from behind by our laddo – Leyton, you stuck your head into the lion's mouth by going back to the docks.'

DS Leyton glances rather sheepishly at DS Jones.

'I know – before you say it, Emma – another one of my nineteen lives.'

DS Jones grins – that he has raised his allocation.

But he continues in an optimistic manner, gesturing to Skelgill with an open palm.

'Thing is, Guv – they didn't find me – and now we know what the score is.'

Skelgill remains silent for a moment.

'What is the score?'

DS Leyton appears surprised by the question – but he has a ready answer.

'Well – looks to me like they're knocking off high-value cars on the mainland, shipping them over to the Isle of Man – that workshop, it's no chop shop – so I reckon they're recycling them asap – cloning their identities and sticking them back into circulation. We know there's a ready market of millionaires. The reason they're living there is to avoid paying their taxes – just the sort to buy a nice pre-owned motor – a bargain, no questions asked. I wouldn't be surprised if the merchandise is being stolen to order.'

DS Jones is processing what her colleague has suggested.

'Do you think we should involve the Manx Constabulary? They must have knowledge of the car dealers on the island. And a database of locally registered vehicles.'

But DS Leyton interjects.

'I reckon they'll be using cloned UK registrations – bear in mind they're second-hand motors. Easier to hide in plain sight. Most rich folk have a base on the mainland – they only have to live on the island half the year.'

Skelgill, who has been holding his peace, now intervenes.

'Aye – contact them – but maybe not yet. The whole point of what we've just done is to avoid them charging in with their size twelves and compromising the secrecy at our end. Remember – it's a murder we're trying to crack – not a motor theft ring.'

DS Jones is listening carefully – and she detects a note in Skelgill's delivery that suggests an underlying concern. Is there something he has not yet shared with them? However, when she speaks, she directs an alternative query at DS Leyton.

'Did you get any impression that they might be dealing in more than stolen cars?'

'What – like contraband?'

She gives a small shake of her head.

'I was thinking marijuana.'

DS Jones looks apprehensively at Skelgill – he is leaning over the helm again, staring at some indeterminate landmark and minutely adjusting their course. He appears to be opting out of this part of the discussion.

But DS Leyton has nothing to report.

'I don't know if it would be worth their while, girl – I mean what's the population – eighty thousand?'

DS Jones nods, but she persists with her point.

'It could be a stepping stone to Ireland – not an obvious route. Then we're talking over six million people.' She makes a sound of frustration. 'There just seems to be a chain here – I'm not sure how the links are connected – but we have Swinesdale, drugs, the Badduns, Dale Spooner, executive cars, the Isle of Man –'

Skelgill has turned to look at her – but his expression is at best neutral.

DS Leyton picks up the thread – he has a pragmatic take on the matter.

'Why don't we just round up the gang? With a bit of shoe leather and surveillance we can get them bang to rights. Once they're in custody, Spooner might feel safe. I reckon he nicked the Mercedes for them – but somehow got into bed with the Badduns. The gang made 'em pay. Spooner must have hidden and filmed the fire – but he still ended up taking the rap.'

Skelgill exhales resignedly.

'I might as well chuck another spanner in the works.'

He fixes his gaze upon DS Jones.

'Do you know what a sugar daddy is?'

It is typical of Skelgill – the sort of curveball they have come to expect without ever being able to predict its trajectory. DS Leyton's jaw falls slightly open, but DS Jones is more composed.

'Of course – if it's what I think you mean. An older male benefactor. I believe it's a growth industry online.'

Skelgill is nodding.

'Megan Graham – Jess's Ma – she tipped me the wink. I heard a rumour about Jade Nelson at the Christmas party – that she was escorting. Megan says no way – but Sheryl Graham's told her that she's seen Jade more than once in a limo, dressed for dinner, you might say. And Jade seems to have been keeping it quiet.'

'Well, it certainly ain't Spooner chauffeuring her.'

DS Leyton's quip is flippant, but Skelgill has more to add on this point.

'There's talk of there being no great thing between him and Jade Nelson – even that the bairn might not be his.'

DS Jones is quick to take him up on this.

'Is that for certain, Guv?'

Skelgill has to row back a little.

'Probably third or fourth hand. Allow for Chinese whispers. But the limo – and fancy togs – we can take that as read.'

DS Leyton has identified the problem.

'So, what are you saying, Guv – that we can't trust what Jade Nelson says about the hush money? That could be inconvenient – if her story starts to unravel.'

Skelgill appears pained – and DS Jones now understands his terse counsel about this being a murder investigation. But her mind moves swiftly.

'What if the provider of hush-money and the sugar daddy are

one and the same?'

Skelgill glances at her sharply – she can read in his eyes that this is not a new idea to him. He nods for her to continue.

'When you think about it – why would she admit to it? If she's happy with the arrangement. If Dale Spooner found out it might change his attitude to remaining tight-lipped. That would upset her applecart.'

Skelgill is looking like he might buy into this argument. But he can think of a caveat.

'There's still the bairn.'

'But – as you say, Guv – it may not be his. Presumably he would have a fair idea of that.'

Skelgill continues to play devil's advocate.

'She tried to get him off the murder charge – remember, the alibi she was forced to abandon.'

DS Jones regards her superior reflectively.

'Eighteen years is a long time to wait when you're in your early twenties.'

Skelgill is surprised by his colleague's philosophical stance. But he is reminded of his cousin-in-law Megan Graham's words. That Dale Spooner was punching well above his weight. And, for sure, a girl that looks like Jade Nelson is never going to be short of suitors.

He gazes somewhat pensively at DS Jones – for a moment she seems to be sharing the same transcendental plane – when DS Leyton spontaneously thumps the hull of the boat with the side of his fist.

'Alright then, Guv – so what's the story with this old tub?'

Skelgill gives a little start – but, after a second's hesitation, he seems content with the diversion.

He leaves the helm to pick up the advertising board which was hung over the side of the craft. He turns it briefly towards DS Leyton before resuming his station.

'Bit of a shot in the dark. The owner agreed I could take her for a sea trial. I picked up the keys last night.'

DS Leyton looks a little amused.

'I bet he didn't think you'd give it an actual shot in the dark!'

'*She*, Leyton. A widow – lives at High Harrington. This was the husband's. Bit of a mechanic – he souped her up.'

Skelgill's reply suggests he harbours a small sense of guilt about his misappropriation of the boat – after all, there must have been the chance if it being impounded, temporarily, at least. But he had calculated the alternative: the car ferry from Heysham in Lancashire would see them arriving late afternoon. DS Leyton could not have held out – the only option would have been to resort to the Manx police.

'She's been moored in that tidal lagoon for the best part of a year.' He taps the helm. 'Little run out will do her good.'

DS Leyton seems satisfied with the response, although he has a follow-up question.

'Can you have a 'she' called Danny Boy?'

Skelgill glances again at DS Jones, who looks like she anticipates a politically incorrect rejoinder.

'These days, Leyton, you can have anything you like.'

It seems to settle the matter, although DS Leyton's characteristic loquacity is steadily becoming restored.

'So, what do you reckon, Guv?' He knocks against the hull again, as if sounding out its condition. 'You going to put in an offer?'

Skelgill is reminded of the exchange with the thug, and his response when confronted with a similar question. Funny how the natural reaction is to resort to excuses. Despite that Danny Boy is going for a song.

'If I had a boat on the sea, Leyton – when would I fish on Bass Lake? I can hardly find time to get out there as it is.'

His colleagues might disagree with this assertion – but Skelgill's definition of what constitutes sufficient angling time is probably wildly at odds to the average. Rather than dispute the point, DS Leyton continues to make conversation.

'I'm surprised you didn't bring a rod, Guv – trail a line over the back. You could have caught kippers for our breakfast.'

Skelgill is momentarily sidetracked by the string of inaccuracies in his sergeant's suggestion. But he chooses to gainsay what he considers the most heinous aspect.

'That's not fishing, Leyton – that's trolling.'

'Trawling? That's alright, ain't it?'

Skelgill glowers.

'Trolling, Leyton – *trolling*, with an *'o'* – trawling's what you do with a muckle great net – commercial fishing – for a living.'

DS Leyton remains bemused.

'So why's this trolling malarkey out of order, then?'

It takes Skelgill a moment to put his personal prejudice into words.

'Leyton – where's the skill in trailing a lure over the stern and waiting for a fish to hook itself? Using a line with a breaking strain that doesn't even give it fighting chance. Might as well go to the chippy and come out and say you've just caught a cod.'

DS Leyton turns to DS Jones to glimpse the hint of a smile – but perhaps there is something more profound, and they exchange a knowing glance. Skelgill's contention – that the catching is more important than the catch – provides an insight into his attitude towards his job. Not that he would purposefully procrastinate – when the time comes to strike he is suitably ruthless – but that he secretly relishes the relentless stalking that makes for a successful hunt.

Skelgill seems to detect that he is being psychoanalysed. He addresses DS Jones.

'Was there something?'

'Oh – no – well – I was just thinking. This boat – you said the owner lives at High Harrington. That's where the Mercedes in which the Badduns were found was stolen from.'

Skelgill regards her reprovingly.

'Jones – take it from me – that is definitely a coincidence.'

13. UNDER FIRE

Penrith HQ, 9 a.m., Wednesday, January 6th

'**E**xpect Smart any second.'

DS Jones turns from the window of Skelgill's office. Her slender figure silhouetted against the white backdrop makes a bulky Icelandic sweater look chic. But fresh snow is falling and her expression holds a small degree of trepidation, as if she has been rehearsing a journey she will need to make, and the tribulations it might hold. DS Leyton, settled beside the filing cabinet opposite Skelgill's desk, looks more relaxed – it seems the half-dozen days off since his own latest escapade have served him well, and he is still in festive mode. Skelgill's words, however, rouse him, and he sits upright and gives a shrug of his heavy shoulders, rather like a well-fed dog that knows it really must accept the prompt of a walk; there is always that favourite lamppost.

Skelgill rounds his desk and scowls at the standard mug of tea that stands in the centre. He too wears a jumper which might be a Christmas gift – though he does not quite carry it off so well as DS Jones – with unkempt hair and several days' stubble he looks more like an Icelandic fisherman who has come in from a shift at sea.

'I'll get you a fresh one, Guv – that will be tepid.'

Skelgill does not seem to hear DS Jones. He has attended a meeting of his peers, chaired by the Chief, the first of the year, to review cases old and new, to set priorities and allocate resources. There can be some empire building, and a combination of determination and bravado may be required to fight one's corner. DI Smart is renowned for dramatising his predicaments and exaggerating his staffing requirements. Skelgill is often angered by the obligatory horse trading – DI Smart constantly trying to poach his team, not least DS Jones, for whom he has made another play that needed a vigorous rearguard action. But, while Skelgill has won the formal argument, it has been at the cost of having to reveal more of his hand than he – and possibly the Chief – would have preferred.

But now, before DS Jones can execute her offer of a replacement beverage, Skelgill's door is darkened as he predicted.

DI Smart loiters, preening. His poses and outfits might be copied from a model in a clothing catalogue; though he is too skinny, too weaselly ever to look entirely the part.

'Morning ladies.'

It is his modus operandi. To sow discord he employs deliberate provocation, either uncaring of or insensible to its alienating effect.

His next move, however, is more unexpected.

He brandishes his mobile phone and, with a locker-room leer, leans conspiratorially to share some content with DS Leyton, whose seat is just inside the door.

DS Leyton cannot but look at the screen.

Skelgill hears a three- or four-second burst of music that strikes a vague chord. It is playing on repeat. There is a background cacophony of excited voices. He sees DS Leyton's eyes widen a little, and his expression become confounded – in the way that suggests a small defeat has been inflicted upon him.

'Amazing what gets around on social media these days, eh, cock?'

Before Skelgill can object or challenge DI Smart's purpose he takes advantage of the disarray to step across to DS Jones – and now holds the screen for her to watch.

Whereas DS Leyton reacted guilelessly, Skelgill sees that DS Jones shows no outward response – evidence in itself of an inner jarring – quite plainly she controls her features and stares unblinking, before glancing at Skelgill.

'Looks like it's going well with your kissing cousin, Skel.'

Now DI Smart turns gleefully to Skelgill. He again displays the phone – but it is apparent he keeps his distance, out of arm's reach. But the screen is close enough for Skelgill to view the video – and he sees what is already coming back to him, as the soundtrack repeats.

It is the moment at Big Mags Graham's party, just after her daughter Sheryl had fallen from the staircase into his arms, when the dancing had broken out, and he had dropped his inhibitions – a short clip painting a completely false picture of his participation, and enthusiasm to do so – Sheryl waving her arms, he swinging her about, culminating in the moment when she had lunged to whisper into his ear – looking entirely like she was kissing him.

Skelgill is tongue-tied. He does not look at DS Jones. His expression darkens, verging on the thunderous. DI Smart does well to be on other side of desk. But he has gained the upper hand. He has disoriented his opponent, and now comes the thrust.

'Word is, Skel, you're sniffing around more than just your relatives – the Workington underbelly.'

He stares at the stupefied Skelgill for a moment, and then turns to DS Leyton.

The latter senses that Skelgill is stymied and – frankly – is more likely to answer DI Smart with a punch than a sentence. But he feels exposed, too. They know that DI Smart has cultivated a small army of informers; there is the sudden realisation on DS Leyton's part that he may have inadvertently approached one of them. However, he contrives to parry DI Smart's suggestion.

'I'm working countywide. After Carlisle and Barrow, Workington's got the highest number of recorded car crimes.'

DI Smart regards him disparagingly, but ignores his explanation and addresses Skelgill, although his eyes are fixed upon DS Jones.

'I had a word in the Chief's ear.' His rather unseemly phraseology suggests an intimacy that Skelgill doubts exists. 'She's okayed it for Emma to liaise with me. Once she's up to speed –' (now he changes into the first person) 'any queries you've got, any visits you want to make' (flexing bony fingers he takes hold of one of his lapels) 'I'll take care of you – a bit of hand-holding – someone more your own generation, speaks your language.'

Skelgill jolts in his seat, but before DI Smart can be gainsaid he skips past DS Leyton and turns in the doorway. Then a text alert bleeps from Skelgill's mobile telephone, which is lying on his desk. DI Smart leans forward, peering to read it. Skelgill snatches it away and places it face down. But DI Smart grins conspiratorially – for he has detected a reaction caused by the message.

'Love you and leave you, ladies.' He winks at DS Jones and moves away, but he has a final word for Skelgill. 'You're getting likes from all round the station.'

And he is gone.

There is a stilted silence. Skelgill is quietly fuming. Social media is anathema to him, but its all-pervasive presence – and role in solving crimes – cannot be denied, and he knows enough of it to be suitably irked. He had noticed that DI Smart had hung back at the end of the meeting, and now he wonders if he showed the video to the Chief. But the 'generational' jibe has stung him even more – there are only a couple of years between DI Smart and himself.

DS Leyton no doubt detects something of Skelgill's turmoil, for in typical style he tackles the awkwardness head on.

'You're a good mover, Guv – you could be on Strictly! Those lifts are not easy – especially when the lady's not exactly – well – you know – built like Emma.'

He realises he has dug a small hole for himself – and now DS Jones rises and takes up Skelgill's untouched mug, evidently intending to carry out her offer of obtaining a refill. She meets Skelgill's gaze with a curious look, but one that certainly carries an element of reproach, despite a little smile.

'I suppose it's one way of passing the time of day.'

Her choice of words is a reminder that she had paid attention to his earlier account of his endeavours.

Skelgill is obliged to defend himself.

'It's not what it seemed. She'd just fallen off the stairs and I happened to be standing underneath. Then she started jiggling about to the music – I didn't want to look like the party pooper. I was under cover, remember.'

DS Jones glances back over her shoulder as she leaves the office; there might be the hint of a flounce in her naturally buoyant gait.

Skelgill scowls – although now he is more concerned that she may have gone quickly in order to have a word with DI Smart. He looks to DS Leyton, who returns an expression of sympathetic resignation. But again he does not shy away from a contentious point.

'Guvnor – how does Smart get his information?'

Skelgill shakes his head regretfully.

'In the meeting – I explained that we've found a drug farm in Swinesdale – it's the justification for getting the Spooner case files. Your car thefts investigation – aye, it's been longer running – but I had to cover that, to make it clear you've got your hands full – obviously I didn't mention the Isle of Man scam. Chuck into the mix me being in Workington – private family party or not, there's a glimpse of Jade Nelson in that video clip – Smart would recognise her. So, we're talking Swinesdale, Spooner, car thefts, Jade Nelson, Workington – all on the same page. Even a donnat like Smart can join the dots.'

DS Leyton is nodding understandingly.

'You're right, Guv – he'll be like a cat on a hot tin roof if he thinks there's any chance the Spooner case will be re-opened.' The sergeant shifts position and pulls at the back of his jacket, as if his shirt is sticking to him. 'I can't help wondering if I've been speaking to one of his snouts. That Mason Milburn, for example.'

Skelgill gazes reflectively at his colleague.

'Not a lot you can do about that, Leyton. Just be cagey.'

'No fear, Guv. After my boat adventures I'll be extra vigilant. Don't want to end up in Davy Jones's locker – *hah* – speaking of the Joneses!'

DS Jones re-enters bearing Skelgill's favoured outsize mug; she seems rejuvenated.

'I told DI Smart I would contact him if I find anything contentious.'

She smiles in a relaxed manner. DS Leyton seems to get the gist of her sentiment.

'Very clever, girl – he'll be bricking it – I wouldn't want you going through my dirty laundry.'

DS Jones laughs – although her expression registers mock displeasure at the image he conjures.

Skelgill, meanwhile, appears somewhat relieved. Without further prompting, he begins to pontificate.

'We've obviously got limited resources – and there's been a flood of cases over Christmas. I've managed to convince the Chief to lay off us this week – that's probably another reason Smart's suspicious – plus she's lumbered him with the theft of an HGV carrying a load of sanitary protection from Stobart's distribution centre. But as far as setting up surveillance to collect evidence on the Workington car gang and the Swinesdale drug farm – we're more or less on our own – with what DCs we can spare off other jobs. Obviously, we can't risk taking any of Smart's crew. I reckon you both need to come up with a plan – that we can put to the Chief if we want more bodies.'

'At least it sounds like she's batting for us, Guv.' Skelgill frowns, but DS Leyton continues on this more optimistic note. 'I don't see why we can't manage. The trick is to understand when to go in – when to nab the right people red-handed.'

Skelgill folds his arms.

'The right people being?'

His sergeants shake their heads under his scrutiny. But DS Leyton remains buoyed.

'A bit more leg work yet, Guvnor. I reckon I should have a word with the Isle of Man Constabulary – find a contact I can trust – I won't give anything away. And the local beat cops in Workington – find out who are the likely candidates for running the car operation.'

He looks at Skelgill, who nods – and who looks at DS Jones – but DS Leyton interjects.

'I can see Emma's champing at the bit to read those statements.'

She grins a little self-consciously.

'You find any nuggets on the car front – fire 'em over to me, girl.'

DS Jones acknowledges his request. Then it is she that puts a query to Skelgill.

'What about you, Guv?'

Skelgill glances at his displaced mobile – as if there is some small matter of guilt.

'I'll see what comes up.'

When they are gone, he stares at his phone.

The text has been forwarded by Megan Graham – its originator, Sheryl Graham. The language is graphic, but the gist is clear. Sanitised, it reads:

"Someone's given Jade a good hiding."

14. CLUES

'Sir Mallory? I'm Detective Sergeant Jones of Cumbria CID – I phoned yesterday afternoon?'

'Ah, yes – come in out of the cold, young lady. I'll put the kettle on.' The elderly man leans out of the cottage doorway and through keen blue eyes gazes perspicaciously at the inscrutable grey skies. 'I should say gingerbread is called for, wouldn't you agree?'

Skelgill's common rejoinder of "Don't mind if I do" springs to DS Jones's mind, though it always sounds a little presumptuous (not that Skelgill would realise) – and instead she settles for an engaging smile.

The interior is a mixture of slate and distempered stucco, stone-flagged floors and dark beams, and the walls of the passage and cosy firelit sitting room into which he leads her are adorned with antiquated climbing gear and memorabilia, framed yellowed news cuttings and faded sepia photographs of hooded men with sunburnt faces and frost in their beards. It is like a cross between a cottage museum and perhaps a traditional alpine guest house that has been decked with gleanings from antique shops – except this is all real, the life and trappings of one of Britain's most auspicious mountaineers, an audacious pioneer of the Karakoram, author of a score of books on the subject (several of which spawned films), ninety-three-year-old Sir Mallory George. Though long retired to his modest Cumbrian birthplace, she knows from TV documentaries that he is fiercely independent, and is still seen determinedly abroad in the local fells, despite his advancing years.

While she waits she finds the dark eyes of those climbers upon her – and she wonders what she sees in them. How many, for instance, came back to tell their tales? The attrition rates in the early days of mountaineering made fighting in bloody wars seem safe. Perhaps these young men – she supposes in the 1950s it would have been – had missed the terrors and adrenaline suffered by their forefathers, and sought their own jeopardies, by their own free will.

'Here we are, young lady – help yourself – don't stand on ceremony.'

Her thoughts are interrupted. With surprising steadiness of hand, the man lays down a tray upon a thick oak coffee table. She sees that he is far from frail – attenuated by age, yes, but he is wiry and strong – not a big man, a climber's build – and his pale blue eyes are alert.

They each help themselves, although in momentary silence, like the courtship dance of grebes their ritual movements are an ice-breaker of sorts. DS Jones can tell that the man suspects she is a little overawed, perhaps something he is accustomed to as a venerable celebrity. She ought to be getting used to it – she ought to get to the point.

'Sir –' But she immediately stalls – for there is the anomaly of calling an actual Sir, a Knight of the Realm, "sir". He seems amused. But she also feels a little guilty – that she is operating by necessity with a cover story. The man seems so trusting. She employs the collective pronoun to make herself feel better. 'We believe there may be a long-term pattern of thefts in this area. I mentioned when I rang that I hoped to speak with you about a matter that you reported –' She hesitates again, to correct herself. 'I should say, a matter that you mentioned to one of our officers.'

'Really?'

He cocks his head a little to one side, but otherwise seems untroubled by her account. She continues.

'Yes, sir. Our records state that you had a possible intruder – on the same night as the incident in Swinesdale that became known in the media as the Badduns Murders.'

What DS Jones does not say is that, in her opinion, an appallingly cursory interview was conducted, and scant notes were taken. Worse still, was the sentiment expressed: "Claimed intruder 10 p.m. Householder in bed. No signs of breaking and entering or other disturbance or theft. Elderly witness probably unreliable."

DI Smart's lackey, in conducting house-to-house enquiries, was plainly going through the motions. It was a box-ticking exercise. The interview was dated a week after the burning of the Mercedes, by which time Dale Spooner was in custody.

Despite that it was a cursory report, and that DS Jones had speed-read the copious files, this entry did not escape her laser-like scrutiny. Her colleague DS Leyton had requested any nuggets she might find. It may not be a nugget, but certainly it had glinted like a flake of gold in the prospector's pan.

For a moment Sir Mallory George does not respond, and DS Jones feels a twinge of doubt – that the report may be right – and the elderly man anyway might struggle to recall the events of over three years ago.

'K2 sorted it out.'

'K2?'

She knows enough that this was one of his famed ascents. Is he rambling?

'The mountain?'

'My German Shepherd – alas now gone.'

She must look perplexed.

He regards her with a twinkle in his eye.

'You're thinking it should be K9?'

'Well –'

The man chuckles.

'I suppose if I kept having dogs, I could work up to K9 – but – well – I'm too old for another, it wouldn't be fair on the poor beast.'

'You look very fit, sir.'

DS Jones has spoken before she knows it, and now she finds him gazing rather wistfully at her.

'Not fit enough to woo a young lady like you.'

His remark may be a little gauche, but his tone is gentlemanly and she is too intelligent to be inflexibly woke. She smiles gracefully.

'You said, sir – that your dog sorted it out?'

He hesitates, but then he nods and gestures with a slow movement of one hand towards the exit to the hallway.

'We rarely lock doors around here. It was summer. I couldn't swear now that I hadn't left the back one open – I mean literally open – a fox might have wandered in. Whatever it was, K2 got his teeth into it – there was a smear of dried blood on his muzzle. I looked around in the morning – but there was no sign of a dead fox – or anything, come to that.'

DS Jones wants to ask, did he tell this to the investigating officer? Fox or not, there may have been traces of evidence that should have been captured. But it is not for her to suggest a failing on the man's behalf – most likely he tried to explain and was dismissed as senile, batty – or attention-seeking. And he is plainly none of these things.

But DS Jones feels that her pulse rate has risen ... she finds herself reaching for another slice of gingerbread.

*

It has taken her just fifteen minutes to drive from Sir Mallory George's cottage in the hamlet of Mungrisdale, and – when she could have called at any of several properties – she finds herself at the picnic spot beside the river, introduced to her by Skelgill as the scene of the blazing inferno that engulfed the Baddun brothers.

On the face of it, Skelgill seems more inclined to DS Leyton's side of the inquiry, the Workington connection. And she sees the rationale. The trail leads back from here. The car was found in Swinesdale. Dale Spooner had almost certainly stolen it. He likely supplied the gang. They operate out of Workington. If the gang were responsible for the killing of the Badduns – retribution for stealing the car intended for the buyer they had lined up – then Dale Spooner will be in no doubt about his own or his loved ones' fate should he talk.

But she is uneasy.

She asks herself, is she simply in irrational competition with this logic? She has her own findings and wants them to work out. But that is not her nature – she is a team player; it does not matter who gets it right, or who gets the credit. No – the discord she feels is of a different kind. It is that uncomfortable feeling of knowing you

189

are deluding yourself, of trying to make the facts fit when intuitively you recognise they do not. It is akin to wrestling with a cryptic crossword – and of inserting a solution that matches only one half of the traditional two-pronged clue. The excuse, that it is simply one of those obscure clues that she does not comprehend – the compiler's mind works in a mysterious way, or uses a turn of phrase that she is too young to have experienced, or that is outwith the ambit of her general knowledge. Setters often employ cricketing terms and abbreviations, for example. *"Caught a second time for all the players" (4 letters)* – it was a clue that stumped her only last week. "All the players" might have been a sporting reference – TEAM or SIDE. Or maybe musicians – BAND? But the first prong of the clue, "Caught a second time" – what was that all about? A replay, perhaps? A re-release? Then she had solved an intersecting clue that made the first letter C. It ruled out all of her putative synonyms. Against her better judgement she had settled upon CREW. But then another intersecting word made the third letter S. Crew was wrong – as she had suspected all along. Eventually, experimenting by dropping letters into the two spaces in "C_S_" brought to mind the word CAST. Of course, *that* kind of players – actors! And then she saw the corroboration: *caught* was C, and then A on its own, and *second* was S, and *time* was T. Caught a second time. C-A-S-T. Using coded conventions the compiler had spelled it out before her very eyes.

What is being spelled out before her very eyes in Swinesdale?

If the Badduns came here of their own volition, why? Skelgill had alluded to a rogue dog that was shot where it transgressed. And there was his casual remark when she had challenged him about the unlocked gate behind the Moot Hall Café. What had he said – the first principle of burglary? Make sure your exit is clear. But there is no exit from Swinesdale – unless you are prepared to take flight across the fells. For the seasoned criminal, it is far from an ideal rendezvous.

Has Skelgill been hinting to her, to press on, open minded? Let her senses do the work? After all, he too had drifted back to Swinesdale – whether or not he was keeping a watchful eye upon her, he was in investigative mode, and simultaneously identified the shed where marijuana is being grown. And in that, as she pointed out, they have something that is surely too much of a coincidence.

He had, of course, given her the credit. Is he hedging his bets?

But there are other aspects that niggle at her.

Revenge upon the Badduns by the gang is a plausible motive. But revenge upon the car? Why would they incinerate a perfectly good Mercedes? Why not reclaim it and ship it to the Isle of Man? The forensic reports concluded that the Badduns were almost certainly unconscious before the car was set alight – it is not as though the fire was a special form of torture. She tries to think of a counter argument – perhaps the vehicle was bespoiled in some way – but she remains unconvinced.

Today, there is Sir Mallory George's account to stir into the pot. What if it were not a fox? Is that a conclusion Sir Mallory has reached in retrospect? The interview notes might have been sparse, but they did use the word 'intruder' – that it was the first impression. A sneak-thief abroad on the same night as the inferno? Another coincidence?

DS Jones climbs out of her car.

It is eerily overcast; the sky might almost be frozen like the silent snowscape. And yet something pervades the atmosphere – it has been so from the very first – there is an ineffable quality about the dale that is discernible if impossible to describe.

She sniffs the air.

Does she detect the sticky scent of marijuana?

Surely it cannot be, this far up in Swinesdale. She must imagine it. As she surveys the descending valley, she sees that smoke is rising vertically in fine columns – from Jacob Floxham's miner's cottage, a quarter of a mile away; from the shadowy pines that surround Fellbeck, where Katrina Darkeness must also be at home; and, further, from the farmsteads, and the hamlet – a distant smudge.

Perhaps the smell is the wood they burn, some conifer or other. She is reminded of Skelgill and the juniper, and she takes a few crunching steps through ankle-deep snow to a straggling bush and pulls off a sprig. She removes a glove and crushes the spiny foliage – it pricks her flesh – but she inhales the aroma. It is invigorating –

piney, turps-like, as pungent as smelling salts.

The sensory burst is the catalyst for a sudden cascade of images, of incomplete thoughts, fragments chipped from her subconscious, tumbling fleetingly past her mind's eye.

The cast.

What if they are actors in this together?

The shepherd, the writer, the farmer, the herbalist.

And others, perhaps.

Could a drugs farm operate here without the locals knowing?

Does Hugh Larkfield run a little under-the-counter service?

Or something greater, in which they each have a vested interest?

They were all living here at the time the Badduns were killed.

Has she not been met with a subtle wall of silence?

Could this be the corroboration, the solution to the second prong of the cryptic clue that is Swinesdale?

But no sooner than this notion begins to take shape, it is overshadowed by a returning feeling of disquiet – and where before it was a sense of doubt, more disconcertingly it is now one of danger.

She has revealed herself to all of them but Hugh Larkfield. If there is some conspiracy – or even if it is just a local grapevine – he too will surely know her purpose by now.

She glances across at her car; it is distinctive, easily recognisable.

Quite likely they are aware of her presence.

She is alone in the rat trap.

Skelgill cannot be watching from above a second time.

She tells herself the fear is irrational.

And then a text message arrives on her mobile.

*

'Looking for inspiration, madam?'

'Oh!'

DS Jones turns, surprised by the suave voice close at hand.

Kendall Minto touches her upper arm; her reaction is an excuse to offer reassurance.

'Sometimes it's the only way to get a scoop.'

DS Jones frowns reprovingly. Though she understands he means that, for a reporter, creeping up on one's victims comes with the territory.

Now he refers to the book she holds; she had been engrossed in the blurb.

'I interviewed her for the launch – she did a signing in the Carlisle branch.'

With a flourish he waves a hand, the long smooth fingers neatly manicured, to indicate their present surroundings, a smaller satellite outlet of the same chain. His text – his suggestion that they meet ("New Year catch-up?") – had come as a relief; a reprieve from her circumstances; torn and unsettled as she was, it had seemed a better option than it might ordinarily do. And there was the commitment she had made to her colleagues in this regard, despite Skelgill's reservations.

Tomes Books in Keswick's Market Square suits her for several reasons, not least the latter. The town is only half an hour from Swinesdale, and it is neutral ground. The store has a secluded café on its top floor. Skelgill – a frequenter of Keswick tearooms – is unlikely to set foot in a book shop.

She feels a small amount of guilt on this last point. But she sees it as a practical matter. Kendall Minto is good-looking, and he knows it, always stylishly dressed and fashionably coiffured, and he is of her own age, a peer of their schooldays. The idea of an information exchange is a channel that DS Jones has, if not exactly encouraged, reluctantly kept open. While she can tolerate his effusive charm, there can also be his unwelcome persistence as a prospective suitor. Lurking always in the back of her mind is the question of how much he wants to keep up with police developments – versus how much he just wants to meet her. Whereas she can find a way to give him a fair hearing, Skelgill is more likely to give him a thick ear. There endeth any useful purpose the inquisitive journalist might serve.

'This one?'

She turns the book to display the front. It is the novel by "K.T. Darke" with the striking black-and-orange cover, successive sightings of which had earlier led her to realise she herself was with its actual author.

'That's right – *A Blind Eye* – it was released to great fanfare in October. Intriguing title, yes?'

Kendall Minto looks at her penetratingly. She does not doubt that his antennae are already twitching, despite that her interest must surely appear incidental.

'I got a book token for Christmas. I was thinking of buying it. Shall we go and order? You can tell me if it's any good.'

He laughs, as if to suggest that surely she does not expect that he would read that kind of novel.

Notwithstanding, she takes the book and they ascend to the second floor. Serendipity should not be sniffed at – not exactly one of Skelgill's maxims, but certainly one of his sentiments. However, she bides her time, and when they have collected their drinks and settled in a corner there ensues some festive small talk. Her mind, however, wrestles with what she might say. She is acutely aware of words to avoid, the likes of "Swinesdale", "Spooner" and "Badduns". While she knows she can trust Kendall Minto to remain firmly in their camp, as DI Smart has already demonstrated, in a manner of speaking, walls have ears.

Kendall Minto is easy company, not least because he is happy to talk about himself. Like most men he simply seeks approbation. She appreciates that underneath he is good hearted, but he is not her type; he is too showy, for one. And, rather hopelessly, he is inclined to express his wishes, not sensing that this is exactly how to diminish their chances of coming true. But a journalist is a good foil for a police officer. Like a Cocker Spaniel they can be sent into the undergrowth to flush out game where it would otherwise be unseemly or inappropriate. The journalist has professional permission to lack moral compass; a blind aim is all that it takes. In the latter respect, she has to tread carefully.

But she will probably have to give him something – he is too smart that she can interrogate him and not create suspicion. However, she has an opening gambit – to play to his ego.

The novel lies upon the table. She leans forward and places a hand on the cover.

'How on earth did you pull it off? I've heard she doesn't give interviews.'

Kendall Minto affects a casual response, but DS Jones detects the pressure of simmering immodesty trying to escape from within, a discernible puffing of the chest. A little to her surprise, however, he resists an actual boast and leapfrogs to what might be a subsequent point in the conversation. It makes her wonder if the direct answer is not exactly to his credit.

'She's incredibly pragmatic – about literature I mean. Do you know – she doesn't read any contemporary crime fiction? To avoid unconscious plagiarism, she says. She was very forthright – you know, she declaimed that half of Agatha Christie's plots are bonkers – that they'd never get published in this day and age.'

He regards her with an expression of exaggerated shock, as if this were the challenging of some long-standing tenet of the flat-earth degree of magnitude.

DS Jones gives a non-committal murmur. Having conducted her own interview, she is drawing the comparison to his impression of the woman she knows as Katrina Darkeness.

'I asked her about sex, of course.'

This is more like it. The old Kendall Minto, who does not quite appreciate the difference between when he may impress a girl or embarrass her. DS Jones folds her arms and tilts her head a little. Strands of her fair hair fall across one eye. But she gives him the benefit of the doubt.

'And?'

'Well – her books are known for being a bit earthy at times. I asked her if it was drawn from personal experience.'

DS Jones cannot entirely suppress a laugh.

Now he affects offence.

'You can mock – but she didn't deny it.' He indicates to the book. 'There's stuff in those novels that you couldn't make up – eye-watering. I mean – for a woman to write.'

DS Jones is shaking her head; her large hazel eyes, however, show patience.

'Kendall – a woman is allowed to use her imagination.' She sips rather demurely from her coffee. 'Besides – I thought you didn't read this sort of thing.'

He looks a little confounded.

'Naturally, I – er – I skim-read some beforehand – and looked them up, the synopses.'

But on this point DS Jones, as she herself let slip to the author, is equally skating on thin ice. She casts a little diversionary pebble.

'That said – it's K.T. Darke's elusive social life that the public really want to read about.'

Kendall Minto looks like a thwarted adolescent.

'You sound like my blinking editor.' He takes a gulp from his mug before realising it is still too hot and for a moment appears as if he might explode. He swallows with difficulty and fans his face. 'I can tell you – I had a good mind to cook something up. I did all the research I could, but there's nothing particularly juicy in the public domain.'

It is a convenient segue for DS Jones.

'She's from Edinburgh, right?'

'What? Oh, yes.' He looks for a moment like he has been dragged away from some other thought – perhaps the scandal he ought to have invented. "Yes – brought up and educated there – private school, of course. Studied English Lit. at St Andrews University. She married an Edinburgh lawyer – considerably older – he's some kind of chief prosecutor in the Crown Office – good for material, I should think. Name of Farquharson, if I recall – they have a daughter, Elizabeth. They're separated now – I'm not sure if they're divorced – probably too costly. She worked as an administrator in the law firm where she met him. She got her breakthrough novel in her twenties and has never looked back.' He gestures again to the book cover. 'They've televised some of her DI Scawthwaite series – she must be worth a packet.'

Now he sighs, as though such good fortune will be forever out of his reach.

DS Jones is thinking that she might need to reveal something of her hand, something that will prompt him and keep his interest – but, more pertinently, she is also wondering how he can be of use in this regard – when he turns the tables on her.

'So, what has she been up to?'

He grins boyishly. DS Jones is reminded she underestimates his acuity at her peril. She is obliged to show a card.

'Did you know she has a holiday home in Cumbria? More of a writer's retreat, in fact.'

Kendall Minto looks unwilling to admit that he doesn't know.

'Has she been burgled?'

His attempt at deflection takes DS Jones by surprise.

'Er – no. Why do you say that?'

'Just a shot in the dark. I thought you were about to tell me the Star Creeper is back in business.'

DS Jones is perplexed.

'What are you talking about?'

'Oh –' Kendall Minto gives another theatrical wave of one hand; it is a dismissive gesture. 'It was before your time. I mean – when you were away in London – it was one of my first assignments as a cub reporter – me not having the brains to go to Uni.'

She indulges him a little.

'Kendall, you have the brains.'

Gallantly, he now backtracks.

'But not the application – unlike you.'

'You have it now.'

'Ah – maybe I've found my forte.' Then he plies her with an artless grin. 'I still find myself skiving off to meet attractive ladies.'

She has to bring him back on topic.

'The Star Creeper?'

Rather absently he runs his fingers through his hair and then spends a moment carefully rearranging it. He casts about as though he is hoping to be in sight of a mirror, but there is none.

'It was my idea to give him a name – make a bogeyman out of him, like the national tabloids do?' (DS Jones nods obediently.) 'Actually, the first time it was thought that it might be something political. You know how the radical Welsh occasionally torch a holiday home – there was a case over towards Maryport – a Manchester United footballer owned a converted boathouse. Obviously it would be easy to tell when he was away on match duty – they were playing Plymouth Argyle in the FA Cup. The property was damaged by fire – but it turned out the burglar had made himself at home – got smashed on vodka, tried to fry chips – fell asleep – the chip pan caught alight – and he scarpered empty-handed when the place went up in smoke.'

DS Jones nods and he seems content to expound.

'There followed a couple more instances. An actor from *Ennerdale* – she plays that raunchy barmaid with the buck teeth and pneumatic bosom – had her cottage in Kendal broken into, when she was attending the BAFTAs in London. And then –' (and now he laughs sardonically) 'there was an MP from Liverpool – actually a Cabinet Minister at the time. His place in Windermere was done and a valuable fur coat taken. It turned out it belonged to his secretary – he tried to hush it up, but she was having none of it. The story soon morphed into a minor version of the Profumo Affair. What was she doing in her boss's second home in the Lakes when his office was in Whitehall? Interest in my Star Creeper became somewhat eclipsed.'

DS Jones has listened implacably. Now she reveals something of her interest.

'How long ago was all this?'

Kendall Minto makes a face of exaggerated trepidation.

'Worryingly, I'd say five years – and I'm still in the same job. And look at you. Within touching distance of Inspector rank.'

DS Jones lowers her eyes; she brushes at some invisible contaminant on her jeans.

'You're more senior, now.'

He harrumphs.

'It's a very small pond. In which I am a jack-pike-of-all-trades. If I may mix my metaphors.'

DS Jones smiles sympathetically.

But he recovers his mojo. He leans forward and taps the cover of the novel.

'You have cleverly distracted me again. What's the story with K.T. Darke?'

She has no choice but to be cagey. But she also knows it might work out in her favour.

'I can't say any more. It may be nothing. But if you could point me to the coverage of those break-ins and your interview. Ideally,

I'd like the unedited version. I'll make sure you get the story, if and when anything unravels.'

'Hmm, you drive a hard bargain. But discretion is the better part of valour, as they say. I'll see what I can come up with.'

He glances casually at his designer wristwatch.

'Jeepers! I have a meeting with the powers that be.'

'When?'

'About ten minutes ago. Another written warning ahoy! How time flies when one is having fun.' He rises, regarding her somewhat forlornly. 'Although I suspect you only came to pump me. You always did prefer the older guys – more mature, I suppose.'

His bemoaning of his fate is a fishing-for-compliments of sorts, for reassurance. But she does not bite.

'Kendall – it's always nice to catch up.'

It is a rather back-handed rejoinder, but she deigns to partake in the French-style formality of kisses on each cheek – but opts not to comment upon his cologne.

She leaves a few minutes after him, having returned to the shelf the copy of K.T. Darke's latest crime thriller, *A Blind Eye*. Her conclusion is that she should play to her strengths, and reading is one of them – although it is the case files that she has in mind. But before she returns to the mountain of admin, there is something she hopes to find out in the fells.

*

It could be her imagination, but a barely discernible talcum-like powder seems to be falling as she descends into the pines that surround Fellbeck. It is so fine that it almost might be materialising out of thin air, microscopic ice crystals literally condensing from the frozen ether. Or perhaps it is invisibly cast from the trees themselves?

The white roadster is parked beneath the makeshift shelter.

A thin column of pale smoke rises from the chimney stack.

DS Jones is relieved to see that Katrina Darkeness must still be here. When she telephoned ahead, the woman had sounded guarded – not at all like her open manner of their conversation over cocoa; her voice was strained and her words had seemed stilted. She cranes up at the first-floor window. Is there still the impression of a face – that doll, set back on the sill? Despite the daylight she can see little better than before – only the surroundings reflected, grey sky and white mountains. But it is disquieting; the idea of such inanimate surveillance rekindles her sense of isolation.

Yet as she emerges from her vehicle she quickly realises she is not alone. A familiar engine – the quad bike – is approaching at speed. She hears the simultaneous thrum of tyres and rattle of bars as it passes over the cattle grid. A couple of seconds later it swings into view and slews to a halt, sliding a little on the compressed snow between her and the property. It seems she is the object of the rider's haste.

'Sergeant – I was planning to call you. Then I saw your car. I have found something that may be of interest.'

Jacob Floxham looks like a model from a workwear catalogue location shoot. His rugged outfit and manly pose, astride the horned quad like it might be a steer he has subjugated; his dark curls and modish beard; his tanned complexion and penetrating stare; a confection that is just a little too perfect. Another handsome guy. Two in two hours. But somehow the comparison makes her uneasy. She feels an inexplicable pang of fondness for the ingenuous if occasionally asinine Kendall Minto.

'What is it?'

'They, actually. A couple of discarded petrol cans.' He gestures over his shoulder. 'I thought you would want to see straightaway.'

DS Jones glances at the house. She is torn – but she knows she ought not neglect that he might have something.

'Can I drive there?'

He grins, and pats the seat behind him.

'Just hop aboard. You ride well, remember?'

When before she had spontaneously taken up the challenge, for some reason she is reticent.

'Where is it – I mean, how far?'

She touches the front of her jacket with both hands, questioning the suitability of her outfit.

'You'll be fine. It's no more than a couple of minutes – up at the lead mine. We should go while there's enough light.'

He shifts to make room on the pillion. With a second glance at the house DS Jones steps forward. She straddles the seat – but she feels more inhibited now about taking a grip of his overalls. She squeezes the machine with her legs and presses hard against the running boards.

Jacob Floxham wastes no time. They exit the track from Fellbeck and turn left up the dale, skimming past his cottage and the picnic spot where she parked earlier. A minute more and the lane peters out. He stops proficiently and switches off the ignition.

Now he points up the fellside.

DS Jones follows his indication – she sees the old mine workings, long-abandoned grey stone ruins, more like a modest chapel perched precariously, a couple of hundred yards up the steep incline. There is no obvious path, but a small beck, a minor tributary of the Caldew seeps down black and glistening.

'I won't risk the quad. The simplest thing is just to walk up the stream bed. You never know what's under the snow. Might turn an ankle.'

He leads the way, picking a course around boulders. In general the snow is not melting. The stream is just a trickle of groundwater, barely half an inch deep. He is correct that it makes easy going. In places there are patches of thin ice, some suspended above the water, that disintegrate underfoot.

The stream flows directly from one of the workings, an arched stone entrance, a tunnel. DS Jones knows about these things, an adit or drift mine it is called. Adits were sometimes driven to intersect with vertical shafts, for drainage and ventilation. Skelgill has often warned of them. He has related some disturbing tales stemming from his volunteer capacity in the mountain rescue. Jacob Floxham makes a move towards the cave mouth.

'Inside?'

He seems relaxed.

'Yeah – not too far, though. But I suppose that's why they weren't found.'

'How did you find them?'

'You put me on my guard.' He regards her with a knowing expression, a half-smile. 'But I can't claim too much credit. One of my dogs chased a Swaledale ewe in there. The dog couldn't flush it out so I went back for a torch.' He wields it now, and switches it on.

DS Jones hesitates. She knows she ought to call Skelgill.

But if there is nothing – it would be embarrassing. Jacob Floxham could be mistaken.

Then again, there is the opportunity of a breakthrough achieved of her own initiative.

Jacob Floxham is going in.

'Watch your head. Do as I do and you'll be okay.'

She follows. She has to crouch, but not so low as to be uncomfortable.

His outline is silhouetted against the light cast along the passage. He blocks much of the view, but in the bobbing beam of the torch she gains an impression of corroded iron arches and rotted timber posts, between them sections of stone walls roughly built to hold back loose rock and scree. The stream covers the floor, winding unevenly, muddied and opaque. There is a pervading smell of mould spores and sheep urine.

He stops.

'There.'

She moves closer; the passage is too narrow for them both and he turns and backs against the wall to let her get halfway past him. Then he reaches forward with the flashlight. About six feet ahead the stream seems to come to a stop in a wider pool, at a heap of debris that blocks the way, a collapse perhaps, of rubble and projecting lengths of decayed pit-props. Lying to one side of the front of the mound are two red-painted metal petrol cans, gallon size.

DS Jones can feel her heart racing, hear it, almost.

She tries to think – what to do? The cans do not look that old. Should she have expected more rust, especially in the dank environment? Or perhaps the conditions have preserved them? And should she salvage them now – present them as trophies to Skelgill? But if this is a bona fide piece of evidence she ought to call in a forensic officer, potentially a crime-scene manager.

Jacob Floxham detects her uncertainty.

'I thought you would want a photo? I can keep the torch steady. It will light the background – your flash will get the detail of the cans.'

He is right about the photograph. The petrol cans could disappear before she can get them recovered – despite that the odds of such are small. They may have lain untouched for over three years.

And yet something feels wrong. Is it the dale again, the watching wilderness, the sense that she is being followed, suspicion pervading the stifling atmosphere?

'Take a photo – before we start to get cold.'

She is distracted by the dilemma, and perhaps just needs a nudge; his words prompt her to act.

She takes out her mobile and attempts to compose a shot. The light is poor and the autofocus struggles to zero in.

'Move closer – I'll direct the beam over your shoulder.'

She does not know why, but her feet feel strangely heavy. Maybe the water is leaching into her boots. Is it deeper where it widens out? She crouches and edges forward.

She feels Jacob Floxham close behind; he seems to be adjusting his stance. A hand comes to rest against the small of her back.

'Jacob!'

The hand is withdrawn.

The voice – urgent, eerily resonant, echoing – belongs to Katrina Darkeness.

'Jacob – are you in there?'

DS Jones senses that bizarrely he seems to want to huddle down, as though it were a children's game of hide-and-seek.

Then the voice comes again – more strained now. Is it anxiety – or is it a note of warning?

'Jacob – I'm looking for Lily!'

15. JADE

'It's for your Ma – a cod to replace the one I brought and took away again at Christmas.'

'She's gone t' bingo.'

'Just stick it in the fridge – tell her when she gets back, will you?'

'Danny – come in for a mash – a drink?'

Skelgill hesitates.

'Are you on your own?'

His cousin Sheryl Graham plies him with a curious look.

'Nay – Jade's here.'

Skelgill hesitates. Sheryl Graham does not.

'Come on – Jade won't mind.'

Skelgill rather ostentatiously looks at his wristwatch.

'I'm supposed to be meeting a colleague.'

'You never came back after.'

Skelgill understands she means after the party.

He sways back a little on his heels.

Then he winks at Sheryl Graham.

'Aye, alreet – if you make it worth my while.'

Sheryl Graham gives a throaty laugh and steps aside.

'Go into the lounge – the fire's on.'

He can hear a radio playing faintly, it must be through in the kitchen, because the door that immediately gives on to the living room from the hall is wide open. Sheryl Graham sticks her head around the jamb and calls out.

'Here's us big cous – Danny Boy.'

Hiding his discomfiture Skelgill ducks under a sagging Christmas decoration to see more of the same, overdue for removal, including a tree that is almost entirely bereft of needles and looks more like something washed up by the tide. The furniture has been restored to its regular layout, and Jade Nelson is seated upon the sofa of a three-piece suite, arranged around the hearth, collectively angled towards a massive television set in one corner. Some daytime TV chat show is playing, although the volume is muted. Despite that the room is lit only by the weak natural light of winter, she is wearing large-lensed wrap-around sunglasses. She has on a loose-fitting pink velour shell suit. He detects no make-up. Her long blonde hair is drawn back severely and held by an elastic band. Trendy shades excepted, it is a different proposition to the glamorous model looks of their previous encounter.

He is searching for a quip – something about the dark glasses – maybe the snow – or whether he has interrupted them about to have a session with a sunlamp, when she begins stiffly to rise. As he reaches out a palm to exhort her not to get up, she pre-empts him.

'I won't cramp your style.'

She has obviously overheard the exchange on the threshold – and has drawn her own conclusions. Perhaps Sheryl has made more of their acquaintanceship than is actually the case. Skelgill's alarm is heightened when he thinks of DI Smart gleefully spreading gossip.

'It's alreet, lass – sit back down. I'm not stopping long.' He indicates in the direction of the through-lounge and the other way into kitchen, whence can be heard the rattle of crockery. 'Just for a mash.'

Jade Nelson lowers herself gingerly. There is an uncapped plastic water bottle on the broad arm of the settee and as Skelgill squeezes past he appears not to notice and clumsily knocks it over.

As it topples and rolls off the upholstered arm they both make an instinctive dart – Skelgill quite remarkably stoops to snatch it out of the air before it hits the carpet; Jade Nelson, in her lunge only succeeds in dislodging her sunglasses. She flaps at them, and restores them to her face, her expression pained.

She too was quick – but not quick enough to hide the vivid yellow-and-purple bruise around her right eye.

Her body language hints at some mixture of guilt and

embarrassment.

Skelgill waits to see if she will speak. He stares unblinking at the hearth; the room is warm and the hiss of the gas fire soporific.

'Jade.'

The sound of her name seems to cause a jolt to pass through her slender frame.

He inhales to speak, but pauses for a second.

'I take it you know what I do for a day job?'

Plainly she does not want to look at him – at least, not to face him – and he cannot see her eyes.

She nods, however.

'These Grahams can be a dodgy lot.' He laughs to himself, as if recalling episodes that would bear him out. 'But I wouldn't stand by to see an injustice done to one of them.'

She turns her head a fraction, and leans forward a touch. She waits for him to elaborate. When he does not, she shrugs and sinks back.

A silence ensues. Clanks continue to emanate from the kitchen. Sheryl Graham seems to have turned up the radio and is accompanying it inexpertly.

'Who did that to you, Jade?'

Jade Nelson first appears to freeze, and then perhaps to shudder. PTSD. Skelgill is conscious of the minefield.

After half a minute she contrives an utterance.

'I fell on the stairs.'

'That was Sheryl – and I caught her. And I'd catch you just the same, lass.'

Now he has made more explicit his offer as protector.

But she shakes her head.

Skelgill waits another half-minute.

'What else is there?'

He senses she is digging in her heels – but that is progress. It must be apparent that he is not going away and she is stuck with him. And perhaps, deep inside, there is a voice that beseeches her to tell.

Without warning, she turns her head to face him.

She pulls down the pink fabric of the top to expose her left shoulder.

He sees a gold bra strap. Smooth bronzed skin.

On another day it would be a seductive pose.

Except for the bruise where she has been roughly grabbed and held – and he realises there are more dark contusions on the sides of her neck.

She retreats, and cowers, as if something bad will happen. That the act of defiance was summoned at great expense. He detects pain in her movements. Now she holds her midriff.

He senses there is more. Something worse than this. But it is not his specialist subject – perhaps only the retribution.

Time to strike.

Despite that Sheryl is now lost in full-blown kitchen karaoke, he lowers his voice.

'Listen, Jade – I'm not as daft as I'm cabbage-looking. I know about Dale. I know there's something being hushed up. I know about the threats. You've got yourself into a hole. Don't dig any deeper. While there's still time – let me give you a hand out.'

She cowers again – and for a moment he has a dreadful feeling that she thinks he is trying to bargain – that here is the frying pan route out of the fire. A sordid quid pro quo.

'All I want, Jade – is to know where Dale's mobile is.'

Though his qualifying statement seems to assuage her worst fears, still she does not respond.

He reaches, and gently touches her upper arm with the tips of his fingers, keeping them in place but not moving; an earth to conduct away the tension.

'Look at you, lass – this is not the worst it's going to get. Their patience will run out.'

It is a speculative assertion. But the suspicion that has dogged him since hearing about an assault on Jade Nelson has crystallised in seeing her. Cages are being rattled. Nerves are fraying. Insiders are being suspected. Jade has fallen victim to these circumstances.

Finally, she cracks.

'He won't talk. Not while he thinks – there's – the threats.' She seems to correct herself, but Skelgill lets it pass.

'Jade, if I can find the phone, I can make it look like it was on our initiative. In the meantime we'll move you and your bairn to safety.'

Immediately he senses that she is predisposed to reject the idea as a hollow promise, an official platitude of the type trotted out down the decades to gullible would-be witnesses. Safe for how long? He knows the story all too well.

But there could be another sentiment at play – and this is one he has not quite yet bottomed in his own mind. She may not be weighing up the odds of survival, but of something else altogether. That – as he fears – she is complicit in her own abduction. Despite the beating, whatever assault she has endured, her loyalty has shifted, the scales have tilted to organised crime, the 'high life', the gangster's moll.

Just when he is thinking his ploy has failed, she confounds him.

'He said it's at his work.'

Skelgill stares, taking in the words.

'His work. What does that mean? Has he still got the garage at the back of his Ma's?'

She shakes her head.

'There's no garage. I don't know what it means. It were what he told me when he were first remanded. He won't talk about it no more. He's too scared, now. He just said it's safe at his work.'

*

Skelgill stands at his sergeant's desk in the open-plan office. He affects disinterest and grimaces as he sips from a recyclable paper cup, as if he might be passing the time of day, filling a few minutes of boredom in mundane conversation, having visited the drinks machine.

In fact, he is wishing not to attract unwanted attention; one of DI Smart's constables sits just a few workspaces away.

DS Leyton is shaking his head. He speaks quietly, almost under his breath.

'I can't make head nor tail of it, Guv. I checked out the garage situation – and it's right, what you were told. Spooner's Ma's moved house long since – and most latterly he was living in a flat that didn't even have its own parking space.'

'He must have had a lock-up, Leyton.' Skelgill is staring aimlessly across the workroom. He utters, hardly moving his lips. 'A place where he stashed stolen cars until it was time to ship them on.'

DS Leyton makes a face of frustration.

'I've been through the case notes – there's nothing mentioned in the investigation that surrounded his arrest.'

Skelgill glances in the direction of DI Smart's subordinate. The officer is watching him, but turns his head back to his work under Skelgill's disparaging glare.

'All they were interested in was nailing him for the Badduns murders.'

DS Leyton's thoughts are still bogged down by the elusive garage.

'There must be five hundred flippin' lock-ups around Workington, Guv.'

Skelgill scowls; the exaggeration sounds unduly pessimistic.

'There's a row of them at the end of Town Quay, opposite the docks. Run down. Quiet spot. Perfect location.'

DS Leyton appears to flinch – perhaps because he recognises the address as being in the proximity of the lagoon – but there is also the practical challenge. From past experience lock-ups frequently change hands and it can be impossible to establish ownership. They are often rented out or even hijacked without an absent owner's knowledge. It can be like searching for a needle in a haystack.

'There's no chance of Spooner spilling the beans, is there, Guv? Now that Jade Nelson's come on board.'

Skelgill looks especially doubtful.

'We can't risk going there, Leyton.'

DS Leyton gives a slow shrug of his broad shoulders. At a distance he and Skelgill might seem to be bemoaning the misfortunes of the England football team.

'Thing is, Guv – they've obviously got access to warehousing at the docks – surely that's where Spooner was taking the motors. Ready to be spirited away to the Isle of Man on the next high tide.

They'd want them off the mainland asap. But from what I saw it was just an empty hangar – four bare walls. I can't see him hiding the phone there.' He runs the fingers of one hand through his thick dark hair. 'More likely the workshop at Douglas.'

But Skelgill seems to dismiss this notion. Their conclusion has been that Dale Spooner was a freelancer. The idea that the Manx gang would let him in on their operation seems unlikely. Spooner's involvement almost certainly ended when he handed over a vehicle, perhaps not even at the Port of Workington. There remains in the background always the possibility of one such a rendezvous being Swinesdale – despite the improbably far-flung location.

He grinds his teeth in frustration. He knows he has a gem – but realistically little to go on. The suggestion that the phone is safe is tantalising. But as a clue it is cryptic. *"At his work."*

Dale Spooner was like some peripatetic character from a folktale. Jack Frost, the Sandman, Wee Willie Winkie. Unseen, he visited the properties of private citizens, their driveways, their garages, the lamplit streets outside their houses. That was where Dale Spooner's real work was done, in the small hours while those good folk slept.

As is his habit when he is stymied, he changes the subject.

'What about the Manx Constabulary? Where are you up to with them?'

DS Leyton looks more enthusiastic.

'I've made what sounds like a decent contact. A sergeant in Douglas. DS Mona Quirk, she's called – experienced, local woman, sounds like she knows the ropes. I'm waiting for her to get back to me. I explained we think there's a scam afoot and that we received a tip off of activity in the past couple of days – inter-gang rivalry – and whether they've had any sniff of that. I mentioned there might have been some shenanigans in the port area.'

He pauses, and winks knowingly at his superior – the 'shenanigans' to which he refers being well known to them.

'I also asked her about vehicle records – seems they keep a database of all residents' cars, like we thought – but not UK-registered motors. But she reckons they've got a working knowledge of what's on the road, especially the fancier cars owned by dual nationals or non-native Manx citizens. She also hinted that they've got a fair idea of the types who'd not be averse to taking on a pre-owned motor, so to speak.'

Skelgill is pensively swilling around the last of the dubious-looking sludge in his cup.

'How did she react to the suggestion of an organised gang?'

'Took it seriously, Guv – but, reading between the lines, I don't reckon they know it's going on.'

Skelgill suddenly realises that DI Smart has materialised beside his subordinate's work station and is staring over at them. For a moment he is alarmed that they may have been overheard. He even wouldn't put it past Smart to have learned how to lipread.

He knocks back the last of his tea and begins to move away.

'Let me know when you hear owt.'

He strides from the open-plan office, crushing the paper cup as he reaches the exit and tossing it into the recycling bin marked "plastic".

*

Somewhere a church clock is striking three. Skelgill is surprised he can hear it. He closes the office window and stares out across the steadily consolidating snowscape.

He rues that fishing is so limited at this time of year.

And in these conditions even those waters that have no close-season are frozen.

It is another attraction of the sea.

But he has been reminded that sea fishing – other than from the shore – is as much about seamanship as it is about angling. Whereas his boat on Bass Lake is really like an extension of his being. It needs no fuel, causes no pollution and little disturbance, he can manoeuvre it on a sixpence.

Nevertheless, he finds himself humming *Danny Boy*.

But any deeper reflection is overshadowed – for Sheryl Graham's use of the epithet is called to mind, and a resurgence of the unease he has suppressed since leaving her and Jade Nelson.

He has to admit, Sheryl played a blinder.

Jade can have had no idea that the 'chance' meeting was a set-up. Sheryl going along with it, having seen the battered condition of her friend. Not that she missed the opportunity to tap him up for a wad of cash. He gives an ironic growl. It is hardly the sort of bung he could put on his expenses, handed out to a fellow clan member, and the Graham clan at that. Though he does not doubt that in similar circumstances DI Alec Smart would have the brass neck to submit such a claim. He is reputed to wield the biggest expenses account outside of the Met.

He wonders fleetingly why he has received no further direct interest from his fellow inspector. Perhaps he is keeping something up his sleeve for tomorrow's regular Friday catch-up with the Chief – a lurid revelation intended to embarrass or belittle. He seems to have an inside line on Skelgill's movements and contacts in Workington. But today's encounter was kept close – solely his cousins Megan and Sheryl Graham who know that the short visit was not the passing call to drop off a cod that it was made out to be. Megan had used her sway over Sheryl – and Sheryl had succeeded in coaxing Jade to visit her. Jade was probably glad of the company, of the respite – and she probably felt quite safe under Big Mags Graham's roof. Whoever she is tangled with, they would be unwise to trouble her on Graham territory.

But his disquiet remains.

He must, however, tease out the competing strands of his sentiments. Truth be told, the most potent emotion he suffers is not a healthy one, for it is of vengeance. He would like to get his hands on whoever it was that did – what they did – to Jade Nelson. No man should get away with that. Man? It is not a man that assaults a woman. It is a worm.

He recognises the obstacle to progress. Jade Nelson is not about to tell him who did it, nor why or what was their motive. He must take it as further impetus to solve this case. A question that has been troubling him, however, he is now convinced has been answered. Sheryl Graham's account passed on by Megan Graham – that had culminated in the 'sugar daddy' theory – is mistaken. If Jade Nelson were ever a willing participant, she is no longer. And he doubts that she ever were. More likely she was coerced, taken advantage of – perhaps making the mistake of believing it was the right thing to do – and, yes, perhaps being tempted by the high life – only to find herself no better off, a hostage to fortune, and – though he baulks at the thought – to all intents and purposes, a concubine.

She might still be embroiled, but she must desire freedom. Only fear traps her.

Besides, if Jade had not wanted out, why did she confide in Sheryl in the first place? Surely that was a forlorn cry for help.

That she has been assaulted convinces him that time is running short. Someone suspects something. It may be the actions of his own team (he included); or clumsy prying by DI Smart, thrashing about in his desperation to get to the bottom of what Skelgill is up to; or an inadvertent slip-up by one of the people they have interviewed, a resident of Swinesdale, a petty crook like Mason Milburn, or even Jade Nelson herself.

He stares while more snow begins to fall. The cold spell shows no sign of relenting. Does it make life harder for the predator, or for the prey?

How long will Jade and her child be safe? Spooner, come to that?

And Sheryl. Megan. Others perhaps.

And how safe can he keep them?

On which note, he wonders, where is DS Jones?

16. SOLUTIONS

HQ, 10 a.m., Friday, January 8th

At his desk, Skelgill sits upright, his hands folded in front of him, his thumbs winding as though he is practising some obscure angling technique, a method of steadily retrieving a dry fly, perhaps.

In fact he is reflecting upon the Friday review meeting.

Without overtly or explicitly stating what has so far remained between Skelgill and the four walls of her office, the Chief had nevertheless made it known that it was about time his team produced some concrete result from their now-laboured investigations.

DI Smart, behaving like a starved dog that knows it can reach a pan of sizzling sausages left carelessly close to the edge of the cooker, was at the limits of his tolerance. But under the reproachful eye of the Chief he somehow contained his frustration.

Skelgill is reminded of DI Smart's attempt to get DS Jones to consult with him – that he might accompany her, even – and of her tactic to escape his attentions, in which presumably she has so far succeeded.

Come to that, she has been elusive now since yesterday morning – and that cannot all be about avoiding DI Smart. He is just beginning to feel unnerved by her prolonged absence, when suddenly she walks into his office.

The first thing that strikes him as unusual is that she is empty handed – at least, in the tea department.

And then there is her appearance and demeanour. Not so different to usual, probably invisible to the casual observer around the station (and she attracts plenty of those) – but to one familiar with her there is some indefinable tarnish upon her normally pristine exterior, and a flatness about the regular spring in her step.

To his credit, Skelgill manages to summon up a small degree of empathy, if inauspiciously expressed.

'You look like you've not slept well.'

DS Jones contrives a grin and settles into her regular seat before the window. In winter, Skelgill's office is rarely at an adequate temperature, and she gives an involuntary shiver. She straightens the batch of materials upon her lap.

'I suppose I have been burning the midnight oil.'

When she does not elaborate, Skelgill shows a further modicum of concern.

'You alreet, lass?'

DS Jones visibly gathers herself.

'I'm not quite sure where to start, Guv. With what happened yesterday.'

It is as though she is still processing some events – but it would seem more for their meaning than the simple issue of in which order to relate them.

'There is a matter – which I think will merit forensic investigation.' She begins falteringly.

'Wait.'

Skelgill gets up. He leaves the room, to return in short order with two machine teas. He hands one over and resumes his seat.

'Stop gap.'

DS Jones seems appreciative – and in the short hiatus appears to have reached some inner consensus.

Now she relates the incident in Swinesdale – of her return the second time and the encounter with Jacob Floxham. His news of the petrol cans. The lead mine. And events that culminated in the curious arrival upon the scene of Katrina Darkeness.

Skelgill listens with arms folded and brows increasingly knitted.

There is a silence, but just when it seems Skelgill will pontificate, DS Jones beats him to the draw. Her features become wrapped in an expression of self-reproach.

'I don't know what I was thinking – about bringing those petrol cans out myself. I mean – they could carry traces of whoever put them there. If it were Dale Spooner – then ...'

Neither of them needs to finish the sentence. If it were Dale

Spooner, it would not look good for him – nor would it for their investigation.

But Skelgill does not seem too perturbed by this notion.

He encourages his sergeant to expand upon her narrative.

'So, what did you do?'

'I just decided to get out of there. Not make a fuss – to play it down. I wanted to move them both away from the mine. I taped off the mouth of the tunnel. I don't think there's much chance of some random walker going in – but I thought we should mobilise promptly – that you would want to check it out this morning.'

Skelgill nods.

He waits for her to continue; clearly there is more to come.

'I knew I should look in greater detail at the case files. There were things I wasn't sure about – but I just couldn't put my finger on what was disturbing me. I was over at the archives until late last night.'

She shifts uneasily in her seat and pats the collection of papers on her lap.

'There's a mountain of material. A lot was collected and much of it I think was rejected or simply ignored. The first thing I checked was the report of the search of the area, of the vicinity of the car fire. It mentions the mine – but merely in a list of sites on a photocopied map.'

She glances at Skelgill to be met with an expression of cynicism. It would be no surprise if there had in fact been no search, or lip service paid to one, at best. Skelgill can picture DI Smart shining a torch into the mouth of the adit and ticking the box on his clipboard. They had their man and why waste time?

However, DS Jones is willing to play devil's advocate – not to get ahead of her potentially significant find.

'The cans could have been dumped since. Very recently, even. To be honest, Guv – to my eye – they didn't look as if they had been there long enough.'

Skelgill gazes past her, out of the window. Of course, they can bottom this; he seems to be assessing the conditions; there is an established pattern of snow showers, and a worsening weather forecast.

DS Jones breaks into his reverie.

'Okay, then I found this.'

He gazes back at her a little vacantly, his mind still momentarily adrift.

She reaches over to slide a clear plastic evidence bag across his desk. He lifts it to see it contains a beermat advertising a popular brand of what DS Leyton refers to as 'cooking lager'. It is stained and a portion is torn away. On it there is spidery capitalised writing in blue biro, an illegible scrawl, it seems.

She gives him a moment to absorb it, but does not wait for him to inquire of its provenance.

'This was among several boxes of potential evidence that were recovered from the Badduns' caravan. It appears at a glance like an untidy effort at a pub quiz. Notice the household names.'

Skelgill gives the exhibit a less cursory second inspection.

'Do you know about the Star Creeper, Guv?'

He shakes his head – and as she begins to relate Kendall Minto's account he frowns with increasing severity.

'I was assigned outside the county – but I reckon I would have heard if the crimes were treated as connected – that there was some sort of campaign.'

His response reflects the young journalist's bemoaning of his unsuccessful efforts to create a Lakeland bogeyman, as he had put it.

DS Jones, however, is undeterred.

'On that list – there are seven names that I think I can decipher. Possibly one or two more were torn off. You could speculate as to why – but maybe for no reason other than it was being compiled in a bar and the person got fed up – like doodling – or maybe there was a disagreement.'

Skelgill is watching her more intently now.

'Anyway – two of the three people that Kendall Minto mentioned are named on that beermat. The professional footballer and the *Ennerdale* actor.'

She pauses, perhaps for a small dramatic effect.

'Guv – I think the Star Creeper was not one person but two – the Badduns. I think it's a list of victims they intended to target.'

Skelgill inhales to retort, but she continues quickly.

'Sir Mallory George is on the list – I interviewed him yesterday morning.'

This is news to Skelgill, that she has visited the famous mountaineer – but his special status stills Skelgill's scepticism.

DS Jones relates her discovery in the case files of his reported 'intruder', dismissed as an elderly man's fancy – and of his revised version as told to her. That he now attributes it to having left his back door open, and a fox that was chased off by his dog. That there was blood on the hound's muzzle, but no fox's corpse.

Skelgill seems mildly amused by the naming of the dog, K2.

DS Jones extracts a weighty document from her stack of files. Now she stands and lays it before Skelgill. She flips over several pages to one that is marked with yellow highlights.

Skelgill scowls at the prospect of the wall of text.

'This is the pathologist's detailed report of the autopsies conducted on the Badduns. Obviously the bodies were severely disfigured by the fire, and external and indeed internal injuries were not easy to determine. But what was categorical was that the gunshot wounds that they both received were anterior – they were shot from the front. Jake Baddun in the thigh and Boris Baddun below the knees.'

Skelgill is staring implacably.

'But look at this. It is referring to Boris Baddun.'

DS Jones leans over to indicate a marked paragraph. Skelgill seems to be drawn towards her; perhaps it is her musky deodorant, activated by stress.

She seems able to read upside down without difficulty.

'*"Lacerations to right biceps femoris and left gastrocnemius."* That's the back of one thigh and the opposing calf. The pathologist speculated that he may have injured himself climbing over a barbed wire fence, perhaps in the act of escaping.'

Now she stares at Skelgill.

'I think he *was* trying to escape – not from the killer or killers – but from the fangs of K2.'

She waits for a moment.

'Guv – I believe the Badduns were housebreaking in

Mungrisdale parish on the night they were killed. Picking off celebrities from their list. Properties where they expected to get a good haul.'

Skelgill regards her pensively, but with growing appreciation.

'They were chased away from Sir Mallory George's cottage. But only by a dog – and if they felt the alarm had not been raised, why wouldn't they have gone on to burgle Katrina Darkeness? She lives just a few miles further – and within a stone's throw of where they were found dead.'

If Skelgill is working out what are the implications of his colleague's logic he gives no clue to what he thinks they might be. However, his shrewish expression is telling.

'She didn't report anything.'

DS Jones places a hand on the plastic sleeve containing the torn beermat.

'Guv, most of the people on that list didn't report anything. The rich and famous often don't want the attention, especially if the items stolen may be controversial – look at the case of the Cabinet Minister. It's well known that Katrina Darkeness goes to considerable lengths to keep a low profile.'

Skelgill folds his arms. There is an obvious question, which he fully expects his sergeant has considered – but he poses it in any event.

'You didn't ask her?'

Now DS Jones becomes rather wide-eyed. She seems uncharacteristically agitated.

'I was going to, Guv. That's why I went back to Swinesdale. Jacob Floxham intercepted me before I could knock on her door.' She stands upright and inhales and turns to gaze out of the window. There are flakes of snow swirling close – though her focus is lost somewhere in the middle distance beyond. 'But – like I said – I felt – well – my instincts were bidding me to retreat.'

She looks back at Skelgill and perhaps sees some understanding; she exhales, and resumes her seat, seeming to relax.

'I thought of an alternative approach. I've briefed DC Watson – she's contacting local glaziers and locksmiths, to see if they have any records of repairs undertaken in Mungrisdale parish generally and Swinesdale in particular. It's a bit of a long shot – most of these firms are just one-man bands and may not have kept records.'

Skelgill strikes a note of optimism.

'They might have a decent memory.'

DS Jones does not look entirely convinced. There is a silence, and Skelgill still senses the unfamiliar downbeat quality that has pervaded her manner. He is just mulling over whether to make a congratulatory quip about her outshining Miss Marple when they are interrupted by a small cameo that might equally owe its origin to the world of fiction.

Unannounced, DS Leyton skids into Skelgill's office and then – clearly struck by self-doubt – looks every inch the cartoon character that has run beyond the edge of a cliff, and pedals frantically in mid-air, unable to reverse.

He stops – and stares rather helplessly at a bemused Skelgill. Then he realises DS Jones is present.

'Emma.' He nods a greeting – but then he too seems to detect some disquiet in her demeanour. 'Are you alright, girl?'

DS Jones does not immediately answer, and now Skelgill inserts a quip.

'Late-night clubbing with that Minto – she claims it's the only way she can get him to talk.'

DS Jones glowers at Skelgill and directs an urgent shake of her head at DS Leyton. The ball seems to have travelled back to his court, and now he gathers his wits, realising he has the floor and is expected to explain himself.

'Guv – it's this Spooner's work malarkey.' Then it dawns on him that this is not something that either he or Skelgill has committed to reports that may be shared among interested parties on the intranet. 'Emma – do you know about this?'

She gives a half shake of her head and glances apprehensively at Skelgill. Accordingly, giving due credit to his boss, DS Leyton conveys Jade Nelson's revelation, the operative phrase *"at his work"* in relation to where Dale Spooner is said to have concealed his mobile phone.

DS Jones regards Skelgill interrogatively, that he has somehow succeeded in eliciting such a confession from the controversial young woman.

But Skelgill is looking impatient.

'Spill the beans, Leyton.'

DS Leyton again looks like he is having second thoughts. But he summons up what courage there remains of his doubtful convictions.

'Well – what it is, Guv – what say "at his work" means a motor?'

He sees that his colleagues are perplexed, and he hurriedly continues.

'I mean – what say he was in a tight spot – a bit like me?'

Skelgill is about to interject – but DS Leyton raises a hand.

'Hear me out, Guv. Take a step back – he'd nicked a car that was supposed to go to a customer. Then it was half-inched, by the Badduns – or he stupidly lent it to them – and suddenly he can't fulfil his part of the contract. So what does he do? He nicks another car – a replacement.

'All well and good, except the gang's not happy. It's maybe not the make or model or age they ordered. There's a question mark over timings. They decide they can't rely on Spooner and perhaps they suspect their operation's at risk of being compromised.

'They let Spooner deliver the back-up motor to the docks – but they're plotting against him – maybe teach him a lesson – but maybe worse. Or maybe it's about what they're going to do to the Badduns. And – like me – he overhears them. He makes it look like he's scarpered – when the only thing he could do was hide in the back of the motor. There – he hears even more mutterings about what fate awaits him when they get their hands on him. And it won't just be to roll him in the stinging nettles.

'So – what does he do – he makes a recording of what's happening to him. At the time he was thinking of self-preservation. Create some evidence – maybe a recording of the threats – against him – the Badduns.'

He pauses to mop his brow with the sleeve of his rather crumpled white shirt.

Skelgill is gazing somewhat sceptically at his perspiring subordinate, the second to experience such a reaction, despite the chill of the room. The hypothesis seems improbable, despite DS Leyton's plausible candour. He could be excused for wondering if his sergeant has suffered another bump on the head.

'So where's the phone, Leyton? *At his work* – you still haven't dealt with that.'

'Ahem.' DS Leyton produces the kind of little cough that is normally a precursor to an inconvenient admission. 'Well – here's the thing, Guv. And I never mentioned this. Remember I said there was a load of picnic gear in the back of the Land Rover Discovery – and I'd hid under a blanket? Well, there was some food. Four packets of popcorn.'

He glances appealingly from one colleague to the other.

'I was flippin' Hank Marvin – anyone would be. So I scoffed the lot. Gave me a right old bellyache, I tell you.'

In spite of the serious timbre of their discussion, DS Jones cannot suppress a giggle, and even Skelgill is grinning. Perhaps it is the image of the imprisoned DS Leyton determinedly and silently munching his way through one bag of popcorn after another. Skelgill is plainly impressed by the heroic scale of the achievement. But DS Leyton resists any such distraction.

'Point being – I didn't want to leave any trace that I'd been there. These motors – like a lot of cars – they have inspection panels in the boot section – often they're quite well concealed. It looks like continuous lining. It's so's you can get at the light clusters to replace a blown bulb – or sometimes where the jack and wheel brace are stored. That Land Rover had one on each side at the back. So I crushed the packs and tucked them away inside the cavities. I doubt they'll ever be found. Even if someone changes a bulb, they'd have to reach down well below the light fitment. Who would bother their backside to do that?'

Now he stares at his colleagues. He sees there is no need for him to elaborate. The corollary is clear. Dale Spooner's definition of "at his work" could be the car – and the hiding place could be exactly what DS Leyton has described.

Instead he proceeds with his theory of Dale Spooner's train of thought.

'So Spooner hides the phone as an insurance policy. He wasn't thinking about the Badduns being done in. He maybe didn't know that was going to happen. He was just thinking that if he were to be stood in front of a firing squad, he'd be able to say that he's hidden evidence of what's been going on.

'At some point he made a getaway – maybe he escaped from the car before it was locked up – maybe later. Or maybe he blagged his way out. If they searched him, they'd find no phone on him. But he didn't need to risk carrying the phone. He'd have been able to return to the Isle of Man at leisure – locate the car – piece of cake for him to break in and retrieve the handset. He had no idea he was going to be banged up as a suspect for the Badduns murders. But all of a sudden he's got an alibi. He'd realise that once his mobile tuned in to the network, any video or photo would be assigned a timed GPS location tag. He could hardly be in Swinesdale and the Isle of Man at the same time. Trouble is, it blows open the lucrative car-smuggling operation – so the gang issues the threats. It's a standoff. They all know Spooner's not guilty of the murders, so they expect he'll be acquitted and the whole thing will blow over. But that's where their plan falls down – and where we joined the party.'

DS Leyton pauses to assess the reactions of his colleagues. DS Jones is looking intrigued – and a little confounded as she no doubt recalibrates her own knowledge and theories against her colleague's proposition. Skelgill, when he might be expected to be a picture of cynicism, actually seems to have zoned out, and is staring at the wall above DS Leyton's head, where his map of the British Isles is hung. Perhaps it is the sheer weight of conjecture to which he has been subjected in the past hour.

But now DS Leyton can supplement his suppositions with some facts.

'There's been a couple of interesting developments. First, on the Manx front I've heard back from DS Quirk. They've had no reports of a break-in at the docks area – a small point, but significant, if you ask me.'

DS Jones is nodding. A fox does not draw the hounds to its earth.

'And here's the bigger thing. I interrogated the stolen car

register for the week before the Badduns were murdered. Yes – there was the Mercs in which they were burned. But three days later, early doors on the day of the night of the murders, a black Chevrolet Suburban was stolen from Barrow-in-Furness. It's never been recovered. Not a trace. Now that workshop in Douglas – like I said before, that's no chop shop. I had a good butcher's and they're not re-spraying. There's just a lathe and some vices and small-scale kit. I reckon they're just changing the ID, removing any obvious marks, chassis number, so on. Recycling as fast as they can.

'Now, DS Quirk put out a request and an officer's come back saying he knows of a Chevy Suburban. It must be British registered because it's not on their database. The officer's going out this morning to see if he can locate it and check out the reg – details of the owner's address and so on – all incognito, like. What she could tell me is that it's black, same as the one that was stolen. Not easy to miss, a big American job like that.'

DS Leyton sees that Skelgill is now staring directly at him; but there is something decidedly unnatural about his expression.

'What is it, Guv? You look like someone's just walked over your grave.'

Skelgill has become the third person to break out into a sweat; the hair on his arms bristles, and a bead of perspiration trickles down his spine.

He does not respond to his sergeant's concern, but fires a terse question.

'When do you expect to hear back from the Manx police?'

'Maybe by lunchtime. They seem quite efficient – but I'm not sure they expend much energy spying on their own citizens – they don't want to scare away just the kind of folk they're trying to attract. Without the rich, they can't afford their low tax rates.'

'And if they find the car – the Chevy?'

'I don't know, Guv. Obviously, we could brief them about the idea of the hidden phone. They could ask the owner if he or she is prepared to allow a search.'

Skelgill glares, now doubly alarmed.

DS Leyton raises his palms; he backtracks on his suggestion.

'I know, Guv – it risks non-compliance – and warning-off the owner, if they're any way involved. The trouble is, how would we get a warrant to impound the car in a foreign jurisdiction and with no evidence?'

'Send in Spooner under cover of darkness.'

DS Leyton knows not to take the sardonic quip seriously – but he is more surprised when Skelgill rises and reaches for his outdoor jacket.

'Where are you heading, Guv?'

'Competing theories, Leyton – let us know the instant you hear about the Chevy. In the meantime, we're off to check for Spooner's fingerprints on some petrol cans up in Swinesdale.'

Leaving one sergeant bewildered, he indicates with a jerk of the head that the other should accompany him.

17. PITFALLS

11.30 a.m., Friday, January 8th

'That's Sir Mallory George's place – the one set back amongst the bare trees.'

'Aspens.'

'Sorry, Guv?'

'They're aspens. They spread underground – live for centuries. Longer. The leaf-stems are flat so the trees are wind-resistant. When they've got leaves.'

DS Jones, driving, is unable to look again. The main route through Mungrisdale parish is 'main' only in primacy – in many places it is single-track in width, especially as it twists and turns – zigs and zags, even – between what seems like a haphazard string of properties clustered beneath the towering fells to their left, the west, the Skiddaw massif, into which are cut the various tributary dales. Then there is the snow on the road. And more falling sporadically.

She gets the impression that Skelgill has digressed because he does not want to admit not knowing exactly where the venerable climber lives.

He might even be a bit grumpy about it.

There is a simple solution.

'The Moot Hall Café will probably be open. Think we can risk a snack without raising suspicion?'

Skelgill needs little encouragement.

'Maybe get a carryout.'

DS Jones nods. She has not formulated a plan as regards the marijuana farm. But she is reminded that, if the Badduns were operating in the area – as seems increasingly possible – then the fate that befell them is consistent with the cutthroat nature of the illicit drugs trade. Far more so than had they become tangled with a gang of car thieves. And likewise with the self-contained business of housebreaking, when being chased by an Alsatian would seem to be the upper limit as regards occupational hazards. Logic says drugs are still the most likely connection, and yet she has become increasingly uneasy about the idea.

They are both silent as they pass through the hamlets of Mungrisdale and Bowscale, and finally into Swinesdale.

DS Jones takes the valley road and immediately pulls into the parking area for the café.

Skelgill unfastens his seatbelt.

'I'll go, Guv – I think he's getting used to me.'

Skelgill scowls, as though he thinks she anticipates he will put his foot in it.

'Want me to leave the engine running?'

'Nay, I'll be fine.'

She hesitates, as though she finds it slightly unusual, leaving him alone in the car, somewhat impotent.

She departs into a fresh flurry of snow, large flakes that stick to the vehicle, and quickly envelop it.

Skelgill, too, is unaccustomed to the situation. He is not good with sensory deprivation, and it compounds the bout of cabin fever that had assailed him in his office, which had prompted his abrupt departure. Swarmed by conjecture, there had been the sting in the tail of DS Leyton's account – the news of the black car, that is inviting an uncomfortable connection he has so far resisted. Now, with the view disappearing behind an opaque veil, he casts about for some distraction. In his shooting brake there would be a map tucked under the sun-visor, but his colleague is content (misguidedly so in his opinion) to rely upon her mobile for navigation.

He peruses the controls.

He looks in the back seat – there is just DS Jones's shoulder bag.

He opens the glove box.

On top of the regulation faux leather folder containing the owner's manual and service record is a paperback novel. The cover has a striking design in black and orange, but it is the title and, in

particular, the author's name that wins his attention. *A Blind Eye* by
K.T. Darke.

*

'Here we go, Guv – this one's got sugar. *Guv?*'

DS Jones has approached without Skelgill noticing – he is
entirely cocooned – but more than that, he did not even stir when
she placed her purchases on the bonnet to open the driver's door,
and now has ducked inside and leant across with his hot drink.

To her amazement he is engrossed in a book.

Cold air and snow are blowing in. She slots his disposable cup
into the console, retrieves her own and the paper bag containing
scones, and jumps in and starts the engine for the heater.

Skelgill, without looking at her, now speaks.

'Have you read this?'

The strained note in his voice invites the question, "Why?" –
but instead she answers precisely.

'Oh, no – I've been meaning to. Katrina Darkeness gave it to
me – I keep forgetting that I left it in the glove compartment.'

Skelgill's mouth is dry.

He drinks, seemingly inured to the near-scalding state of the
liquid.

He does not take his eyes off the book.

But it seems to DS Jones that he is staring through and beyond
the open pages, rather than reading their words. Curiously, he is at
a point about halfway through. He must have happened upon it by
chance.

He hands it across, keeping open the spread.

DS Jones notes, with a small amount of dismay, that he has
cracked the spine and bent over the top corner of the right-hand
page. It is the start of a new chapter. He points.

'Read it – from there. In fact, read it out loud.'

She glances at him; he is plainly not joking.

'From the top? Where it says *"Mummy – he says they're going to –"*
– oh.'

Her face registers apprehension – more than that – something verging upon foreboding.

Skelgill waits.

She gathers herself – she is already scanning ahead – her eyes narrow.

She begins to read, enunciating clearly, her soft Cumbrian accent adding a depth of feeling to the narrative that has Skelgill, after a few lines – and despite the alarming content – settling back and closing his eyes, and breathing intermittently, as if he is not sleeping but in a state of meditation.

After a couple of pages, the passage reaches its conclusion.

DS Jones – who, too, has become absorbed – gives a shake of her head, like a person prodded from a daydream. Instinctively she switches on the wipers, as if to clear snow from the screen will somehow let them see what they have both just heard.

She is first to speak.

'Guv – that can't be a coincidence, surely?'

Only now does Skelgill open his eyes. He folds his arms.

'That would be one too many, I reckon, lass.'

DS Jones places the novel carefully face down on the dashboard, now unconcerned by the ruined spine, and slowly rubs her eyes.

'But what does it mean? Is it allegorical – or is it autobiographical?'

Skelgill turns his head to present her with a look of reproof.

But she is struck by another thought.

'*Lily!* That's the name she used when she came and called into the tunnel. She said she was looking for Lily. She has a daughter – in real life, I mean – she's Elizabeth. Elizabeth is sometimes Lilibet – or Lily.'

Skelgill is gazing at the drifting snow and does not respond. DS Jones interjects again.

'And *Sandy* – the woman's partner in the story – it's short for Alexander. That's her ex-husband's name. Alexander Farquharson.'

Skelgill now reacts to this point. He pulls his mobile phone from his jacket and glowers at the screen. He has just the semblance of a signal.

'Let's check sommat.'

He retrieves and selects a number, and switches the handset to speaker mode.

It seems to take an age to find the network and finally connect.

DS Jones leans across to read the screen. The contact is displayed as "Cam".

'DS Findlay?'

She refers to a Scots colleague and long-time friend of Skelgill's.

'Aye.'

'Guv?'

She means why is he ringing the man, but the call is answered and Skelgill holds up a silencing hand.

'Dan Dare!'

Skelgill readies himself for the customary banter, and a dressing-down for only ever getting in touch when he wants a favour.

'Guilty as charged, Cam.'

Skelgill, however, cuts to the chase – on the grounds that his line hangs by a thread.

'Cam – can you look up a shotgun licence for us?'

'Aye, nae bother – I'm logged in, the now. Who is it? What's the address?'

Skelgill turns to DS Jones. She looks suddenly panicked – but Skelgill makes do.

'No address – except it's Edinburgh – but I reckon you'll get it on the name, Alexander Farquharson.'

They hear a mixture of murmuring, deep breathing, and the clicks of a keyboard. Then a triumphant expiration of breath.

'Och, aye. Alexander James Farquharson – here's yer man. Stays in Ann Street – very nice. He's coming up for renewal in May. It's every five years.'

Now the Scotsman gives a low whistle as he reads out the make and model of gun. He remarks that it goes with the exclusive address.

Skelgill knows his way around a firearms licence application.

'What does it say about where he shoots?'

More perusal ensues.

'Aye – here we go. Gleneagles Shooting School. Estate of

Duke of Buccleuch. Isle of Colonsay – gives the laird's name. It's like a list from Burke's Peerage.'

'Owt down here?'

'Haud yer horses.' Now DS Findlay reads under his breath, muttering indistinguishable Scots words. 'Aye – here we go – Skiddaw Forest, estate of Todd Hall – does that sound right?'

Skelgill confirms it does.

'I don't suppose there's anything on the ammo – the make of cartridges?'

'Negative. It isnae generally recorded. The inspecting officer might make a note if there's a great arsenal kept away frae the guns. Nothing here. But a gun like that – I tell ye one thing, he's not going to be using yer bargain basement shells.'

Skelgill glances at DS Jones. She nods meaningfully. He has not advertised her presence; she realises it is for practical convenience. Indeed, it takes only a moment's hiatus for DS Findlay to shift into conversational mode.

'So, how's the lassie – young Emma? Danny, if I were your age I'd be –'

'Cammy –' Skelgill hurriedly interjects. 'I'll get back to you on this – we need to check something – you know how it is with shotguns.'

The elderly sergeant might be a trifle offended at being so cut off, but he perhaps also reads between the lines, and facilitates an economical ending of the call.

Skelgill looks again at his sergeant. She is plainly conflicted.

'What is it?'

'I'm thinking less allegorical and increasingly autobiographical. But, Guv – why would she write about it?'

Skelgill has put aside any chagrin regarding her superior vocabulary. He answers phlegmatically.

'Good material.'

DS Jones flashes him a questioning look – he might have a point, but she seeks a more nuanced explanation.

'It's like you would keep a diary. Almost as if – as if to exonerate yourself – one day, if you needed to.'

Skelgill shrugs.

'It's proof of a sort, right enough. I don't know about exonerate.'

DS Jones is clearly shaken. When new facts and old feelings collide, it can be an unsettling experience – of excitement, but also of the risk of jumping to the wrong conclusion – like the crossword, of fitting an attractive solution to a clue that is not fully understood. Now she takes the lid off her tea and drinks, staring pensively towards the snow-shrouded buildings of the Moot Hall Café. Skelgill takes the opportunity to grab the paper bag and begins to make short work of his scone.

'How was the marijuana farmer?'

He grins, as though he enjoys the ring of the rhyme.

DS Jones starts, disturbed from her reverie.

'Oh. He asked about you again.' She gestures to indicate their two cups. 'Obviously – I'm with someone. He's a creep.'

Skelgill gives a small ironic laugh.

'That aside – what do you reckon to him now – what he's up to?'

She understands Skelgill means in the light of what is unfolding.

'I don't know. It might still stack up – in a way we can't yet see.'

Skelgill despatches the last of his scone and gulps down some tea.

'Howay, lass. Finish up and we'll look for those petrol cans. Breath of fresh air's what we need. Get us heads straight.'

She nods – although her memory of the lead mine is not particularly one of fresh air.

She puts her cup into the console and slides the car into gear.

Skelgill is looking acquisitively at the brown paper bag.

'You going to eat that scone?'

*

'How did you get up there?'

Skelgill is scanning the fellside that rises towards the old mine workings.

'He suggested we should follow the bed of the stream – to

avoid rocks hidden under the snow.'

Skelgill's scrutiny becomes more critical.

After a few moments he makes an observation.

'Someone's trekked across – see – from further down the road.'

There is a just-discernible line of tracks, masked by fresh snow, ascending at a diagonal.

'Perhaps that was Katrina Darkeness. We all came back down the same way. The stream.'

Skelgill stares in silence. It is plain that something disturbs him.

'Should we go up, Guv? I mean – in case she decides to leave.'

She indicates loosely behind them. As they drove past, a wisp of smoke rising from the pines had indicated that the author was at home, and the shepherd's quad bike stood outside his cottage, its pillion capped by an inch or so of snow.

It is the case that neither of them is quite ready to tackle Katrina Darkeness – the revelation borders upon the incredible, and thus is entirely disorienting. Could it really be that what she has written is in all actuality somewhere between a witness statement and a confession? To confront her with this charge without corroboration leaves them open to being made complete fools of – for an author's imagination has no bounds, and anyone should know that.

And for DS Jones it is doubly confounding. There is the sinister atmosphere of the dale and the guarded and confusing interactions with its inhabitants – most recently her unnerving episode at this mine.

She is content, therefore, to go along with Skelgill's suggestion that they stick to their original purpose, a practical distraction that should indeed clear their heads. The conditions are certainly bracing. The arctic air that has Britain in its icy grip is unrelenting, and the grey blanket of low cloud is hard to read; sometimes there is snow, sometimes not; in between, their origin defying explanation, ghostly flurries pass, like giant wraiths that stalk the fells.

But they are well equipped. Skelgill did not yield to his colleague's offer to drive without decanting tackle from his own car. They each have a torch, waterproofs, wellingtons – and Skelgill wields a wading staff, hand-made from an ash pole, with blue baler twine where a commercial model would have a leather thong looped through a hole drilled at the grip end.

A brisk, almost cavalier ascent brings them to the cave mouth; but now Skelgill is patently more circumspect. The halt is not just for breath. He inspects the structure and its environs, to acquaint himself with any vulnerability. After some reflection he ducks beneath the strand of police tape into the tunnel, and turns back to flash a somewhat macabre grin.

'I reckon an avalanche is the worst thing that can happen.'

DS Jones is looking like she does not need additional worries, but she steels herself and follows suit. Skelgill moves swiftly – she notices this – jabbing ahead with the tip of the long staff, although she knows from her own visit that the murky stream water is just an inch or two in depth. She also knows he is no fan of caves; he craves the horizon as his object and the sky as his ceiling; perhaps that accounts for his hurry to get the job over with; to see the petrol cans for himself and beat a smart retreat.

She realises they are nearing the point where the stream widens – and indeed she glimpses the red paint of the cans, discarded at the base of the collapsed rubble – when Skelgill utters an oath and abruptly thrusts out a hand to stop her in her tracks.

'What is it, Guv?'

'How close did you get?' His tone is severe.

'Where you are, I suppose – I took the photograph from about there.'

He does not answer – instead he probes at the surface of the water in the centre of the small pool. His staff must be the best part of five feet in length. As he bends lower it disappears right up to the loop of blue baler twine, and still meets no obstacle. He smears a hand across his chin, as if he has just witnessed a narrow escape.

'This is a shaft. It could be fifty foot deep – a hundred. This is a death trap.'

For a second time in this place, but for a different reason, DS Jones can feel her pulse racing. That she was here – the breath of Jacob Floxham palpable upon her nape – the touch of his hand at the small of her back. And then – the voice. Katrina Darkeness. The redeemer.

Skelgill appears unfazed when DS Jones turns tail and splashes back to the mouth of the passage. When he reaches her a minute later she is still gulping in the mountain air. He waits, and watches. When she seems more composed, he lays a palm on her shoulder. He grins.

'I reckon you're right – those cans look too new to me. Red herring.'

His words might be intended as a casual diversion from her shock – but his use of the idiom is ambiguous, and for a second her dismay is rekindled.

'Do you mean as a coincidence – or as a lure?'

But Skelgill does not get the chance to differentiate.

There comes the muffled ping of a text notification. He tugs his phone from a pocket of his jacket.

'It's Leyton. Must have been while we were under ground. He wants me to listen to his voicemail.'

But now Skelgill curses his telecoms supplier. He shakes the handset, and waves it about, but to no avail.

'That's the signal gone again – why didn't he just put it in the text?'

'Maybe he was driving – a long message?'

Skelgill scowls in frustration.

DS Jones locates her own mobile.

'I don't have coverage, either. We could ask to use the landline at Fellbeck?'

The suggestion prompts Skelgill to glance down the valley.

'Hey up – talk of the devil. That's her car, isn't it?'

DS Jones follows his line of sight.

From their elevated position on the fellside they have a clear view to Jacob Floxham's cottage. A white sports roadster is slewed across the lane, apparently having skidded in the snow, and a woman – Katrina Darkeness it seems – is leaning in at the open driver's door – and she gives several blasts on the horn. As they watch, she abandons the car and begins to skirt the building, her movements frantic, her arms flailing, banging on doors and peering into windows. Skelgill wastes no time.

'This feels like part of the story.'

He sets off at a diagonal, making a beeline for the property. He takes loping strides and is sure-footed in the snow – but after about twenty yards of progress he suddenly halts and turns to DS Jones, slip-sliding in his wake. As she nears he extends the wading staff and hands it over.

It takes Skelgill a minute to reach the lane just short of the old miner's cottage, and DS Jones spills down close behind. Katrina Darkeness is behaving like a woman possessed. She scrambles back to her car to resume sounding the horn – when she catches sight of their approach, and recognises DS Jones.

She is plainly distraught.

She makes a rush at DS Jones and grabs her by the wrists.

'Help me! He's taken Lily!'

'Your daughter? She's been staying with you?'

DS Jones is experiencing flashbacks – the face at the window – the trendy training shoes in the hallway – the two helpings of sweet cocoa that were ready before her arrival.

'Yes – he's taken her! He must have her this time!'

'You mean Jacob Floxham?'

Katrina Darkeness is plainly fighting against extreme panic. Her eyes are wild and she clings more fiercely to DS Jones. But she seems to realise that she must explain to win their support. Her words come quickly, urgently – but now more coherently.

'We both knew you were going to find out. I'll tell you what happened. The shooting – the car fire – it's not what you think. But Jacob – he's not right – I mean, he's crazy – a psychopath. He's been watching you – he believes the net is closing in – he was with me when you rang yesterday – he overheard – he's growing desperate. And now he's taken Lily – you must help me – you understand? Lily knows what he did – she saw from the window. She saw the flames.'

DS Jones remains calm.

'Where do you think he has taken her?'

Katrina Darkeness glances desolately at the cottage.

'I don't know –' Her voice rises, regaining a note of hysteria.

'Yesterday – when you were here – I thought it was the same thing – but she had walked to the café. She sometimes does – she likes a little independence. But I just phoned Hugh – she's not there.' Now she stares pleadingly at DS Jones. 'You must help me. Radio for help – stop him before he gets away. They can't have gone far on foot, surely?'

Skelgill has been a spectator to the exchange. DS Jones turns to look at him. They have neither radio nor functioning mobiles right now. But they also have something that is stupendous. The blurted if incomplete confession – for that is what it is shaping up to be – tells them they have an existential emergency on their hands.

But the woman is half-dressed. She is trembling violently, and it cannot just be the stress of the moment.

Skelgill pulls off his jacket. He steps forward and wraps it around her shoulders. The action seems to be a kind of final straw, and she collapses sobbing into DS Jones's somewhat hesitant embrace.

Skelgill reminds himself that he must remain detached. The woman's emotive account could be misguided. What if the teenager is simply visiting the shepherd of her own accord? What if there is tension between mother and daughter? What if there is a complex relationship afoot?

But as he turns to address the simple prima facie matter – whether Jacob Floxham is holed up in his cottage with the missing girl – the throb of an engine halts him in his tracks.

Into view through flurrying snow, like a great horned beast lumbers a vintage tractor armed with fork-lifts, and sitting – no, standing – astride the growling monster is an ice-encrusted Brian Watts.

And Brian Watts looks furious.

He brings the machine to a juddering halt and clambers down, and limps urgently up to confront Skelgill.

'That Jacob. I reckon he's cracked!'

Skelgill holds up his hands; there are expletives to be disentangled from the protestation – and he recalls, from back in the day, you don't want to be rugby-tackled by 'Forty' Watts when his dander is up. But he sees also that, beneath the surface ire, in the honest farmer's eyes there is indignation and alarm.

'Go on, marra.'

The man needs no encouragement, but Skelgill's accommodating response seems at least to get him onside.

'Danny, lad – I were int' back kitchen – heard sommat – went out – he were int' yard starting up the Defender. I shouted, what the Dickens are you playing at? He about ran us down – he had a look in his eyes like the devil hissen!'

Multiple questions are jostling for prominence on Skelgill's lips. But one commands priority.

'Forty – your shotgun?'

The farmer is not expecting this – he brings a hand up to his chin. His agitation subsides to a mood of reflection.

'Aye – it's int' back, reet enough. Like when thee last saw it.'

'Is it loaded?'

Now the man's voice gains a plaintive note.

'Danny, lad – I allus keep it loaded – what am I to do when there's a fox tekkin' me chickens?'

Skelgill hesitates for a moment. This is no time to replay their previous conversation about gun safety.

'When was this?'

'Just now, lad. He took the Defender about ten minutes ago. I saw him head up the dale. I told me Ma to lock hersen in and I got me clobber on and came after him ont' tractor. Thought I'd have him blocked in, like. Then I met him – comin' at me head on. I stopped – but he veered off – smashed through a gate – up across t' fell – looks like he's heading for Bowscale Tarn – he can get on the track – there's a gap int' wall – and descend to Bowscale and then away. Unless he thinks he can drive right through to t'other side of Skiddaw Forest.'

Skelgill's thoughts are racing. Brian Watts seems clear that Jacob Floxham is making some sort of getaway. Does he know more of their mission than he earlier revealed – and now of their heightened quandary?

But Katrina Darkeness has pulled away from DS Jones. She paws imploringly at the farmer's threadbare Barbour jacket.

'Lily – did you see Lily?'

'Aye – that's why I carried on up – see if you knew what were amiss. She were int' back – clinging on. She were alreet, like – just looked a bit dazed.'

That he adds the rider is a response to Katrina Darkness's schizophrenic expression of hope and horror.

She turns urgently to Skelgill – she seems to appreciate that he alone calls the shots.

'You have to stop him – he's dangerous – murderous, I tell you! *You must save Lily – I beg of you!*'

Skelgill stands stock still, his arms akimbo – but like green-flecked lasers his eyes traverse the broad white slopes of Bowscale Fell.

Abruptly, he addresses all three.

'Get to the nearest landline. Ring 999 and ask for mountain rescue. They're on exercise on Grisedale Pike. Give them my name. Tell them where you are – they'll know what to do.'

And with that he turns and strides towards the far corner of the cottage, where Jacob Floxham's quad bike is stationed.

He wrestles the handlebars to displace the snow – perhaps also an attempt to break the steering lock – but the keys are revealed to be in the ignition. Another farmer that does not listen to police advice.

He sweeps snow from the seat and in short order has the engine fired and revving, as he familiarises himself with the controls.

Just as he kicks it into gear and it begins to roll down the slope, preparing to accelerate away from the bemused party, DS Jones thumps down on the pillion behind him.

*

Skelgill's glance over his shoulder encompasses not just his mutinous colleague – but a sight that makes him doubly smile. Brian Watts is taking him literally. The nearest landline is evidently inside the shepherd's cottage – and the tractor is lining up to break open the front door with its projecting forks.

'Can you do this, Guv?'

Skelgill growls scornfully.

'Why would four wheels be harder than two?'

He refers to his Triumph – albeit a road bike – but his motorbiking skills aside, Skelgill is no stranger to these machines – his youth spent helping out on local farms has given him plenty of experience, across a medley of contraptions. It crosses his mind that in present conditions, the tractor would be superior – in every aspect except speed.

Accordingly, he does not spare the gas. DS Jones seems reassured, but for good measure she clamps her arms firmly around his waist.

Skelgill exclaims at the point where the Land Rover has clearly left the road. Its tracks reveal a sharp banking turn into a gateway – the shattered timbers – a shallow descent to the river, thence across the packhorse bridge and up the rising paddock. He follows doggedly.

DS Jones recognises it as the way she came with Jacob Floxham, a means of reaching the trackway that links Bowscale hamlet with its mountain tarn. It is a viable escape route, if circuitous.

As they steadily gain height across a stretch of gently undulating terrain, she leans close to Skelgill's ear.

'Do you think he's taken the girl as a hostage – to secure safe passage?'

Skelgill, grappling with the handlebars, effects a non-committal shrug.

'Going by your pal the writer – sounds like he's lost his bottle. He'll be thinking on the hoof. Happen he met her on the lane.'

DS Jones is squinting; rogue flakes of snow are being driven into her eyes.

'I haven't been able to find anything on him – his family must be in New Zealand. It's anyone's guess where he might head for, if he can get out of the Lakes undetected.'

Skelgill is scanning ahead – standing now on the running boards, to improve his view.

'How!'

His war cry is the cattle-herding call of the hill farmer.

DS Jones cranes around him, the better to see.

And there is the Defender!

It is on the level, already headed down the dale, but it is clearly stuck, canted over at one corner.

As they circle and mount the track they see that a front wheel has slipped into a deep pot where groundwater gushes from a scar in the embankment. The remaining tyres spin ineffectually, polishing the compacted snow further into ice.

As Skelgill slews to a halt the frantic revving stops.

Jacob Floxham must have glimpsed them in his wing mirror.

He leaps out on the passenger side and stands, half crouched, ready to spring. He snarls like a cornered panther, and it seems to DS Jones that the dark romantic features have become possessed by an altogether malevolent creature.

They are some seven or eight yards apart.

The detectives dismount, one either side of the quad bike and begin cautiously to approach him – when he makes a sudden dart and wrenches open the back door of the Land Rover – and yanks out Lily Darkness by her wrist.

For DS Jones there is a sudden déjà vu – a flashback to the face at the window at Fellbeck. For Skelgill it is just a shivering sixteen-year-old who is far from suitably clad – trainers, jeans and a hoodie – and in appearance a more sylphlike, untarnished version of her mother. And the same intelligent deep blue eyes.

But only a split second is spare to take in such details – for Jacob Floxham also grabs the shotgun.

Roughly, he hooks an arm around the neck of girl, and thrusts her in front of him.

He raises the weapon.

Skelgill's first instinct is to shield his colleague – but they are too far apart. Instead he takes a couple of paces forward.

'Get back! Start walking down the hill!'

Jacob Floxham indicates with a jerk of the shotgun.

Skelgill realises he means to take the quad bike.

He begins to move steadily – but towards the man and his victim.

The twelve-bore swings to point directly at him.

Skelgill stops, the tips of the barrels just three feet from his chest.

He sees a red dot above the thumb-piece that tells him the safety catch is off.

The finger on the trigger flexes.

The girl is staring at him – she seems uncannily calm. Then she blinks quite decisively twice and lowers her eyes purposefully down to her right.

Skelgill's gaze follows.

She opens her palm.

Skelgill lurches forward.

The trigger is pulled.

An empty click. Another.

The butt is smashed into Jacob Floxham's face.

The man staggers backwards.

The girl gives a cry – it could be alarm or pain or both – but she is released and is sent spinning to the ground.

Both Skelgill and DS Jones leap to her aid.

Jacob Floxham sinks to his knees, blood spattering the snow.

DS Jones wraps a protective arm around Lily Darkeness, and begins to draw her away.

Skelgill urgently casts about. The shotgun has disappeared into a deep drift of snow – but within a few seconds he locates what he seeks.

He stoops to pick up some small item – and again another close by.

And now, when he opens his hand, in his palm are two live cartridges.

He shakes his head in disbelief.

The girl, with extraordinary presence of mind, had removed them from the gun.

Then comes a sharp warning from DS Jones.

'Guv!'

But it is too late.

Jacob Floxham is on his feet and haring for the idling quad bike. He leaps aboard – drives at them, scattering them – and on past the

Defender.

Skelgill clenches his fists in frustration – in a few minutes the fugitive might reach the valley bottom and steal another vehicle.

But – not so fast!

Just as the quad bike is about to disappear behind the first spur, clanking around the same curve comes Brian Watts and his ancient tractor – and, clinging on grimly behind him, wearing Skelgill's jacket, Katrina Darkness.

In the game of chicken there is only one winner.

The quad bike is driven off the track. It topples and its rider tumbles down the snow-covered slope.

For a moment he does not move – then he struggles to his feet – he staggers, limps – and begins to trot, gathering pace with every stride.

He might still escape.

But not if Brian Watts has anything to do with it.

Disregarding his damaged ACL, in a glorious re-creation of his heyday the former Wath Brow Hornets outside back leaps from the tractor and, like a ginger-tipped missile executes a flying tackle that brings down his opponent. Brian Watts is not a big man and Jacob Floxham resists furiously. He could yet get the better of the contest – but for an incapacitating blow to the jaw: Skelgill joins the fight. Immediately the farmer produces a coil of baler twine and begins to truss their captive's legs, like a spider would entangle a juicy fly.

Behind them there is an emotional reunion in progress.

Katrina Darkeness has made an equally adrenaline-fueled charge for her daughter, whom DS Jones has handed into her arms. Skelgill's jacket is passed on again.

And now Skelgill looks up expectantly – for, belated, but welcome nonetheless there is the *dub-dub-dub* of the airborne cavalry — and descending through the mist comes the search and rescue helicopter.

Skelgill sees that DS Jones is approaching – she has a pair of handcuffs at the ready. They are swiftly applied.

Brian Watts continues to hold the captive face down in the snow, none too gently.

Skelgill rises and pats him on the shoulder.

'You always were a fierce little bugger, Forty.'

The farmer seems pleased with the compliment; though he nods ruefully, and again Skelgill has the impression that the farmer is somehow not surprised by what has unfolded, as if he has been harbouring doubts about goings-on in the dale.

But there is no time for reflection. Skelgill addresses his colleague. He jerks a thumb in the direction of the hovering aircraft; a man with a collapsible stretcher strapped to his back is already descending on a winch.

'I'll brief the lads.'

But DS Jones is momentarily distracted.

'Look, Guv.'

She indicates in the direction of Swinesdale hamlet.

A distant line of winking blue lights snakes cautiously along the snowbound valley road – the mountain rescue have passed on the message.

'Just hang tight – it'll take them a few minutes to find their way up the fell.'

DS Jones nods – but there is something in her expression that holds Skelgill back.

'What is it?'

She glances at the prone figure of Jacob Floxham. She turns away a little and lowers her voice.

'It was when he spoke – did you hear his accent?'

Skelgill looks puzzled – and perhaps impatient that she has noticed some minor foible.

'Will this keep?'

'Er – yes – of course.'

'Reet.'

DS Jones watches as Skelgill strides across to where the helicopter is depositing the mountain rescue crew. Already now two men are on the ground – the second has a first-aid rucksack – and a third is almost down. Snow is swirling like a mini tornado beneath the rotors of the chopper, and the noise is intense, and Skelgill gathers them into a tight huddle. The three break away – two head for DS Jones; the other, unfurling a space blanket, moves at a tangent towards Katrina and Lily Darkeness, huddled beside the Defender.

DS Jones sees that Skelgill is talking on a borrowed radio – he seems suddenly stiff – as if alarmed – and, before she knows it – before she can begin to react – he steps into and clips on the hoist harness, waves a signal to the winchman – and is drawn up into the belly of the great bird – which makes a one-eighty-degree turn and rises into the mist.

18. KINGPIN

Workington, 2 p.m., Friday, January 8th

'Cor blimey, Guvnor – I wondered why you wanted to meet here!'

Skelgill glances about his surroundings – they stand inside the deserted speedway track; it seems a sad relic on the post-industrial wasteland of Workington's Northside. They both watch as the coastguard helicopter banks away, its next mission already scheduled.

Skelgill shrugs phlegmatically. He sticks his little fingers into his ears and waggles them as if he is trying to displace water. Despite a headset the fifteen-minute trip has left them ringing.

'The pilot reckoned it's a good spot to land.'

'I thought it might have something to do with the Badduns' caravan having been nearby.'

Skelgill shakes his head. He stares a little vacantly at his colleague, as though something has distracted him.

'How did you get on, Guv? Is that a drop of blood on your sleeve?'

Skelgill starts towards DS Leyton's car.

'It'll have to wait, Leyton – we're not out of the woods yet.'

DS Leyton has more questions, but he has to scurry to keep up with Skelgill, and once inside the vehicle the latter orders him to head for the town centre.

'Leyton, tell us in full what you said over the radio – I could barely hear you for the racket.'

DS Leyton takes a moment to set them on course. The access road has seen little traffic and the snow is challenging for a regular family car. But at least the coastal terrain is flat, and when he has a steady roll on he composes himself.

'Right then, Guv. Well – I reckon the Isle of Man cops know

more than they first let on. That car – that black Chevy – seems they've had tabs on the owner. They suspect him of having his fingers in a few pies – organised crime – but he's kept a low profile – to all appearances a respectable settler. But one of his lines of work is dealing in second-hand executive motors.'

He glances expectantly at Skelgill. But Skelgill is staring ahead, listening implacably.

'He must be our kingpin, Guv. He's called John Silverbach, forty-two, originally from Croydon, where he's got some business interests. No actual criminal record, but a few cautions and two acquittals – one for a bullion job at Heathrow Airport and the other for GBH on a known London mobster. Complaints of domestic abuse from two former partners, but the charges never stuck.'

Skelgill is nodding grimly.

'Anyway, Guv – like they promised me – they went to check on the fancy motor. When they got the registration number they realised it was a cloned identity – it's driving around with the same plates as some Ford Mondeo in the south of England.

'I don't know if they accidentally rattled his cage – or maybe we spooked him, breaking into that lock-up – or he got wind of it somehow – or even if it's just pure coincidence – but, like I said to you over the radio, *he's on the move.*'

DS Leyton pauses for breath – and perhaps a little for dramatic effect.

'He caught the eight o'clock ferry from Douglas this morning – that put me in a panic. Crikey – what if he's been tipped off, thinks we're interested in the motor? I mean – if he's calling the shots in the car-theft ring, he must have claimed the Chevy for himself. In which case he would know it's knocked off. What if he intends to make it disappear before we can search it? Jeez – no car – no phone.'

Skelgill jerks his head around to stare at his colleague. Swept up in the snowstorm of events – a squall that still swirls about him in a dizzying fashion – he has overlooked the suddenly diminished significance of Dale Spooner's mobile phone. His eyes widen in alarm – should he disabuse his colleague of this fact? But if the phone has become moot, their need to find the black Chevrolet has not – the urgency of their task could hardly be more pressing.

But DS Leyton merely interprets his superior's reaction to be in accord with his own.

'Then I thought – wait a minute – he's taken the ferry to Heysham. Why not Liverpool? He must be coming north. And, sure enough, ANPR cameras picked him up – first on the M6 at Burton-in-Kendal services, and then on the A66 just west of Penrith, about an hour ago. Obviously, Guv – this is why I've been trying to get in touch with you – it looks like he's heading for Workington. It's the only logical explanation.'

Skelgill checks his wristwatch – the time is approaching two p.m. The car ferry is about a four-hour journey, and a couple more by road from Heysham to Workington. By both measures, the conclusion must be that John Silverbach will already have arrived.

'Do we know if he's alone?'

'The Manx police say he boarded the ferry on his tod, Guv – but there's no knowing if he's picked up someone on the way.'

'More likely one of his local oppos.'

'Hmm – I wish I'd managed to get tabs on the Hawkins geezer.'

'We might meet him soon enough.'

Skelgill scrapes the fingers of both hands through his hair, damp with melted snowflakes. His features, naturally craggy, are markedly strained.

'We need to find Jade. We'll try her place first.'

There is slow traffic, as drivers exercise caution that is probably disproportionate to the risk. Some fresh snow is falling, but the main roads are gritted and for the most part clear.

A little to Skelgill's frustration, DS Leyton seems to resign himself to their pedestrian progress.

'Last time I can remember snow in London, Guv – I reckon I was a nipper. Good for the kids, the North – we actually get a winter.'

Skelgill folds his arms.

'I can see you've not had much practice on it, Leyton. You should get a set of chains.'

'They can slow you down, though, Guv.'

Skelgill makes a scoffing sound in his throat.

'Not compared to being stuck on a hill. That might be another thing you've noticed about the North, Leyton – most of it's on a slope.'

They have reached a neighbourhood of narrow streets lined by austere terraces, nondescript, basically homogeneous stone and some harled, which the snow does little to make more appealing. Here the roads are unsalted, and cars carelessly abandoned make navigation trickier still.

'It's on the left – pull in after that white van.'

'No sign of the Chevy, Guv.'

Skelgill is staring at the road surface ahead, but if he is looking for tracks the criss-crossing of tyre marks is just too complex to decipher.

'Hang fire, Leyton. I might just pass as a local.'

Skelgill gets out, taking care not to slide on the icy pavement.

There is no doorbell. He knocks, and raps at the letter box.

No reply comes.

He moves to peer in at the window. The curtains are drawn back, but no light is on and he can see that the gas fire is off. Before the hearth are a child's toys – dolls and clothing and a doll's pram – but no semblance of activity. He is pondering his next move when a female voice calls out.

'She's not in, chuck.'

The Manchester accent grates, and Skelgill turns to see a middle-aged woman lounging in her doorway. The way she is dressed and her dishevelled hair make her look like she has just got out of bed. But she holds a half-smoked cigarette, and he can hear the canned sitcom laughter of a television emanating from behind her.

There is the decision at times like this of if and when to reveal his identity. Closing of ranks is a predictable reaction in a tightly knit community. But Skelgill senses that another human motive may underlie her emergence from the warmth of her living room.

He drops his plan to remain incognito.

He half-crosses the street.

He produces his warrant card.

The woman seems unfazed.

'When did you last see her?'

'She came last night in a taxi. Had the taxi wait. Carried the bairn out in her nightie. I saw her old Ma leave after that. There's been no one there since.'

'Did you see the name of the taxi firm?'

The woman inspects the end of her cigarette.

'It were one of them minicabs. They all look the same.'

Skelgill is distracted. Had his meeting with Jade prompted her to jump ship? To move her daughter to safety? She has evidently not gone to her mother's place. Or has she heard another way – or simply sensed impending danger? Or is he reading too much into the situation, making five when there is only two plus two?

'Someone else were looking for her.'

The woman sees she has his attention. She relishes her moment in the limelight. She drags languidly on the cigarette.

'When was this?'

'About twenty minutes ago.'

'What did you see?'

She inclines her head towards DS Leyton's car.

'Big black limo. There were two of them.'

'Two men?'

'Aye.'

'Have you seen them before?'

She hesitates tantalisingly.

'I've seen the car before, once or twice. The windows are tinted – no one got out.'

'What about today?'

'Aye, they did.'

'Did you recognise either of them?'

The woman seems to reflect, then she shakes her head.

'Can you describe them?'

'One were stocky – jeans and a hoodie – had the hood up, like. Bit of a scruff.' (That is ripe, Skelgill is thinking.) 'The other were tall, much taller – smarter – he were the driver. Both about fortyish.'

Skelgill is becoming gripped by a strong urge to leave. The danger to Jade feels palpable. With some work they might be able to trace the taxi journey – but not in the few minutes that are available.

He backs away. He raises a hand of thanks.

She begins to retreat inside her door.

Then a thought strikes him.

'Wait – did you speak to them?'

Now she looks a little guilty – it is the face of one who does not want to inform but knows they must.

'Aye.'

'What did you tell them?'

'I said she might have gone to her pal Sheryl's – that they knock about together.'

Skelgill cannot contain a note of alarm in his voice.

'Did you give them the address?'

'I don't know where Sheryl lives.'

Skelgill nods curtly. The fact offers a small respite. And the woman now loiters – he realises she might be hoping for some remuneration – for perhaps this same information produced a tip first time around.

But he turns and strides for DS Leyton's car.

'We need to get to Big Mags' place.'

'Righto, Guv. Ain't that where you were filmed doing your disco dancing?'

Skelgill's response leaves his subordinate in no doubt that the subject is not up for discussion.

And he impresses upon DS Leyton that there is imminent danger.

They can be at their destination in fewer than five minutes – but so could have been the black Chevy, twenty minutes earlier. Outsider John Silverbach may not know where to go. But if the stocky companion is local crook James Hawkins – then he would soon be able to find out where Sheryl lives. Her mother, Big Mags Graham is infamous.

Skelgill barks out instructions.

DS Leyton puts on a much-improved show of snow driving.

When they turn into Big Mags' street Skelgill is torn between alarm and relief when he sees no sign of the black Chevrolet.

'Take it slowly, don't stop.'

DS Leyton understands the observational tactic.

The house in question is mid-terrace; in this street the properties are a shade larger, with a yard of space walled off to accommodate a bay window, instead of opening flush to the pavement. Beside the bay is the front door, and above it on the first floor a single narrow bedroom window.

As they pass Skelgill glances up – and he glimpses what he thinks is a blonde-haired doll – when its face breaks into a silent tearful wail, terror occupying the staring eyes.

'Leyton – drive round the back!'

'Where, Guv?'

'Hang a left – there's a lane that runs between the back-to-backs.'

DS Leyton does as commanded, sliding first one left turn into a side street and then seeing the narrower entry to which Skelgill refers.

As he slews around, the skid helping with the tight angle, they see ahead of them – blocking the way about halfway down – the black Chevrolet Suburban.

Skelgill does not need to explain to his partner what they might face and what they might have to do. It is plain from his demeanour that action is imminent and they may yet be in the nick of time to avert some unspoken horror. Right now, the threats that have been bandied about as hearsay – to Dale Spooner, Jade Nelson and their child – threats that are ten a penny in the criminal fraternity and which could have been taken with a pinch of salt, are threats that suddenly seem very real indeed.

'Stop here.'

They will go the last yards on foot, to keep the chance of the element of surprise on their side.

The lane is untidy. There are overflowing wheelie bins, their contents spilled by scavengers; and household rubbish of all kinds – including a stack of lopsided kitchen units, a ripped sofa with stuffing bursting out and, propped against one wall, a urine-stained double mattress.

They tread softly in fresh snow.

The back gate beside the black car is closed but off the latch.

Immediately there is the smell of cigarette smoke.

Skelgill raises a hand – he peers through a crack – and DS Leyton finds an adjacent fissure.

They hold their breath, lest clouds of condensation penetrate the gaps in the flimsy timber.

Standing guard outside the broken back door is the thuggish dog walker. There is a cigarette in one hand and the heavy dog chain in the other – and again no dog. The shillelagh is propped against the wall. Weapons of choice that can be carried in plain sight. He looks cold, and angry.

Skelgill's heart and mind are racing in equal measure. The image of the little girl's face drives him.

DS Leyton turns gingerly, and mouths "James Hawkins".

He draws an imaginary razor across his throat – it is not entirely clear whether he means this is the threat the man poses, or what he would like to do to him.

Skelgill nods. Two against one – although they are unarmed – and how will they cross the yard before their opponent can summon help and begin to lash out?

Skelgill casts about frantically.

Idea.

He beckons to DS Leyton – he points at the mouldy mattress and makes a wrapping motion. DS Leyton looks baffled – and alarmed – but he falls in and grabs the rear as Skelgill picks up the front.

Skelgill, whistling jauntily, shoves open the gate with his boot and enters – they could just pass as two local removal men. He sees the man, and seems surprised.

'Delivery. Where do you want your mattress, marra?'

The sight must be sufficiently plausible and convincingly acted – and the fact that the man's presence is illicit and he would not want to reveal such – causes him to react as though he is indeed the householder expecting a delivery.

He steps forward into the centre of the small yard – at a loss for words – and only then in this instant does he tentatively recognise Skelgill – and too late – and perhaps not as an obvious adversary –

and the detectives surge and enfold him, and topple him, pinioned, to the ground.

He makes surprisingly little noise – mainly muffled porcine grunts as he struggles to free himself.

While DS Leyton uses his own bulk to good effect to subdue movement and stifle sound, Skelgill is rummaging in the shed where he shared a drink with Big Mags' disreputable beau on Christmas Day. He emerges with a coil of washing line – and between them they secure the bundle.

Skelgill is quickly back to his feet.

'Just watch him, Leyton – I reckon he's the one who knocked you on the head.'

The man's eyes are just visible above the top of the mattress.

'There ain't a can of paraffin in that shed, is there? I'm thinking pigs in blankets.'

The eyes shift about nervously.

Skelgill simply pats his colleague on the shoulder.

'I'll holler if I need you. Watch him like a hawk.'

DS Leyton notices the club.

'Want that, Guv?'

Skelgill considers for a second, but shakes his head.

'You can't swing a cat in there, Leyton. Call for back-up. The station's under a mile away.'

He pushes open the damaged door and steps into the kitchen.

The way ahead into the hallway is open and from above there are sounds of panic and commotion.

Most distressing is the muted cry of a child.

A woman – Jade he thinks it must be – seems to be shouting that she "doesn't know".

And another voice – Sheryl? – screaming "go away!" repeatedly.

And in answer – a violent banging – and the wrenching and splintering of wood.

He steals beneath the unguarded stair where he caught Sheryl and there ensued their infamous dance.

He reaches the foot of the flight.

At the head of the staircase on the left is a bedroom door. A big man dressed in smart clothes is savagely stabbing at it with a vicious-looking commando knife.

The girls are barricaded in.

But the wood is not solid and the blade has cut a foot-long gash.

'Police! Stop! You're under arrest!'

Skelgill cries out a warning but his deeper instincts have taken over; the tribe is threatened; his oath to Jade is put to the test. So while he has followed protocol he does not wait to see if the man desists and indeed gives himself up. He charges up the stairs taking two at a time.

The man turns and with a snarl plunges the knife at Skelgill.

John Silverbach might hold the high ground, but Skelgill has gravity. A left-hander, he grabs the descending wrist and with an unexpected twist and a wrench of his body, diverts the blow with a judo-like throw. His assailant flies over the top of him. Skelgill falls face first onto the staircase – he braces with outstretched arms. The man has no such control – he makes a vain grab at thin air and flips over the unguarded edge to land with a sickening crack on the back of his neck.

Skelgill raises himself up. He stares for a moment. The knife is lying in the hallway at the man's feet. But he chooses to leave it. He clambers panting to the landing and puts his mouth to the rent in the bedroom door.

'Sheryl – it's me.'

There is a silence – a pause as if its occupants are frozen by fear and mistrust.

'Danny?'

'Aye – it's alreet – you can come out. The danger's passed. We've got more officers on the way.'

He hears scraping noises – furniture being moved – he peeps through – he sees that they have tipped a wardrobe across the door and jammed it with a bed against the far wall – but it was only a temporary defence as the flimsy plywood panels gradually disintegrated.

The door opens.

It is Sheryl – she hugs him – envelops him – and he is sure she would snog him if he gave her the chance – but he politely puts her aside to check on the others. Jade seems to be in a state of shock, sitting now on the bed – perhaps revisited by the trauma of her last experience at John Silverbach's hands. Her small daughter, a three-year-old, a pretty mini-me of Jade, seems recovered. She kneels beside her mother, stroking her hair.

Skelgill steps forward.

He picks up the girl; she does not protest.

'Come on, lass – let's get you some sweeties.'

She is quite unfazed; she brightens immediately.

'I want a Happy Meal.'

Skelgill looks at Jade – she contrives a tearful smile.

He grins, and pulls a crumpled note from his back pocket. It is gleefully accepted by her daughter.

'I think I can stretch to that.'

He leads the way out – he nods to Sheryl that she should chaperone Jade.

As they descend the stairs there comes the wail of police sirens, and flickering blue lights from the open lounge door.

The man, supine, is unmoving.

Skelgill realises he has his eyes open.

He hesitates.

The man hisses.

'I can't feel my legs – my arms – my fingers.'

Skelgill hesitates – but before he can respond the girl speaks.

'Is that my Dadda?'

Skelgill is shocked, he shies away protectively.

'Nay lass.'

'He hurt my Mummy.'

Close behind him Sheryl is helping Jade down the stairs.

When Jade sees the man – she stops and bends over him.

She stares for a moment, as though uncertain of something.

Then she spits copiously into his face.

Sheryl pulls her away.

With his free hand Skelgill unfastens the front door and steps across the threshold – he converges with a team of uniformed officers and paramedics – he hands the child to a WPC with orders to pass via a drive-thru en route to hospital for checks.

While the paramedics begin to attend to John Silverbach, Skelgill briefs the police constables. They seem eager for action and march through to relieve DS Leyton of his charge. Skelgill exchanges a few words with Sheryl – to confirm that John Silverbach is indeed the person with whom Jade has been involved in a forced relationship. A minute later the uniformed officers bring out a protesting James Hawkins. He hardly notices Skelgill – but if his time rolled in the mattress were not enough, the sight of his incapacitated overlord receiving emergency medical treatment seems to knock the stuffing out of him. He proceeds meekly to the waiting police car.

Skelgill picks his way through to the back, and finds DS Leyton in the small yard, experimentally swinging the shillelagh at an imaginary foe, rather like a golfer might try out a club he is thinking of buying.

He looks at Skelgill in alarm, as though he is just reminded of his superior's role in their mission.

'You okay, Guv – you look a bit peaky?'

'I'm fine.'

'What happened?'

'He tried to knife me. He fell off the stairs.'

'How is he?'

'It's not looking good.'

DS Leyton stares pensively at Skelgill – but when he sees no sign of remorse in the grey-green eyes he seems reassured.

'That just leaves the motor.'

'What?'

'The Chevy, Guv – Spooner's mobile phone.'

Without another word they exit into the lane.

DS Leyton pops open the lift-gate.

19. A BLIND EYE

DI Skelgill's office, 6 p.m., Friday, January 8th

"I shot them both."

DS Jones leans forward to pause the video. Her laptop sits on the corner of Skelgill's desk, and they are crowded in upon it. It is her just-completed interview with Katrina Darkeness. It seems that she feels the blunt admission merits time to be allowed to sink in. After a moment, she restarts the recording. The camera angle is from above and behind DS Jones's left shoulder, and the definition is not so good that her interviewee's expressions can easily be discerned. The main thing is the voice, and the general body language. Both her tone and her demeanour seem largely unrepentant.

"They were going to rape us. Possibly kill us. Can you imagine? Lily was just thirteen."

DS Jones – the interviewer – responds evenly.

"Could you explain what happened?"

"It was exactly as I wrote – almost to the letter. Apart from some of the names. Sally being my alter ego."

"Can you explain for the record how it came about."

"I have already told you something about Alexander – Sandy – how he is the most meticulous person you could ever meet. He thinks of everything. He anticipates every hitch before it happens. It's probably why he's such a successful lawyer – he only takes on the cases he knows he will win. And I think his profession – perhaps like yours – makes him acutely aware of risks – from crime, I mean. To add to which he spent eight years in the SAS Reserve. So he had a plan – if we were ever invaded – that whoever can do it, should go for the gun. Once you've got the gun, you're at least on equal terms. They may have a hostage – but if they harm them, you shoot. It might be a stalemate, but that's better than the alternative. And then you look for a chink in the armour – that split second in which to get a shot in. He had walked us through exactly what took place. It might seem unlikely – but the thing is – he was right, wasn't he?"

DS Jones is scanning the notes of a provisional statement. She does not reply directly. After a moment she looks up.

"Boris Baddun was holding a knife to your daughter's throat and had an arm round her waist. She managed to raise her legs and you shot him in the area of his shins. You then turned and shot Jake Baddun in the thigh as he charged at you wielding a knife."

"Obviously, at the time, I did not know their names. But I assume you have them in the correct order."

DS Jones hesitates. Katrina Darkeness adds a rider.

"I still have the knives – they are beneath the floorboards in the lounge. I burnt the old ones and replaced them because of the bloodstains. But I thought – well – that I should keep some evidence. It was an afterthought."

DS Jones has reacted with surprise, and is scribbling.

She looks up again.

"Can you tell me what happened next."

The woman lifts her hands in an appeal for understanding.

"I was in shock – I mean – I was in shock from the moment they came in through the conservatory doors – but I was doubly so after I'd fired the gun."

"What about Lily – Elizabeth?"

"She, too, I imagine – although she was remarkably composed. She has an old head on young shoulders – but I don't need to tell you that. I took her upstairs – away from the scene – I told her to stay in her room."

She hesitates now, and bites her lower lip; she seems to be fighting a little internal battle. DS Jones waits patiently.

"My first thought was to call Jacob. Apart from the fact that he was only a minute away – well, it just seemed the natural thing to do." She is clearly finding this aspect uncomfortable. "Our relationship, you see? It was more than just neighbourly."

DS Jones, though her back is to the camera, must react in a way that is suitably non-judgemental, for the woman continues.

"And he came within seconds. He took complete charge. He seemed to know what to do – as if he had been ready for something like that."

A copy of the novel, *A Blind Eye* is lying on the desk. DS Jones rests a palm upon it. The autobiographical account ends with the words *"Jump, Lily – JUMP!!"* and the narrative resumes its own entirely different and unrelated course.

"What was the condition of the Badduns?"

The author does not answer directly.

"Jacob told me he would rush them to hospital. That it was far quicker than calling an ambulance – which made sense. They had a fast car outside. He insisted I should look after Lily – which was also what I knew I needed to do. I never went back into the lounge after the shooting until Jacob had gone. When I pulled Lily away they were on the floor, groaning. Next time I went in, Jacob had dragged them both out. I robotically began mopping up the blood. I threw the rugs out the back and Jacob burnt them later with the floorboards."

Here she visibly shudders – and it is reasonable to assume it is the association of the fire.

DS Jones offers a prompt.

"So, Jacob Floxham moved the Baddun brothers into their car, and as far as you were aware set off to drive them to hospital?"

Katrina Darkeness is nodding.

"He returned about an hour later."

"And you hadn't rung the police."

Though phrased as a question, DS Jones's intonation is that of a statement.

"He had said he would take care of it when he got back. That I was in trauma and shouldn't have to deal with it on my own. I wanted that – for him to be with me. But when he arrived I could tell immediately that something was wrong."

"What do you mean?"

"I don't know – it was something about Jacob – his manner.

Something about him had changed – there was a side I had never seen before. Something hard and cruel – and he was excited."

DS Jones remains silent.

"He told me there had been an accident – that the car had caught fire and he'd had to leap out. I didn't quite believe him – it seemed too impossible – another impossible thing on an impossible night. Then he said we needed to forget it ever happened – deny any knowledge whatsoever if the police came – that the police would probably come in the morning."

There is another pause.

"He said that they were almost certainly known criminals – that the police would think it was a gangland killing – that they would never in a million years suspect a reputable author in her holiday home."

She puts her hands on the desk and leans forward earnestly.

"I know – as the saying goes – you couldn't write it. Except – he – Jacob – was another one who was more or less right."

In DS Jones's manner there can be detected a certain discomfiture. But she avoids any temptation to excuse herself – that it was not on her watch; she has the good sense not to magnify what will surely become DI Smart's embarrassment when he is obliged, along with the Chief, to review the tape.

Katrina Darkeness continues with her account.

"So I acted as if nothing had occurred. I kept Lily away from the police – they never knew she was at Fellbeck. Jacob had frightened me by mentioning that I could be part-culpable. That the police could get it wrong and pin the whole thing on me. That it would be so bad for Lily. She relies on me – since Alexander and I split up it hasn't been easy for her. So I was afraid. And as facts emerged I realised there was something else – that I was in deeper than I first thought."

"What do you mean?"

"When I heard that the car was found burned out at the head of the dale. That Jacob had never driven it towards Keswick in the first place. When I challenged him – well, mildly questioned him – he went half berserk – I'd never seen him like it before. He called me all sorts of names and threatened me – *and the safety of Lily.*"

There is a rising note of disquiet in the woman's voice and she half reaches forward as though she wishes to touch DS Jones.

"It was then I began to suspect that he had a criminal background."

DS Jones does not respond, despite the suggestion that the writer seeks some affirmation. However, perhaps she does convey a hint unseen by the camera, for Katrina Darkeness sits back in her seat, and seems to be reassured.

"I was trapped. While I had become ostracised from Alexander and our circle of friends in Edinburgh Jacob had grown very important. But I see now that he had insinuated himself into my life with his good looks and charm, and by seeming to care. I don't mind admitting that there was a time when I was infatuated with him. But after the incident – gradually I began to feel like a victim of coercive control – like an abused wife. I had no choice but to go along with him. He is incredibly manipulative. Kind and cruel in the same breath. He knows just when to pull the levers to make you bend to his will."

DS Jones folds her arms and sits back. It is not difficult to discern that she is experiencing a moment of self-reproach.

But she gathers her wits and now, despite her sympathetic manner hitherto, brings forth a reminder that Katrina Darkeness is far from a mere witness in this matter.

"An innocent man has spent three years in jail for murders he did not commit."

The woman puts her head in her hands.

After a moment she looks up imploringly, parting her long dark hair with fingers that tremble.

"What could I do? Jacob said the police would never believe me – that he would kill Lily if I ever so much as breathed a word of what took place. He undermined my grip on reality – and kept me in a state of perpetual fear." She shakes her head regretfully. "And yet, he was all I had."

There is a pause while she drinks water from a glass. Again, DS Jones bides her time and the woman continues.

"Naturally, I have been following the case. I assumed that since the poor man Spooner couldn't have done it, he would have been released – acquitted – set free on appeal."

DS Jones now offers a little solace.

"It is true, you cannot be held responsible for that. There is no evidence to suggest that he was framed. His arrest and subsequent conviction were unrelated to you."

Katrina Darkeness seems to be looking at DS Jones with some bewilderment.

"You sound like my defence counsel."

"I am just giving you reasons why you should be entirely candid. You acted in self-defence. You have a witness – the Badduns cannot contradict you, and the forensic evidence supports your claim. You believed that Jacob Floxham was taking them to hospital. Thereafter you were coerced into silence under the threat of harm to your daughter. I can tell you that your suspicion of Jacob Floxham is well founded – we believe him to be a dangerous criminal –"

Rather curiously, DS Jones's voice seems to break with sudden emotion – so much so that the woman does reach out and place a palm briefly over hers. And, indeed, it is she that picks up the thread.

"I shall take all the responsibility. I have an explanation – but not an excuse in the eyes of the law – I realise that. My only concern is for Lily – she has borne the burden of the secret with extraordinary maturity. But I don't doubt she will need counselling – I'm just so glad it can happen." Now the woman sighs, and puts her hands to her face. "Only – if I am in prison, I shan't be able to support her."

DS Jones has regained her composure.

"I would be surprised if it came to that, madam."

The woman stares at her for a moment, then she gives a peal of laughter that is just slightly hysterical but certainly tinged with hope.

"It didn't seem to do Jeffrey Archer's career any harm. And I should never again be short of material."

Their respective sentiments seem unsynchronised, but on this particular point there is a note of harmony and DS Jones indicates again to the book on the desk.

"So, you wrote it into a novel."

Katrina Darkeness nods slowly. She inhales through her nose, her lips compressed pensively.

"I had to get it off my chest somehow."

"Was it also a cry for help?"

The author gives a small ironic laugh.

"A message in a bottle?"

DS Jones does not answer, though she indicates with an open palm that the woman may expand. She obliges.

"I suppose it was a small insurance policy. A kind of poison pill."

"Against Jacob Floxham, you mean?"

"Yes. I didn't know for how long I could trust him – not to harm us."

"Was it not risky? Jacob Floxham had a copy in his cottage."

"I know. But once it was published, there was nothing he could do about it. With so much time having passed, I managed to convince him that no one would ever be sufficiently astute to draw the connection. Obviously, I have been desperate for a way out. To be honest, my prayers were answered when you came calling."

DS Jones looks up from her note making.

"Is that why you gave me the book?"

The author nods.

"I don't know if you noticed – I folded over the corner of the page."

This appears to mark a hiatus in the proceedings, but just as DS Jones reaches to pause the recording, DS Leyton begins to clap – he directs his impromptu applause at Skelgill.

'Whoa – there you go, Guv! Astute to go along with all your other talents!'

Skelgill is caught fleetingly between brazen bravado and poorly affected modesty – but perhaps he suddenly doubts the sincerity of DS Leyton's compliment, and he resorts to some irony of his own.

'Nay, Leyton – it was all down to Jones – she kept going back to get high on the fumes of that weed – that's what did the trick – following her nose.'

Skelgill's crudely worded insight raises a chuckle – but in DS Jones's eyes the deep truth is there for all to see. She was continually drawn back – but the subliminal pull of Swinesdale had blinded her to the hidden danger.

She gives a shake of her head – she has some notes to hand out, and she seems glad of the practical distraction.

'DC Watson has identified a glazier from Penrith who made a repair to the sliding doors at the rear of Fellbeck. Katrina Darkeness told him that she had to break in when she arrived from Edinburgh late at night and had forgotten her keys. It was a week after the Badduns incident.'

DS Leyton makes an exasperated "tch" – such elementary police work overlooked. They all understand his point – and DS Jones has more in this regard.

'If they had spent time looking into Jacob Floxham. The fact that I couldn't locate a tax or national insurance profile was a red flag – he was my next target for background checks.'

She makes a face that tells she wishes she had done it sooner.

She pulls a transparent evidence folder from her pile and hands it to Skelgill.

'After you took off in the helicopter we searched his cottage. Here is a passport – a British passport – with undoubtedly his photograph and the name Jason Fordham.'

She gives her colleagues a moment to examine the exhibit.

'A similar alias is a means to achieve continuity of signatures and suchlike. But that's only the beginning of it.'

Now she refers to her report.

'A Jason Fordham has been on the run from Essex Police for over five years – timing that corresponds to Jacob Floxham's arrival in Swinesdale. Jason Fordham is wanted for questioning over the suspicious death of an elderly farmer – at a smallholding near Chelmsford where he had been employed as a labourer. He completely abandoned a steady relationship he was in with the man's niece. If she is to be believed, she has never heard from him since.'

She pauses – and reads silently before she looks up.

'And – as you can see – there is one striking coincidence. When the farm was searched, a marijuana-growing operation was discovered in one of the barns. The theory that was developed was that this was a kind of 'cuckooing' – that Fordham had taken over and had got the farmer at his mercy. Something went wrong – the old man died – and he cleared out.

'We've pulled the files on Jason Fordham. He has a prior criminal record. So we're just waiting on fingerprint and DNA analyses from our "Jacob Floxham" for confirmation. I have no doubt it's him.' She glances at Skelgill. 'Remember, Guv – when I said there was something about his voice, his accent – it was a lapse from his fake New Zealand persona – Jason Fordham is originally from south London.'

Skelgill is nodding.

DS Jones continues.

'There must be a strong possibility that he had struck up a similar arrangement with Hugh Larkfield – the chicken shed at the back of Moot Hall Café. I have applied for a warrant to search the place and to bring him in tomorrow. Hugh Larkfield could be a co-conspirator – or it might be that he has been acting under duress. The latter would be no surprise, given what we have learned.'

Now DS Leyton offers a view.

'That Fordham geezer – or Floxham – whatever he calls himself, he sounds like a nasty piece of work all round.' He sweeps a hand through his thick dark hair. 'But here's a question – looking at it from my perspective, dealing with the motor scam – why did he torch the Mercedes – and the Badduns inside it?'

Skelgill seems content that DS Jones should answer.

She takes a moment to compose herself.

'First of all, I doubt he will tell us – he's not cooperating and I think his strategy will be silence and his defence denial. But I don't think he's the cleverest crook. I think he has survived on a mixture of cunning and charm.'

She glances a little apprehensively at Skelgill, but he has reclined in his seat and closed his eyes.

'I suspect it was an impetuous decision – obviously, he couldn't have known the home invasion was going to occur. But I imagine he saw the situation as a threat to his cosy arrangement in Swinesdale – and his freedom from his past. You heard what

Katrina Darkeness said – that he told her it would look like a gangland killing – that the police would misread the situation – and – well – they did.'

She stops.

Skelgill awakens.

In his eyes there is the faintest glint of triumph – but he evidently decides not to enter the land of gloating – not yet, at least. Perhaps there are still too many I's to be dotted and T's to be crossed. And, perhaps – just perhaps – he feels the tiniest smidgeon of sympathy for DI Smart, for it is easier to be magnanimous in victory, and there is always that haunting principle of "there but for the grace of God go I".

His colleagues seem to get this.

DS Leyton shifts the conversation back to one of its more gory details.

'Scary thing is – those Badduns, sounds like they could have been alive.'

There is a pensive silence, until Skelgill, speaking without emotion, has something to add.

'Say they'd succeeded in doing what they intended at Fellbeck, Leyton – a defenceless woman and a thirteen-year-old lass. Would you have put the fire out?'

Skelgill in fact uses a more uncouth phrase for extinguishing the flames, and it is one that hints at where he might stand on the issue. When there is no answer from either of his sergeants the moral dilemma detains him no longer.

'I can't believe Smart didn't suspect Floxham from the start.'

His colleagues look at him for an explanation.

He gestures to the pile of reports that DS Jones has placed for convenience on one corner of his desk.

'What did it say in his statement? The first thing he knew was when the police woke him at eight. *Eight?* What kind of shepherd's still in bed at that time of the morning? He was keeping a low profile – he didn't want to draw attention to himself. On a normal day he'd be the first to notice. It was near his cottage and he'd be up and about. Instead – it's me that detects the smoke from a mile away.'

DS Leyton is again looking somewhat disgusted – that the original police investigation left so many obvious stones unturned – but for DS Jones a more nuanced expression troubles her countenance. When she speaks, the issue that has shaken her confidence finally sees the light of day.

'He knew we were closing in – in particular that I was closing in, despite that I couldn't see the wood for the trees. He must have spotted me earlier – Katrina Darkeness said he called round straight after I'd interviewed her. Then when I went back he intercepted me. The story of the petrol cans. The idea of walking up the little beck.' She glances at Skelgill. 'I realise, from what you said – it meant we left no tracks. And the petrol cans. A red herring. A lure. The submerged shaft.'

She looks intently at Skelgill.

'Guv – when Katrina Darkeness came to the lead mine – I think she was doing more than just looking for Lily. I feel rather in her debt.'

Skelgill is staring at her, his features pained, as if he has known this all along.

Then he punches a fist into the opposite palm and throws his hands up in the air in an act of mock despair.

'I can't leave either of you – look at what happened to Leyton!'

DS Leyton responds robustly.

'Hark at the kettle calling the pot black – you've just nearly been shot at and knifed in the same afternoon, Guv. Besides – if I'd not got myself whacked on the head – we might never have busted that car ring.'

'Aye – and look at the crackpot ideas it gave you!'

DS Leyton makes a show of being offended. He folds his arms defensively and rocks from side to side in his seat. But their exchange has acted as a pressure valve. He addresses DS Jones.

'I don't suppose you're exactly up to speed with this, girl?'

As they have arrived hotfoot from Workington, DS Jones has hurried likewise from her interview with Katrina Darkeness – and her news understandably has taken priority.

'The mobile phone?'

'Sixty-four-thousand-dollar question, Emma.'

DS Jones nods expectantly.

DS Leyton seems a little reluctant to continue.

'And the tuppeny-ha'penny answer – maybe the phone ain't gonna be so easy.'

'You didn't find one in the Chevrolet?'

'Not a phone, not a sausage. As clean as a whistle.'

But DS Jones is quick to appreciate the corollary. She turns to Skelgill.

'I suppose it's academic now?'

Skelgill frowns, as if he is not entirely convinced. But DS Leyton continues – he seems keen to emphasise the positive.

'Exactly. Just what me and the Guvnor have been saying. Spooner ain't gonna have to prove he was somewhere else now, is he? Any half-decent defence counsel is gonna tell him to keep schtum. He's off one almighty hook – no point getting himself back on another lesser one – not just to please the Crown.'

DS Jones nods pensively.

Then a thought strikes her and she inhales to speak – but checks herself – as if realising she should choose her words diplomatically. She addresses Skelgill in as deferential a manner as she can contrive.

'Are we saying there is not actually a phone, after all?'

She refers to their conversation at the outset – that it could have been a ruse to trick the police into reopening the investigation.

'Jones – don't even go there. The last thing I need is the Graham crowd on my back. Let's face it, if it weren't for Sheryl, we wouldn't have picked the case up. And we've caught everyone that counts.'

DS Jones has the hint of a smile at the corners of her mouth.

The tension is ebbing, and they all have reasons to be both relieved, and satisfied with their work.

'What about the others in the car-theft gang?'

Skelgill glances at DS Leyton – again he delegates a response.

'The Manx police have picked up a couple of suspects this afternoon. We've got James Hawkins in custody. John Silverbach's under guard in West Cumberland Hospital.'

DS Jones is listening closely – she glances at Skelgill, but his expression is implacable. She turns to DS Leyton for an explanation. He shrugs phlegmatically.

'He made the mistake of tangling with the Guvnor – came off second best.'

She looks back at Skelgill – but now he is staring trancelike, grimacing at nothing in particular.

After a moment's silence he seems to snap out of it, and looks urgently at his watch.

He springs to his feet and reaches for his jacket.

'I need to get to a shop – and back to Workington.'

*

'Danny – come in for a minute.'

The voice is honeyed.

Skelgill finds his eyes popping a little at the sight of Megan Graham. Despite having queried Jade Nelson's glamorous appearance, she has made a fine job of dressing to the nines. Heels, hair and striking cosmetics – along with sheer stockings, a figure-hugging low-cut dress and a lacy shrug; it is an ensemble that will surely require an overcoat to combat the elements.

'You make me feel underdressed.'

'Actually, I was thinking how smart you look. I'm used to seeing you needing a shave.'

She impudently reaches up and touches his smooth jaw.

'I have been known to make an effort.'

She chuckles throatily.

'Come through to the kitchen – have a quick drink.'

He notices that her speech is moderated – there is less of the local accent to which he is accustomed. She turns without waiting for an answer. He follows, thinking he should remind her he is driving – whereupon entering the kitchen a slightly balding middle-aged man in a dark lounge suit rises from a chair holding a glass of red wine in one hand.

'Danny, this is Bill. Bill Turner.' Megan Graham now giggles and Skelgill realises she is a little tipsy. 'Bill is my new boss – now that I'm Finance Manager, I'm directly under him.'

There is a note of innuendo in the woman's tone, and the man looks positively sheepish.

He must be, Skelgill deduces, proprietor of Turner's Paints, and is clearly finding awkward the impromptu ménage à trois – but Skelgill also detects a hint of defiance in the businessman's eye. Though, when he offers a hand to Skelgill, the grip is rather feeble.

Megan Graham is reaching down a wine glass, but Skelgill pre-empts her.

'I shan't stop.' Now he raises a small branded gift bag. 'I brought you this.'

'Chanel!'

Megan Graham swoops upon him.

She delves into the bag.

'Chanel No.5 – I've always wanted some!'

She plants a kiss before Skelgill can defend himself.

'But there's two bottles?'

'Aye – well – I thought you could pass one onto Sheryl – a late Christmas present, like.'

Skelgill has other details of explanation for both gifts – but he sees that Bill Turner is looking a little upstaged – and instead he makes his excuses and nods a farewell to the man, who smiles rather wanly.

'I'll see myself out.'

Megan Graham seems to understand it is the best arrangement. She presses the gift to her bosom.

'See you, Danny.'

Outside, the night is clear and crisp and stars twinkle faintly beyond the streetlamps. The snow has a crust of ice and Skelgill crunches back to his car, his breath coming in clouds that drift away on the light breeze like little fractions of his spirit. He glances at the house as he turns to fasten the gate. There is movement in the front room – a putting on of coats, perhaps. A taxi pulls up facing his car.

He slides into his shooting brake and promptly starts the engine.

'Sorry about that.'

'How did it go?'

Skelgill looks to his passenger. In the taxi's headlamps there is a sparkling apparition, highlights of blonde hair, gold earrings, and a top that shimmers – as if the glittering crystals outside are also within.

'Good choice – thanks. Good decision.'

'Maybe you should make the next one.'

Skelgill contrives a hopeful expression – boyish almost.

'I hear the Taj Mahal's under new management.'

In response comes a sardonic chuckle.

'Anything that doesn't involve dancing.'

'Jones – you know me and dancing – strictly business only.'

POSTSCRIPT

Excerpt from an article in the Westmorland Gazette, by Kendall Minto

A COURTROOM DRAMA was played out this morning in a special hearing to deal with the fallout from the case that was popularly known as the Badduns Murders – believed originally to be a gangland-style execution, for which local small-time thief Dale Spooner, 24, received a life sentence.

Gazette readers will recall gripping events earlier this year – in which your humble correspondent played a small but pivotal role in directing Cumbria Police to the key that unlocked the true nature of the crime. Today Dale Spooner's conviction was quashed on the grounds of irrefutable new evidence. Mr Spooner is now a free man, happily reunited with his fiancée and their child. It is understood his legal team will be presenting a claim for compensation to the Miscarriages of Justice Applications Service.

In a second sensational development – which saw media throng the steps of Carlisle Crown Court – famous crime writer K.T. Darke (real name Katrina Darkeness, 43) was acquitted of all charges laid against her in relation to the Badduns incident, following her earlier guilty plea to a charge of withholding information that might be material to the prosecution of an offender, for which she received a suspended sentence of one year.

Ms Darkeness's summary acquittal came in the wake of a catalogue of charges laid against a south London man, Jason Fordham, 33, who at the time of the Badduns murders worked as a shepherd in Swinesdale, where the charred bodies of the deceased were discovered in a burnt-out stolen car. Mr Fordham was wanted by Essex Police in connection with the death of Chelmsford farmer, Ely Ede, 72 – and it is alleged he went on the run and successfully took up a false identity in Cumbria. In addition to charges in relation to this latter incident, Mr Fordham was formally charged with the murders of Jake and Boris Baddun, attempted murder of a police officer (two counts), threatening behaviour, coercive control, and various drugs-related charges under the Proceeds of Crime Act. The Gazette understands that the explosive evidence which saw the dropping of charges against Ms Darkeness will underpin the Crown's case against Mr Fordham.

A parallel investigation by Cumbria Police into the stolen car in which the Baddun brothers perished also led to charges. A criminal gang operating out of the Isle of Man – and which had been under surveillance by the Manx Constabulary – was comprehensively dismantled, with the arrest of its mastermind, career criminal 'Long' John Silverbach, 46, who appeared in the dock in a wheelchair, to which he is now permanently confined, being paralysed. Silverbach was charged with a series of offences related to the handling of stolen property, but more heinous, the attempted murder of a police officer, possession of an offensive weapon, along with charges of sexual assault and of causing actual bodily harm. Several associates of Silverbach have been committed for trial in the Isle of Man, while local Workington man, James Hawkins, 44, a previously convicted car-thief, was also arraigned at Carlisle Crown Court, on charges of handling stolen property, assault upon a police officer, possession of offensive weapons, and resisting arrest.

Finally, Swinesdale resident and café-owner Hugh Larkfield, 52, was charged with withholding information that might be material to the prosecution of an offender. Mr Larkfield's legal representative, speaking to the court on his behalf, explained that, while her client will be pleading guilty to the charge, mitigating factors will emerge during the trial of Jason Fordham, and a request was made to delay sentencing until these can be fully appreciated.

Addressing the scrum of media after the hearing, Cumbria Police spokesperson DS Emma Jones – a rising star in the constabulary's ranks – deflected criticisms that an earlier inquiry by a different CID unit had failed properly to investigate the Badduns murders. A paragon of professionalism, DS Jones insisted that there was compelling forensic evidence which linked Mr Spooner

274

to the incident. She also pointed out that he was well known to the authorities for his light-fingered approach to high-value vehicles. However, it would appear that his time spent in wrongful custody has more than cancelled out any such misdemeanours, and it is hoped for the sake of his family that he will turn over a new leaf in this regard.

As a final postscript, in an exclusive interview with the Gazette, a gracious DS Jones was able to give credence to a theory developed by your very own correspondent – namely that the so-called 'Star Creeper' who targeted the homes of celebrities was almost certainly a double-act in the shape of the deceased Baddun brothers. Perhaps the talented detective and the intrepid reporter should team up more often?

**

Next in the series ...

Murder in the Fells is scheduled for publication in July 2022. In the meantime, books 1-17 in the Inspector Skelgill series can be found on Amazon. Each comprises a stand-alone mystery, and may be read out of sequence. All DI Skelgill books can be borrowed free with Kindle Unlimited, and also by Amazon Prime members on a Kindle device.

FREE BOOKS, NEW RELEASES, THE BEAUTIFUL LAKES ... AND MOUNTAINS OF CAKES

Sign up for Bruce Beckham's author newsletter

Thank you for getting this far!

If you have enjoyed your encounter with DI Skelgill there's a growing series of whodunits set in England's rugged and beautiful Lake District to get your teeth into.

My newsletter often features one of the back catalogue to download for free, along with details of new releases and special offers.

No Skelgill mystery would be complete without a café stop or two, and each month there's a traditional Cumbrian recipe – tried and tested by yours truly (aka *Bruce Bake 'em*).

To sign up, this is the link:

https://mailchi.mp/acd032704a3f/newsletter-sign-up

Your email address will be safely stored in the USA by Mailchimp, and will be used for no other purpose. You can unsubscribe at any time simply by clicking the link at the foot of the newsletter.

Thank you, again – best wishes and happy reading!

Bruce Beckham

Printed in Great Britain
by Amazon

75082888R00166